Praise for
BEHIND THE FOURTH WALL

"Powerful and poignant, with mystical elements ... A five star read that tears at your heartstrings."

–Liz Berg, author of *Jewish Folk Tales in Britain and Ireland*

"A cleverly written tale that delivers a riveting plot wrapped in a tightly-paced narrative ... filled with ... wonderfully flawed characters who stay with you long after the last page."

–Karoline Barrett, author of *Raisin the Dead*

"A compelling read, *Behind The Fourth Wall*, is one man's emotional journey from the depths of despair."

–Jeanie Roberts, author of *The Heron*

"If you like ... the magic of theatre, and magical realism ... this is the book for you!"

–Judith Pratt, playwright, author of *Siljeea Magic*

"Go inside the exclusive world of ... theater ... as a playwright struggles with unimaginable loss and mysterious redemption. Solomowitz writes with the authority and expertise necessary to make an incredible story powerfully real."

–Ben Sharpton, author of *The Awakening of Jim Bishop: This Changes Things*

For Katharine –
Who turned my world around and makes me a better human being.
First to critique, first to encourage, and first in my heart.

For Kevin David, Joshua Caylen and Marc Evan –
Who motivate me, enlighten me, and always make me proud.

For Mom –
Who inspired me to become a writer and
would have enjoyed seeing my first published novel.

With Gratitude

I t wasn't easy finding other writers who challenged me to take a hard look at the manuscript and offer productive critiques and solutions, but somehow I managed. I'm especially indebted to the guidance of Liz Berg, who helped me see where revisions were needed. Karoline Barrett and Ben Chapman added their insightful notes. I'm grateful to all three authors. Novelist and playwright, Judith Pratt, provided feedback on a number of the production aspects of the play in the story and introduced me to my publisher. Diane Gedymin was there early on to help with the editing.

I owe my friends Jeff Bennett and Jill Linden special thanks for all they taught me about the craft of directing theater. Also Lynn Antunovich, who graciously invited me to sit with her one summer as she directed *The Sisters Rosensweig* at Bare Bones Theater. My evolution as a director is due mainly to them along with the dozens of talented actors I've had the pleasure of collaborating with over the years.

I learned much about the technical side of theater production from Cliff Broffman, whom I was fortunate to have alongside me when we produced children's theater in New York. And I wouldn't have had community-theater experience without encouragement from Jo Ann and Stan Katz and Michael Casano of the Northport One-Act Play Festival. I'm appreciative to each of them.

To my Brooklyn College and NYU professors who encouraged me to pursue writing, I thank you. A special thanks to Professor Carole Grau. And to the few that discouraged my literary ambitions, I absolve you.

To my always supportive first readers—Kathy, Josh, and Kev—thank you for your candid and dependable notes, edits, feedback, and enthusiasm. I love you guys.

To my once-removed second cousin, Susan Mandeltort, who introduced me to Cape Cod (and lobsters) in 1981—unlocking a lifelong love affair—my unceasing gratitude. And to all the others along the way who enabled me with the insight and experience to write this book, I thank you as well.

– Michael Solomowitz
May 2021

BEHIND THE FOURTH WALL

"Yes, I have tricks in my pocket, I have things up my sleeve. But I am the opposite of a stage magician. He gives you illusion that has the appearance of truth. I give you truth in the pleasant disguise of illusion."

–Tennessee Williams, *The Glass Menagerie*

Prologue
An Intriguing Proposition

Noah Miller clenched the velvet box with a sweaty hand, leery of leaving it in his front pocket, unguarded, where it might wander off like a lost sock from a coin-operated dryer. The 18-karat gold ring with the chic sapphire stone he had just purchased, using the entire line of credit on his Visa, was too important for complacency, or its once-removed cousin, negligence. He smiled on the way to his car anticipating her reaction. He was going to surprise her tonight at dinner. Then it occurred to him. He stopped and checked how much cash he had left in his wallet.

He found parking up the street from the restaurant. It was after seven so he did not have to pay the meter. Good thing because he never carried change and was pretty sure he had overextended the limit on his only credit card. He knew he was late but assumed Jessie would forgive him once he presented the ring and the question that went along with it. The rain started just as he reached the canopy outside Butera's.

The pretty hostess in the black chiffon dress led him to Jessica's table. He leaned in to give his girlfriend a kiss, quickly swiping at his damp upper lip before contact, unsure if it was due to nerves, the rain, or from following a hostess in her tight clinging dress too closely.

"Not drinking?" he asked a bit surprised, mindful she normally enjoyed a glass or two of red with dinner, except that time when she was pregnant.

"Waiting for you," she told him.

"Yeah, Jess," he said apologetically. "Sorry about that. Friday night traffic."

"I was a little late myself," she confessed, chuckling at her ambiguous admission.

Ronaldo, their waiter, waited for them to get settled before handing them each a menu and requesting their drink order.

Jessica sidestepped the question. "I'm in the mood for baked clams," she said. "Will you share them with me?"

Noah fidgeted in his seat. "Sure. Sounds good."

"Half-a-dozen on the half-shell," she told Ronaldo. "And more bread, please. Starving."

The waiter turned to Noah.

"A Scotch, thanks," he said. "A double."

When Ronaldo left, Noah emptied the entire contents of his water glass.

"You okay?" Jess asked him.

"Great. I'm great," said Noah, dabbing at his temples with his napkin. "Really, I'm fine."

He waited until after dinner before surprising her, allowing Ronaldo to assist in hiding the ring in her mound of orange sherbet. She managed to excavate it on her second scoop, shifting her gaze from the crystal blue sapphire—posing on the basin-end of her dessert spoon—to Noah's beaming expression.

"How 'bout it, Jess?" he asked, circumventing the formal proposal he was hoping she would not insist on. He preferred not to make a scene.

"How about what?" she asked, choosing absolute clarity when it came to a question of this magnitude.

"You know, me and you? You and me?"

"Well," she said, still holding the spoon in place between them. "Which is it? Me and you? Or you and me?"

Noah courteously confiscated the spoon from Jessie's hand and dropped the scoop of sherbet into what was left in his water glass. He snared the ring out with a spoon, buffing the gemstone with his cloth napkin. Then he rose and came around the table to her side, dropping to one knee. She was going to make him work for it.

The diners at the tables around them hushed as they watched the side act unfold. Soon the entire restaurant was silenced. And staring.

Noah was aware of the sudden stillness in the room but did not let that hold him up. "Jessica Sagamore," he announced, holding the ring before her, a determined gaze never leaving her sight. "I love you with all my heart." He had practiced the lines all day anticipating her response. "Will you be my wife?"

Jessica scrutinized the ring. "It's beautiful, Noah."

"It better be …" he cautioned under his breath, switching gears as he placed it on her proper finger. "Promise me you'll never take it off."

At that, she peered profoundly at him. Noah could feel the imprint it left on his soul.

"I promise I'll never take it off … with one condition."

He cocked his head to the side, his mouth slightly ajar, too dumbfounded for words. Not the response he was expecting.

"I'll only remove it," she said, her forehead crinkled like a pleated skirt, "to save you."

A bewildered look surfaced on his face. "Save me? … From what?"

Her eyes smiled. Her lips followed. She had given him her answer.

Noah waited a moment until he realized that was all he was getting. He considered her intriguing proposition and determined he could live with it. "I accept your terms, madam."

"And I accept yours, Noah Miller. Yes, I'll marry you."

He leaned in and kissed her gently. With that, the patrons of the restaurant cheered and applauded. The waiter swooped in and popped the cork from the champagne bottle.

Noah accepted his glass, noting the brand. "Dom Pérignon?" he questioned, forcing a smile. "Did I order that?"

"It's the only one we serve," said Ronaldo.

"Great," said Noah lifting his glass, concealing a renewed sense of trepidation. "Only the best for my bride-to-be."

1
Exit Stage Left

The gusty breeze snatched the slip of paper from Noah Miller's lap. He watched as it darted untouched on an urgent crusade across the ferry deck, plunging overboard to its sodden end before he could react, taking with it his list of reminders and a phone number he had not yet logged on his phone. He groaned cathartically, then pulled a pad from his knapsack and scribbled what his memory would allow. In a pinch, he still preferred pen to technology.

When he finished what he could, Noah leaned back on the hardwood bench atop the Cross-Sound ferry's sundeck, closed his eyes and inhaled the early summer afternoon. He was just on the verge of toppling off the cliff and plunging deeper into that quiet hemisphere of serenity when his calm was shattered by the pattering of four tiny paws maneuvering around him. Noah's amused gaze followed the rambunctious pug as it swaggered down the aisle, rebuking each pair of threatening legs it passed with a muted yelp, a rattled impulse from a defiant pup. "No, Reggie," scolded its master, a smoldering cigarette in her hand conducting a procession of liberated fumes. She tugged at its leash with each infraction while the two made their way to the empty deck astern where the obliging canine raised his hind leg and relieved itself into a puddle of condensation from the ship's compressors. "Good boy, Reginald." On their return midship, the pug, detecting a Jack Russell terrier nearby, raised its bulky head and yanked its leash, causing a fierce and unwelcome tug-of-war.

Noah chuckled and shut his eyes allowing the late day sun to console him. With his car safely below deck, this was so much better than coping with Connecticut weekend traffic and endless highway construction. But the road ahead concerned him. Long Island's Gold Coast properties and miniscule lighthouse islands he had observed as they departed Orient Point had long since melted into the horizon and all that lay ahead were open waters and an undetermined future he was not yet ready to face.

It had all evolved so quickly Noah wasn't quite sure how it happened: his job at the firm; his sublet house admiring Northport Bay; his family. But he didn't want to think about that anymore. This was a sensible decision. The right decision. The only decision, really, once he stepped back and considered his options. He needed to abandon his predicament for a while and, when the opportunity presented itself, Noah realized, with some encouragement from his depreciating bullpen of friends, colleagues, and loved ones, that this temporary relocation was the ideal solution.

Relaxing onboard the Cape Henlopen, a recommissioned WWII landing craft, which he learned, had stormed Omaha Beach on D-Day, Noah recalled the conversation that day with his college crony.

Jerry Ziegler, a producer of off-Broadway and, lately, off-off-Broadway productions, had called him at the office, told him he was in town and had some exciting news. Noah was in no mood for more Jerry-antics—that is how he referred to his escapades—but when his friend informed him it concerned Noah's play, he relented and agreed to meet him.

"I hate delicatessens," complained Jerry, as he slid the cumbersome steel table forward so he could fit his overindulged girth into the cramped booth.

Noah smiled. "Then why'd you pick this place?"

He peered at Noah with those culpable brown eyes. "What do you mean? So we didn't have to wait for a table in one of those fancy restaurants. I know you're a busy man."

Noah awaited the punchline. There was always a punchline. "Besides, I'm a sucker for kosher pickles."

After the busboy filled their water glasses, the waitress came by. "What can I get you boys?" Jerry was still assessing the lunch specials.

"Small garden salad," said Noah, "balsamic vinaigrette on the side."

"Boring!" objected Jerry without looking up. *"That's* what you're eating for lunch? I take you to a bona fide New York City deli with pastrami, corn beef, and tongue on the menu and you order a garden salad with boring dressing? Who are you and what have you done with my old roommate who used to share eggs-over-easy pizza with me at three in the morning?"

"Sorry Jer. Not very hungry."

Jerry teetered his head from side-to-side then turned to the waitress. "I'll have the Reuben, dear, with swiss on whole wheat. That comes with fries, right? And see if you can find sour pickles, you know the real sour ones? The lighter the complexion, the better. They should look anemic, like they're waiting for an ambulance."

The waitress grinned and collected the menus. "I'll send out a search party."

"I think she likes me," whispered Jerry after she left.

"You think every waitress likes you."

"Not all of them. Just the young hot ones. Can I help it if I'm a likeable guy?"

"No, Jerry. You can't do a thing about it."

"Nice tush, huh?"

"Didn't notice."

"How could you not notice that tush? Tight, hard, round. What's not to notice?"

Noah shook his head. He had not changed.

"And what's with the garden salad? You dieting or something? You ought to be ashamed. I'm telling your mother."

Noah pondered the ramifications. "I don't think so, Jerry."

"What? You don't think so? You don't think you're dieting or you don't think I'd call your mother? What's her number? I'm calling her now."

"Mom passed away."

"Oh my God? Your mom ... too? Noah, I'm so sorry. When? Why didn't you call me?"

Noah looked up from his water glass. "Three years ago."

"Your mother passed away three years ago and you're just telling me now? What kind of person are you? I loved your mother."

"We tried getting in touch at the time but your office said you were unavailable."

"Unavailable? They said that? Give me the name of the person you spoke to and I'll fire the bastard. Who was it?"

"I really don't remember and even if I did, Jer, what's the point? You're not a funeral guy. I understand."

Jerry picked up his water glass and replaced it. "Sorry we weren't there. Sheila and I were devastated."

Noah took pity. "I got your card and the babka cheesecake. Thanks."

"*Juniors.* Did you notice it was from Juniors? The original. In Brooklyn."

"Very thoughtful."

"Only the best for my buddy." And then, more soberly, "Really, we would have come but we were in Budapest last summer and couldn't get back in time." He took a sip of water. "You know I'm here for you, pal, whatever you need."

Before Noah could say anything, the waitress was back with a small pewter platter of pickles and coleslaw.

"You found them," beamed Jerry. "I love you."

Then he picked out the biggest one and took a bite. And, as she left, he called out, "Keep 'em coming!"

He munched it down before Noah could change the subject. "So, what's this great news you have for me?"

"I love sour pickles."

"I'm aware of that, Jerry."

"They're an art form, you know? Only in this city."

He wiped his mouth with his oversized napkin, pulled himself up in his seat and placed both hands on the table like he was about to deal a hand of gin rummy.

"So, my friend … what would you say if I told you that the Cape Playhouse in Dennis, Massachusetts, wants to produce your play?"

"What?"

"I know. Incredible, right? A one-month run in August. That's prime tourist season."

"In Dennis? But how?"

"I sent your script in. One of their directors—I met this guy at one of those real estate marketing dinners a couple of months back, you know, where they try to sell you a timeshare—he'd seen it during its run downtown, loved it, and convinced the board. They couldn't get the rights to the play they originally slotted so they needed a backup. Besides, he owed me a favor. The only thing is, they're putting their schedule together as we speak, and I need to get back to them right away."

Noah mulled over his offer. Barely. His full-length comedy, *Committed,* had had a somewhat successful three-month engagement at the Orpheum Theater a couple of years ago.

"I'm really touched, Jerry, but considering all that's happened, I'm not sure this is the best time to be staging a play. But thanks for thinking of me."

Jerry removed his glasses, picked up a pickle, and held it like a lethal weapon. "Don't make me use this, Noah B. Miller."

"You know you're dripping pickle juice on your pants."

"See what I'd do for a friend? Look, I understand you've been through a lot in the past year."

"Please, Jerry … not the big-brother lecture."

"It's not a lecture. Okay, maybe it is. Call it what you want. But as your manager and friend, I think this is exactly what you need to get your mind off your … you know, off of things for a while."

"Look, it sounds great. I'm appreciative. And if it was any other time, I'd certainly think twice about their offer. But I've got a busy job and just don't see how …"

"Think about it, pal. The Cape. A couple of months away from the city, from your job that you hate."

"I never said I hated …"

"… Who you kidding? We both know you can't stand critiquing plays, especially ones not as good as yours. I'm not even sure why you took it. Besides, you love Cape Cod. You always said that. What could be a better distraction?"

Noah looked around the bustling diner for the waitress, hoping she would swoop in and get his mind back on pickles … and tush.

"I don't know, Jer. I just don't know if it's the right time."

Noah started the engine of his SUV and waited his turn for the crewman's signal, waving him off the ship into New London. At the light, he crossed the Amtrak tracks and proceeded onto I-95 North towards Providence. Traffic was light this Saturday evening. He turned on the radio, searching for something Classical and found a Connecticut station playing Haydn's *String Quartet in B-Flat Major.* It would have to do.

Crossing the Gold Star Memorial Bridge, Noah recalled the last time he was here, visiting the Eugene O'Neill Theater Center while researching the Nobel laureate and Pulitzer Prize-winning playwright. O'Neill's famous actor father, James O'Neill, had built a summer home in nearby Waterford he named Monte Cristo Cottage after his most celebrated lead role in *The Count of Monte Cristo,* a stage production he appeared in for nearly 40 years.

Passing the Mystic exit, Noah laughed and shook his head. Getting a leave from work for the summer had been easier than he thought. Besides, he needed a break from the grind. His theater reviews for the Associated Press had been mostly unfavorable lately and beginning to get noticed.

Noah poured himself a third cup of coffee and made his way back to his desk in the far corner nearest one of the panoramic windows facing

Jersey. At 42, he was older than most of his AP colleagues and lucked out with a choice cubicle when his esteemed predecessor, Melvin Garbowitz—Garbo to his colleagues—who had been with the service since the Carter administration, retired. Noah prioritized the assignments on his desk: a couple of on-air scripts, his syndicated entertainment column, *Make My Day*, and two theater reviews.

The phone rang. It was his boss asking him to stop by. While it seemed a bit unusual—his boss normally came to him when he wanted something—Noah did not look too far beyond the summons. Too much on his plate these days. He picked up his mug and proceeded to find out what was up.

Barney Saperstein was more a father figure than a boss to Noah. His son, Harry, had been Noah's next-door Northport neighbor and friend for years and the three often found themselves barbecuing together on holidays and disputing the Yankees' and Mets' chances that season.

Barney had met Noah and his wife, Jessica, at his son's place about five years ago. After getting to know him better, he hired Noah to replace Garbo.

"You rang?" inquired Noah, stepping into Barney's office and heading for the sofa.

"Close the door."

Noah paused. "I don't like the sound of that."

Barney gave him his "Not today" look followed by a simulated smile. "Will you close the door, please?"

Noah retreated. "When you put it that way."

He shut the door and placed his coffee mug on the Elvis Presley coaster on Barney's desk, next to the red-pencil holder, and sat on the chair opposite. He waited, watchful, as his boss sifted through a stack of papers.

The apprehensive interlude made Noah feel vulnerable. He surveyed the wall of pictures, diplomas and awards adorned with ribbons and embossed gold seals, and noticed one photo of a youthful Barney Saperstein standing between Bobby and Teddy Kennedy.

Finally, the tension got to him. "Are you firing me?" he inquired, laced with equal shares of insecurity and relief.

7

Barney ceased his movements, raised his eyebrow, and hesitated just enough to send a chill down Noah's spine. "Do I have a reason to fire you?"

Noah took a long sip of coffee. "Not necessarily, unless someone's pissed off about the cash payoffs I've been receiving for my lousy reviews."

A slow smile came to Barney's lips. "Why would they pay you for a lousy review? Is it like *The Producers?* Do they want a lousy review?"

Noah played along. "They try to bribe me for a great review but I can only offer them a fair one."

"That's what I like," said Barney. "An honest crook. We need more good men like you. By the way, what's the payoff these days for a lousy review?"

Noah smirked. "What do I get if I tell you?"

Barney dropped his pencil on the desk and sat back in his chair. "You get to keep your job … maybe."

"I want my lawyer," said Noah, surrendering.

Barney came around the desk and plopped down on the couch, the convivial duel over.

"I called you in here, Noah, because, frankly, I'm concerned. I've read your last seven reviews—seven, mind you—and, I have to tell you, I'm seeing a pattern."

Noah let him finish.

"You're ripping the writer, the actors, the director, jeez, the only one you haven't attacked yet is the lighting director. Are you telling me you couldn't find one redeeming element in seven plays?"

Noah took a deep breath before responding. "What can I say? They're producing real crap these days. Most of them should have closed in previews. The only reason they have any life at all is because of the tourists. The big shows have been sold out for weeks—or just too expensive—so they take whatever's left. If a show is on a New York stage, they figure, it's got to be good. They don't bother reading reviews. Who reads reviews anymore? They see one or two quotes, out of context, the producer has plastered on their website and a ticket is sold. So, the show endures out of survival of fulfillment. Take what you can get. It's my new evolutionary theory of the Broadway ticket industry.

"Nobody cares anymore what's being produced, just looking for something to do while they're visiting the Big Apple. The producer fills seats, the actors work, the tourists see a show. It's a win-win-win for everyone. Even me. I'm just doing my job, boss, giving them an honest review."

Now it was Barney's turn. "Look, I accept your theory. *Maybe.* But I still think you can use a break."

"I don't need a break. I need a breakout star. A hero with a story. A show worth reviewing. I need the next *Hamilton.*"

"You need to get off the theater beat for a while and regroup. A change of pace. Why don't you go somewhere and write another show. About … Ben Franklin. Now *he* was a character with a story!"

"*Barney!*"

"Noah, I'm not kidding. You've been through a lot the last few months and it could be affecting your judgement. I know you took time off after Jessica passed but I'm not sure you were ready to come back. Why don't you take a couple of weeks and go somewhere? Visit someone. Do something fun, you know, something you enjoy."

There was no getting around Barney once his mind was made up. Noah knew him well enough to know that.

"Well, now that you mention it. There is something I might want to try."

"Good. I like it already. What is it?"

"The only thing is I'll need more than two weeks to see it through."

Barney brought his head closer as if he was in on the secret. "Are you going to keep me in suspense?"

"This theater company on Cape Cod wants to produce my play."

Barney leaned back. "You wrote another play?"

"No, the same one. You know, from the Orpheum."

"That's great news, Noah. Wonderful news. I think you should do it."

"Thanks. But it means I'll need the entire summer off." Noah was expecting at least some hesitation. "Is that okay?"

"Okay? Are you kidding? Take the summer. Take the winter. Noah, what's to think about? Go to the Cape and produce your play. I think it's a wonderful idea."

Noah decelerated to the speed limit as he turned east onto I-195 and made his way past the three giant smokestacks in downtown Providence. Another hour to go before reaching the Cape. He passed a billboard, *Make the Most of Now.* Noah regarded the message and laughed. That is exactly what he was doing. And it could not have come at a better time. He needed to get away and unwind. That was for sure.

He laughed again, realizing that it had come full circle. This was simply the end result to something that had started right here. Funny, he thought, how life connects the dots. His mind drifted back to his first visit, some twenty years prior, when his cousin invited him to a beach house she had rented in Truro. It was a full house of people—some he knew, most he did not—but it didn't take long for the group to click with the aid of day-long happy hours and some loose joints.

He remembered that weekend, the pure fun of being in his twenties before a mortgage, a baby, and family responsibilities kicked in. He recalled, too, how much they laughed. It was easy to laugh then. He especially remembered how effortless it seemed to make a certain woman laugh, a woman he met that weekend and wound up dating.

Karen Luccelli was a friend of a friend and a guest at the beach house. Noah could not take his eyes off her. But he was shy around women and never came on too strong. Eventually, he found himself alone with her in the kitchen and made an innocent observation. She responded, and the relationship took off from there.

The next night, the two of them were taking a sequestered swim under a full moon. She would become his second true love and, when she ended their relationship a year later because she believed their religions—he a progressive Jew, she a devout Catholic—would impede on a long-term commitment with consideration to raising children, Noah's heart shattered in every direction. It took months before he could collect most of the pieces and move on.

Years later, he used scraps of that breakup as the basis for his first full-length play, *Committed*, which his college roommate/manager/agent Jerry Ziegler, used to convince a hard-up off-Broadway producer, and a pretty poor bluffer when it came to Poker, to give the play a two-week run at his East Village theater. When the reviews arrived, the show had a pulse and ran for 89 performances. Noah Miller was a successful playwright his first time out and the industry awaited his next venture.

It never came.

Now he was heading back to the Cape where it all began. By the time he reached Fall River, Noah noticed he was going 80-mph. It was after ten o'clock and he was anxious to get into bed. Jerry had booked him a room for the night at the Sandy Neck Motel on 6A in Sandwich, not far from where he had rented houses for them, but that would have to wait until tomorrow.

He followed Rt. 25 to 6 West and signs to the Sagamore Bridge along the northern coastline of the peninsula. He was too tired to pull over at the scenic rest stop to admire the quaint bridges that spanned Cape Cod Canal, that tourists and locals had been admiring since 1935. If he had, Noah would have noticed that the Sagamore and its sister bridge, the Bourne, were nearly identical except the latter had a longer approach.

Noah slowed the car down and opened his windows. He was anxious to breathe in the Cape oxygen. With no traffic, it only took him a moment to cross the Sagamore as opposed to up-to-half-an-hour during the busy summer months with the tourists coming and going on the weekends.

Cape Cod had always been a sanctuary for Noah. His last visit there was a couple of years ago—he and his wife had rented a house on a Barnstable beach for a week, off-season, with their daughter, Erica, who had just turned a year old—but the familiar feelings always returned. He felt freer here than any other place on earth. His heart beat slower and he never had trouble falling asleep. Everything seemed more vibrant too. He could not explain it. The sun was brighter, the Hydrangea bluer, the locals friendlier, the sunsets lovelier. He could taste the brine in the air.

Noah pulled into the motel parking lot and picked up his key at the front desk. There was a message from Jerry. "Call me if you get in before 11 p.m. or I'll see you at 9 a.m." Noah checked his phone. It was almost 11:15 p.m. He grabbed his bag from the back seat and found his room.

Entering, he sensed a hint of tobacco in the air. The room was a throwback to the '70s with heavy dark drapes reaching the floor, a rotary phone, and a step up to the bathroom. One window held an air conditioner that looked as dated as the building. He turned it on high, carefully removed a Daddy Long Legs spider making its way across his full-size bed and carried it outside. Then he undressed, used the bathroom, and got into bed with his book.

Now that he was a playwright again, Noah commended himself for accepting the challenge and agreeing to the terms. The one provision he had requested and received was the additional title of Assistant Director so the actors would not have reason to object to his presence at rehearsals and he would have input in the audition process. Choosing the right actors was essential to a play's success, especially Equity actors. They were on a demanding schedule. So was he. Two days of auditions starting Tuesday, the following week in meetings with the production team—the set and lighting designers, the costumer, the theater's marketing and program people—then nearly four weeks of rehearsals. There was a lot to get done in little time but that was the frenetic life of the theater. And Noah was looking forward to every moment.

He dropped his paperback—Dan Brown's *Angels & Demons*—on the floor by the side of the bed and grabbed the pull chain of the ceramic whale lamp on the nightstand. The room went black. He yanked the tucked-in sheet out from under the mattress and rested his feet on top. That was better. It was good to be back.

He lay there awake, pondering how working on his play would take his mind off his troubles. Barney was right. So was Jerry. He knew they were looking out for him.

The last year had been a private hell and his play would be a perfect distraction so he could stop thinking about the dark secret he had been carrying around along with the empty hole where his heart used to be.

2
The Overture

The knock at the door whisked Noah out of a deep, restful sleep. He opened one eye and glanced at the alarm clock on the nightstand. Jerry was early. Immediately, he realized he had forgotten to set an alarm.

"Okay," he shouted. "Coming," and opened the door.

"Did I wake you?" inquired Jerry, facetiously, peering through the crack. Noah opened it all the way, inviting him in.

"As a matter of fact."

Jerry stormed into the room. "Didn't you get my message?"

Noah looked on impassively.

Jerry grunted. "Well, you know what they say?"

Noah was still waking up and quite sure he did not.

"The early bird may catch the worm, but it's the second mouse that gets the cheese."

"Never heard that one."

"That's because you sleep late."

"I'm not even sure what it means."

"It means, you don't have to be first on line for a big sale, but if you're last, there's probably not going to be much left."

Noah thought about it. "I don't think that's what it means."

"Yeah, well, you're still in your underwear."

"Give me five minutes to shower."

"No problem."

"And another five to brush up."

Jerry headed for the door. He knew this act.

"And *another* five to get dressed."

Jerry opened the door. "Why don't I come back in, say, fifteen minutes?"

"You mean," said Noah, closing the door, "when your message said you'd be here?"

After Jerry bought them breakfast at the 6A Café, they drove about ten minutes to a jarring, potholed Foster Road and parked in front of a house that could easily be branded the runt of the neighborhood. The lawn was smothered with daisies, dandelions and crab grass, and the mailbox was hidden within a bouquet of thorny vines.

"This is *your* place," said Jerry.

Before stepping in, Noah noticed a decaying marker besides the unlocked front door with peeling paint. He wiped away the muck revealing the year of construction: 1827. Something else was hiding below it. Scratching at the remaining sludge on the small oval plaque, it crumbled under the pressure of his hand.

"It was one of the last houses available for the season," Jerry added. "Very affordable."

Noah soon learned why. In the parlor, an oversized Victorian-era love seat crowded the room beside a scratched Art Deco coffee table, both facing a fireplace strewn with cobwebs. You could see the smoky outline where artwork had hung on the walls.

"They stuck their heads into the cramped bathroom. The sink was positioned where the showerhead was aimed, adjacent to the toilet, leaving little room to maneuver.

"Cozy," said Jerry, moving on.

"You're kidding?" said Noah, wincing.

The narrow bedroom contained side-by-side twin beds, more like army cots, arranged between two walls with no space between them so one would have to climb in from the foot of the bed. An old pine armoire leaned up in a corner in place of a closet. It had once been off-white but Noah would not begin to classify its color now. One of its hinges was broken and its door hung askew.

In the kitchen, an antiquated fridge and potbelly stove had not been cleaned, well, ever. A free-standing tub served double duty as a sink. A slashed screen door with a gaping entrance for flies and mosquitoes led them out to the backyard. There, a dilapidated rusty card table was set up against the backdrop of an endless watery salt marsh. In the distance, beyond a string of beach houses, one could make out Cape Cod Bay.

"Here's where you'll be working," said Jerry.

"This is more like it," said Noah, finally pleased with something.

Jerry nodded. "As far as the house goes, it's just a place for you to knock off at night. You're not going to be throwing any lavish parties here. We'll do that at my place, just up the road."

They moved towards the marsh. "I was told it's an original New England Cape," said Jerry.

"No doubt about *that,*" said Noah, not bothering to hide the sarcasm.

"Lots of history. May even be the original homestead in this area."

Noah turned back to the house. "I think the demolition crew missed this one."

Jerry placed a hand on his friend's shoulder. "The cleaning ladies were supposed to get here before you and make it habitable. Sorry. They're coming today. And, I'll call someone about the screen door."

The two began making their way to the car. Noah peered back at the shoebox with the steep-sloping roof.

"If you really object," added Jerry, "we'll try to find you something else."

"Don't bother," Noah told him. "We writers are used to roughing it."

Jerry's BMW crossed over a single train track—used primarily for the town's "trash" railroad to discard rubbish, Noah would learn later—and, just up ahead, turned onto Salt Marsh Road, a secluded scenic dirt road running alongside the marsh.

Jerry parked on a crunchy gravel driveway leading up to a splendid grey-weathered house and staircase. Upon closer inspection, Noah noticed the "gravel" was actually vast quantities of crushed seashells and clamshells. There may have been shards of lobster shell, as well.

The steps led them onto a wide composite deck with cushioned wicker furniture and Jerry unlocked the glass door with a polished platinum key. Entering, they were welcomed inside with the sweet summer scent of fresh-cut rhododendron, housed in an oversized ceramic vase with vibrant red pedals on a marble-top table.

"This is where I'll be based," explained Jerry, "but I'll be all over the map this summer so feel free to use this place when you want. At least, when my wife's not around."

Noah admired the lacquered wooden beams spanning the high-ceiling room and made himself comfortable on the white leather recliner, raising his legs.

"I may just do that," said Noah.

He noticed the walls were tinted an icy grey and followed the contour up to the two circular skylights resembling oversized portholes. On the far side of the house, his attention was drawn to the panoramic windows overlooking a back deck engulfed by grassy dunes and more white wicker furniture. A propane grill stood in one corner and an outdoor shower in another.

Jerry joined him by the windows and pulled open the sliding door. They stepped out onto the deck and noticed an inground pool off to the side of the house. The bay breeze tussled Noah's hair. He breathed it all in and followed the 50-foot catwalk to the edge of the dunes with Jerry in close pursuit. The staircase at the end led down to a private empty beach and the grey-blue waters of Cape Cod Bay.

"This must be costing you *a fortune,*" said Noah as they made their way to the shoreline.

Jerry picked up a flat stone and skimmed it into the bay. "Actually, it's a write-off from Sheila's company. What can I say? Nice to have a wife with a business background."

They headed west along the dormant shoreline, maneuvering past glistening rocks and cumbersome boulders.

"I'm having a party tonight," Jerry told him, "so you'll get a chance to meet Pete Benson, our director. Asked him to invite the production team and a few others connected to the theater so everyone can meet everyone else. There'll be food, music. Casual. Should be fun."

"Sounds good," said Noah. "I look forward to meeting them. What's Pete like?"

"We've only met a couple of times but he seems like a decent enough guy. Single, divorced I think. Been directing plays on the Cape forever. Lots of experience and connections. Also met our stage manager when I was here last week. She's something else."

"What do you mean?"

"Nothing. Strictly by the book.' I'm sure you'll like her. I've been told she's one of the best at her job."

They watched a seagull hang above the water searching for prey then fly off disappointed.

"Well," said Jerry, "I've got an early lunch date so I'll take you back to your place and let you get settled. Here's your key and this one's mine."

Noah put them in his pocket. "I'm going to hang out here for a while, if you don't mind."

"You sure?"

"I can walk it from here. You go ahead. I'll see you later."

"All right. But do us both a favor and bring your happy face tonight. Okay?"

Noah laughed. "I'm *always* happy, Jerry. Just a happy-go-lucky kind of guy."

With that, Noah removed his loafers and headed down the shore. He sensed Jerry watching him before leaving for his meeting.

Donna Summer was singing *Hot Stuff* when Noah made it back to Jerry's place. The door was unlocked and the music blaring so he did not bother knocking. The house was full of people Noah never met as he made his way inside keeping an eye out for his friend.

A server walked by with a tray of champagne so Noah helped himself to a glass. A while later, appetizers were passed around and Noah grabbed a plate and a couple of crab cakes off the tray. Standing there enjoying them, he realized he hadn't eaten since breakfast.

Just then, Jerry, in khaki shorts and an exotic Hawaiian button-down, approached him. "Glad to see you made it. How's the food?"

"Tastes just like Cape Cod."

"I told you you'd like coming here."

A couple who had walked in behind Noah stepped between them and gave Jerry a hug before heading over to the bar on the far side of the room.

"Leeches," groaned Jerry, who picked out a half-dozen pigs in blankets from a nearby tray.

Noah noticed the cocaine embedded in one of his friend's nostrils and tapped his nose. "Hey, you might want to freshen up before you make the rounds."

"Thanks pal. Don't go anywhere. Some people I want to introduce you to."

"Where would I be going?"

"I don't know," Jerry called out, making his way through the crowd. "That's what bothers me."

Noah headed to the other side of the room and waited for the bartender to finish chatting. When she turned around, his eyes applauded the vision—still attractive in her thirties, probably a model when she was younger.

"What can I get you, cowboy?" she asked, her high cheekbones rising higher. Noah detected the hint of a southern drawl.

"Bass Ale," he told her, then added "please."

"A *polite* cowboy," she said, impressed. "Rare breed around here. What makes you think we have it?"

"It's my friend's favorite and … it's his house."

She kept her eye on him as she reached into the mini-fridge. "As a matter of fact," she said, pulling one out and flipping the bottlecap off. "Glass?"

"If you don't mind."

She grabbed a glass and smiled. "I get paid not to mind."

While she poured, Noah noticed the top three buttons of her blouse were undone. *"Nice pouring,"* he blurted out then wished he hadn't.

She smirked and bit her lower lip.

Noah attempted to reload. "Sorry. What I meant was, um, you didn't spill a single ..."

"... I know what you meant, Sundance."

Noah wondered if she was flirting. "Good. That's good," he said, a bit flustered from his indiscretion, his face a pale shade of humiliation.

"Anything else I can ... do for you?"

"Chardonnay and a white Russian, hon," interrupted some guy in tight leather jeans. Way too tight.

She rolled her eyes. "Come back for a refill," she told Noah, "and you can watch me ... pour some more." Then she was off.

Noah downed about half his glass and turned to face the room. Standing there in his long sleeve white linen shirt and beige slacks, he detected a sense of comradery. The crowded room made him feel invisible. Carol King was singing *I Feel The Earth Move* and Noah swayed to the beat.

After a moment, he perceived someone next to him, singing along with the lyrics. A young woman, early twenties, with charismatic auburn hair and pale green eyes, was monitoring him. "Nice party," she said, taking the lead.

Noah peeked at the room, acknowledging, then back to her. "It is, isn't it?"

She emitted a warm glow. For a moment, Noah thought she seemed familiar. "Aren't you a little young for this group?"

"Probably. But that never stopped me before." Then she flashed him a smile, a bewitching one that lit up her face.

Before he went on, he noticed the music slow down, like a vinyl album running at thirty-three rpms instead of forty-five. He decided to ignore it, chalking it up to an obsolete sound system.

"I'm Noah," he said, switching hands awkwardly with his beer.

"Emily," she told him, giving his hand a cordial squeeze.

"A pleasure to meet you, Emily," he said.

"Emma," she corrected him, cautiously. "Friends call me Emma."

A brief intermission ensued as they sized one another up.

"You must be Noah Miller."

Noah seized his glass with both hands like a bear protecting its cub. "How did you know?"

"Sorry. I overheard you mention that you're Jerry's friend and put two and two together. I'm with Sotheby's. I found your houses. Just finished filing the paperwork this morning."

Noah exhaled. Before continuing, he noticed the guests in the room seemed to be moving sluggishly, a museum crowd milling about the Venus de Milo. It was an eerie feeling he decided to ignore, keeping his curiosity focused on Emma.

"So you're responsible for my dingy little prison cell?"

She started to laugh, then stopped. "Jerry told me you needed something inexpensive near him, and that was the best I could do on short notice. A lot of history in that house. And you've got a nice view of the marsh."

Noah smiled, easing the moment. "It's fine. I'm over it. The cleaning ladies came this afternoon. Great view. Love the view. Besides, I'll probably spend most of my time here."

"Well," she asserted, giving the room a courteous glance. "*This* house is one of the best rentals in town. I'd buy this place ... I mean, if I could afford it."

"Perhaps someday," said Noah, noticing the pretty bartender peeking his way. He acknowledged her with a grinning nod, then noted her lack of movement and wondered if she was staring at him. The decelerating music was becoming annoying.

"The music's a bit off, isn't it?" he offered. "Mind if we go outside?"

The two snaked their way through the stagnant crowd. On the back deck, Noah slid the glass door closed, muffling the music and collective chatter. "That's better," he said, coming over and placing his near-empty glass on the railing.

It was quiet there except for the periodic breaking of waves in the distance and the light gusts of wind weaving through blades of grass on the dunes.

"I heard you wrote a play for the Playhouse."

Noah chuckled and shook his head, expressing his incredulity. "Did Jerry bother to mention that I wrote it four years ago? It ran for a couple of months in New York. It's not a new play."

"I think that's exciting. A real live playwright in our midst."

Noah sighed as he took that in. "That's not my day job, you know. I'm *not* a full-time playwright. I cover the theater circuit for the Associated Press."

She nodded, acknowledging. Noah reached for his beer and downed what was left.

"I'm looking forward to seeing it, anyway," she told him.

Noah was flattered but did not know how to respond. After a moment, he realized he was staring at her, trying to place her. He laughed uneasily and she laughed with him, easing his tension. He no longer noticed a lag in motion.

"You know, Emma, I'm sure you've heard this before and I promise it's not a line, but you really do remind me of someone. I just can't put my finger ...."

This time Noah thought he saw compassion in her eyes. He took a step back lost in a puzzle of confusion. Something seemed to be going on, something much deeper, almost disturbing. No, Noah realized, it was more disconcerting.

Just then, as if on cue, the moon retreated behind a cluster of clouds— the spotlight shut off—and, just like that, whatever sensation he was feeling, dissolved.

The sliding door opened, distracting him.

"There you are!" bellowed Jerry, a Bass Ale in his hand, sounding more than a bit intoxicated. "I've been looking all over for you."

Noah's focus shifted to his old friend. "Well, you found me."

"It's always the last place you look," said Jerry. "Why is that?"

Noah took a step towards his friend. "I think it's because you stop looking after you find someone."

"Well that's not very nice."

"No, it's not," agreed Noah.

"Should have known I'd find you out here by yourself."

Noah exhaled. "I wouldn't say I'm alone, old chum. I believe you know ...."

Turning, his arm extended in her direction, he realized Emma had vanished. "Where'd she go? She was just here."

Jerry grabbed Noah's shoulder like a father with his rambunctious son. "C'mon pal, I know that game. You don't want me thinking you're out here all by your lonesome so I won't feel sorry for you. Well, it's not going to happen. I do think you're out here by your lonesome and I do feel sorry for you." Jerry evaluated what he just said. "Or is it the other way around?"

Noah took Jerry by the arm and led him towards the glass door. "I'm fine. Really, you don't need to worry about me."

Jerry stopped. "You're a big boy, I understand. But I don't want *you* feeling sorry for yourself. I won't let you."

Noah dropped his head. "Message received." Then added, "thanks."

Jerry studied him before letting him off the hook. "Let's go in and meet the team, shall we? I'd like you to get comfortable with everyone before tomorrow's meeting." He slid the door open, allowing the music to infiltrate their space, and stepped inside.

Before following him in, Noah surveyed the beach. It was dark out there, but the scrambling clouds allowed some moonlight to slip through and, when it did, he thought he could make out her silhouette by the water.

3
Enter Molly

~~~

Noah slipped into the back of the room not wishing to disturb the production meeting.

"Morning, Noah," Roz called out. "We're just finishing up."

Noah winced and acknowledged the stage manager he had met last night with a wave of surrender before finding a seat. "I'm early. Please, don't mind me."

Roslyn Harris finished barking out notes to her attentive staff then pulled out a gold pocket watch. "It's eleven-fifty-seven. I'll see everyone back here at one o'clock sharp. If you haven't met our playwright and assistant director, Noah Miller, please introduce yourself."

Noah acknowledged the enthusiastic crew members before the room cleared then waited as Roz finished jotting notes into her black marble notebook.

"I'd hate to see your 'to do' list for the week," said Noah, coming up to her.

Roz extended her hand and he reciprocated. "I'm strictly a day-to-day person," she replied. "I can't think in terms of weeks. For me, it's what do I need to get done today."

She stood. "That's where this comes in," she said, raising her notebook for emphasis before placing it inside a khaki green knapsack she left on the table. "I'm old school. I'd be lost without it."

She wound her way backstage and Noah followed. "We have sets to build, a lighting program to work out, costumes to coordinate, props to gather, blocking, rehearsals, sound, it never ends, and that's what I love about my job. Keeps me on my toes."

She passed through a doorless threshold and approached a midsize fridge. "Peter should be here soon," she informed him. "He's usually on time."

Noah took in the theater's utility kitchen with a sink, electric coffee pot, microwave, and a couple of beat-up cabinets. "I like your watch," he offered, changing the subject. "Didn't know anyone still used those things?"

Roz removed the watch from the tiny front pocket of her Levi jeans. "Grandpa worked for the old New Haven Railroad line out of Boston. He was an engineer. Loved what he did." She admired the delicate timepiece before handing it off. "When he retired after 52 years, they gave him that."

She paused, reminiscing. Noah sensed she was holding back emotions. "Guess they don't do that sort of thing anymore," she added.

He inspected the elaborately etched engraving and opened the casing before handing it back.

"Good times," she said, taking a final sentimental look. "He'd let me drive the engine on special occasions." She smiled at the memory before replacing the watch in her pocket. "Of course, his hands were always on top of mine just in case."

Roz opened the fridge and retrieved a brown paper bag from the top shelf. "Something to drink?" She pulled a pink soda can off the door.

"I'm good, thanks," he said, giving her an inquisitive look.

"It's TaB," she told him before popping the tab.

"Didn't know that was still around."

"Guess I'm the only one that still drinks it."

Returning to the big table, they sat catty-cornered as she pulled out a turkey and swiss sandwich—wrapped in translucent waxed paper.

"Not eating?" she asked, pausing for an answer, and, when it didn't come right away, taking a ravenous bite.

He shifted in the hard steel chair trying to get comfortable. The folding chair felt cool, reminding him of grammar school days.

"Had a late breakfast," he said, lying to her and to himself.

He watched as she devoured her Kaiser roll and bit into the half-sour pickle.

"They never have those real sour pickles anymore," she said, finishing it.

Noah smiled to himself and crossed his legs.

"I understand you write full time," she mentioned.

"Associated Press. Theater reviews mostly."

"Yes," she said. "So I've heard."

Noah was not sure what to make of that and Roz did not bother to elaborate. He let it go.

"And, you know," he continued, "this play ran for three months. Off-Broadway."

"I know," said Roz. "I saw it."

"Sorry I'm late, everyone," announced Jerry Ziegler, bursting into the room and coming over beside Noah. "Had an early meeting in Plymouth this morning. Where's our director?"

"Should be here any minute," said Roz to the show's producer as she cleaned up her mess.

"How'd it go?" asked Noah.

"The meeting?" Jerry sighed. "Who knows. Nobody makes commitments anymore. Getting harder and harder to make a deal no matter how you slice it."

Jerry sat and began sniffing. "Was someone eating a kosher half-sour dill pickle?"

Noah scrutinized his friend. No getting anything by Mr. Pickle.

Roz turned to him. "What can I say? I like 'em."

"I do, too," admitted Jerry, "but whole sours are so much better."

"I'll try to remember that," she offered, giving Noah a look.

Changing the subject, Jerry went on. "I was looking over the schedule," he said, "and noticed we have less than one day from the closing of your current show and our tech rehearsal. Are we going to be able to break everything down on stage and get the lights, sets, and mikes ready in time for final tech?"

Roz did not hesitate. "It'll be tight but we've done it before. The crew knows what to expect."

Noah waited to see if Jerry had a follow-up. He did not. "So, what did you think?" he asked her.

She started to respond then stopped to face him. "What did I think of what?"

"My play?"

Roz placed her knapsack on the floor beside her and reached inside. "Well," she said, mulling it over. "Overall, I think you did a good job."

Noah was not buying it. "Thank you. But what did you *think?*"

She pulled her notebook out and placed it on the table in front of her.

"Well, it was a few years ago, understand, and I've seen a lot of theater in between." Noah continued to stare.

"From what I remember, the theme was universally appealing and I thought you did a good job developing the characters." She stopped there hoping she had answered his question.

"And?" he prodded.

Now she looked for her pencil and, finding one, gazed back at him. "You know you're putting me on the spot."

"I'm just asking you to be honest. Believe me, Roz, I have plenty of experience with criticism. I do it for a living. Don't feel like you have to sugarcoat it for my sake."

She pondered that before going on. "Okay, here's *my* review of your play. I loved the dream sequence at the end. It was different and memorable. There were some good lines in the show. Your characters were more or less clichés although I believe a stronger cast might have made that less noticeable."

Noah grinned and shook his head. Couldn't fault her for her frankness. Besides, he had asked for it. "And what did you think of the ending?"

Before she could answer, Peter Benson strolled into the room. "Everyone, good morning," he said in a vigorous tone without raising his voice, trying not to sound hungover.

"It's afternoon," Jerry informed him, giving Noah a side glance.

Peter placed his bag on a chair. "Tomatoes, to-ma-toes," said Peter, finishing up a soda, then chucking it towards a garbage pail, missing.

"Since you didn't bother showing up at our little soiree last night," said Jerry, "you didn't get to meet our playwright."

Peter extended a hand towards Noah and Noah stood to receive it.

"Peter Benson. Nice to meet you, Noah."

"Pleasure," said Noah.

"Sorry, Jerry," added Peter, "I had something last night. Hope you all enjoyed yourselves." Then sitting, "Are we ready to discuss the schedule?"

Roz opened a file folder and distributed calendar pages to each of the attendees. At the top, it read "Production Schedule – *Committed*; Opening August 3rd, Closing August 28th."

"Roz," continued Peter, "why don't you walk us through it?"

For the next twenty minutes, Roz went over the schedule, day by day, leading them up to opening night.

"Thank you," said Peter. "Just one change I need to make. I can't be here on the 21st, personal thing, so we'll have to switch it with the open date."

Noah jumped in. "I'd be happy to take over for you that day, I mean, if it's okay with you."

Peter studied him before responding and Noah took advantage of his ambivalence. "We'll be two weeks in by then. You'll let me know what you want to work on. That way we can leave the schedule as is as well as the open date."

Peter considered the offer. "I'll take you up on that, Noah."

"Good," said Jerry, standing. "Is that it? Are we done?"

Peter pushed his chair away from the table and rose. "I think that will do it for today as far as you guys are concerned." He turned to Roz. "You almost done setting up for the next show?"

Roz nodded. "We're on schedule."

"Excellent," said Peter, flashing a faux smile. "Then I'll leave it in your good hands. Auditions tomorrow. I'll see everyone at 10 a.m."

After Jerry ran out and Peter left, Noah found Roz in the kitchen. "Is he normally that talkative?"

Roz finished rinsing a knife in the sink. "He's complicated," said Roz, shutting the water. "Always has a lot on his mind."

In the next room, they could hear people shuffling in, some crew back early from their lunch break.

"Nothing to worry about," she continued, drying the knife with a dish towel. "He's a good director. Been here for years. The actors like working with him."

"The actors?" said Noah. "And the *crew?*"

Just then, on cue, Will and Maggie entered the room heading straight for the coffee machine as Noah stepped out of their way. Will filled up the pot with water while Maggie cleaned out the filter and refilled it with fresh ground coffee.

"Make it strong, Mags, okay? The last pot you made was as weak as my bad knee."

"Stop complaining," she ordered, raising her coffee spoon. "You're beginning to sound like my ex. Without the perks!"

Coming closer, Will added, "You mean the wild sex every night and twice on Sunday?"

Maggie shook her head. "*No,* I mean the regular paychecks he brought home every Friday."

"Okay you two," chided Roz. "That's enough of that."

The two culprits shot each other a look before laughing it off. Roz turned back to Noah. "The crew is *my* responsibility."

Noah nodded and left it there. "See you tomorrow."

The next morning, Noah pulled into the Playhouse parking lot just as Jerry was getting out of his car, carrying an extra-large cup of Dunkin'.

"How you doing, buddy?" asked Jerry.

Noah nodded. "I'm good."

"Great day to start working on a play, don't you think? This is why I love the business. We have a venue, got our actors coming, and, of course, the Cape. It doesn't get any better than this. What do you say?"

Noah breathed in the muggy bay air. It was going to be a hot one. "Doesn't get any better … as long as there's air conditioning."

Jerry took note and placed his arm around Noah's shoulder as the two headed for the backdoor. "And you. Away from the city. Out here on beautiful Cape Cod. Working on your play. This must seem like heaven to you."

Noah gave his pal a facetious glance. "Just like heaven."

"I'm serious," said Jerry, goading him to agree. "Doesn't this beat being cooped up in an office, writing reviews for pathetic excuses for shows—phones ringing, colleagues interrupting, deadlines, interviews, traffic, noise, garbage, New York City subways—*must I go on?* I mean, really, how can you compare that to this?"

Noah opened the door. "Got to hand it to you, Jerry. No complaints from me."

Jerry stepped through the doorway. "I hope you're serious."

An hour later, as Roz and her crew were busy installing the main set for the Playhouse's upcoming production of *Deathtrap,* Noah, Jerry, Peter, and Peter's summer intern, Bobby Callahan—a Boston College senior majoring in theater—were holding auditions in the back room. They had six major roles to cast plus one minor role and two extras for understudies and every out-of-work actor from Providence to Provincetown was hanging out waiting for their name to be called.

"Call the next one, Bobby," said Peter, squeezing the skin between his eyebrows then popping a couple of Advils as they crawled through the interminable audition process.

Jerry was whispering lunch options in Noah's ear when Molly Talbert stepped up to the table and handed her photo-resume in Noah's direction. Peter intercepted it. Noah was immediately transfixed and the only one, apparently, who recognized her—the bartender from last night's party—to whom he never did get back.

"Molly Talbert," announced Bobby.

She smiled seductively at Noah. "Bass Ale?"

"My favorite," said Noah.

"Is one your limit?"

Noah grinned, taking his time, assessing her slender build and firm breasts. He wondered if they were real, then decided they were. Everything about her appeared genuine. "When it comes to indulging, I can only handle one at a time."

She chuckled at his playful response.

"I like Bass Ale," said Jerry, attempting to trespass on the conversation.

"Excuse me," interrupted Peter. "I'm trying to run an audition here and we've got an endless line of actors waiting their turn to ride Space Mountain. So, if you don't mind ..."

"Sorry," said Noah.

"Molly," said Peter, "nice to see you again. If you would, please read from the middle of page 10. Bobby?"

"Ready," the intern answered.

When the scene was over, Peter gave her two more pages to read.

"Thank you," said Peter, "we'll be in touch."

Molly showed off her minty-fresh smile. "Thank you," she said to no one in particular. And, as she turned to leave, "Hope to hear from you."

"Mmmmmm," whispered Jerry to Noah. "I think I'm in love."

Noah's gaze did not leave her until the door behind her closed.

Later that night, Molly received a call from Bobby requesting that she return the next day.

On Wednesday, callbacks proceeded a lot quicker since there was a much smaller pool of actors to choose from. Peter, Jerry and Noah discussed each performer they auditioned and narrowed the list down. Noah did his best to remain objective through the entire process and not flirt with Molly when it was her turn. A day earlier, he chastised himself for his behavior and decided that a relationship now, with her or anyone, would not be advisable. This was not the time ... definitely not the right time.

So, in an act of deception, which he had virtually no experience at, Noah tactfully struggled to influence the decision against Molly getting a part in his play. But Peter had worked with Molly before and was familiar with her abilities. He advocated on her behalf and there was little Noah could do to change his mind.

Jerry remained neutral as long as he could to support his pal until it came down to a final vote between Molly and another actress. "I'm sorry, Noah," he said, "but I have to agree with Peter. He knows her and he's worked with her before and we agreed to choose the best actor for each role. Besides, I think she'll be great."

By the time they left the Playhouse at three that afternoon, the cast for *Committed* had been set and Molly Talbert had gotten one of the lead roles.

4
Six Feet

I t was raining that day—a miserable day—all the more appropriate, considering.

Maybe our guests would not show up because many do not enjoy driving in that kind of downpour. They worry about their brakes, smashing into a telephone pole, running someone over. Most drivers do not change their wipers until after they are in a heavy rainstorm or blizzard and realize they cannot see five feet in front of them. They do not recognize the importance of a twenty-dollar pair of wipers until it is too late. And then, just like that, their lives are altered. Forever.

That's the kind of day it was. Dismal. Dreadful. Just the way I felt. A little rain wasn't going to keep them away. They were going to pay their respects, God bless them, and relish that free lunch if it was going to kill them.

Of course, this meant that I was going to have to face them.

It was called for noon and I was running late but I really had no excuse. Just taking my time. All the preparations—the catering, flowers, cleaning crew—had been taken care of by Jessica's friend, Dee Dee, who stepped up and took over when she realized I could not deal with anything that week. The only checkbox on my list that day was to show up dressed for the occasion—a pressed suit, dark tie and dress shoes. Shined.

I have no idea when the last time my shoes were shined. Probably fifteen, twenty years ago. But they still looked new right out of the box. I had only worn them for special occasions—weddings, graduations, an occasional Bar Mitzvah—but there have not been many of those lately. Well, until that day.

I arrived about an hour late and was whisked into the office to handle the bill. God forbid they could manage a funeral service for your wife prior to some pathetic schmuck taking care of the tab.

I forgot to bring a check so they had to accept my Visa. I got credit for the miles, probably enough to get me to some remote Caribbean island where I could live out my life in a beach house and you *do not* need a car with a good pair of wipers. Unless, of course, you're foolish enough to drive around in one of those hurricanes with a name.

Of course, the questions would come. Not that I had any answers but who were they going to ask? They did not give a damn about me and how I was going to get through all this as long as they could walk away grasping the big picture. Well, I wasn't going to hand them any eight-by-tens. *There were no* eight-by-tens. Hell, not even wallet size.

They escorted me into her room to identify the body. She was so beautiful, even dead, I could hardly believe she was gone. Someone handed me an envelope with her personal things. I removed her sapphire ring, the one that doubled as a wedding band. She had promised me once she would never take it off and I wasn't going to let her break that promise now. I slipped it back on her finger.

It was a lovely service. Not that I had much to do with it. The Star of David Memorial Chapel had to provide extra chairs to accommodate everyone. You know the rigid kind, unpadded, intolerable for any long period when you had to sit through a service that, mostly, you did not want to attend but knew you had to make an appearance.

A couple of people got up to say something, stories about what a wonderful person she was and how much they loved her and were going to miss her. I appreciated that.

Jessie's Great Aunt Cecilia, 93, the last full-blooded Mashpee Native American from the Wampanoag tribe, stood up from her wheelchair, her shoulders back, waiting for the room to quiet. She spoke a gentle prayer in her native tongue. Then her aide translated: *"I am the noble owl's flight,*

I am the silenced moon at night. I am the glacial winter's blast, I am forgotten days of past. Keep me near within your soul, I'll stay with you, will keep you whole. Keep me dear within your heart, I'll endure with you, will not depart."

When they were done, there were hushed whispers around the room. Then the rabbi tactfully looked my way, giving me one last chance to say something. You know, be a mensch. I blew up my cheeks and raised my eyebrows, giving him the high sign. Didn't dare shake my head, which would have given away what a wimp I was. Still not ready.

I mean, what could I possibly add to the conversation? I was searching for answers myself. I guess I could have put her life in perspective. Given people closure. Made them feel better. But who was going to make *me* feel better?

When it was over, we formed a processional behind her casket to the hearse. That is when most of the guests bolted but not before extending a hand or planting a kiss and letting me know how sorry they were.

How sorry were they? Sorry that I have to spend the rest of my life without my beautiful wife? Sorry that it was me and not them? Sorry that I will grow old without my companion and best friend, keeper of shared memories and private jokes by my side? *That sorry?*

"Too bad, Noah, you had a fifty-fifty shot there but you blew it. She went first, you understand, and, well, you only go around once. She's gone, you're not, and I'm late for tee time. Been nice. Great service. Loved the Rabbi. Keep in touch, okay? We'll have you over for dinner sometime."

Yeah, right. Probably kill myself first.

At the cemetery, everyone took a turn tossing dirt in the grave. A Jewish thing. Then I commandeered the shovel and buried her casket. Not all the way, mind you, just enough so it was not visible anymore. It's a mitzvah. A good deed. You collect them like Coney Island arcade tokens, save them up and turn them in when you need a favor at a critical time in life. Not many people know that.

About ten friends stood around with umbrellas. I did not mind the rain. It was more a light drizzle at that point and cooled me off. Concealed my tears anyway. Dee Dee tried guiding the dirt into the grave with her foot until she realized what that was doing to her suede pumps. I would have appreciated some help but there was only the one shovel. Live and learn.

Most of us were listening to the rabbi chant Psalm 23 from a prayer book while I focused on the effect the wind was having on the top of the trees. I watched a maple leaf gently descend from a branch high above our heads. It tumbled lazily back and forth, ferried by a September breeze, and I followed its flight all the way down until it struck its intended target, the rabbi's balding forehead, just as he was finishing the chant.

The ambush startled him as he was stuffing the prayer book in his jacket pocket, causing him to drop it about six feet. *Into the grave.*

No one knew what to do so we all just gawked at him for guidance because if there was ever a time you needed an answer to the question— *What do we do now?*—this was one of those times.

I mean for God's sake, do we leave it there? Retrieve it? Ask for volunteers? Call in a SWAT team? What is the protocol for a dropped prayer book into an open grave?

The Rabbi must have been mortified but somehow kept his composure. I give him credit for thinking on his feet and coming up with what, I guess, he figured was his most compelling argument.

"Some people believe there are no such things as accidents. Things happen for a reason. We may not understand what the reason is now so we'll just have to accept it and leave it at that."

Then he went on to let everyone know that lunch was being served at my house and we were all invited back. Oh sure, smart guy, put the ball back in *my* court.

When I think about that day, this is how I like to remember it. The rabbi's faux pas gave people something to talk about, a story to gossip with all the freeloaders who never made it to the cemetery and only showed up for the catered lunch.

In truth, I contend, he was right. There are no accidents. I also believe that my wife was somehow involved. I imagine she plucked that leaf off the tree and guided it down to its intended target—the rabbi's noggin—causing him to drop that book into her grave. Not because she was an avid reader. I think she did it for me.

You see, she knew me best and would have known how uncomfortable I would be having to face everyone that day. That dreary day. She gave them something to talk about so they would ease up on me.

Even in death she was looking out for me. Still taking care of things.

That was my Jessica.

5
Reverberations

T he next day was a balmy summer day and Noah took advantage by working on the script in his backyard. It was an off day for everyone except three crew members who were setting up lights for the new show. Peter had discussed some minor fixes with him the night before and Noah agreed to make the changes. It was just after noon and the marsh before him was nearly still, save for some restless flies, mosquitoes, lady bugs, and lily-pad hoppers, busy with their lives in the obscure insect universe.

Noah was finishing up a slice of Sweet Tomatoes' personal pizza he had picked up earlier along with a cup of iced coffee. He had come to realize that he was no longer in the city and if you needed something you had to go get it yourself, delivery service was not always an option on Cape Cod. Sweet Tomatoes did offer "drive up service," he learned on their website, so there was no waiting time since he had called ahead, a tolerable concession he would have to live with.

Comfortable in a beach lounge chair he had recovered from a below-deck storage locker at Jerry's place, Noah read through the first draft rewrite on his laptop. The changes Peter had requested were not really essential to the show, just adding lines to the non-pivotal roles to give them, as Peter put it, "more three-dimensionality." He also suggested building in some backstory for one of the main characters so her actions at the end were more credible. Noah didn't think it was truly necessary for that last suggestion, but decided not to object, figuring Peter would feel more invested in the show if his script recommendations were taken seriously.

"Hello? Noah?" He heard a woman's voice calling from inside the house. "Anyone home?"

"Out here," he called back, not recognizing the voice right away and wondering who it could be. He turned in his chair in time to see Dee Dee Donaldson, his late wife's dearest friend, coming through the duct tape-repaired screen door and rose to greet her. She had insisted on being called that instead of her given name, Donna, after her divorce. She thought it more exotic and necessary now that she was back in the game.

"Dee Dee," he said, giving her a heartfelt hug and compulsory peck on the cheek. "What are you doing here?"

"Believe it or not," she said, "I was in the neighborhood." She stopped there, taking in the captivating picture before her. "Now you're talking," she said, admiring the view. "This is beautiful. And peaceful. So peaceful out here. It's like another world."

"Thank you," he replied. "I do love it here. Please." He pointed to the seat at the table and returned to his lounge chair.

On the table, she noticed the pizza box and opened it. "You don't mind, do you?"

"Help yourself," he offered. "It's good, in a thin crust, low-sodium, non-Mozzarella cheese sort of way."

She inspected what was left. "That doesn't sound too appetizing."

"Try it," he suggested. "It's different than New York pizza but has its merits."

Dee Dee separated the last two slices. "I hardly had any breakfast this morning."

"Want me to nuke it for you?"

"That's okay. I'll try it like this."

She picked one up and folded it. It cracked.

"Probably cold by now," he said, "but still good." Noah watched her take a bite.

"Interesting," she conceded. "Not as greasy."

He waited until she swallowed. "So how did you find me?"

She was about to take another bite then decided against it. "Believe me, it wasn't that hard. We came up yesterday—I'm here with my girlfriend, Joanie—and we were looking for something to do this weekend and thought it might be fun to see live theater. I saw your name on the Playhouse website. That's great they're producing your show again, Noah. Good for you. I think that's marvelous. Anyway, I stopped in Dennis to pick up our tickets for *Deathtrap*, and started talking to this lady. I told her I was a friend of yours. Someone made a call to Jerry, who said it was okay to give me your address and, well, here I am. Hope you don't mind that I came by. I didn't interrupt you or anything, did I?"

Noah shut the laptop. "Not at all, Dee. It's good to see an old friend." He stretched out in his chair. "So where are you guys staying?"

Dee Dee took another bite of pizza then crossed her legs showing off her chiseled, supple thighs. She often wore a tight blouse and short skirt to accentuate her modeled features, fully aware of the power of a seductive body.

"We rented a beach house in Dennis."

Noah nodded, having exhausted the limits of his small talk.

She pulled a tissue from her leather clutch and dusted the crumbs from her lips. For a moment they just sat and stared at one another—Noah fearful that Dee Dee had brought an agenda with her and was about to unleash it.

"So," they said in unison, unwilling to let the quiet persevere another second. Then they laughed, genuine nervous laughter. Hers genuine. His nervous.

"Noah," she began, giving him advance warning that the assault was at hand. "You know I love you, right?" Before he could respond in any sensible manner, she added "and I know you know how much I loved Jessica."

Noah tried to take a breath to calm his rising pressure but his lungs were too compressed to inhale. "Dee," was all he could muster, but that didn't stop her.

"I wanted to apologize to you."

He felt a physical release inside his chest cavity with some relief. "Apologize? For what?"

She leaned forward, placing her hand on his knee. "I knew Jess was unhappy. I was with her the night before she … you know … and we talked about things. She opened up to me." She paused. "We cried a lot that night." Dee Dee let that settle before moving on. "She was so lost and confused. She told me she wasn't sleeping, wasn't eating, she was just so depressed over what happened, she didn't know how to handle it."

She stopped there and Noah watched as she raised her head, peering straight into his hazel-green eyes. "I'm so sorry I didn't say anything."

He waited. "It's okay," he offered, unsure whether she heard.

"Should have said something," she murmured to herself.

Then it started, and Noah watched a single tear well up in her eye and descend her cheek, grasping onto the bottom of her chin before letting go.

"Maybe if I had told you …"

Soon the onslaught was upon him, a heavy rainstorm of tears that propelled him to embrace her. They sat in that position for what seemed much longer than it was, until her tremors subsided and he began stroking her upper arms.

"Thank you," she said pulling back.

"For what?"

She stood up. "For letting me get that off my chest."

He got to his feet, "You know you can tell me anything, Dee," and realized he sounded like Mr. Rogers. "I'm glad you said something."

She gazed at him again and used the tissue she had crunched up to wipe away what was left of her tears. "I've been wanting to tell you that for some time."

He watched her blow her nose.

"I understand. It's been tough on everyone."

She smiled but Noah could sense the pain. Then she started to make her way in and he escorted her to the screen door. "I'll be back in August to see your play."

Noah shook his head. "Don't feel like you have to."

She smiled again. This time it was more like a laugh. "Don't be silly, Noah Miller. Of course I'll be here."

He grinned, embarrassed, and pulled the door open. "Enjoy your time on the Cape."

Dee glanced at him—just under the time limit he might consider it uncomfortable—and headed inside. She stopped and turned back. "You know … she loved you very much."

He stood there a moment after she left until her car pulled away then went back to the table, gathered up the garbage and placed it in the pizza box.

He looked out on the marsh. The insects were still buzzing about though he sensed there was more at play. He knew there was a pecking order in the insect world just like anywhere else. Grasshoppers devoured plant life. Spiders and praying mantises consumed other insects. There was a hierarchy in the bee family with queens, drones, and workers, each with a job to do. Everything had a place by design. Each life form had a reason for living and a challenge to face.

Noah sat at the table, contemplating what Dee had told him. He rested his chin in his hand and sensed the familiar agony of lost love brewing inside. He thought about Jessica and how much he missed her and how hollow everything felt since she left him and how it all just seemed like a dreadful dream he could not wake up from. It had all been there, right in front of him, and then, like that, it was gone.

He was her husband and had vowed to look after her in sickness and in health. That was his commitment to her. He had given his word in front of the rabbi and their families.

It was on its way. No stopping it now. He perceived that tsunami wave of agony coming at him, about to engulf him, flowing closer and closer and crashing down on his coastline, shattering whatever remnants of his heart remained into billions of shards of abandonment and despair, his penitence for a job poorly done.

The last thought he had before his own downpour started, was—how had he missed the signs of his wife's suicide?

6
Abel's Hill

Friday was a full day for Noah and Peter. At 9 a.m., they met with Roz and her crew to work out the lighting design for the show. Some dramatic lighting was needed for a couple of scenes and the lighting designer and technician were both pros. Noah could tell they brought a vast amount of experience to the table.

After that, a husband-and-wife-team in charge of set design, came in to finalize plans from the script that had been emailed to them a month earlier. Since the action took place in a small apartment, and the dining area and living room were the main sets, there were no apparent complications.

Noah was a few minutes late to his briefing with the costume designer. She offered a number of helpful solutions for the main characters and described how their wardrobe would change from scene to scene to enhance the action.

After lunch, Roz and Jerry joined them to discuss minor changes in the rehearsal schedule over the next few weeks because one of the main actors had requested two days off for a Warner Bros. film she had auditioned for several weeks ago. The agent for Mindy Russell, had called Peter last night to advise him that Mindy had just learned she was chosen for the role and regretted having to make this request after the schedule was compiled. Peter was not pleased to make the concession but he admired Mindy and agreed to give her the time off. Other things could be worked on while she was away. Besides, he was not about to lose her over this.

Then, Jerry, Peter and Noah met with the theater's marketing team to discuss ideas for online ads, local sponsors backing the show, the program, and other marketing suggestions that needed their input. That briefing was anything but that, lasting nearly three hours.

Noah's final meeting with the team that day, which turned into a dinner meeting, concerned the show's budget, which covered everything from salaries, advertising, cost of props, sets, lighting, costumes, sound, technicians, music, printing, and miscellaneous, to anticipated profits. By the time he returned home after 9 p.m., the last thing that went through his mind before conking out was tomorrow was Saturday and there was nothing on his agenda except the prospect of sleep.

On Sunday, Jerry had invited Noah to sail to Martha's Vineyard and a brunch outing with a couple of friends he wanted him to meet. While Noah was not eager to confront new people and answer personal questions about his life, Jerry convinced him that the more he got out the less of an issue it would be for him. Besides, Noah loved sailing and had not visited the Vineyard in some time. When Jerry promised that they would rent mopeds in the afternoon and visit John Belushi's gravesite on the far side of the island, Noah relented. Belushi had been one of his favorite performers.

Noah and Jerry drove to the Harwich Port marina with the top down, arriving in plenty of time for their 8 a.m. excursion. They boarded the *Valiant 42*, a magnificent sailing vessel that Ed and Amy Kaufman had owned for more than twenty years. Amy had been Jerry's psychology professor at Northeastern and, taking an interest in his theater work, had remained a good friend. She had even persuaded Ed to back some of Jerry's shows when he was first starting out as a producer.

The couple had retired in their early fifties when Ed sold ninety percent of his business—Innovative Designs Encouraging Alternative

Solutions, or IDEAS, a thriving enterprise that developed, patented and marketed new inventions—keeping ten percent and a seat on the board so he was not completely divested. They had spent most of that time sailing the double-ended cutter-rigged sloop from Maine to the Caribbean in a carefree lifestyle their friends envied.

Ed and Amy enjoyed the quiet, often unexplored destinations and avoided larger ships, ferries, and barges whenever they could. When they sailed to the Vineyard, they stayed away from the main tourist towns of Oak Bluffs and Vineyard Haven.

After giving a quick refresher course in crewing, Ed kept Jerry and Noah busy rigging the sails and other seaman's duties, giving each a turn at manning the teak steering wheel for their more than two-hour voyage to Menemsha, a remote fishing village in Chilmark on the east coast of the island. Noah and Jerry both had some sailing experience but needed to go over the seaman's terms so there was no misinterpretation of orders that could cause the boom to knock someone overboard or, worse, capsize the boat.

It took them about an hour to navigate through the harbor and rig the sails properly for Nantucket Sound, and once they were on their way on open seas, the two were relieved of their duties for the time being.

Sunning themselves at the bow of the ship, Jerry explained that he had mentioned Noah's situation to Ed and Amy.

"Why'd you do that?" asked Noah, annoyed. "Why didn't you let me handle it the way I wanted? I thought this trip was supposed to help me, you know, work through this?"

Jerry sat there with his puppy-dog face until his friend had had his say. "I'm sorry, Noah," he told him. "I didn't want you to be uncomfortable. This way it's out there and, hopefully, there'll be no awkward questions."

Noah shook his head. "You're amazing, you know that? And sometimes you're a complete buffoon."

"But you love me, don't you? You know I'm always watching your back?"

Noah grinned, shaking his head. "Why is it that my back only needs watching when you're around?"

Jerry sat back. "That's love, boychik. You might think it's paranoia, but it's called true love in my book."

After docking in Menemsha, the group headed over to the Beach Plum Inn & Restaurant, a working farm with cows and chickens, overlooking scenic Vineyard Sound. Ed and Amy were friends with the owner who always saved the best table for them and their guests when they knew they were coming.

"Did you receive my package?" Ed asked Matthew, the proprietor, as he sat down.

"The Dom is safe and sound," replied Matthew. "Mimosas okay with everyone?"

They all nodded and Matthew left to retrieve a bottle along with four glasses of orange juice.

"They don't serve champagne here?" asked Jerry.

"They don't serve any liquor," explained Amy. "Chilmark is one of the island's 'dry' towns. It's BYOB, and we like to send it ahead so we don't have to lug it up the hill."

"How do you know Matthew?" Noah asked Ed.

"He and I worked together on some invention ideas he came up with some years back. A couple of them were popular for a while."

"Anything I might have used?" inquired Jerry.

Ed and Amy shared a smirk. "Have you ever milked a cow?" Ed asked.

Jerry chuckled. "Not recently."

"I didn't think so," offered Ed. "Another one assisted disabled people with cracking an egg open."

Jerry's smile downsized. "Probably never used that one either."

After the mimosas were poured, the group feasted on lobster omelets, pan-fried asparagus, warm blueberry muffins, and an exotic house specialty dessert that featured stewed plums.

"That was amazing," said Jerry, lengthening his belt a notch.

"Delicious," added Noah. "Thank you for taking us here."

"We love coming to places like this," said Amy, "and it's always nice to bring friends along."

Ed added, "We're blessed to find places like the Plum off the beaten path. When people go exploring a new area, most of them don't really take the time to look for the obscure restaurant or whatever it is they're after, which is too bad because they miss out."

"You're lucky you have the time," said Noah. "Jerry mentioned that you don't work anymore and spend a good deal of your time traveling. I'm envious. I'm also curious. Do you ever miss working? I mean, it seems like you have plenty to do with your boat and your travels and finding great places to eat." He stopped there to allow them to digest his words. "Do you ever feel like you made a mistake retiring when you did?"

When Ed did not respond, Jerry intervened. "I think what Noah's trying to say is ..."

"I got this, Jerry," Ed interrupted, with no apparent anger in his voice. "It's a deep question you're asking Noah, and I needed a second to think through my answer." He gave his wife a look, who appeared to know what was coming. "I believe the key to early retirement, to any sort of retirement, really, is staying busy."

Noah nodded gradually, hoping for more.

"Shortly after I sold my business," Ed continued, "I felt this emptiness. Not at first. I mean, you work so long to put it together, then, when it's gone, you're relieved. We had enough money for a comfortable lifestyle. I didn't have to worry about bills, returning phone calls, or any of that stuff we all have weighing us down every day." Ed took a sip of his cooled coffee. "Then something happens. I don't know. It just comes out of nowhere. It's probably like being a star ballplayer for most of your life then finding yourself sitting in the stands and no one recognizes you. That's what it felt like, a shot to the gut. The phones stopped ringing, the mailman stopped delivering, almost as if you dropped out of life. Like you're invisible. Dead and buried."

Ed caught himself there, realizing his metaphor might have been inappropriate. "Eh, sorry Noah," he offered. "That was a poor analogy. I didn't mean anything by it."

Noah nodded, forcing a smile. "That's okay. Didn't take offense."

After a brief moment, Ed continued. "I've got one more but this one has a positive spin. Remember that movie, won best picture—*Shawshank Redemption*? It had a great line in it."

"About getting busy—living or dying," said Noah.

Ed smiled. *"Yes."*

"It's a good line," agreed Noah. "A good philosophy."

"And it's *so* true," Ed added. "You can feel sorry for yourself and melt away or you can get out there and enjoy life. What's left of it. The world has so much to offer if you're willing to look for it. I believe people retire too late because they're afraid of running out of money and they want to pace themselves. Then, when they're ready, they're either too old, too lazy, or too scared. You've got to do it when you can still get around. Still see it for yourself. So I asked Amy to retire not too long after I did so we could continue our journey together. Move forward with our lives." He took Amy's hand. "And we've never looked back."

"I certainly have no regrets," added Amy. "Sure, I miss teaching. Miss my students and the people I worked with. But buying a boat and seeing the world has been a treasure I wouldn't trade for anything. No regrets here."

After brunch, the group hiked down to the beach, got their feet wet in the choppy blue water, and a stroll along the shore. After an hour or so, they headed into town. Ed was meeting an old friend there and Amy wanted to get to the fish market to check out what they were catching. She was planning a dinner party on their boat later that week. Noah and Jerry were hoping to rent mopeds for their afternoon excursion but had to settle for what they could find, electric bikes. They set the time to meet, which gave them a little less than four hours for sightseeing.

"I didn't exactly agree to this, you know," complained Jerry as they got underway.

"Come on, Jer," said Noah, "we got a beautiful day, empty roads ahead and the wind at our backs. What could be better than this?"

"Give me a minute," said Jerry. "Oh, yeah. Anything else!"

Noah laughed as he took the lead, rising up from his seat and pedaling away. "There's a hill up ahead … going down. Come on, Jerry, put your heart into it!"

Jerry struggled to keep up. "It's not my heart that I need right now. It's my legs, my thighs, my knees, and my butt. And they're all telling me to call an Uber!"

Then Noah took off down the hill, expanding the gap between them, and slowed down at the bottom waiting for his friend to catch up.

"That was incredible," said Noah. "I forgot how much fun it was to take a hill like that. We must have been pushing fifty."

"I think the speed limit is thirty around here," said Jerry. "Just so you know. You could have been ticketed if there was a cop around."

Noah let him ramble.

"I don't understand. Why do you seem to be going that much faster than me?"

Noah looked over Jerry's bike. "It helps if you turn on your motor," then twisted the handlebar to the "on" position. "Now you're set."

"Oh," said Jerry, embarrassed. "Thanks. I was trying to save on energy, you know, with climate change and all."

Noah shook his head, laughing it off.

Fifteen minutes later, they pulled off South Road at the Chilmark Cemetery, also known as Abel's Hill Cemetery, and dismounted. This side of the Vineyard seemed deserted, even forsaken. They stood their bikes on the kickstands near the entrance. Inside, the graveyard emitted a tranquil sensation as if everything had stopped centuries ago.

"If Belushi wanted a quiet resting place," noted Noah, "he couldn't have picked a better spot."

Searching for his grave, Noah recalled his favorite Belushi movie. "*Animal House* was definitely number one on my list," said Noah. "I remember getting very high the first time I saw it and couldn't stop laughing."

"A classic movie," Jerry agreed, "but I think my choice would have to be *The Blues Brothers.* Some great lines in that movie." He quoted from the list of desperate excuses Joliet Jake pleads to his former fiancée for leaving her at the altar, ranging from running out of gas to an earthquake, a flood, and locust.

Noah laughed recalling the scene. Then they moved on. Belushi's grave was not hard to find, framed within its own split-rail fence, not far from the entry gate. It was littered with beer cans, wine corks and cigarette butts, no doubt left by fans paying tribute. Sometime after the funeral, his body was moved to an unmarked grave so only friends and family are aware of his actual resting place. This one was purportedly contrived in fear that his admirers might parade through the cemetery and ravage the grounds in search of their hero.

The headstone before them read: *"Here lies buried the body of John Belushi – January 24, 1949, March 5, 1982 – I may be gone, but Rock and Roll lives on."*

Standing there, Noah was aware that the official cause of death was attributed to a drug-related accident. He envisioned all the potential fans who never got the chance to know him.

"What a waste," said Jerry, who could have been reading his friend's thoughts.

Noah looked towards the grave with sadness. "Thirty-three years old. Too young to retire."

He was touched by the loss of the comedian and what effect that loss had on those close to him. Noah especially empathized with Belushi's family and friends. He wondered what Belushi must have been going through to risk giving up the acclaim and popularity he enjoyed at the height of his career. He considered his own recent loss and whether his wife and his favorite comedian shared a similar disorder or whether they merely surrendered to their sorrow, too depressed or disillusioned to move ahead with their lives.

After they had paid their respects, Jerry began making his way towards the entrance. "Coming?"

"If you don't mind," said Noah, "I'd like to explore a little. We still have some time. What do you say?"

"I need to take a break. That ride was a little too much exercise for one day. Actually, for a lifetime. I'm going to head back to the bikes and wait for you there."

Noah told him he wouldn't be long. Wandering further in, he passed sparse headstones with eighteenth-century dates on eroded hard-to-read markers. Each one featured a skull and crossbones. The further he advanced the further back the years went. He noted the overgrown vegetation and the mildewed footpath. No one had visited these graves or worked these grounds in some time.

He came around a bend and made his way down a pitched incline. Abel's Hill. Trudging down it, Noah wondered how long it had been since Abel descended his own hill. By the time he reached bottom, the sky had darkened and he could hear rumblings in the clouds. He thought that strange since the forecast had called for sunny skies.

The unmarked graves were nearer one another here and the massive trees—Noah recalled the colossal Sequoias he visited when he lived on the west coast—inflicted an eerie complexion out of an Edgar Allen Poe verse. He perceived he had found the original burial grounds.

Just then a streak of lightning attacked a nearby tree. Noah jumped. When the smoke cleared, he discovered dozens of bodies strewn across the grounds he would swear were not there a moment before. Dead bodies. When he approached them, he noticed they were Native Americans. And the lightning did not kill them. They appeared to have been gunned down and stabbed. He could see the wounds and musket holes and dried blood, the horror of the slaughter.

Something else was bothering him. More disturbing. Stepping carefully past them, Noah realized that except for a few elderly men, they were all women and children.

Then he saw something move—someone move—a man bending over two bodies. He was shirtless with long coconut white hair, a single reddish feather in his headband. He rose and turned towards Noah, who noticed a scar across the man's forehead. Then Noah panicked. Was he responsible for the massacre? He was not about to find out.

Noah ran up Abel's Hill. By now the winds had picked up, impeding his progress like a vindictive chest-bumping bully blocking his way. Punitive raindrops pelted him further undermining his ascent. Noah clambered up the steep muddy hill resorting to crawling when his footing gave out. When he did make it to the hilltop he kept running as if his motor was turned on, not bothering to verify whether he was being pursued. He ran all the way back, the length of the cemetery, to the gated entrance where he found Jerry on the grass, leaning up against the rusty fence.

"Jerry," he screamed out of breath. "Get up. We have to go ... now!"

"What?" said Jerry, who had been napping. "What's going on?"

"There's a guy back there. And a lot of dead bodies."

"What?" Jerry repeated, getting to his feet. "Of course there are dead bodies. Did you forget where we are?"

"No," said Noah, trying to regain his breathing. "The bodies aren't in graves. They're lying on the ground."

"Well maybe he was burying them?"

"No, you don't understand."

"What, Noah? What are you trying to tell me?"

"There were dozens, mostly women and children. Like some kind of massacre."

"What?"

"And thunder and lightning and a heavy downpour. Didn't you see it?"

"Noah, calm down. You're not making sense."

"And this Indian, Native American, was bending over the bodies. He could be responsible and he may be after me. Come on, we have to get out of here."

Jerry looked into the cemetery. There was no one in there as far as he could tell.

"Noah, get a hold of yourself. Rain? Lightning? Dead bodies? What are you talking about? It's been sunny all day. And there's no one following you. Look for yourself."

Noah peered up at the cloudless sky then into the graveyard. "But it was raining. And lightning and ..."

"What's gotten into you, pal?"

"I saw it. Saw them. Him. I swear, I'm not making it up."

Jerry took a breath. "Do you want me to walk back there with you? We could check it out together."

Noah stiffened, shaking his head. "I'm not going back in there. Sorry, I just can't."

"Are you sure?"

He took his time answering. "No. No way. I'm not going back in."

On the voyage to Harwich, there was little conversation. Noah chastised himself and questioned what he could have been thinking to want to visit Belushi's grave, which only spurred more guilt and isolation he thought had already been resolved.

As for what he thought he saw afterward, that would remain a mystery.

7
Lingering Fumes

T he trip to Martha's Vineyard was still weighing on Noah's mind the next day, July 4th, and the week-long celebrations, local parade, fireworks, and patriotic decorations tattooed on store windows and cars did not help lift his mood. Noah slept late that morning, thinking about his wife and preferring to spend the day alone. Jerry stopped by in the early afternoon, presumably to invite Noah to a holiday cookout at his beach later but Noah was convinced he was checking up on him after yesterday's ordeal. Besides, he did not feel like attending any parties.

"Don't make me start with Jake and Elwood," said Jerry in a serious tone. "Cause *you know* I will if I have to."

"Noah looked at him realizing he had no choice. "Okay, I'll go," conceded Noah. "Just please don't quote *that* movie again."

After Jerry left to see to his arrangements, Noah worked on the house. He needed to stay busy. First, he decluttered—throwing out broken things, moving furniture around so it was easier to come and go—then he laid out a couple of personal items he had brought with him, a family picture of the three of them and an early crayon drawing his daughter, Erica, had made for him. She had told him it was her family standing in the front yard of their house with a weeping willow and a rainbow fence. The drawing elicited mixed emotions.

He had been at the Cape for over a week but was still hesitant to remove the items from his bag. He spent the rest of the afternoon finalizing his script rewrites and laying out in the backyard reading his book. Then he showered and shaved and drove to the party.

He found Jerry and his guests on the beach, sitting around a makeshift bonfire, drinking beer and wine. Noah counted a dozen people in all but the only one he recognized was Peter. Someone was playing guitar, leading them in *The Night They Drove Old Dixie Down.* Noah came over and Jerry handed him a beer from a small cooler before plopping down on the sand and joining in the song.

When it was over, Jerry introduced him to the group. "Noah's play is at the Playhouse next month," Jerry told them. "I'm producing it, Peter's directing, and we expect to see all of you there in a few weeks. No excuses!"

One of the women, sporting a red, white and blue tie-died tee shirt and jeans with gold-stitched flowers on her thighs as if she was just back from Woodstock, asked "What's your play about, Noah?"

Noah smiled, embarrassed. "It's called *Committed*, about a couple that's been dating for a while and she's at the point of pressuring him to make their relationship more permanent while he's beginning to have second thoughts."

"The story of my life," said Penny, Peter's date, an attractive veterinarian Noah later learned. She playfully smacked Peter in the arm, then added, "Why is it always the guy who gets cold feet?" They laughed.

"Well, to tell you the truth," said Noah, "the show is based on two women I dated and molded into the female lead. I met Cyma while I was away at college. Karen I met a couple of years later here on the Cape." He hesitated before going on. "I was young, carefree and believed in the magic—you know, love conquers all. The truth is, Karen's the one who got cold feet and wouldn't commit."

Some cross discussion followed until Penny asked, "Why didn't you write it that way?"

Noah picked up a handful of sand, letting the grains sift through his fingers. He wavered on the degree of sincerity he wanted to share with a group of people he did not know. "She broke my heart," Noah admitted, his attention fixed on the mound of sand before him. He swallowed hard, then raised his gaze to meet Penny's. "Maybe I should have. All I know is it was easier to write it that way. I could still use the pain and vulnerability I felt then but could redirect it in a more accessible way. Just the choice I made at the time."

No one had anything more to add, except Noah. "If you come see it, I hope you'll let me know what you think."

Jerry popped the cap off another beer. "Of course she's coming. You're all coming. I thought I made myself perfectly clear … otherwise, I'll have you quartered, shot, and walking the plank. In that order."

When his stomach began gurgling, Jerry corralled Penny and her friend, Gloria, to join him in the house and the three returned with platters of cooked shrimp, mussels, crab legs, and cut vegetables. They feasted on the holiday buffet, and after, enjoyed a rousing version of *American Pie* as the day grew darker, culminating with a blazing sunset that stretched across the bay.

Noah pulled off his socks and stuffed them in his shoes then left the campfire for a walk along the shore. He allowed the gentle waves to spray him, then, found himself swallowed up by the soft damp sand and prowling tides pecking at his toes.

A little while later, he stopped to admire the fireworks light up the sky.

"Ooooh, pretty," said a voice coming up behind him.

Noah turned to find Emma, the real estate agent he had met that first night at Jerry's.

"Hello there," he offered. "The last time I saw you, you were there. Then were gone."

Emma let that one alone. "I love a good fireworks show. Don't you?" She strolled along the water.

"Where you been hiding?" he asked, keeping pace.

She giggled a bit nervous. "Working. Selling. Renting. This is my busy season. The plight of the real estate agent." She stopped there to remove her dark leather sandals, placing her hand on his shoulder for support. "How's your play coming?"

Noah picked up a stone and threw it into the water. He did not see it land. "Keeping me busy. Rehearsals begin this week. I'm psyched."

They continued up along the coast. A couple of rambunctious kids ran by waving sparklers, towing their lagging parents behind. None of them seemed to notice the pair.

He studied her face when reflecting light allowed. "Are you from the Cape? I mean, originally?"

She watched the colorful spectacle. "I was born in Quincy, actually," she said, turning her attention to him. "The Boston area. Most of my family is from the Cape. My grandmother had a house in Chatham and I spent my summers here when I was growing up."

"That must have been fun," said Noah.

She peered out on the bay enjoying the perpetual reverberation of the placid waves. "I loved coming here. Spending time with my cousins. Grandma and Aunt Sylvia gave us cooking lessons. We took turns making dinners, baking desserts. I really enjoyed being here and decided this is where I wanted to live."

"What about your parents?" he asked.

She took her time. Noah noticed her hesitancy. "I lost my parents in an accident."

"Sorry, I shouldn't have …"

"It's okay. It was … a while ago."

They stood on the beach admiring the show. When the finale began, they were mesmerized by the onslaught of sound and fury as the frantic outburst ignited the night, watching in silence until the lingering fumes from the final blast died, dropping wearily from the sky.

"Now that you know my story," she said, "I'd like to hear more about you."

He started back towards Jerry's place. "Oh, I'm not that interesting."

"Tell me about your family."

He glanced at her, wondering. But she had opened up to him. "What do you want to know?"

He was procrastinating but she was ready. "Whatever you'd like to share."

He appeared to be struggling, troubled, his expression shifting with each memory. "I had a daughter. Erica. She had a stuffed animal she took to bed with her every night. She loved that thing." He stopped there then added, "she was very smart. Started reading before she was four."

"*Had* a daughter?" she questioned. And, when he didn't respond, added, "Noah, what happened?"

He took a breath, almost imperceptibly. She was the first one in some time to ask. He questioned whether she was the right person to confide in but thought if he could just get it out—say the words—perhaps it would stop weighing on him so heavily. "She drowned. Last summer. July. It was an accident."

He did not understand why he was opening up to her and yet he continued. "She was so sweet. So smart. I miss her."

Emma did not prod any further, allowing him the moment.

"She had just turned four. It was a pool party. One of her friends. Monica. Monica's birthday."

A painful smile followed. "Jessica took her. My wife." Then blurted "I lost *her* three weeks later."

He stopped there.

"*Noah,*" she offered. "I'm sorry. Terrible thing to lose a child. *And* your wife, my God."

He did not respond, just stood there, disorientated, lost in a bleak world as if he was the last burst of light from a summer fireworks' show searching for the other vanished flares. Talking about it failed to relieve him of anything.

Sometime later, he realized he was still standing on the same spot. He looked around but it was too dark, like he had been sucked into a black hole and every ounce of light had gone with him. He breathed in the night, refueling his lungs, but could not see a thing even if she was right there beside him. The beach was deserted. He called her name but there was no response.

He headed back to the party and found Jerry, Gloria, and another couple sitting around the waning fire, tossing whatever they had in to keep it going.

"Who is that?" cried Jerry, more than a bit inebriated. When he sensed Noah's presence, "Noah, is that you? Is that *you*, Noah?"

"Hi Jerry," said Noah, sitting beside him.

"Where the hell have you been?"

Noah pulled a tissue from his pocket and dropped it on the dying embers. It flared briefly. "Took a walk. Watched the fireworks. Did you see it?"

"How could you miss it?"

Jerry opened the cooler to offer his friend a beer but there were none left. "You were out there all this time? By yourself?"

Noah took his time. "No. I ran into …"

He stopped there, then reached for the last scrap of food on the platter in front of him. A piece of stale broccoli.

"Yes?" Jerry inquired. "Who'd you say you ran into?"

Noah finished chewing. "No one. No one you know. Great fireworks, huh? They really know how to celebrate the holiday around here. Thanks for inviting me, pal."

Down the shore about a mile away, the chilled tide ebbed and flowed over vanishing footprints.

8
Drama Versus Comedy
❧⦿❧

We used to laugh a lot more.

We were young, still in our twenties, and nothing bothered us that much, at least, no one let it. Everything seemed easier then and we thought our problems were silly and if you left your keys upstairs—who cared?—you ran up and got them. No one bothered chalking the climb up the stairs to your aerobic step count for the day.

Of course, you didn't forget things as much when you were that age so you weren't required to run up too many flights of stairs. Having a sound memory was a right, not a privilege.

Summers were longer and winters shorter and spring tulips and autumn foliage took your breath away and made you feel good to be alive to appreciate it. There were weddings to attend and parties and more picnics, open bars and low-interest credit cards, and everyone was healthy and looked good in a bathing suit.

In our thirties, things were a bit more sobering. We were conscious of our careers and paychecks, paying down college debt and the relentless bills, who our friends were, how we spent our free time, and shedding a couple of pounds so we could still fit into our favorite jeans.

It was time to start thinking about moving out of the city, planning a wedding, finding a house somewhere with grass and a backyard and shrubs where you could walk your dog without having to pick up after it, getting an annual checkup, starting a retirement account.

We also decided to start a family then but that did not happen right away. So we kept trying. And trying. Eventually, we wound up at a fertility clinic—more doctors—and, somehow found a way to pay for it, thanks to understanding parents.

But we learned to our dismay that invitro fertilization is not guaranteed and, for a while, we mourned the process and our diminishing hope of return on investment.

Somehow, we got through it and when Jessica became pregnant and our precious little Erica was born, everything seemed to change.

Besides, we learned we had a support system behind us so even when unexpected problems popped up—the car wouldn't start and we were out of diapers, the pediatrician's office cancelled and the rash looked worse, the babysitter called in sick—family and friends were there to step up. We found a way to keep moving forward.

Our forties were a wakeup call, like someone pounded the big gong of life and no one was at the front door.

But it was more unnerving than that. The alarm clock goes off and you realize you're late for your first day at the new job. The officer turns on his flashing lights behind you and your mind goes blank when he asks what the emergency is? You just threw a wild pitch, allowing the winning run to score in the final game of the World Series, and you have to face your Hall of Fame-bound teammate who announced his retirement before the game.

It is time to think about starting a college fund, take a vacation for the historical landmarks instead of the beaches, hiring a lawn guy because you don't want to be the only one on the street mowing your own lawn, losing weight because your doctor ordered it.

We sweated the big stuff along with the small stuff and found out it's not all small stuff.

But none of that mattered anymore. Our family was complete and everything else would take care of itself.

We don't laugh as much as we once did, probably because, considering everything we have been through, we now believe that life is no laughing matter.

9
Character Development

A fter Noah, Peter and Jerry finished up their meetings the other day and made final decisions on sets, artwork, props, and music for the show, Peter and Noah found a quiet spot to discuss the rewrites. Jerry did not bother hanging around since he needed to get back to New York for business and to pick up his wife who planned to return with him to the Cape for the summer.

This morning, the cast and crew of *Committed* were finally coming together to begin a grueling four-week schedule of rehearsals. Before they began, Peter had the cast run through a couple of exercises to help them get better acquainted. He asked them to sit in a circle on stage and name each of the actors around them by their real names. Then, he asked them do it again using their characters' name. Once everyone was familiar with one another, the company went into the back room and sat at the table to receive the rewritten pages and begin reading through the script. Roz Harris, the stage manager, and Peter's intern, Bobby, also joined to take notes.

"Each of you have received the new pages Noah's been working on," said Peter. "Please replace them in your scripts and let's go over them. We'll start with Act I, Scene iii, pages 29 to 45, the anniversary dinner scene between Charlie and Wendy. Why don't we read through that first so everyone gets the gist of what was changed." He waited for them to find the page.

"Basically," he continued, "we added a couple of pages to the scene to delve a little deeper into his infidelity and the effect it has on their relationship. Charlie admits he's been seeing someone on the side, although he swears it's platonic, that doesn't really appease Wendy. To her, it's just as bad as if it were of a sexual nature because it's severed a trust between them and she's outraged he needs someone to talk to behind her back while he's pondering making a commitment. There's a lot of back and forth while they play off one another and some funny lines as you'll see—good job, Noah—and I believe the humor helps tell the story. Humor leads to pain, leads to anger, leads to confrontation, a vicious circle, that sort of thing, which culminates when she dumps the salad bowl over his head ending the scene. Any questions?"

Molly, scribbling notes in the margin of the new pages, asked, "Can we talk a little about Wendy? I mean, what's her story? Has she ever been married? Was she burned before? It doesn't sound like this is her first relationship. Seems to me, she's seen this, I mean, Charlie's infidelity, and she's not going to put up with it, sexual or otherwise. I'm just trying to get a handle on her character so I understand what I'm going into the scene with."

"Good question," said Peter. "Noah, can you offer some backstory on Wendy's and Charlie's characters for Molly and Wayne?"

Noah placed the pen he used to jot his own notes on the table. "With pleasure. Let's begin with Charlie. So, Charlie has been seeing someone else because of his fear of commitment. I made his affair platonic because, obviously, he's our protagonist and I didn't want the audience to turn against him. What he's doing is acceptable, even understandable, considering he's a guy who's never been in a committed relationship. He's scared, and this is his way of dealing with his fear. Although it's wrong, I think the audience will accept it because it's something a guy might do without crossing the line. It's forgivable."

"*That's* debatable," said Molly. The room laughed.

"Perhaps," admitted Noah, grinning, "but my sense is that the majority of the audience *wouldn't* chastise Charlie for his indiscretion— they'd understand his fear and his choices in this case—so we keep them in the plus column."

"Oh?" Molly added, "so we're keeping score?" More laughter.

"Also a guy thing," said Noah, playfully. This time, even Peter joined in the laughter. Molly glanced Noah's way, holding it in, then nodded, giving him his due.

"As for Wendy's character," Noah continued, "she's more complicated. Obviously, Wendy has been burned before as Molly guessed. She's seen this behavior in a previous relationship and recognizes Charlie's fear. But here's where it deviates. Wendy loves this guy and is seriously considering marrying him. Even though she's angry and hurt, she's going to give him a chance to fix this. How does she do that? By breaking up with him. By separating from the situation, she's going to test him. And, only if Charlie truly loves her and understands this was a juvenile act that has no place in a committed relationship, will she take him back."

The discussion of character motivation and relationships continued for some time and Peter was so impressed with Noah's descriptions and backstories that he had him outline the remaining four characters as well. After deliberations, the group took a fifteen-minute break before they began reading from the script. They proceeded through it twice, stopping often to ask Noah about a particular line and character choices.

Peter mentioned that he would begin blocking—tracking of the actors' movements on stage—at rehearsal the next day.

"We'll work on blocking this week as we go through each scene. I expect that to take most of the week. I'll need everyone to memorize their lines so we're off book by Monday. That means no scripts on stage after Saturday morning's rehearsal. You'll still be able to ask for a line if you need it but I'm expecting you all to know your lines by then. Is that clear?"

Most of the actors consented in one way or another.

"Any other questions?"

When rehearsal broke, Peter, Noah and Roz stayed behind to discuss a few details that still needed attention before the next rehearsal. It was nearly six o'clock when Noah left the playhouse. Making his way through the parking lot, he found Molly leaning up against his car. "More questions for the playwright?" he asked.

"Actually, I think I have some answers."

Noah was intrigued. "Really?" He opened his side door, laying his bag on the passenger seat. "Well, I'm all for answers. What have you got?"

"I think you're Charlie," she started. "And this play is about you."

He grabbed a water from a mini cooler in the backseat. "Wow, so we're getting personal."

He looked her over, deciding how far he was willing to go. "You think you know me that well?"

He was stalling and she knew it. And, he knew she knew it.

"No, not really," she said, keeping it serious. "It's a hunch." Then, to underscore the point, peered straight into his eyes. "Am I right?"

He twisted the cap off his water and drank. "Before I answer your question, tell me why you think I'm Charlie?"

"All right," she replied, leading him away from the theater. "Mind if we walk?"

He followed her without replying, realizing she did not want Peter or Roz or anyone to see them and make assumptions.

They headed into a wooded area behind the lot, stepping on fallen branches and brittle leaves until they reached an exposed layer of sand within the brush.

"You're Charlie," she told him. "He's got your sense of humor and Wendy seems just like the kind of woman you'd fall for. Smart. Confident. Stands up for herself. I'll bet she was one of your old girlfriends. Maybe even your first love."

Noah smirked. "Charlie has my sense of humor because I created him."

That did not deter her. "But you're not denying you're him, or rather, that he's you?"

Noah chuckled, admitting to himself that he was not going to win this argument.

"I'm right," she pleaded, "aren't I?"

He laughed, his poker face shattered.

"Okay," he surrendered. "You're just too clever, what can I say."

"So, Charlie is based on you, right?"

"Yes, your honor."

"And Wendy is modeled after an old flame, right?"

"Uh huh."

"And this show is based on your relationship with that woman. Right?"

"Wrong," he said, getting serious, his entire attitude overhauled. "That's not true."

"What do you mean 'not true?'"

"She and I broke up for completely different reasons that had nothing to do with this story."

"Really?" she said, almost defeated. "I thought I had it figured out."

Noah did not want to say anymore but realized he was exposing too much with his sobering demeanor.

"Sorry to disappoint you. But if Charlie goes through with it and they wind up happily ever after, *and* this relationship is based on me, then that would mean, if you play it out, that I would have married the 'Wendy' character in real life. And that never happened."

"So tell me," said Molly. "What happened with the real-life Wendy?"

Noah took a swipe at a bug crawling up his left sock. "*Now* you're really getting personal. C'mon, let's get out of here. The natives seem to be restless."

Noah managed to turn the conversation to the other characters in the show as they headed back to the parking lot. She waited until they reached her Jeep. "You're not going to answer my question. Are you?"

He gave a quick glance around the lot, making sure it was empty. "Sometimes, you have to stand up and do what your mind tells you, despite what you may be feeling inside."

"What does that mean?"

"Let's just say, for one reason or another, it didn't work out between us." Now it was his turn to focus on her. "Can we please just leave it at that?"

Molly gave him a long stare then pulled her door open, capitulating. "Sure. I understand." She got in and looked back at him. "We'll leave it right there ... for now. See you tomorrow."

Noah watched her drive away then got into his Rogue. The summer sky was still bright and he did not want to go home yet. Did not want to be alone. Jerry wasn't coming back until the weekend so there was no one to join him for dinner. He decided to go to The Pilot House for seafood, where there would be plenty of locals—no one he knew—and a live band playing outside to keep his mind—his heart—distracted. He needed that.

He turned on his Classical radio station and sat there reminiscing, recognizing an old familiar feeling, torment, flaring up inside. He knew what it was. Guilt. Even with the separation of time, he still could not talk about the woman in the show. And tonight, with Molly, would have been the perfect time to let it out of the bottle and eradicate it once and for all. But, just like then, he did not have the nerve. Just like then, he could not bring himself to cut loose the albatross, suspended around his neck, and admit that even though he had loved Cyma, he could not go through with the wedding. He never made it to the courthouse, shattering her fragile heart and his own at the same time.

He started the engine, pulled out of the lot, and headed back to his place. He was in no mood to put on a face, even for people he didn't know.

He was tired of putting on faces.

10
Conflict

❧⟨❧⟩❧

The company of *Deathtrap* was using the mainstage for their final dress rehearsal for most of Thursday morning with the show due to open the next night. Once it did, Noah and Peter would have full use of the stage so their first official rehearsal was delayed until the set was cleared after lunch.

Noah would have liked to use that time to sit with Peter and go over the lighting design that Larry provided. He had a few concerns. He was also anxious to begin breaking down each scene for preliminary blocking of the actors' movements so they would be ahead of the game. But Peter said he was busy that morning and would not be around until one o'clock. Instead, Noah sat by himself in the rear mezzanine behind the orchestra section and watched the dress rehearsal.

While there was down time and before the house lights were lowered, he studied the architecture of the Playhouse. He noticed the high timbered ceilings extending down from the rear and the crossbeams in the rafters. Narrow overhanging loge sections on either side of the stage stretched back towards the steeply pitched balcony. He had read that the theatre was built in the late eighteenth century—used as a town meetinghouse originally—and wondered if the locals had ever gathered here to discuss their Native American neighbors. He was also aware of the tribe's unresolved battle over territorial rights.

The building was moved to its present location in 1927, attracting theater crowds away from sweltering New York City and out to the cooler coastal shores of the Cape. Top Broadway talent such as Humphry Bogart, Henry Fonda, Gregory Peck, and Bette Davis were coaxed away to make their Cape debuts on this stage. The *New York Times* once referred to the Playhouse as the "place where Broadway goes to summer."

Noah pulled out his copy of the *Committed* final draft and opened it to the first page. He pictured the set in his mind and read his own stage directions to himself.

Curtain opens to dark stage as we FADE UP MUSIC (James Taylor's Fire And Rain) *from surround-sound house speaker system. Plays for at least 10 seconds then, as MUSIC FADES DOWN, simultaneously FADE UP LIGHTS SLOWLY to find Charlie Hobson, alone on center stage sofa of living room, laying out tiles in the overturned Scrabble board game box. He is singing along to the music, which is coming from a stereo, stage left. There is room for six players around coffee table. He picks up the mini-hour glass and turns it over, testing it. He pulls out a scoring pencil from game box and realizes the point is broken, then calls out to Wendy (offstage).*

When *Deathtrap* was finished, Noah stood and applauded the actors for their curtain call. Only a handful of people made up the audience, including the producer, director and a couple of the Playhouse marketing execs Noah had met the previous week. Except for one obvious missed lighting cue, the show proceeded seamlessly and Noah wondered how many rehearsals were needed to accomplish that. He made a mental note to ask Roz later.

When everyone broke for lunch and the stage was being cleared, Noah walked out to the far end of the parking lot to check in with his boss. He had not spoken to Barney since leaving New York nearly two weeks ago and was curious to know how his temporary replacement was handling his assignments.

"Noah Miller," said Barney as if he was announcing the winner's name at the Academy Awards. "To what do I owe the honor?"

Noah had not missed his boss' sarcasm. "How you doing, Barney?"

"I'm doing just fine. How the hell are you? And how's Cape Cod treating you?"

Noah proceeded to inform him of the progress of his play and about the friendly and supportive cast and crew.

"Glad to hear it. I'm pleased things are working out."

"How's the new guy doing?"

Barney took a little longer to answer. "Harrison is working hard, pretty much keeping up with the pace. His reviews need some editing here and there but that's to be expected until he becomes more familiar with our style. Overall, I'd say he's doing fine."

Noah smirked knowing full well that the job was more challenging than Barney would admit. "Well," he said, "it appears everything is under control. It was good talking to you, Barney. I'm sure we'll be in touch …"

Barney cut him off. "Noah," he said in a serious tone, more friend than boss. "How are *you* doing?"

Now it was his turn to vacillate. "Okay. I'm … okay."

"Noah, you can tell me. I'm here to help if I can."

Noah appreciated the sincerity. Barney had always been a friend first. "I'm not sure … It's lonely, what can I say? I'm trying to stay busy and keep my mind off my problems. There. Is that what you wanted to hear?"

Barney waited to see if he was finished. "I give you a lot of credit to put yourself out there like that. I know it can't be easy but I think that staying busy is probably the best way to handle it. And, over time, you'll find that it *will* get easier for you. I'm sure of that."

"I hope you're right."

"I'm always right. You should know that by now."

After the conversation, Noah went inside to see if there was anything edible in the fridge. The *Deathtrap* crew had had an end-of-rehearsal party last night and there were still sandwiches and some pizza laying around. While he sat munching on a dried-out chicken salad sandwich, the cast from *Committed* began filing in. When Peter walked by, Noah jumped up and ran over. "Did you get my text this morning?"

"I did," said Peter. "You wanted to talk about lighting? Right?"

"Yes," Noah told him. "And I thought we'd get a head start on the blocking."

Peter opened the fridge, pulled out a slice from the pizza box, and stuck it in the microwave. "The thing is, Noah, it's hard to make blocking decisions in a vacuum. You need to have the actors say their lines as they move on stage so you can see what it actually looks like and whether or not it works. So much easier. Trust me."

"Right," agreed Noah, a bit embarrassed by his own inexperience. "Makes perfect sense."

"Good," said Peter, "why don't you gather up the troops and we'll start at the table. I've got some notes. You and I can talk about lighting after the rehearsal. Okay?"

"Sure," agreed Noah, checking his watch. "Sounds good, although I'm not sure everyone is here yet. It's just one o'clock now."

"Take an inventory and send a text to whoever's late. Even if they're a minute late. Will you do that for me, please?"

The only actor still missing was Molly so Noah shot her a text. She arrived seven minutes later and found them in the backroom. "So sorry everyone," pleaded Molly, walking in. "Peter, Noah, please forgive me. It won't happen again."

Peter bit his lip as he watched her find a seat and get settled. "I know it won't, Molly, because if it does I will have to find someone to replace you. And that will take time out of the schedule so I'd rather not have to do that. Understood?"

"Loud and clear," answered Molly as if she was responding to a drill sergeant, then, realizing that he may have taken it the wrong way, changed her tone. "I mean … I understand. Sorry."

After unlocking her gaze with Peter, she glanced at Noah who turned his head, looking away.

"That goes for everyone in this room," Peter added. "I will not put up with tardiness. When you keep me waiting, you keep everyone waiting. And we have too much to cover before we open. So here's what you're going to do. You should plan to arrive at least fifteen minutes before call time. That way, you make sure you're on time and ready to go. If, for some reason, you're going to be late, you should get in touch with me or, if you can't reach me, call Noah or Roz. Don't text me. Call me. I want to hear your voice. And it better be a real emergency that's holding you up or *I promise* I will replace you and you will never work for me again. Is that clear?" There were varying degrees of consent throughout. "All right, let's get started."

Peter delivered his notes to the group on different subjects—specific line delivery, relationships between characters, use of body language, and character reactions. Mostly, he emphasized how important it was to stay in the moment as if you were in a real life situation.

"That's my biggest concern," he said. "And you're going to hear that from me a lot in the next few weeks. Stay in the moment."

After the table discussion, the group proceeded onstage to begin rehearsing. For the first week, Peter told them, they would go over each scene as much as necessary until they got the blocking down. They would begin using props the second week when they were off book and their hands were free. That would build up a continuity. The last week they would fine tune anything that was still not working heading into "hell week," the final tech and dress rehearsals before opening.

Noah was excited to be part of the team. As playwright, you would not normally be invited to rehearsals unless your name was Neil Simon or Lin-Manuel Miranda. When *Committed* first opened off-Broadway, he was asked to sit in on one rehearsal because the director needed him to rewrite some dialogue he thought seemed contrived. Noah was willing to oblige. But now, as Assistant Director, he was in a position to express his opinion and help make decisions from beginning to end. More importantly, the entire process was keeping him busy so there was little down time. And that was helping with his other problems.

The cast worked through the afternoon and into late evening until scene-by-scene blocking for the entire play was completed, taking only one half-hour break for dinner. Noah gave his opinion freely when Peter was ambivalent how to proceed in a certain scene and, for the most part, Peter seemed pleased with his assistant's contributions.

It was a tedious process made longer because each actor needed to scribble notes in their scripts while Peter gave them direction when to cross, when to stop, when to sit, and when to stand, as they read and moved through each scene. As professionals, they were required to do this expediently.

The entire company was exhausted when Peter let everyone go with instructions to meet the next morning. They would only have until midafternoon because the stage would have to be cleared for that night's opening of *Deathtrap*. Noah and Peter never got around to discussing the lighting plan.

The following day, they began again at scene one to see how their previous day's work held up. It was a constant evolution of changes of movement and positions in these early stages to help keep the actors' gestures and motivations, actions and reactions, in character and as spontaneous and authentic as possible. Noah was captivated by how much two characters moving closer or further apart affected the dialogue or how a simple turn away from the action could influence the overall feel of a scene or line. He was learning so much being there, not only from a director's vantage point but useful information he could leverage as a playwright.

At the lunch break, Noah approached Peter, seated on top of a picnic table. "I have a suggestion for the scene we just finished," offered Noah, "before Wendy dumps the salad on Charlie's head and walks out."

Peter was busy checking his phone messages. "I'm listening."

"What if Wendy actually grabs Charlie's wrists while she's trying to pin him down for an answer about moving in together? Then, we reverse it, and Charlie grabs her wrists when he's trying to explain why he's been seeing Stacy on the side. I think the physical action would really help underscore the dialogue of him feeling trapped in the relationship, unable to move, and also Wendy feeling that not only have her hands been tied the whole time while he's been cheating on her but their entire relationship has been "tied up" and not going anywhere. Do you see the symmetry?"

Peter lowered his phone, turning his full attention to Noah. "Well," he started, "it's not bad. I get the implicit meaning and what it represents. It just may be a little too conspicuous, obvious, you know, over the top, for my taste. So I don't think I want to go there."

Noah was disappointed, convinced that his suggestion was a sure thing. "Okay, I get it. But couldn't we at least just try it and see what it looks like? I mean, the entire comedy is a bit over the top."

Peter lowered his gaze to his phone again. "Look, we're done with act one for today and we only have a couple of hours left because of tonight's opening. I really want to move on to the next scene. Okay?"

Noah couldn't believe his idea was being dismissed before giving it a shot. "Peter, you asked me to speak up if I had any ideas and I'm coming to you with one that I think will definitely help the scene."

Peter stuck his phone in his pocket and stood up. "Look, I've made my decision. We're tight on time today and I don't want to go back. Okay?"

"But how are we going to know if it's right or not if we don't at least take a look?"

Peter began walking away. "It's not right, Noah, and we know that because I just said it."

"Peter, please don't walk away."

Peter came to a stop and spun around. "Noah, that's enough," he said raising his voice so that anyone within distance could hear and anyone that did stopped to eavesdrop. "I've made my decision, understand? I said it nice the first time. I said it as clearly as I could the second time and I'm not going to repeat myself. I'm pulling rank. I'm the fucking director of this show and we're moving on. Is that clear enough for you?"

Noah stood there paralyzed in disbelief as Peter kept walking, looking smaller and smaller as he moved away. He could not believe they had just gotten into an argument over a suggestion and in front of nearly the entire company. It had all been so positive up to this point.

Roz was the only one gallant enough to come over. "How about that? That didn't take long. I won again. A hundred and twenty bucks."

Noah was just emerging from his disorientation. "Huh?"

"I had day three," she explained. "We pick 'em out of a hat like Super Bowl scores."

"Day three?"

"His first meltdown. We run a pool. Ten bucks a man. The crew and anyone from the cast who's worked with him before. Sorry we didn't invite you in but you're new and we weren't sure, you know, whose side you were on."

"Day three, huh?" said Noah. "Is that a record?"

Roz laughed. "You kidding? He usually doesn't get past day two. I think he was on his best behavior." And then, "Thanks."

Noah shook his head.

"C'mon," said Roz, "I'll buy you lunch. You made me a rich woman today. It's the least I could do."

II
Letting Go

11
Letting Go

On Sunday, the weather was steamy and unrelenting and, with the Cape Cod tourist season now in full summer swing, Noah decided to stay local.

Jerry, back on Cape with his wife Sheila, invited Noah over for brunch and a swim, and Noah was relieved not to spend the day alone. The three friends cooled themselves in the pool and later shaded themselves beneath a large umbrella, anchored through a tempered glass table set like a five-star restaurant, complete with crystal champagne flutes and marble napkin holders. They dined on Jerry's famous eggs Benedict brunch.

"How's the play coming along?" asked Sheila, her Michael Kors sunglasses obscuring large brown eyes, peeking out below an oversized sombrero.

"Wonderful," said Noah without hesitation. "We've got a talented cast and we're just about through the blocking stage. I'm really enjoying it."

Noah avoided any mention of his recent skirmish with the director.

"The Playhouse attracts Equity actors," explained Sheila. "We've been coming for years. Many of them have appeared on Broadway stages. We saw Bernadette Peters there some years back."

Jerry refilled his champagne glass from the pitcher allowing a couple of ice cubes to spill in. "No kidding," added Jerry. "Who do you think pays their salary?"

The conversation crossed multiple subjects until the second mimosa pitcher was empty. "Who's ready for another?" offered Jerry.

"I'm sure I've had enough, thank you," his wife told him.

Noah agreed. "I'm good. Thanks."

"Lightweights," said Jerry. "Both of you. But I'm not going to drink alone."

After a while, Sheila excused herself and went in for a nap, blaming the heat for her fatigue. Once she had left, Jerry appeared more serious.

"What?" asked Noah. "I don't like that look."

Jerry raised his eyebrows. "What happened with you and Peter?"

Noah inhaled. "What did you hear?"

"He called me Friday night. Said he didn't appreciate you disagreeing with him, especially in front of the troops."

Noah shook his head and licked his lips preparing to defend himself. "That's an interesting version."

Jerry leaned back in his seat. "Okay, why don't you give me yours?"

Noah thought it through before responding. "I went over to him during the break, just the two of us, and made a suggestion. He listened, decided against it, and gave me his reasons."

"The louse," said Jerry, suppressing a smile.

"Do you want to hear this or not?"

"Stop being so sensitive and finish the story."

"All I said was can we at least try it and see what it looks like because I think it's a good idea and will reinforce the dialogue."

Jerry began nodding. "And what was your suggestion, if I may ask?"

Noah moved over into Sheila's seat and repeated his recommendation about grabbing one another's wrist.

Jerry pondered it. "Okay, I see the imagery. Not a bad idea. So what happened?"

"I don't know. After he turned me down, I just asked if we could look at it before making a final decision and he went bonkers in front of everyone, even reverting to profanity, which I didn't appreciate." Still upset, Noah took his time. "Roz told me they had a pool going since, apparently, Peter's meltdowns are par for the course."

Jerry eyed him. "So, who won the pool?"

Noah winced. "She did."

Jerry stood and removed his terrycloth robe. "I'm going back in. Care to join me?"

"Sure," said Noah, "why not?"

"All I can tell you is this," said Jerry. "Peter told me that if you continue to get in his way, he wants you removed as his assistant and will banish you from rehearsals."

Noah laughed. "*Really?* I make one suggestion, one *good* suggestion, and now he wants to get rid of me?"

Jerry jumped in. Noah waited for him to surface.

"You know he *can't* banish the playwright according to the Guild. Tell him to read the small print."

"Why don't you just apologize and let it go?"

"If I thought I did anything wrong, I would. You know me, Jerry. But, obviously, I believe Peter is the problem here. *He's* the one that can't let it go. Ask Roz, or anyone else that's worked with him."

"You know you're making my job harder, right?" added Jerry.

Noah shrugged and dove into the pool, running his fingers through his hair once he surfaced. "I don't even care whether he liked my idea," he said. "I made a suggestion and asked him, reasonably, to take a look at it. That's *all*. I don't think I have anything to apologize for."

Noah leaned up against the side stretching his arms out along the tile to stay afloat. "So where did you leave it with him?"

Jerry lowered his sunglasses and dropped his head a smidge. "I told him I'd talk to you and pass on his message. That's it. Consider yourself spoken to."

Noah shook his head in disgust. "Incredible. We're dealing with a child."

Jerry shot him a look. "That may be true, Noah, so I would watch myself from now on."

Noah gazed at the clear summer sky then back at his friend. "I thought I was supposed to make suggestions to help the play?"

"I'm not telling you to stop," said Jerry. "You just might want to pick your battles with this guy. That's all I'm saying."

Later, after Noah left Jerry's place, he drove through the town of Sandwich and found himself in front of Heritage Museums and Gardens, behind the old town hall. Since the clouds had rolled in easing the temperature and humidity to more tolerable levels, he decided to explore the 100-acre grounds full of dazzling hydrangeas and enchanting daylilies this time of year and take his mind off Peter.

Upon entering, he passed an indoor museum—housing exotic antique automobiles—and, further down, a 19th century windmill. After checking his map, he passed by an outdoor concert stage in the middle of an empty field then headed for the nature trails taking him through the less-traveled grounds. He was glad for the power walk after laying around for almost half the day. A while later, he wound up on a dirt road by the Shawme Pond Overlook and found a place to relax in the shade below a towering centuries-old oak.

It was quiet there off the main path and Noah was captivated by the view of the pond from the back side. He had never seen it from this angle. He leaned against the tree's massive trunk and relaxed, inhaling the sweet taste of nature hovering before him and the serene solitude. Slowly a picture began to form in his imagination—a white blanket on a grassy field near a lake—and he recalled the Catskill Mountains trip he took with Jessica and Erica last summer. He especially remembered the playful butterfly they encountered and how his daughter was so taken with it. Mostly, he realized how fleeting time is and how those moments come and go.

Coming out of a dreamlike state, he noticed someone on their way towards him. He did not recognize her at first but, as she approached, she began to come into focus.

"Can you smell it?" asked Emma without waiting for an answer. "That's summer."

Noah nodded. "Yes. It's delicious."

"I love the scent of summer," she added, sitting beside him. "It takes me away. Just floats me on a cloud. I don't know what it is. Jasmine. Lilacs. Honeysuckle. I love it, whatever it is."

"Aren't you supposed to be showing houses or something?" he asked.

"I'm playing hooky today," she whispered. "Don't tell."

"I'd like to play hooky from *my* life," said Noah. "Tell everyone."

She laughed. "I couldn't sit inside on a day like this."

"I don't blame you. A beautiful day to be alive."

While they sat there chatting, an older gentleman with a friendly worn face and a cane, waved as he passed them about fifty feet away.

"Do you know him?" asked Noah, not sure which one of them the man recognized.

She waved back. "Eh, that's Mr. McDermott, a client," she told him. "Don't be shy. You can wave too."

Noah obliged.

"Sweet old guy. Lost his wife a couple of years ago and I helped him sell his house." She stopped. "I'm sorry, Noah. Didn't mean to go there."

Noah lowered his knees and stretched his legs out. "It's okay. Bad things happen to good people. I get it."

They were quiet for some time, taking in the fragrant scents of a summer day.

"Did you ever talk to someone?" she asked. "I'm sure you have friends or maybe you reached out to someone, you know, a professional?"

Noah took his time responding but wasn't ashamed to answer her question.

"After Erica and Jessica, you know, died ..." He held up there, talking in spurts, mulling his words over carefully. "It was difficult, I won't lie. I felt ... abandoned. No one to turn to." He waited there not wanting to appear critical. "Jerry was in Europe. Didn't know what was going on. Barney, my boss, urged me to take as much time as I needed, but he wasn't *really* there for me, not every day. I mean, he tried, but ... Our friend, Dee, called. But she was dealing with her own shit."

Noah seemed mesmerized—a prisoner of his own world—trying to make sense of it. Then, "I checked myself in. One of those places you go to find yourself. Knew I needed help. Six weeks. That's why I didn't come back right away. They helped. A little I guess. We talked. Let go of some … stuff." He gulped. "Some of it. There's no magic pill for that."

He lowered his head and plucked a blade of grass, twirling it between his fingers.

"I knew I had to get back to a routine if I was ever going to … you know, move on."

He titled his head without looking her in the eye, lost in his own world.

"I miss them so much. I don't think I'll ever … Ever."

He stopped there. After a moment, Emma took his hand in hers.

"I think you're doing great, Noah. Just the fact that you're here doing your play … meeting new people. That's the way to take back your life. Or start a new one."

Her words gave him strength and he raised his eyes, this time peering into hers. "Thanks."

She smiled warmly. "Your wife and daughter will always be with you. They're a part of you and … you them." She squeezed his hand. "The pain you feel is love. Not a bad thing. Just takes a while to get used to."

After a while, she rose to her feet. Noah did the same.

"Sorry," she said. "Time to get back to work. Don't want to take advantage."

He nodded.

Before leaving, she pointed to the pond behind them. "That's the Shawme Pond, an Algonquin name for Sandwich."

He looked over her shoulder, unfocused.

"There's an old Indian legend," she went on. "A great Mashpee chief named Metacom went to battle the English settlers. This was about fifty years after the Pilgrims landed. Then the Colonists invited him to sign a peace treaty. When he arrived, they sent their militia into his village and massacred his tribe. His wife and son were killed. He brought their bodies here, set them on a wooden pyre and lit it, floating it into the pond. He claimed this freed their souls into the universe. After that, he swore that his wife and son returned to him in his dreams and he knew they were all right."

Noah did not say anything.

"It is said that if you let your pain out into the pond, your loved ones will return to you."

"That's quite a tale," he said finally. "But I'm not sure I believe in that stuff."

Emma looked at him, searching. "Hey ... you never know."

She stepped back. "See you around, Noah. Hang in there, okay?"

Noah watched her walk away until she was out of sight. He stood there a while and thought about the story and the legend. Then he turned towards the pond.

12
Choices

I met my boss, Barney Saperstein, the same year Erica was born, at his son's place. Harry and Rachel Saperstein have been our neighbors since we bought the house in Northport next door. About a year after we got to know them, Harry knocked on the door to invite us to their July 4th holiday barbecue. Said it was a relatively small group of friends and family and hoped we could make it. We asked him if we could bring anything but he told us he had it covered and to just bring an appetite.

The party was called for noon and we headed over about a half-hour later. We brought a couple of bottles of Pinot—a red and a white—because Jessica hates to go to these things empty-handed. We knew Katrina and Larry Williams from across the street and were introduced to the Saperstein clan.

I liked Barney from the start despite his being a diehard Mets' fan like Harry, which was hard to figure since they both seemed so sensible. I followed the Yankees at the time and from then on, whenever we got together, the three of us would compare ball clubs and players. Barney has a wonderful sense of humor and I felt comfortable around him. I let him know that his cheeseburgers were the best I ever tasted but he still refused to give me the secret ingredients he mixed in with the beef. Said it was an old family recipe deemed classified.

I spent most of the afternoon chatting with him and we covered a slew of topics. I told him about some magazine articles I had written and my new play, *Committed*, that was opening at the Orpheum Theater in the East Village in a few weeks. He promised to come see it. Before we left, he asked me to get him copies of the articles and seemed interested in my work. I sent him the articles the following week and forgot about them. When my play opened, I made sure there were four comped tickets for Barney and his wife, Leslie, Harry, and Rachel.

A few months after meeting Barney, he called and asked me to visit him at his office but did not tell me anymore. He is the managing editor for the Associated Press. Since it was a considerable ride on the railroad into the city from Northport, I also made plans to meet my play's director, Tim Holland, at a Soho pub after the meeting. I had an idea for my next play and wanted his feedback.

Barney gave me a quick tour of the place and invited me into his office. He thanked me for the tickets and mentioned how much they all enjoyed my show. He also said he liked my writing style in the articles I had sent over.

"So what are your plans now?" he asked me.

"Well," I started, "I have an idea for a new play. I'm actually meeting my director later to discuss it with him." He nodded and I thought he was going to ask me what it was.

"Let me ask you something, Noah. How long will it take you to write the play and get it on stage? Approximately how long?"

"That would depend on the amount of time it takes to write it," I told him. "Probably a year or so, I guess, I mean, with the casting, finding a theater, rehearsals, and so forth."

"And, if you don't mind my asking," he continued, "what are you going to do for income until then?"

I was blindsided by the question. "Well, Jessie works part time and I have some investment dividends."

"Investment dividends?" he repeated, sounding as if he didn't believe me. Either that or he thought I was nuts.

"I also have some money put aside from an inheritance."

"An inheritance?" His questioning made me uncomfortable.

"Well, what's left of it after we bought the house."

"And all that covers your living expenses, entertainment and everything else?"

I did not say anything at first. He sounded a bit worried, a lot like Jessica did since Erica was born, and I could not believe he was talking to me like I was his son. Son-in-law.

"We make do," I finally told him. "It's not the best situation, I admit, but now that I've had one play on stage, it's opened up the door for my next one. And the one after that."

He sat up in his executive chair, stuck his hand under his chin, and squeezed his jaw like he was wringing out a beard. Then he rose and began pacing the room. "I don't understand," he began. "You're an intelligent guy, a good writer, somewhat successful, with a wife and a kid and a mortgage. But you're not very good at finances. Are you?"

It was rhetorical, I found out, because he did not wait for an answer.

"Frankly, I'm surprised. If I was in your position I'd have had a nervous breakdown by now. How do you stand it?"

He was still not looking for a response.

"I mean, really, Noah, if I was your father, I'd have sat you down and given you the facts of life long before today. I don't know how you sleep at night. My heart is racing right now and I'm the one in the room with a steady paycheck."

Then he plopped back into his padded chair on wheels and stared at me. I was a bit taken aback considering we had no formal relationship, but this time, I surmised, he *was* waiting for a response.

"Well, I'm glad we had this little chat, Barney. What do I owe you for the session?"

He sat up and clasped his hands in front of him like a schoolteacher waiting for his class to simmer down. He was not smiling. "I'd like to offer you a job, Noah."

The next day I mentioned Barney's offer to my wife over breakfast.

"Really?" she said, somewhere between surprised and indifferent. I was not sure which side of the fence she was leaning. "You're not going to consider it, are you?"

Now *I* was surprised. "As a matter of fact ..."

Then her jaw dropped. I could see one of the fillings in her molar.

"Noah, I know money has been a little tight lately but what about that discussion we had a few weeks ago? About choices. You said you wanted to give playwriting your complete attention. You were all in. What happened to that?"

I moved a little closer. "I am all in, Jess. Promise. I'm still ... committed (we smiled at one another) to writing my next play and seeing it up on stage. That hasn't changed. But think about all the advantages of taking this job. I'll be in the city reviewing other productions and making connections. I'll have my own theater column so my name will get around. And with a regular paycheck every week, we won't be so strapped for cash and we'll be able to afford a babysitter for Erica when you go to work. Or, if you prefer, you don't have to work."

I thought that last part would sell it but her expression told a different story.

"I'm just afraid that if you're writing for the AP wire service every day, you'll stop writing plays. And I don't mind going to work knowing that you're here looking after our daughter. With you in the city all day, Erica will never see you. And, of course, having money coming in each week would put my mind at ease as far as finances, but I'm really worried that you'd be selling out your dream of becoming a playwright." Then she rose and began cleaning up, her back towards me, but not before adding, "And I would hate to see that happen, that's all."

I took her by the shoulders and gently spun her around. "Me too, hon. Thanks Jess. My biggest fan. I promise you it'll all work out. There'll be a happy ending. And this job won't get in the way of our dream."

But I could already see signs of disappointment in her eyes, the sense of resignation and withdrawal. It was not an expression I looked forward to facing every day and I wasn't quite sure I had the power to change it. Once you see that in someone, it's usually irreparable, no matter what you do to remedy it—like a somber piece of artwork on a museum wall you can't seem to walk away from. It's from their permanent collection so it's always there, leaving you feeling empty and depressed and longing for something better, hoping they'll replace it but knowing it will still be there staring back at you the next time you visit.

Barney was right. I had to think about our finances and make sure we did not run out of money before my tenuous dream of becoming a successful full-time playwright paid off. And who could predict when that would be? If that would *ever* be?

I took the job at AP and promised myself I would only stay three years. Tops.

13

Living in a Dictatorship

13
Living In a Dictatorship

⎯⎯⎯⎯ ⟡ ⎯⎯⎯⎯

Noah saw Peter on Monday morning at the next rehearsal. Saturday had been a planned away day from the theater since *Deathtrap* performed matinee and evening shows on the weekend and the only time available was in the morning. The actors spent the day together off-site running their lines to get ready for their first "off book" rehearsal when they would have to have their lines memorized without the use of a script.

Peter did not say anything about their incident on Friday and everything appeared to be business as usual so Noah let it drop for the time being and focused on his job giving actors their lines when they asked.

"I need you to be on top of that," explained Peter just as we were starting. "Don't give them the line until they ask for it, but if they do, you need to be right on it. Got it?"

Noah had understood his assignment but appeased him anyway. "Got it."

Only Molly and Wayne, who played the main characters, were needed that morning on stage since they were rehearsing the last scene in act one, the couple's anniversary dinner and subsequent breakup. The other actors would join them after lunch once they moved on in the script. The sets for *Committed* were not yet ready so they used a card table and folding chairs for the dining room where the scene takes place.

"All right," said Peter, "let's take it from Charlie's entrance with the salad bowl at the top of page thirty-two. A lot of movement in this scene, in and out of the kitchen, so please remember how we blocked it last week and which lines you move on."

"So, I'm starting in the kitchen, right?" asked Wayne.

"Yes, you're in the kitchen and Molly's in the living room," noted Peter. "You enter through the door just before her line. Picture a swinging door around here that divides the kitchen and dining area. Roz, can we chalk a line here for the door?"

Roz called her assistant. "Suzy, take care of that please." And she chalked the line on stage by Peter's foot.

"Let's make it a full three-foot door," said Peter. "Measure it please."

After Suzy extended the line, Peter added "Okay, Molly, Wayne, here's your door. Please use it. Any other questions, concerns? Okay. Are we ready to start? Good. Wayne, you'll enter with the bowl and begin tossing the salad on the table. Molly, let him get started with that and then you'll head over to him with your line. Okay, let's begin."

When Wayne enters and goes through the motion of tossing the salad, Molly approaches him.

"Charlie," she says, *"have you thought any more about what we talked about the other night?"*

"What'd we talk about the other night?"

"I'm glad to see I took it a little more seriously than you did."

"Well, I might have taken it seriously if you tell me what it was."

"Stop!" called Peter. "Is that the line?"

"I believe it is," said Wayne.

"Noah?" asked Peter.

"'Well, I might have taken it *as seriously as you* if you tell me what it was,'" said Noah. "You missed a couple of words there, Wayne."

"Sorry," he said.

"Let me hear it, Wayne." He repeated the line. "Better," said Peter. "Thank you. Let's take it from right there."

Wayne said the line again, correctly this time.

"It couldn't have been that serious if you haven't got a clue."

Charlie stops tossing and considers what Wendy just told him. "Is this what I think it's about?"

"Probably."

"I have a clue."

"And?"

"And I did a lot of thinking on the subject."

"And?"

"Hold it, there," said Peter. "Molly, when you say that second 'And?' it's got to be a little different than the first one. Okay?"

"Different? How?" she asked.

"Maybe you hold it a little longer, or the emphasis is different, but it shouldn't sound the same as the first time you say it. Okay?"

"Got it."

"Good," said Peter, "let's start from your first 'And.'" They accommodated Peter and moved on.

"And, I've made a decision."

"Well?"

"I've decided I don't want to talk about it."

"Why not?"

"Cause I don't think it's an appropriate time."

"You never think it's an appropriate time."

"That's not true. This is ... this is ... line!"

Noah hesitated but recovered, "Uh, 'this is a serious subject, which deserves ...'"

Wayne picked up on it.

"This is a serious subject, which deserves a serious discussion. But we're about to eat dinner and I don't want to get upset."

"Why do you get upset every time I bring it up?"

"I'd answer that question but that would only get you upset."

"Charlie, just give me one good reason why you don't think we should move in together and I promise I'll drop the subject."

"All right. I don't think we should move in together because I don't think we're ready for it."

"Why the hell not?"

"Eh, eh, that's another question."

They proceeded stop and go through the scene, pausing for missed lines and directions from Peter. When the scene was over and everyone was satisfied, they took a forty-five minute lunch recess.

The afternoon session began with the full cast. Since it was an off day for *Deathtrap*, they had access to the stage for the entire day. Roz reminded Peter that they would need to be off stage by five o'clock the rest of the week so the stage crew could prepare the set and test the lights and microphones.

Peter let everyone know they would be starting with the first scene of act two, where the three couples gather for another game night at Charlie's apartment. Since Wendy has broken up with Charlie at the end of act one, Charlie now has a new partner, Stacy Becker, whose interest in the game and the company is wearing thin. Stan and Cynthia Urlicht, a married couple in therapy, are good friends of Charlie's.

The scene opens in the middle of a Monopoly game with Billy Corona and partner, Lydia Wilkins, about to throw the die.

"Announcement, everyone," says Billy. *"Corona and Wilkins' Enterprises is now building a hotel on Atlantic Avenue and anyone who visits us will have to shell out 1,150 granola bars for the privilege. Reservations are suggested."*

Billy laughs and counts out his payment. "I love the Parker Brothers," he adds. *"If I ever have twins, I'm going to name my first born after 'em."*

"What'd you say?" asks Lydia.

"Nothing that'll hold up in court," says Charlie.

Peter stopped them there. "I have no problem with your deliveries but I want you all to keep in mind that you're playing a board game at someone's house and you can't just be sitting there staring. You need to be in the moment, doing something. Right? We talked about this. Wayne, perhaps you raise your hand on your line like you're being sworn in to testify. Lydia can be drinking a little too much. Stan might be laying his cards down in some obsessive-compulsive manner. Cynthia could be whispering into Stan's ear. Stacy is bored. You could be filing your nails or peeking at your phone or something else that suggests boredom. Everyone with me on this? If you're just sitting there waiting to say your line you'll put the audience to sleep. Okay? Let's run it again from the top."

"Excuse me, Peter," said Noah. "I think Billy could be counting spaces on the board to see what he needs to roll for 'Free Parking' and then yell out what he wants to roll. 'Big guy needs to roll an eight. Show me an eight.' Or something like that. I can add it to the script if you want. Shows everyone how badly he wants to win. I know I used to do that before my turn when I played."

Peter sighed. "Um, I don't think so, Noah. I don't want to start adding lines at this point. It should all flow … naturally."

"But it's something Billy *would* do," added Noah. "And I just thought if you were looking for ways to …"

Peter cut him off. "I get it. I'm just not crazy about it. Okay, everyone, from the top."

An uncomfortable pause loomed in the room.

"I don't think that's such a bad idea," said Steve, who was playing Billy. "I kind of like the suggestion, I mean, I could see Billy doing that."

Peter turned to him and smiled in a flippant manner. "Thank you for your opinion, Steve, but I already covered it."

Mindy, playing Cynthia, chimed in. "Sorry, Peter, but I have to agree. I think counting spaces ahead of your turn fits Billy's personality and gives him an action that's true to his character. He doesn't even need to say anything, just count. Pretty funny if you think about it."

Peter stood up, incensed. "Let me be perfectly clear, everyone. I appreciate and value your opinions but this is not a democracy. We're not taking a vote, we're not running for higher office, we're just doing what the director tells us to do. *Now* are we clear?" He waited for a response but there was none. "Good. Can we please take it from the top?"

The rehearsal continued through the afternoon and no one offered suggestions or further disagreed with Peter, who had clearly drawn the line and crossed it. The irrational conflict brewing between Peter and Noah was now apparent to all and contributing to a sense of tension that was not doing anyone any good. While the cast secretly sided with and felt empathy for Noah, they knew who was calling the shots and who they needed to support ostensibly so they would not jeopardize the opportunity to be cast in a future show. Peter was a Cape Cod director who hired actors. Noah was a New York playwright visiting Cape Cod for the summer.

At the dinner break, Roz went looking for Noah and found him outside eating alone at a picnic table. "Mind if I join you?" she asked.

"It's a free country," replied Noah. "Check that. I hear we're living in a dictatorship now."

Roz sat down and took a bite of her sandwich. She felt sorry for him. She waited until he finished chewing.

"I did warn you about Peter." No response. "I think there's a screw loose or something." Still nothing. "He's really not a bad director. Believe me, I've seen *bad* directors. But he does rub people the wrong way. Must have something to do with his childhood and an unresolved Oedipus complex."

Noah suppressed a smile. "You're just trying to cheer me up."

"No," she laughed, "I'm serious. I think you represent the father figure and he just wants you out of his way."

Noah took a sip from his water bottle.

"You might want to hold off on your suggestions," she added. "No matter how good they are. Seriously. I think he sees you as some sort of threat and, if you don't watch yourself ..." She stopped there.

"I appreciate your concern, Roz, but I can take care of myself."

"I'm sure you can," she said, "but, right or wrong, if you don't let up, Peter *will* get rid of you. I've seen him do it too."

Noah weighed that before going on. "This is *my* play and it's my job to offer my two cents to make it the best it can be. If I didn't make suggestions, I wouldn't be doing my job as both the Playwright and Assistant Director."

Roz stood up to make her point. "You don't have to convince me, Noah. All I'm saying is if you keep it up, you won't have a job to come to every day." Then she left.

He sat there pondering why Peter refused to support his suggestions. This was not the way he thought it would go.

14
The Understudy

~◦◦◦~

Rehearsal was called for 8 a.m. the next day and for the rest of the week. Act two, scene two, a scene between Wendy and Cynthia in a quiet French restaurant, was first up and Molly and Mindy were there on time, ready for their closeups. Noah held onto his script in case someone needed a line and Roz and Bobby were on hand for notes. Nobody mentioned a word about the altercation the previous day and all proceeded as if nothing had happened. That was fine with Noah, who was not expecting an apology or anything else from Herr Direktor.

Peter sat in a folding chair downstage while Noah watched from the first row of the orchestra. Peter offered the actors some final notes and the scene began. After Wendy enters and the two banter, the conversation turns to Charlie.

"I thought you might want to know how Charlie's doing," says Cynthia. "I saw him last night, you know."

"What makes you think I care?" replies Wendy.

"You care. You're both too much in love to give up so quickly."

"I was in love. He was confused."

After they chat about Charlie's new girlfriend, the plot turns more serious.

"I think Charlie's miserable," says Cynthia.

"Is that it?" asks Wendy.

"I think he misses you terribly."

"Did he tell you that?"

"He doesn't hide it well."

"What about her?"

"I don't think she misses you at all."

Peter stepped in at that point. "Mindy, when you say that line, it's got to be deadpan."

"Deadpan," repeated Mindy, nodding.

"Just straight out flat," said Peter. "No inflection. It's a laugh line that breaks up the gravity of the scene and keeps us involved in the moment with humor.

"Okay," said Mindy. "I see that. Let me try it again."

Noah was impressed with Peter's direction and would have said something similar if he was in charge. Later in the scene, Cynthia admits she had an affair and advised her husband, Stan.

"You live with a guy all these years, you think you've got him pegged."

"Cynthia, he didn't leave you?"

"Are you kidding? Stanley Urlicht facing the uncivilized world without a mother figure to hold his hand? ... The bastard apologized to me!"

"He what?"

"Said it was all his fault. Said he's been too involved with things. I tell you, he was carrying on so, I almost blamed the whole affair on him." (They laugh, but the laughter is filled with irony.) "I learned something from all this," says Cynthia. "I learned that I married myself a hell of a guy. Or a hell of a fool. Either way, I love him more now than I ever did."

Finally, Cynthia reveals the reason she asked Wendy to lunch and suggests a reconciliation.

"You were putting a lot of pressure on Charlie to move in with you," she explains.

"I was ready for a change and he wasn't."

"Maybe he needed more time and you weren't giving him that. Put yourself in his place."

"Let's not. The point is he found someone else."

"Just someone to sleep next to. And that wasn't until after you left him. He wasn't even cheating on you, damn it." (Wendy reacts.) "I wouldn't have blamed Stan if he left me. Hell, I would have left him. But he didn't. And I've come to realize what kind of guy I've got."

"You're a married woman with two kids. You have a lot more at stake than I do."

"That has nothing to do with it. We stayed together because deep down, we really love each other. We really care."

"What are you trying to save my soul so you'll feel less guilty?"

"Maybe I am. But you're the one that's going to lose out if you don't give him another chance."

"Let's hold it there," said Peter, jumping out of his seat. "All right, it's nice but I think we can do better. Mindy, you're doing fine. I think your responses are right on. Molly." He stopped here to emphasize his point. "This is a ping-pong match between you two, wouldn't you agree?" He didn't wait for an answer. "And who would you say is on offense?"

"She is," said Molly.

"Good," he agreed. "She's on offense, hitting balls at you all over the court. Right? And what are you doing?"

"I'm playing defense."

"You're playing 'D.' Good. So let's hear that. I want to hear you being defensive. You're blocking her anyway you can. Okay?"

"I thought I was," said Molly. A look from Peter. "I thought I was being defensive."

"Not enough," said Peter.

"How far do I take it?"

"You're on defense the entire scene."

"The entire scene?"

"All the way through," he told her. "Okay, let's pick it up from 'You're a married woman with two kids.'"

Noah rose. "Eh, Peter," said the playwright, almost reluctantly, knowing he was putting himself on the line again. "May I interject?"

Peter took a deep breath. Roz lowered her head.

"I think your direction is spot on," Noah began, "until you get to Wendy's question about saving her soul. That's not a defensive response. That's where she stops being defensive and speaks from the heart."

"Noah," said Peter, cutting in. "Would you let me direct the show please. I think I know what I'm doing."

Noah took a breath, ignoring that last comment. "I know it sounds like it should be defensive, that she's still hurting and reacting, but that's where the scene pivots. Wendy almost can't believe that someone cares enough about her that she's trying to save her soul, which really translates into saving her relationship with Charlie. To have a true friend not only admit her crime of adultery but to use the lesson she learned—about true love and forgiveness—to enlighten her not to make an unforgiveable mistake and miss out."

"Did you hear what I said?" asked Peter.

"The tables have turned, so to speak. It's Cynthia who answers that question defensively. And, I think, if the audience is to understand the true meaning of what's going on here, and to empathize with Wendy's predicament, it should be played out that way. That's it. That's all I have to say."

Peter appeared transfixed. Everyone else either wet their lips, looked away, or held their breath.

"Noah," said Peter almost gravely, "will you come up here for a minute." Noah left his script balanced on the armrest of his seat and made the isolated trek onstage. Peter moved stage right to converge with him at the top of the steps. Roz shaded her eyes with her hand.

"I'm sorry I have to do this, Noah," said Peter in a hushed tone loud enough for all to eavesdrop. "But I'm going to have to ask you to leave."

"Excuse me?" responded Noah.

"You're fired," said Peter. "I can't have you here. I know you're the playwright and you wrote this thing but I can't direct it with you looking over my shoulder and correcting me."

"But I'm only giving you some insight to help you be a better director."

Peter exhaled and smirked at the same time. "Thank you. I know. I get it. But I can't work this way with you here. I told Jerry that and he asked me to give it a try. So we gave it a try. But it's not working and I need you to leave."

Noah swallowed hard and met his gaze. His voice rose to make sure everyone heard him. "I don't work for you, Peter, so you can't fire me."

"I'm afraid you do. And I can."

"No. Uh, uh. I don't. I work for Jerry Ziegler and the Playhouse. They're the only ones who can terminate my contract."

"I represent the Playhouse, Noah. And I'm telling you you're fired."

Noah didn't hesitate. "Fuck you, Peter. I'm firing you."

Peter laughed. "I don't think so, Miller. You don't have any power in this."

The two men glared at one another as the entire company froze. Peter broke first and looked away. "Let's take a short break everyone." He peeked at his watch. "We'll resume in fifteen minutes." Then he turned back to Noah. "After I call Jerry and fire your ass."

"Peter," said Molly, edging closer. "Noah was giving you some background to help you with the scene."

Peter checked the beams in the rafters before turning to her. "I know what *he* was doing, Molly. I'm not sure what you're doing."

Now she was in front of him. "I'm just saying he's not a threat to you. He's an asset. Why don't you listen to what he has to say?"

"Molly, please," offered Noah, "you don't need to get involved with this."

Molly inhaled. "I think I do."

"He's not a threat?" said Peter in a sarcastic tone that couldn't be missed. *"Really?* He just tried to fire me."

"Oh, come off it, Peter," said Roz, making her way up the steps. "Molly's right. Why don't you listen to Noah instead of working in a vacuum? It isn't often that we have the playwright here to offer his insight."

"There's a reason playwrights aren't invited to rehearsals, Roz," explained Peter, "and you of all people should know that."

"All I know," said Roz, "is that your ego, *as usual,* is getting in the way and instead of listening to Noah's ideas, you'll do anything you can to discourage him."

Peter was seething now. "I don't have to put up with this crap," said Peter. "I've got a call to make and when I get back, I want you gone, Noah!"

Then, taking a hard look at Molly and Roz, "And if these two don't shut their traps, you may have company." Then he strutted off the stage, his chin and body erect. "Bobby," he yelled without turning back. And his intern followed him out.

They waited for the two of them to leave the theater.

"Thank you," said Noah, apologetically. "I appreciate you both standing up for me. I hope you don't get axed on my account."

"We're not getting fired," said Roz. "He can't afford to get rid of all three of us. Don't worry yourself about that." Then, peering in the direction Peter exited, she added, "Some people are too stuck up for their own good." She began walking away. "I've got a phone call to make myself."

Noah stood there searching for the right words. "You really shouldn't have said anything. This could jeopardize your acting career. I wouldn't want that hanging over my head. Why did you do that?"

Molly placed her hand on his arm. "Sometimes," she reminded him, "you have to stand up and do what your mind tells you, despite what you may be feeling inside. Wouldn't you agree?"

He gazed at her as if he'd known her forever. "Seems I heard that before."

A couple of the other actors joined them to offer their support. Noah appreciated the gesture. They stood around chatting until Noah's phone rang. "Excuse me, everyone," he said, checking the caller I.D. "I think someone might be getting fired today." He started walking away.

"We're on your side, Noah," Molly called after him.

"Thanks," he called back.

"Hi Jerry," he said, heading out of the theater while keeping a lookout for his nemesis.

"What part of 'watch yourself around Peter' didn't you understand?"

Noah made it out of the building before going on. "This wasn't my fault. The man is a walking timebomb. I warned you about him."

"I swear you're going to give me a heart attack, Noah. Is that what you want to give me? Because I could think of at least four other things I'd rather have than a coronary."

"I have better things to do than to give you a coronary. Look, I'm not his enemy, even though he thinks I am. I disagreed with something he said. He got it wrong and I was trying to clear it up and he got pissed off and fired me. I'm telling you, Jerry, he's the wrong man for this show. Ask anyone who was there."

"Yes," Jerry said, "I heard. I spoke to Roz. She told me what happened. You couldn't leave well enough alone."

"This is my play. I know it better than anyone. That includes Peter. And I'm not going to let him screw it up if I can help it."

"Well, you helped it all right. Now we have a problem—a real problem—and I have to figure out what to do."

"So what's the good news?"

"*The good news?* You think I have good news to tell you? The chutzpa. He wants you out. Today. Yesterday. Immediately, or he's threatening to quit."

"Good. Let him quit. That would solve the problem."

"Sure, easy for you to say. But with three weeks until the opening, I think someone might notice. And they're going to be pretty pissed over this."

Noah let that sink in. "What are you going to do?"

There was no immediate response. Noah took that time to evaluate all the angles. "I have an idea."

"I'm listening," said Jerry.

The ensuing pause was fraught with tension. "What if I direct the show," said Noah, speaking with a confidence he didn't know he possessed until that moment.

Again there was silence and, this time, Noah thought he might have lost the connection.

"*You?* What do you know about directing?"

Noah thought it through and it seemed like the perfect solution. "Well, I know more about the play than he does, for one."

"Okay, I'll give you that. What else?"

"I've been to every rehearsal and sat in on all our meetings. I've watched him direct and I'm aware of everything he's said to each actor. The blocking has all been worked out. The actors know their lines. They all know me and … I think they'll listen to me. It's only fine tuning from this point, Jerry. I'm pretty sure I can handle it."

"I can't believe I'm even considering this. Noah, are you sure you want to do this?"

"What choice do we have?"

"Well, choice, let's see. I could tell you to go back to New York and let Peter finish what he started. That would be the safer choice."

"Since when have you ever taken the road most traveled?"

"I could start today."

"But you're not. Are you?"

"I might."

As soon as he said it, Jerry knew what he was going to do.

"Listen," urged Noah. "It's your decision and I'll go along with whatever you say. I'm telling you that Peter is a loose cannon and, if you let him stay, he's going to self-destruct before we get to opening night."

"That could help ticket sales, you know."

"*Or*, you could let me direct it. I promise it will turn out fine." More silence. "Jerry, have I ever let you down?"

"Well," he said, pondering the question. "Remember the time we drove to that party in Brookline and you met someone and left me stranded. I had to find my own way home. What do you say to that?"

Noah shook his head. "I would say that it never happened because I never would have left you alone like that."

"Well, it could have happened, I mean, if you actually met someone that night."

"What are you going to tell the theater?"

Jerry sighed. "I have no idea. But I'll think of something. Peter doesn't have a lot of friends on the board so that helps. As for you, I'll just have to sell them on your passion for the show and that you have the actors' confidence. You have as much at stake in it being successful as the rest of us. I'll also remind them we're saving some money by getting rid of Peter. That should help because ticket sales have been slow."

Noah listened with a new appreciation for his friend. "Thank you, Jerry."

"You're welcome. Let me go. I have to give Peter the bad news. Hey Noah, don't let me down."

"I would never do that to you."

"Good. Let's keep your record intact, okay?"

Noah stuck the phone in his pocket and waited a few minutes before heading into the theater. The first one he ran into was Will Hatchwell, who ran the spotlights. "That was awesome," Will told him. "You kicked ass in there."

Noah looked almost sheepish. "Thanks, Will. I wasn't trying to kick anyone's ass. Just stick up for my play."

Will flashed him a wide grin. "You stuck up for your play all right. *And* you kicked Peter's ass." With that, he smacked Noah on the back. "Way to go." Then he left.

Noah stood a moment gathering his thoughts. The show was now on his shoulders. What was he thinking?

"Peter's looking for you," said Bobby, surprising him. "He's in the front lot by his car."

"Thanks," said Noah. "Hey, Bobby? Are you staying with the show or what are your plans?"

Bobby straightened his posture. "I'm in. I need the credits. Is that all right?"

"It's great. Glad to have you."

Bobby smiled, perhaps for the first time that summer. "Thanks, Noah."

Peter was stuffing his bag in a crowded cargo area at the rear of his white-striped Mini Cooper when Noah approached him.

"I'm sorry, Peter," he said. "Really. This was the last thing I wanted."

Peter shut the double doors. "Had a feeling it could turn out this way. Never good to have the playwright around. Too much second guessing."

He dropped into the driver's seat and lowered the window. "I've got another gig in Provincetown. Starts next week."

"That was fast."

"Good to have connections."

Noah stepped away from the car. "Break a leg."

Peter nodded. "Better keep an eye out, Noah. Now *you'll* know what it's like to have somebody looking over your shoulder."

Then he drove his Coop out of the lot.

While standing there, it occurred to Noah that the only reason Peter had wanted "a word" with him was to provoke a sense of fear. That, and to have the final word on the matter.

What a prick.

15
Enigma
—◦◦◦—

On Wednesday morning, Jerry stopped by the Playhouse to make sure everyone was on board with Noah and the new order. The theater execs did not give him much resistance but advised him to stay on top of the production or it would be his ass on the line. Jerry listened as Noah delivered notes to the actors and sat behind him in the orchestra section to see what sort of director he had hired. He left at the lunch break and informed his friend that he would meet him at The Pilot House for dinner at the end of the day.

Noah relished his new position. He appreciated that his ideas were readily accepted and was open to listening to suggestions from everyone. Anything that would help. The actors seemed pleased that Noah gave them the freedom to try their own approach to scenes. This not only built confidence and respect between them but also made the show better.

Allowing actors that freedom was often discouraged by seasoned directors who believed they had to be on top of every single decision, motivation and action. It also helped that Noah was the playwright in case someone came up with a better line than what was on the page. This was a tremendous advantage to Noah, who not only had the right to change the line if he wanted but also receive the credit for it. Directors, normally, did not have that luxury.

But there was a huge difference between changing a line and improving it, and changing a line because you were lazy and paraphrasing. Noah quickly learned the difference and which actors were true professionals who understood their roles and read their lines as written and which ones botched them and needed assistance.

John, who played the role of Stan Urlicht, was constantly rewriting Noah's lines, which caused tension between him and his "wife," played by Mindy, forced to respond to a different reading each time. Susan, too, tried to change her lines as Lydia for no apparent reason other than she failed to memorize them correctly, and every now and then, the rehearsal would have to stop for clarification and guidance.

Noah spoke to each privately so as not to embarrass them—he was learning on the job—and explained why they had to stick to the script as written if only so their fellow actors could follow and respond to their cues. Overall, the players were consummate professionals who did a good job and, by the end of his first full rehearsal as director, Noah felt that the day had progressed well.

When they were done, Noah asked Bobby and Roz to hang around to go over the next day's rehearsal schedule, which was going to include the climactic dream sequence.

While leaving the theater, Noah texted Jerry that he would meet him at the restaurant in forty-five minutes after stopping off at his place for a quick shower. Now that Sheila was out for the summer, Noah found himself spending less time at Jerry's house so he was not imposing on their relationship. And, since cleaning his place up and picking up some used furniture at a garage sale, his house had become more inhabitable and less of an eyesore.

When he arrived at The Pilot House, he ordered a beer from the outdoor bar and put his name down on the waiting list for a table. He found an empty Adirondack chair off to the side where he could wait for Jerry and enjoy the local band, a throwback group called *The Chosen Few*. The band mixed in their own original songs with Classic Rock from the '60s and 70's, Noah had read. The lead singer had a calming voice and stringy dirty-blond hair that reminded him of Carly Simon. Jerry showed up a few minutes later and pulled a chair over beside him.

"Not bad," said Jerry, a beer in his hand, his eye on the lead singer. "Nice voice, too."

Noah raised his bottle toward Jerry. "Does your libido ever take a break?"

"My libido will take a break when I'm no longer around. Until then, I take good care of it so that it keeps me apprised of beautiful women in the vicinity to flirt with. That's its primary duty. I can't help that."

The two sat there taking in the ambiance and enjoying the music.

"I did a little research on Ed's company, Innovative Designs." said Noah.

"What the hell for?" asked Jerry.

"Just curious," Noah answered. "He was a very successful businessman. Wanted to know if there were any skeletons in his closet."

"Find any?"

"Did you know about the problems he had with the indigenous people?"

"The Native Americans?" said Jerry. "Amy mentioned some rumbling about it at the time."

"More than just rumbling," said Noah. "It was more like an all-out uncivil war."

"Really? What do you mean?"

"Well, when Ed was planning to build his factory complex, the tribal attorneys for the Wampanoag made motions to fight him on it. Said he was infringing on their territory. Evidently, there was a dispute where the property line was."

"How was it resolved?"

"Well, the courts sided with Ed and he got to build his factory. But while they were under construction, the tribe held rallies on the edge of the property insisting that the ruling was a farce and the company had paid off the court."

"Wow," said Jerry. "I had no idea."

"Of course, nothing was ever proven, I mean, definitively, so we don't really know the whole story."

"I have to admit," offered Jerry, "I don't know Ed that well so I couldn't say one way or the other. I just hope ..."

"Excuse me," said a tall woman with charismatic eyes and an auburn bob, coming up to them, her girlfriend in tow. "Are you Noah Miller?"

Noah rose to his feet. "I am."

"I told you it was him," she said to her friend. The woman extended her hand and Noah took it in his. "I'm Cindy and this is my friend Naomi." Noah shook her hand as well. "I'm a friend of Mindy Russell in your show."

"Right. Very pleased to meet you Cindy. Naomi." He was taken aback. "How did you know who I was?"

She raised her phone. "I recognized you from your picture online. A blurb on the *Times* website this afternoon said that you'd taken over the directing. *And* you're the playwright. That's really something."

"Amazing how quickly news travels these days," said Noah. "Can't imagine where they got my picture from." He kicked Jerry playfully. "This is the show's producer, Jerry Ziegler. Maybe he can tell us."

Jerry stood. "Had your picture on file from your last production. You know the theater biz. Love to get information out there as quickly as possible. Free local publicity and all. How you doing ladies?"

"Fine," said Cindy. "Doing just fine."

Jerry offered a flirtatious pose. "Well, we'd invite you to sit down at our table," he joked, looking down then back for effect, "but we don't seem to have one." The women giggled. "Would you like to pull over a couple of chairs and join us?"

"Thank you, but we're on our way out. We're actresses too. Just wanted to meet Noah and say hello."

"I'm glad you did," said Noah. "Thanks for stopping by." The ladies moved on.

"That was interesting," said Noah.

"You're a celebrity," Jerry told him. "Get used to it."

Noah finished his beer. "I wouldn't go *that* far," he said.

"Suit yourself," said Jerry.

Just then, the hostess came by and led them to an open table on the other side of the bar. After they had time to browse the menu, Noah ordered the honey-and-almond-crusted salmon and Jerry a New York Ribeye.

"So how did the rest of your day go?" asked Jerry. "Was it everything you hoped? Did the cast respond to you? Anyone I need to take out back and, you know, threaten to call their mothers? You *know* I'll do that."

"It went great," said Noah. "Everyone seems to be on board and so far, no apparent problems."

"That's good to hear. Let's keep it that way."

"Jerry, I told you, you have nothing to worry about. It's going to turn out fine."

"That's what worries me. It's all going a little too easy. First there's the painless transition, then it implodes and everyone's running for the hills. Like those early Japanese Godzilla movies."

Noah shook his head, perplexed. "What the hell are you talking about?"

"Don't you remember? Everything's all peaceful and serene at the beginning. Then bam, chaos. Buildings tumbling down, blood everywhere."

"Well, let me know how it turns out."

"But that's not going to happen to you. You're right." He glanced Noah's way. "I'm just a little paranoid. Never mind me."

When their entrees came, the two friends ate their dinners and enjoyed the piped in recorded music seeping from the speakers. The live band was through for the night.

"Sheila and I are in separate bedrooms," said Jerry.

Noah put his fork down and sipped his water with an eye on his companion. "Jerry, I'm sorry. When did this happen?"

Jerry reached for his beer but it was empty. He snatched his buttered roll and took a bite. "It's been happening for a while," he said. "A trial separation, they call it. I'm the one on trial. She's the one trying to figure out what she wants."

"And yet," said Noah, "she came up here and is living with you and you're still together. That's got to count for something?"

Jerry mulled that over. "Sheila loves the Cape. She has friends here. Theater. The beach. It's a big house and I'm always traveling. I wouldn't read anything into it."

Noah was undeterred. "Well, I read and I take notes. And my notes say you guys will work it out." Then, retreating a step, "I hope you can work it out."

Jerry smiled but Noah saw through it.

"It's not your problem, pal. Sorry I even mentioned it."

"Don't be silly, Jer. Who else you going to talk to?"

"Not my wife, evidently." Then they let it drop.

When he had finished his coffee and dessert, Jerry paid the bill and apologized because he had to get on the road early in the morning. "Oh," he said, "I forgot to mention. Some of the Playhouse execs want to take a look at the play. See how it's coming."

Noah appeared confused. "Is that normal procedure?"

"Well, yes and no," said Jerry. "With a new director in house, they want to see for themselves. You can't really blame them. So you tell me what day you want them to come next week and I'll set it up. They're available Tuesday, Wednesday and Thursday."

Noah nodded, relenting. "Make it Thursday, okay? That'll give us more time."

"Thursday it is," said Jerry.

"Afternoon," added Noah.

Jerry stood up. "Thursday afternoon. I'll tell them."

"I'm not thrilled about this, Jerry," said Noah, joining him on his feet. "It's not ready for an audience yet."

Jerry playfully punched Noah's chin. "Relax my friend. They know there's still time on the schedule. They just want to see where you're at."

"You mean they want to make sure we'll be ready for the opening?"

"It'll be fine, Noah. If I thought it was a problem, I'd step in. Besides, I'll be there in case there's any trouble."

Noah still did not look happy.

"Hey," added Jerry, "I've got your back."

Noah nodded again, yielding to the inevitability and Jerry's position. "Thanks for dinner."

When Jerry left, Noah sat down. He did not want to go home yet and asked the waitress for a coffee refill. He killed time by assessing a couple of people still at the bar chatting and laughing, then took a breath of summer and tried to get his mind on his work. Tomorrow was going to be a big day with the complicated climactic scene.

"Hi there," said Emma, approaching his table.

Noah rose. "Hello," he responded, a bit startled to see her. "How's it going?"

"All is well," she grinned. "And you?"

"Couldn't be better," he told her, hardly persuading. Then, motioning to the empty seat, "would you care to join me?"

The restaurant had just about cleared out by this time but Noah noticed an older couple, three tables away, shaking their heads, peeking at him, and smiling. He wondered if their apparent amusement had anything to do with him.

"Hope I'm not intruding," said Emma, getting his attention as she sat.

He glanced her way. "Not at all. I was thinking about work and could use the diversion."

She smiled demurely. "Well, then I'm glad I stopped by."

The waitress brought him a fresh mug of coffee.

"Would you like something to drink?" Noah asked his guest.

"Just some water," she told him.

But when Noah looked back at the waitress, she seemed to have vanished. All that was missing was a puff of smoke. Noah seemed perplexed. She was just there.

He wondered if she had noticed too. "Did you see that?"

Emma raised a brow. "See what?"

Noah shook his head, deciding not to go there. "Nothing. Never mind." Then he moved his water glass towards her. "Here, take mine."

"Thanks."

He looked her over and took a breath. "So, how's the real estate business?"

"Oh, let's not go there, shall we?" she said. "You don't want to talk about work and neither do I."

"Right," he agreed. "Nothing about work."

She waited for him to suggest another topic but nothing came.

"The last time we met at the park," she offered, "you were telling me how you were struggling after your losses."

He added some sugar and cream and stirred his coffee, buying time while he studied her, wondering how this young woman could be so mature and understanding for her age. But he was not in the mood to talk about pain either. Not now. Not with her. "Sorry. I don't know what compelled me to discuss it."

"No, I'm glad you did. We all need someone to talk to sometimes."

He nodded, agreeing, then tested his coffee. "So, Emma, tell me, are you seeing anyone?"

She paused before answering, reaching for a sip of water, as though she was gauging him. "As a matter of fact, Simon and I have been dating for almost eight months. He's an architect. British. I met him by chance through a business associate." And then she added, "A really nice bloke."

"Glad to hear it," he told her, beaming.

She leaned forward, placing her chin on the back of her hand. "Me too."

She smiled cordially, hoping to put him in at ease. "What about you, Noah? I know it hasn't been that long since, well, you know, but I was wondering if, maybe, I mean, when you're ready to, you know …"

Just then he noticed a low-toned ringing in his ear. He decided not to say anything this time. Probably the sound system though he was pretty sure there had been no music since Jerry left.

"I don't think I'm ready to start seeing anyone, seriously just yet, if that's what you're getting at?"

She slumped back in her seat. "Forgive me. I didn't mean anything. I was only thinking …"

"No need to apologize. I know you were only thinking of me."

She added, "I just hope that when you *are* ready, you'll be open to the possibility of meeting someone else."

He scratched his chin. "Yeah, me too."

Sipping his coffee, Noah noticed the ringing had faded. He wondered why this woman seemed so interested in his life. She was a mystery, appearing at times when he least expected, providing advice that overstepped its bounds. What did she want from him? He was always the subject of their conversation. Noah did not think that was normal. Most people, he found, enjoyed talking about themselves and were probably unaware of it. But Emma was different. She seemed interested in him, even concerned.

Noah studied her eyes, looking more pale grey with the declining light. She was an enigma—he was unable to put his finger on it—but there was something about her he could not ignore.

He removed a five dollar bill from his wallet and placed it under the creamer. "Sorry," he told her, getting up. "Long day tomorrow."

"Did you want something else?" the waitress asked, surprising him. She was at his side as though she had never left.

Noah gave her a queer look. "No, thank you," he told her.

Funny, he had not noticed her standing there. He looked down at Emma. "Guess I'm more tired than I thought."

"Tell me about it," said the waitress. And she scurried off.

Emma chuckled.

"Great to see you again," he told her. Then, struggling to indicate some interest in her suggestion so she would not feel slighted, "I appreciate what you said before and promise I'll keep an open mind."

"Sorry about that," she told him. "Sometimes I talk too much."

"See you around," he said.

Then he left her sitting alone and went home to bed.

16
Snort

An exquisite butterfly darted around our heads before landing gently on my darling Erica's knee. It sat there, content and undisturbed, flexing its colorful wings.

I had never seen a butterfly with those colors before—somewhere between a Tiffany and turquoise blue—its wings framed in midnight black with patches of pineapple yellow. My God, it was spectacular.

Erica and I had just finished reading *Are You My Mother?*, stretched out on a white cotton sheet on the grass by a lake in Olivebridge, New York. It was a sublime summer day. Jessica and I had taken Erica up to the Catskills for a long weekend. It was Erica's first real adventure away from Long Island, not counting our trip to Cape Cod when she was still a babe, and a perfect day to go swimming in the lake with her blowup floaties hugging each arm, adorned with colorful whales, sea horses and starfish.

The balmy weather and boundless aqua blue sky were a perfect backdrop for our weekend getaway. We had talked about going upstate for a while but could not seem to find the right time. I had not been back to the Catskill Mountains in years, since my mother had taken my brothers and me to one of those Borscht Belt Hotels in South Fallsburg before they all disappeared along with the busboy and cabana jobs to make way for the casino industry. I have vague recollections, mostly fond memories of my time there, especially the loudspeaker announcements for a game of *Simon Says* or an archery tournament.

Erica froze at the sight of the butterfly, unsure of what to do. It was her first close encounter with one. "Daddy," she cried in a panic, her mouth wide open.

"It's okay, sweetie," I assured her. "It's not going to hurt you. It just stopped by to say 'hi.' I think it likes you."

"It does?" her question as innocent as a four-year old.

"Definitely. Besides, it has no teeth so he never has to brush them." She laughed at that. "I promise you have nothing to fear."

"No teeth?" she questioned. "How does it eat?"

"Eats things it doesn't have to chew. He's a smart fellow. Just like you."

"I'm not a fellow," she insisted. "I'm a *girl*."

Just then our new friend fluttered its wings and rose into the air, setting itself down on my daughter's other knee.

"You see that, honey? It's playing with you."

She laughed again. "Playing with me?"

"Uh, huh. He's a friendly little guy. Do you want to give him a name?"

"He doesn't have a name?"

"I don't know. Let's ask. 'Excuse me, Mr. Butterfly. What's your name?'"

She waited for an answer and, when none came, smiled at me. "You're silly."

I smiled back, so much in love with this little girl we had waited so long to welcome into our family.

"What should we call it?" I asked, recognizing this butterfly had emerged as the primary topic of discussion for the day. Now she got serious and began searching for a name. She gazed towards the lake and the sailboats and kayaks and swimmers, making a contemplative face in which her lips disappeared. She was on a mission.

I tried to help. "Should we call him Harry? How about Shirley?"

She shook her head, still ruminating. "Is it a boy or a girl?" she asked.

"That's a great question, Erica. I have no idea how to answer that."

She opened the book we had been reading next to her—carefully, so as not to dislodge it from her knee—and began thumbing through pages until she found one to her liking. "Snort!" she announced.

I laughed, glancing over her shoulder. "Snort? What the little bird in the story calls the power shovel?" She nodded. "That's a perfect name, sweetheart. We'll call him Snort."

She leaned in, bringing her head closer to the butterfly. "Hi Snort," she said almost in a whisper. At that, Snort fluttered again, rising awkwardly and moved away from us. "Where's he going, daddy?"

"I don't know, honey. Maybe back to his family, or, perhaps he has an errand to run."

We watched him fly away into a memorable summer afternoon. "Bye Snort."

A while later, Jessica returned from her hike around the lake and Erica told her all about her adventure with Snort.

"I'm sorry I didn't get to meet him," said her mom, thrusting her lower lip forward in a pout. "But I'm glad you made a new friend today."

"Me too," she said. "He was so beautiful and he let me name him. I'll never forget him."

I sat by listening in on the conversation, adoring my wife and daughter, and realized that this moment was the most incomparable and fulfilling of my life—the day, the setting, the butterfly, my family—and, if I had the power to stop time, this would be the one I would save and bottle up in my memory so that I could look back at it and know that I was truly happy. And if there really is a heaven, this is the day I want to relive again and again.

Then Jessica asked her if she would like to go back in the water.

"Do I have to wear my floaties?" our precocious daughter asked about her inflatable life preserver.

My wife turned to me but did not wait for a response. "I'm afraid you do, young lady. We wouldn't want any accidents today. I know I wouldn't. Daddy?"

"Not me," I chipped in.

"And I'm sure your new friend, Snort, wouldn't either. What do you say?"

"No, me either. Not today."

While pulling them up her arms, she had a request. "Show me the ring, please."

Now it was Jessie's turn to smile. She turned her hand over, displaying her stunning sapphire ring, the one she planned to bequeath to her daughter someday.

"Will you ever take it off?" asked Erica, a proud admirer.

Jessica leaned in right up against our daughter's nose. "I promised your daughter I would never take it off ... and what do we do in this family?"

"We keep our promises," Erica said.

"That's right, young lady."

Then we all ran into the lake laughing and splashing.

We talked about Snort often and would make up stories of his adventures—like the little bird in the story—and the people and things he would meet. Sometimes when she wasn't feeling well, she would ask me or Jess to tell her where Snort was at that very moment and what he was doing.

Erica said a prayer for him at bedtime every night.

17
Motivation

━━━━━━━━━━━━━━◦⟨◦⟩◦━━━━━━━━━━━━━━

A t the next rehearsal, all players were on stage for the big game show dream sequence towards the end of the play. Roz had already worked out the logistics of moving the sets around with her production crew as the script's stage directions specified and now it was time to get the actors up to speed so the transformation of set and props would be as seamless as possible. Noah set the scene for the actors and, when everyone was ready, yelled "Fade up lights."

When the scene opens, Stacy, Charlie's new girlfriend, in center-stage bed with Charlie, is quarreling over his friends and their relationship. After nothing is resolved, the two roll over and go to sleep. But Charlie is restless. He tosses around and, finally, sits up to find that Wendy has joined them in bed. He quickly learns that she is a figment of his imagination and part of his dream.

"She's pretty," says Wendy, noticing Stacy on the other side of Charlie.

"It's makeup," he replies.

"An actress, huh? Have I seen her in anything?"

"Nothing that'll ever win an Oscar."

"What restaurant does she work at?"

"Some dive on Melrose."

"Must be a good chef."

"She'll bite her nails before she steps into a kitchen."

"A good conversationalist?"

"Does her share of complaining."

"Smart?"

"Only reads things with the word 'Catalogue' printed on the cover."

The conversation moves on and Charlie asks Wendy if they could get back together.

"I couldn't answer that," she tells him.

"Why not?"

She laughs. "Cause you're dreaming."

"Oh yeah," he realizes.

"But," she offers, *"having had a glimpse of your subconscious, I will let you in on some insight."*

"Yeah? What's that?"

"This isn't a game."

Suddenly, as lights flicker, the bed is shoved to the far stage-right corner, and game show music is playing. Charlie lays back in bed. Stacy remains asleep. Billy enters wearing a tuxedo and stops at center stage. Wendy rises, strips off her pajama top, and is wearing a one-piece bathing suit with a "Ms. Right" banner across her body. Cynthia enters downstage as the "cue card" gal. A flashing lightbox sign is lowered from the rafters with the title of this mock television game show, You're A Shmuck, Chuck!

"Thank you ladies and gentlemen," begins Billy. *"I'm Billy C., your host this evening, welcoming you to the world's number-one-rated game show,* You're A Shmuck, Chuck! *Here our contestants—divorcees, widowers and losers—compete for the woman of their dreams (points to Wendy). And now I'd like to introduce our beautiful hostess—a former Miss Angel Cake, Miss Sweet Cakes, Miss Plum Cake, and my main squeeze, would you please give a rousing hello to the talented and lovely, Lydia Wilkins!"*

Lydia enters and crosses to center stage wearing an outrageous outfit, a blend between a Fruit Loops bird and a Carmen Maranda getup, carrying an oversized banana. Cynthia raises her cue card for "Applause."

Noah held them up there and explained to Cynthia how he wanted her to handle the cue cards, twisting her body from side to side so the entire audience could view the card. He also told Lydia to do some kind of Flamenco dance when she hits center stage and had Wendy wave and blow kisses like a "Miss America" contestant when Billy points to her. He asked Roz to add a bouquet of roses to the list of props for Wendy. Finally, he reminded Stacy and Charlie to remain still in bed so the audience would not notice them.

Noah picked it up from Billy's entrance. After Billy introduces the first contestant, Stan Urlicht, he calls for Charlie, still asleep in bed. He wakes, disoriented, and is encouraged to join Billy at center stage.

"What are you doing in my bedroom?" asks Charlie.

"We're not in your bedroom, Mr. Hobson," replies Billy. "You're a contestant here on the hit game show, You're A Shmuck, Chuck! *And this is our studio audience." (Billy points to the theater audience as the house lights come up so that the theater audience becomes the studio audience.)*

"What am I doing here?" asks Charlie.

"You're competing for the woman of your dreams," replies Billy, pointing to Wendy behind them. "If you decline, then we're going to let Mr. Urlicht here have a crack."

Charlie notices Stan for the first time. "Stan," he says, "what are you doing here?"

"Well," he replies. "Wendy's free bait. Me and Cynthia split up again, so I figured I'd give it a shot. Besides, they've got lovely parting gifts."

With some urging from the audience, Charlie agrees to play the game and "ring his Ms. Right" by tossing a hula hoop engagement ring over Wendy. He misses on his three attempts as the 'biological clock' runs out of time.

"No," pleads Charlie, "give me another chance. Please!"

"Sorry, can't do that, Mr. Hobson," says Billy.

"Why not?" Charlie asks.

"Audience?" says Billy, appealing to them.

"You're a shmuck, Chuck," screams the audience at the cajoling of Cynthia's cue card and the flashing overhang.

"Please, one more chance!"

Just then the studio lights flicker, the music lowers, the players exit, the house lights come down, and the set is converted back into Charlie's bedroom with Stacy still asleep in bed next to him. She is awakened by his screams.

"Give me one more chance!"

Stacy shakes him and he responds.

"One more chance," he begs.

"Charlie," she says. "Wake up. You're dreaming."

"Wendy, huh?"

He sits up, noticing Stacy.

"Charlie, are you okay?"

He looks around the room. "No, I'm not."

Then he peers directly at her. "I'm a shmuck!" (Blackout)

Noah was pleased with the performance and gave the team a one-hour lunch break. After lunch, they were going to run it again.

When the rehearsal was over later that afternoon, Molly found Noah and Bobby in the backroom at the big table. Noah was marking his script with notes. "After the final scene," Noah said to him, "I want to run the entire second act straight through. No stopping."

Bobby noted it on his production schedule. "Got it," said Bobby. "Oh, you asked me to remind you about the lighting cues in the restaurant scene."

"Right," Noah remembered. "Let's talk to Roz and Mitch about that in the morning before we get started."

"Okay," said Bobby.

They noticed Molly standing there. "Molly, hi," Noah said to her.

"Sorry," she said, "Didn't mean to disturb you."

"No worries. I think we're done. Bobby, are we done?"

"All done as far as I can tell."

"See, we're all done."

Noah tapped his shoulder. "Thank you, Bobby. Good job. See you tomorrow."

While Bobby was leaving, Noah got up from the table and began packing his bag without looking up. "Now, what can I do for you?"

Molly watched him momentarily, picking her spot. "A few of us are going out for dinner—quiet place, inexpensive, Mexican—and we thought, maybe, well, I thought, perhaps, you'd like to join us?"

He stopped packing and turned to her. "Oh," he said, because that was all he could think of at the moment. "That was nice of you … I mean, to think of me."

She seemed a bit flustered with him gazing at her. "Only if you're not busy. I mean, if you have other plans, we'd certainly understand …"

"I don't have any other plans tonight. In fact, this is the first I'm even thinking about it."

"Well, that's great. So, what do you think? Will you join us?"

"Sure. I'd love to. Would like that ... as long as no one objects."

"Anyone object?" she called out, peeking around the room. "I think you're good. Doesn't seem to be any objections."

"Great," he said. "Glad to hear it." Then, after considering it, "Should I meet you there?"

She studied his face almost missing the question. "Meet you? Oh, no, that's okay. It's only ten minutes from here. So, if you'd like, you can leave your car and I'll drive."

He did not read anything into that. "That sounds fine. I mean, if you don't mind?"

After a beat, "I get paid not to mind."

He nodded his recognition with a grin. "Great. Meet you outside in five?"

She nodded. "See you outside."

At the restaurant, a place called C.U. Mañana, the group of seven were led to a large round table with a colorful frilly tablecloth in one of the rooms in the back. Along with Molly and Noah, there was Steve, John, and Susan from the cast, and Will and Maggie from stage crew. They ordered two pitchers of sangria, which didn't last long, and several of the house specialties, recommended by Molly and Susan, who were regulars there and knew the manager, Manuel, who brought them two more pitchers.

To get to know everyone more intimately, Maggie suggested they go around the table naming the college they attended, their field of study, and what they hoped to be when they grew up. That was good for a few laughs and surprises.

"You wanted to be a vet?" Maggie questioned Will. "You can't even take care of yourself."

After that, Will changed the subject and started talking about other productions he had worked on and some of the hilarious incidents that went on there. That seemed to be a popular topic since everyone had a story to contribute. After a while, the group noticed that each tale seemed to get more and more incredible until Molly questioned the validity of one of Steve's recollections and the focus of the game shifted to whether or not the memory was true or false.

All the while, the samples of food kept coming out and the empty sangria pitchers kept going back in until Manuel cut them off and began serving tea, coffee, and ice water instead. By the end of the evening, they all agreed on two things: that C.U. Mañana was the best Mexican restaurant in the universe and no one was going to eat another thing for at least forty-eight hours.

On the drive back to the theater, Noah did not say much.

"Have a good time?" Molly asked him before pulling into the parking lot.

"I did, yes. Thanks for inviting me."

Then, before she could say anything more, "It was fun. I enjoyed it. A nice mix of people."

"You know," she added, "the guys are really glad you're directing."

"Huh?"

"It's true. Everyone thinks you're doing a better job than Peter."

Noah lowered his gaze, a bit embarrassed. "Glad to hear it. Thanks."

"That includes me."

Noah smiled to himself.

She parked next to his Rogue, the only vehicle in the back lot, and killed the ignition. It was quiet now and Noah felt the perspiration begin to surface like morning dew.

"I think I needed a night out with the gang," he said, his voice a pitch higher than usual. "Sometimes you don't get to know the people you work with and you miss out. Don't you agree?"

Then she was on him, slow reserved kisses, gently brushing against his lips. He sighed and she opened her mouth, granting him free reign. Soon he embraced her, his hand on the nape of her neck, angling his head at different degrees to get deeper and deeper inside. By then, her tongue was all over his like a Jackson Pollock painting.

He breathed in her scent. She smelled good too. Aroused, he closed his eyes, sensing a ravenous hunger and groans emanating from the depths of her throat. Or were they his? Then the heavy breathing started, slowing the pace as heartbeats raced. Kissing Molly felt too good and he missed the intimacy. It had been too long since he held a beautiful woman in his arms, since he held Jessica, and he tried putting her out of his mind.

But that was impossible.

He lifted his head, retreating, waving the flag of surrender. "Molly," he began.

She cut him off. "You don't need to say anything."

"I think I do."

She moved her leg away.

He chose his words prudently. "This has nothing to do with you."

Now she shifted further, towards the door, giving them space. "I'm sorry, Noah. This is my fault."

"No, it's not," he objected. "It's no one's fault." Then, "Why does it always have to be someone's fault?"

She placed her hand on his arm. "I shouldn't have done that," she went on. Conscious of her hand, she removed it. "You're not in a position to get involved with one of your actors. I understand. It could get you into a lot of trouble these days. I would never do that to you. I get it. And I'm really sorry. I ... couldn't help myself."

He let her have her say and waited to make sure she was done.

"It's not that, Molly. I wasn't even thinking about that. All right, maybe it passed through my mind, but really, that's not what this is about."

She bit down on her lip before they disappeared.

"The thing is," he went on, "I'm just not emotionally ready to get involved with someone right now. Believe me, it wouldn't be fair to you if I did."

Then she smiled, putting on her best face. "I understand."

"I'm sure you don't."

Something about the way he said it. It was not your boilerplate response and she sensed there was more to it.

"Are you married?" she asked him, almost accusingly.

He weighed the question and took his time answering. "My wife passed away last year. I'm sorry. I don't really want to talk about it."

The pain in his eyes illuminated like a glittering billboard on a dark mountain road.

"Maybe if you did ...," and she held up there.

Now it was his turn for a protective front. "I don't know, Molly. I don't know anything anymore. None of it makes any sense."

He stopped to gather his thoughts.

"I loved her," he continued, "and miss having her with me. It's a struggle each day and I do whatever I can to keep her out of my mind. Because, if I think about her ..."

He delved into her disappointed eyes and stopped again. This time for good.

"I understand," she told him. "You need time to deal with your pain. But it has to be hard to get through this alone. I can help, Noah. If you let me."

His silence gave her his answer.

They sat there for the next few minutes, neither one knowing what to say. He felt like an abandoned puppy and wondered why every woman he seemed to meet lately wanted to save him.

He exited the car like he was trying to get out of bed without waking her. "Thank you, Molly ... for everything."

She watched him through the open door. "Please call me if you want to talk. I wasn't just saying that. I *really am* a good listener."

He smiled but it did not last. Then he nodded and got into his car.

He drove straight home and fell into bed and spent the rest of the night awake thinking about Jessica.

18
Neglected Transgressions

⎯⎯⎯⎯⎯⎯⎯⎯⎯⎯⎯⎯⎯⎯⎯⎯⎯⎯

J erry received the call after he had left the house. It was Roz. Noah had not shown up for rehearsal and no one was able to reach him by phone. Everyone was concerned.

"I'm on my way to Boston," said Jerry. "Just went over the bridge. Don't have to be there 'til lunch so I've got a little extra time. I'll circle back and check his place."

When he arrived, he found Noah in bed and shook him as if he wasn't trying to wake him. "Wake up, bubala. Time for school."

Noah yawned twice and leaned on his elbow. "Jerry? What are you doing here?" Then, before his friend could respond, "Am I late?"

Jerry sat at the end of the bed. His expression gave Noah his answer.

"Shit. What time is it?"

"Nine-thirty-five."

"Must have slept through the alarm." He stretched and yawned.

"Your phone's off," said Jerry. "Rough night?"

Noah squeezed his lips together and nodded.

"You okay?"

Noah shifted past him, ignoring him. "I should call Roz."

He gathered his clothes and removed some clean underwear and socks from the dresser.

"Why don't you get into the shower and eat something," advised Jerry. "I'll call her and let her know you'll be there by ... 10:30?"

Noah nodded and left the room. "Thanks."

When he was showered and dressed, Noah joined Jerry in the kitchen. "There's coffee, toast and eggs," said Jerry. "I'm not the best chef in the world, maybe not even in the room, but I know how to crack open an egg."

Noah hedged. "I should be going. I don't want to keep everyone waiting."

Jerry placed his hand on Noah's shoulder. "Sit, my friend, and tell me what's going on. I'm sure they're not all waiting around telling war stories."

"I'm really not hungry. Big dinner last night. Mexican. The food just kept coming."

Jerry pulled out the chair. Noah gave him a defeatist look and followed orders. "All right, maybe there was a little sangria but I swear, most of it was fruit and ice." Then he settled down.

Jerry served the food and poured the coffee, joining him at the table. "Are you going to tell me what's on your mind or do I have to do my Luciano Pavarotti impression? And let me warn you, people have paid *not* to hear me sing!"

Noah added milk to his coffee. "It's nothing," said Noah. "I didn't get much sleep last night. That's it."

Jerry made a face.

"What do you want, Jerry? Got a lot on my mind. I overslept. I'm sorry. That's all there is."

Noah finished his toast and washed it down with the coffee.

"Noah, I know you. We go back a long way. Please. Tell me what's going on."

Noah slouched back in his seat, tilted his head up and followed the rustic pattern of the copper-tile ceiling. He didn't come out with it right away. "I was thinking about Jessica. She was on my mind all night."

Jerry stayed silent, drifting back to more innocent times.

"I was wondering what she was going through, you know, in the end. What kind of hell she must have been going through."

Jerry poured himself some coffee.

"I wasn't there for her, Jerry. I didn't help her. I didn't know what to do. What if she thought …"

Silence filled the room as Noah deduced a mental checklist of motives. Finally, he came out with it. "What if she thought I blamed her for Erica's death?"

"Noah!" bellowed Jerry. "Now you're being irrational!"

But Noah had already started to lose it. "She *needed* me, Jerry. She needed my support, my understanding, my love, and I couldn't give it to her. I wanted to, but …" His voice began to tremble and break up. "I didn't know how. I was hurting too and didn't know what to say. Didn't know what to do to help her."

He lowered his head and let it sway, gazing at the linoleum floor, a century of filth imbedded in it. "We never talked about it. Never resolved it. Erica died and we didn't say two words to each other. Like it never happened. Neither one of us. It was all so cloudy. It was all a big …"

Noah rose, unsteady, separating himself from the table.

"If we didn't say anything, maybe it would go away. Maybe we wouldn't have to face the questions. Look for answers. Maybe we could just go on with our lives like it never happened. Maybe, maybe, maybe."

He made his way to the window.

"Can you believe how stupid that was? Like it *never* happened?"

He stood facing the window, hands on the sink, his eyes glazed over in confusion, lost in a world of ambiguity.

"I don't know what else there is to say, except … it was my fault. I'm the only one who could have done something. I could have helped Jessie. Could have saved her. Could have been there somehow instead of neglecting it … neglecting … *her.*"

"You can't blame yourself," said Jerry. "It could have been one of six hundred things. You don't know what was going on inside her head. Why take the blame and do this to yourself? It's not healthy. And I don't think it's going to help you resolve this."

"I'm not sure I'm ever going to get over this," Noah admitted. Then he dropped his head again and sobbed.

After a moment, Noah realized they were not alone. A nosy bumblebee, hovering on the other side of the window, was eavesdropping. He watched it, suspended in space—its blurred wings flapping at the speed of sound—and wondered if it wanted to join the conversation. He opened the window leaving the screen in place between them.

Jerry rose tactfully and patted Noah's shoulder letting him know he was there. "I know someone you can talk to," he told him. "She's good."

But Noah's attention was fixated on his new guest. He watched the bee monitoring him, mesmerized by the encounter.

"... I've only been seeing her a couple of weeks," Jerry went on, "but I like her. Knows her stuff."

Now the bee was inside the house as if it magically transcended the screen.

"... Gives you immediate feedback."

Noah checked the screen for holes but couldn't find any.

"... Not like some other good-for-nothings that call themselves doctors."

Then, without warning, the bee raced out of the room.

"... She's right here in Barnstable. Let me give her a call."

Noah dashed out too, following it.

"Hey, where you going?"

He rushed into the small hallway by the front door. He could still hear the buzzing. It was above him. He raised his head and watched as the bee slipped through a tiny narrow crack in the ceiling.

"Where'd you go?" asked Jerry, joining him.

"Does this house have an attic?" asked Noah.

Jerry looked around. "I don't know. I don't see any pull chord or stairs. Why?"

"Just wondering."

Jerry checked his watch. "I think it's time you got to work, don't you?"

"Right," agreed Noah.

He escorted Noah to his car. It was going to be a blistering day.

"Thanks for stopping by," said Noah.

Jerry opened the door for him. "Think it over, pal. About the shrink. I really think you should talk to her. If not her, someone else."

Noah managed a conciliatory smile. "I'll think about it."

He got into his car and started the ignition. "What do I tell everyone about this morning?"

Jerry took a moment. "Blame it on the Mexican food."

Noah nodded then took off. Jerry peeked at his watch and got into his car. He was no longer sure that having Noah come up here and taking over as director was such a good idea.

When Noah arrived at the Playhouse, the actors were running through the final scene with Roz apparently in charge. He watched them from the rear until Roz stopped them when one of the actors missed their cue. Joining them on stage, Noah apologized to everyone, mentioning something about a stomach problem. No one questioned him further and the incident was forgotten. He read off some quick notes he had prepared for the scene and they started again from the beginning. They rehearsed it for the next two hours until lunch was called.

After the break, Noah gathered his actors on stage. "As some of you may know, because of a contractual obligation, Mindy will not be with us tomorrow and Monday. She's shooting a movie in Arizona over the next three days, so we're going to run through her scenes for the rest of today. Tomorrow we'll work on the remainder. On Monday, we should have our sets in place, and, from what I understand, most or all of our real props will be available so we won't have to keep imagining them. Any questions?"

No one took him up on that so he continued. "Last thing. Next Thursday, we're getting a visit from some of the theater brass who want to take a look at our show." Several of the cast grumbled. "I know, I know, I'm not happy about it either but there's nothing we can do. They have a right to see how we're coming along so I'm giving notice now so no one is surprised when it happens. That's it from me. Let's begin with act one, scene one."

The afternoon rehearsal went smoothly and ended a little earlier than usual. Afterwards, Noah found Roz in the backroom and thanked her for running things that morning while he was incapacitated.

"No problem," said Roz. "Glad to do it. How's your stomach?"

"I'm fine. It was a rough morning but I got through it."

She threw her bag over her shoulder. "We were concerned when we couldn't reach you. You should really keep your phone on all the time, just in case."

"You're right. My bad. Sorry about that. Thanks again for your help. See you tomorrow."

While they were talking, Molly had come by to check on him. He grabbed his stuff and the two proceeded through the building.

"Was it the food last night?" she queried.

"Must have eaten too much," he lied. Then, to placate her, "but I had a good time and I'm glad I joined you."

"You'd tell me if it was something else? Wouldn't you?"

He looked away. "Probably."

He continued to his car then noticed he had left her behind. Or was it the other way around? He circled back so they were within proximity and there was no need to shout, his behavior modified, casting his boyish charm aside. This time he flashed his hazel eyes at her. "Thanks again."

"For what?"

He took his time responding, as honestly as anything he ever said to anyone. "For not giving up on me."

He took another step then looked back at her. "Goodnight, Molly."

He left her there.

She was still standing there by the time the realization set in, unaware how much time had lapsed. During that span, Molly had become aware of a feeling—a feeling she had not sensed for some time; a feeling she felt only one other time in her life; a feeling, she knew, some people never experienced because they were not willing to step onto the firing line and take an arrow through the heart.

She was having the same problem that her character, Wendy, was having in the play.

She was falling for him.

19
The Newport Madam

Jerry encouraged Noah to take some down time off Cape to help relieve his stress and called his former professor, Amy Kaufman, to see if she and her husband, Ed, were in town this weekend and available to go sailing again. Perhaps another day on the water would be the ideal prescription for Noah's tattered nerves.

The couple were planning a day trip to Newport, Rhode Island on Sunday—Ed was meeting a business associate in town—and were happy to have Jerry and Noah tag along. Noah asked if it would be all right to bring Molly with them as she had recently mentioned how much she enjoyed sailing. There were no objections from the hosts.

Noah was not quite sure why he included her—to reciprocate for her invite to dinner or because he could not stop thinking about her since the other night—but he was looking forward to spending the day together.

Sunday was a flawless summer day to be out on the water and their early morning departure would give them plenty of time on open seas for their journey. The winds were expected at ten-to-fifteen knots with gusts up to twenty, perhaps a bit breezy for novices, but Ed was an experienced sailor with a crew at his command.

During the excursion, the group learned that Molly had spent a good deal of time on the water while growing up and was more proficient at handling the sails than either Jerry or Noah. Before long, Ed was relying on Molly's skills as his first mate so there was no need to depend as much on the other two.

"Told you there was a good reason to bring her along," kidded Noah to Jerry.

Once the gusty winds died down and the boat was rigged properly, everyone settled in. Molly went below to assist Amy with a plate of diced apples and peanut butter along with sesame flatbread crackers and a French brie. There was also fresh coffee.

"You're our guest," Amy told her. "You don't need to help me."

Molly smiled. "Hey," she replied almost in jest, "everyone works on the boat. No slouches."

"I wish all my guests were as considerate as you," Amy told her.

Sailing on, they passed other sailboats and Ed and Molly took turns pointing out the type of vessels they were while Noah and Jerry eavesdropped.

Ed was impressed. "Where did you learn so much about sailing?"

Molly gave Noah a glance before responding. "I grew up in the south on the water," she explained. "A place called Skidaway Island. Just east of Savannah."

"We know that area," said Ed. "Pass by it all the time. It's lovely down there."

"A great place to grow up," said Molly. "Quaint and mellow. Very rustic. There's a group of islands there and everyone knows how to sail from the time you're seven. We had a ten-foot Sailfish. Everyone starts with a Sailfish or a Sunfish or something small like that. Easy to get around. All you need is a place to dock it, which is just about anywhere. I was sailing a boat this size before I learned how to drive."

Ed stepped away to make a minor course adjustment as Molly went on with her story. "There's a big fishing industry in that area so there was plenty of opportunity to be out on the water whether you were working or with your friends."

"I'd have never taken you for a Southern belle," said Jerry.

And with an enchanting drawl capturing true Southern gentility, Molly cited the Scarlett O'Hara line about not being a gentleman. They all laughed at Jerry's expense.

"I gave up my charmed accent when we moved north," she went on. "Daddy didn't think it a good idea since there was a negative connotation attached to being from the South at the time."

"And still is," Amy added.

"That's true, unfortunately," said Molly. "I wasn't happy about leaving my friends but I was certainly old enough to understand."

"Why'd you leave Georgia?" questioned Ed, who had rejoined them.

Molly reminisced. "The fishing industry in that area dried up," she said. "Dad lost his job. Couldn't find anything. He wasn't really qualified to do much else. Me? I was seventeen. Still in high school. What was I going to do?" The group eyed one another uncomfortably.

"Where did you go?" Noah asked.

"Mom had an older sister in Plymouth at the time. Just off Cape. The family had some connections and was able to help dad find something. Fixing air conditioners. Dad was always good with his hands and mechanical stuff. Wasn't much but it paid the bills. I finished up at a local high school then went to a small college in Boston. Been here ever since."

Later, Ed returned to his post at the wheel and Amy went below to put away the food and tidy up, leaving Molly, Noah and Jerry topside.

"I was a communications major," said Molly in response to Noah's question. "Didn't really know what I wanted to do but it sort of fit me. My first job out of college was with a radio station. I'd interned there the summer before graduating and they offered me a job when I got my degree. I thought I wanted to be a reporter but that didn't pan out. It's a small circle. Not a lot of opportunities."

"I worked for a radio station after college," offered Jerry. "In Minnesota. When I got there, they were losing money hand over foot."

Molly and Noah laughed.

"What's so funny?" asked Jerry.

"You said 'hand over foot,'" explained Noah. "The expression is 'hand over fist.'"

Jerry winced. "Let me tell you something. They were losing money hand over fist, over foot *and* over a barrel. They didn't know what they were doing. I came up with a list of ways the station could reverse course—even put a marketing proposal together—but the station manager told me I was just a kid out of college and what did I know? I don't even think he read it. They went out of business a year later. Serves 'em right, the bastards."

"What about you, Noah?" asked Molly.

He gazed out over the starboard bow. "I never worked for a radio station," he said. "But I did give television a shot. Went out to L.A. a couple of years after graduation and made connections any way I could. Met a group of writers from this theater company. Had my first play produced there. A one act. I worked closely with one of the directors. Watched the way she handled it. Picked up a few things. It was a supportive group. We were all young and learning on the job. Even took a directing class at U.C.L.A. A fun time in my life."

"What happened with television?" Molly wanted to know.

"I wrote a couple of spec scripts for a network show and even got one to the producers. Sometime later, I got a call from this guy who told me he liked it but couldn't use it for one reason or another. I kept sending them around, hoping to get a writing gig. Eventually, I got an agent but he wasn't much help. A few months later, I'm watching that show on TV and I hear a punchline that sounds familiar. Then another one. And another."

"What was it?" asked Molly.

"I counted six jokes they lifted from my script and used in one of their shows. *Six!*" He chuckled, frustrated. "That shmuck I spoke to wouldn't hire me or buy my script. He just took what he needed and tossed the rest away. Me included."

"Did you tell your agent?" asked Molly.

"Of course," he said, shaking his head. "I was pissed. But he couldn't help me."

Jerry jumped in, "Why not? Couldn't you get in touch with the union?"

Noah took a deep breath. "Like you said, Molly, it's a tightknit circle. The guys with the jobs are making the money. They don't want anyone new cutting in on their good thing. Besides, what was my agent going to do? It's a catch 22. He wants to maintain a good relationship with the network, the producer, so he can find jobs for his clients. Think he was going to put himself on the line for me? Not a chance."

"What about suing them?" asked Jerry.

"Sure," said Noah, "I could have sued if I had a few hundred thousand dollars. How many lawyers do you think the network has on staff? Even if I won, probably wouldn't have covered my legal fees. And do you think any producer would hire me after that? Ever hear the term 'blacklisted?'"

"Well, at least you proved to yourself that you were good enough to write for TV," said Molly.

"Yeah," added Jerry, "look where that got you."

Molly objected. "Don't listen to him. He's just jealous."

"Actually," said Jerry, "I'm half serious. If Noah had gotten a writing job in L.A., and you had become a reporter, and my marketing plan had worked in Minnesota, we all might have different lives right now and wouldn't be working together on Noah's play or sailing to Newport on this beautiful day."

The group spent the final hour of the voyage to themselves—reading, sunning, sleeping—enjoying the wind on their faces and the warm summer air. Approaching Rhode Island, Amy was at Ed's side, taking over the helm for a while so he could get a break.

Ed explained to everyone that he would be busy most of the day and not available for lunch but would meet up with them for an early dinner. He planned to cast off around 6 p.m. so they would have enough light and a spectacular sunset for the ride home. That gave everyone a few hours to explore the city.

After docking and choosing a restaurant where they would rendezvous later, Ed took off to meet his friend. Amy guided them to a Mediterranean snack bar she knew in town where they could get a quick bite to eat. After lunch, Jerry agreed to escort Amy to a couple of home good shops she wanted to visit. Molly and Noah ventured off to see what they could find.

Down the main avenue they explored shops then hit the side streets to see what else was around. Mostly they were searching for antique stores, where, they agreed, they both enjoyed spending time. They stopped in one with a marquee that was hard to miss, Aardvark Antiques.

Entering, they noticed the open beamed ceiling with stained glass pendant lamps suspended like constellations in the night sky. The store had considerably more square footage than it appeared from the street and they took their time strolling the aisles, rummaging through vintage treasures.

In a backroom, they combed through a pile of black and white eight-by-ten photos of Rhode Island from its heyday between Prohibition and the Beat generation. The price was reasonable so Molly picked out one she liked with a bird's eye view of downtown Newport. It appeared to be a Depression-era scene judging from the automobiles cruising the main dirt road. The cost of leaded gasoline at the Esso filling station: twelve cents a gallon.

"Now that's what I call affordable pricing," quipped Noah.

Molly studied the photograph. "I think I'll have it framed," she said, enamored. "I've got the perfect spot in my hallway."

When they left they still had about two-and-a-half hours before meeting the others so they continued on.

A few blocks off the avenue, on an isolated street with a storefront that appeared somewhat out of place for the neighborhood, they approached a dark glass-pane door with an unassuming pink-neon sign—"Psychic Readings." Below it read "Tomorrow's news, today!"

Molly stopped there and beamed at her companion.

"No, no, no," he said, shaking his head. "Don't look at me. Not interested."

"Oh, come on, Noah," she implored. "Don't be like that. It could be fun."

Noah peered at the sign then back at her. "You think you're walking into this place for fun? I think you're nuts. But hey, what do I know? If you want to shell out twenty-five bucks to have someone tell you that one of your dead uncles thinks he knows where the family jewels are buried, be my guest."

Molly took his arm. "C'mon," she urged him, "you never know about these things. Besides, what else is there to do?"

Noah thought it over. "I'll go in and sit with you if you want but I really don't believe in this stuff. And I'm not having my palm read. Is that clear?"

She nodded in agreement and they went inside.

Opening the door, they heard a bell jingle. "See what I mean?" whispered Noah. "If this psychic was legit, would she seriously need a bell? Wouldn't she know when someone came in?"

The room was dark and cramped and the floors groaned in pain as they made their way towards a small table with a crystal ball. "We're not in Kansas anymore," said Noah. They sat at the table in heavy upholstered chairs and observed the metaphysical artwork besieging them. "I'm not even sure we're still on planet Earth."

"Do you smell something?" Molly asked, ignoring him.

He sniffed. "Like a garlic clove past its expiration date. Let's get out of here." Noah started to rise.

"You promised to see this through," she reminded him, grabbing his wrist and pulling him back.

"Unhand me, madam," he cried in jest. "I never promised you a rose garden. Or a rose by any other name, for that matter. And, since everything's coming up roses …"

Molly cut him off. "Are you finished?"

"No, I missed one. Take time to smell the roses, and make sure you throw out the garlic."

Just then a woman who appeared to be in her mid-seventies with a maroon turban and gold amulet around her neck, approached them from the back.

"Hello, my dears. Thank you for coming. I am Madam Sweeny and I will be your guide to the spiritual world."

She sat with them at the table and took her time observing each, then shut her eyes. The overhead lights were lowered. After a moment, she offered her hands to them. "Please enclose the circle."

Molly took her hand and offered hers to Noah. He, too, accepted the medium's hand. Madam Sweeny peered into the crystal ball. After a while, she began to sway her head as if trying to position herself for a better view.

"Three children in a park, a boy and two girls," the madam began. "The older one comes from a noble lineage. Centuries old. She wears a blue cap. The younger one carries a doll. Each day they meet at the park and play together and don't bother with the other children. Then one day, a great bird shows up over the park. It is massive with talons like an eagle's. It glides down and abducts the little girl and flies off with her, leaving her doll behind."

Just then, something moved in the room. Molly and Noah both heard it.

"Her friends are frantic. They chase the bird through the streets and out beyond the neighborhood into the hills. But it is no use. They lose sight of the bird and the little girl."

A faint indistinct sound was heard nearby. For a moment, Noah thought perhaps the air conditioner had kicked on but the nebulous humming wavered, more like a distant breeze.

"The boy and girl find themselves lost," continued the medium, "and don't know the way home. Then, the older girl thinks she sees her friend up ahead in a tree. She runs toward it and disappears into a crevice in the earth. When the boy catches up all he sees is her cap left behind. He is distraught. He doesn't know what to do—go for help or climb down into the earth and search for her. He can't decide. Instead he crawls up under a bush."

Now the breeze picked up, becoming louder, like wind was blowing through the room. Molly looked at Noah.

"At first, the boy is despondent and feels a sense of abandonment but remains in the bush, not ready to find his way back."

Papers began hurtling through the air. A bronze bust of Morgan le Fay—an apprentice of Merlin—is knocked over, and the thud causes Molly to jump. She opens her mouth to say something, but nothing emerges.

Madam Sweeny, her eyes closed, raised her voice above the tumult. "Then, his feelings turn to anger and, in his mind, lets his rage out on all that have conspired against him. He feels resentment and can't help believing the world is his enemy."

Now a tempest billowed through the room. Molly instinctively released her grip and struggled to rise but the force of the indoor storm kept her bolted in her chair, which began to shift along the floor. Noah grabbed the table with one hand and Molly with the other.

"What's happening?" cried Molly, alarmed.

"I think the meter ran out," said Noah, trying to calm her and himself with humor.

But Madam Sweeny didn't seem aware of what was happening in the room. "Then, sometime later, a new girl shows up and finds the boy hiding in the bushes. She offers her hand and he takes it and she leads him back to his neighborhood. But she walks fast ahead of him and, though he tries, can't keep up with her. When he turns the corner, he sees her laying in the street and everything stops."

With a jolt, the ruckus in the room ceased, like a runaway house—whirling beyond a Kansas Cyclone—slamming to the ground. Molly's chair came to an abrupt halt. Noah's heart pounded violently. He let out a deep sigh, stunned, trying to get his bearings.

In the aftermath, papers floated listlessly to the pallid hardwood floor as Madam Sweeny opened her eyes and gave her guests an impartial nod. "I trust this story has meaning for you," she said as if the chaos they experienced was typical. She lifted her head and turned from one to the other.

Molly returned her gaze. Noah felt too exhausted to respond.

"I sense a warning here," the madam added.

Neither of them responded. Noah had hardly paid attention to the story and could not wait to get out of this spook house into the open air. Molly came to her feet, left her payment on the table, and the two exited without a word.

Outside, they hurried up the street—away from the tenebrous door with the unnerving magenta neon tubing—fearing the wind might blow them back inside. But as they headed towards Main Street, Noah noticed that the sun was still blistering and the air static. The wind was not blowing and people were milling about as if all was as it should be.

"Oh my God," cried Molly, once she was able to find her voice. "Oh my God. What the hell was that?"

Still in shock, Noah shook his head. "I think Disneyworld opened a psychic store in Newport, Rhode Island and didn't bother telling anyone."

Molly shuddered. "What did she have a wind tunnel in there?"

"I sure hope so," said Noah, "because if that was coming out of her crystal ball then we need to contact someone from Area 51."

"And what about that story?" asked Molly. "Did it mean anything to you? Because I felt no connection to it whatsoever."

Noah shook his head. "She lost me after 'three kids in a park.'"

Continuing up the street, Molly checked her watch and stopped.

Noah came up beside her. "What's up?" he asked, noting her puzzled look.

"How long would you say we were in there?"

"*Too long* if you ask me."

"No, really, how long?"

"I don't know. Twenty minutes, half-an-hour tops. Why?"

Molly raised her gaze to meet his. "Either my watch is broken or we're late."

"*Late?* What do you mean 'late?'"

"It's ten after four, Noah. We were in there for over two hours."

"Two hours? No way. I don't buy it."

She showed him her watch.

"That's got to be a mistake."

He pulled his phone out of his pocket. "I don't believe it. What's going on …? How could we have been in there …? It's not possible."

Molly appeared dazed. "Nothing about that place seemed possible. Gives me the creeps. Sorry I suggested it. Just *so* weird."

She took two steps forward and turned back. "We should get moving. They're probably waiting for us. Besides, I don't want to think about it anymore."

Noah joined her at her side. "What do we tell the others?"

Molly took her time. "If it's all the same with you, I'd rather not discuss it. I don't even believe it myself."

Noah regarded her trepidation. "I agree. This is one odyssey off the beaten path I'd rather not share with the rest. They'll think we're nuts."

When Noah and Molly arrived at the restaurant, the other three were already seated at a corner table.

"*There they are,*" cried Jerry, raising his martini glass towards them in a mock toast. "And only twenty-five minutes late. We thought you two had been kidnapped by aliens."

Noah and Molly gave one another a look.

"You never know," said Noah.

"Sorry we're late," said Molly. "My fault. I was going through these old photographs in one of the shops and couldn't decide. A women's prerogative, right?"

She retrieved the photo from her over-the-shoulder bag and passed the black and white memento around the table, relieved that no one questioned them any further. She wouldn't have known anyway how to explain their bizarre day.

After dinner, the group headed down to the marina and set sail back to the Cape. The evening ride home was carefree and without incident, and as they headed further and further away from Newport, Noah and Molly relished a guarded sense of relief. The two had decided to put the episode behind them and not mention it to anyone. Whether it was a hoax or magic or delusional, or a combination of the three, they figured it was better to write it off and leave it at that. They did not want to know the truth. It was just too freaky.

Disembarking the ship, Noah watched as Molly dropped the photograph she had purchased into a trash can on deck.

20
Keepsakes

J essica and I never saw the need to rub elbows with our Northport neighbors so when it came time to decide a theme for Erica's fourth birthday we did not encourage her to choose some popular Disney heroine film like *The Little Mermaid* as others did. Instead, we suggested she pick a story she loved and a character with whom she could identify.

True to herself and her emerging sense of humor, Erica chose Hans Christian Anderson's *The Ugly Duckling*—not the graceful, enchanting swan at the end of the story—but the wretched lost soul at the outset. We could not have been more proud.

During the afternoon celebration, we received more than a few confused looks and comments from acquaintances, one who went so far as to complain about what type of message we were sending to the children. We dismissed the criticism explaining that it was Erica's choice and assured them we were harboring no clandestine viewpoint. We also reminded them the fable had an encouraging outcome.

As a concession to those who might have suspected we had a hidden agenda, convinced we were Communists, or something worse, the birthday cake featured an edible white chocolate swan with five candles mounted on its tail. It was a satisfying ending for all, even Erica, who confessed she appreciated the surprise gesture after some of her friends made fun of her unorthodox choice.

Overall, Erica had a wonderful day enjoying her guests and the thematic games we had set up, the magician who performed (he *did* turn a duckling into a baby swan to the delight of all), and the goody bag featuring a softcover copy of *Hans Christian Anderson Fairy Tales.* The book was Erica's clever idea and the feedback we received from parents was that the party was an overwhelming success.

After everyone left and we all pitched in to clean up the mess, none of us were in the mood for real food so we refrained from any leftovers and got right to the cake and ice cream. Since Erica had already opened her gifts with her friends here so she could thank each one personally, it was time to present her with our gift. I handed her the rectangular box and watched as she opened it. Her elation emanated from those grateful green eyes working its way down to a beaming smile.

She lifted the gold butterfly pendant from its slot on the satin padding and tried reading the scripted name in block letters. She turned to me for help.

"Snort," I told her.

"SNORT!" she screamed then hugged me. "It's beautiful. Thank you daddy. Thank you mommy. I love it."

Jessica clasped the gold chain around her neck and Erica examined her new treasure in the mirror. "Now I have special jewelry too, just like mommy."

Later, as I was tucking her in at bedtime, she pulled herself up close and whispered, "Snort will be with me forever."

She laid her head back on her pillow, running her fingers over the letters beneath her chin. "Where do you think he is now, daddy?"

My heart danced. "I think Snort has just been tucked into bed and is about to fall asleep."

"Do butterflies sleep?"

"Of course they sleep, honey. Just like bunny rabbits, and puppies, and kittens, and …" I placed my hands just above her hips, "… cute little girls that just celebrated their fourth birthday." And then I tickled her in her sweet spot and she giggled with delight.

I sat beside Erica for the next fifteen minutes, reading to her from *Goodnight Moon.* Pointing to each word, we sounded out the letters together.

"Daddy," she said, just as I was pulling up her sheet.

"Yes, sweetheart."

"When I grow up I want to have a pretty garden so Snort and his family can come visit me all the time."

I kissed her forehead. "That sounds like a wonderful plan."

She yawned. It had been a fulfilling day, and a long one, and she was asleep before I turned out the light.

Erica cherished that pendant and it became her favorite keepsake.

21
Two Tenors In A Verdi Opera

It was Tuesday morning and Mindy—Stan Ulrich's wife, Cynthia, in the show—was back from her film shoot. The day was overcast and humid with rain in the forecast and people were milling about a bit slower than normal. It was the first time the entire cast would work together with all props and sets in place and, while there was a slight buzz in the air, the weather seemed to be sucking the life out of everyone. Noah could not seem to shake it either and was hoping the caffeine would soon kick in.

Before they got started, he had Roz and Bobby assemble the cast and crew in the back room and joined them after pouring himself another cup of coffee.

"Nice to have everyone here together again," announced Noah, making his way around the room. "Mindy, I trust your shoot went well and you can now afford an exotic two-week vacation in Paris or Rome or whatever European resort you've always dreamed of visiting."

A couple of people laughed and one snickered. "It was a lot of fun," replied Mindy, placing the script she had been scrutinizing on the table. "I didn't earn as much as you think. More like an exotic week or two in Santa Fe. But I did get to work with Kate Winslet."

"Well, that's exciting," added Noah. "I'm glad it went well and, more importantly, that you're back."

Someone in the room whistled in appreciation.

Noah pulled out his notepad and double-checked his notes. "This week, we're going to go through the scenes that still need work. I want to finish them up no later than Thursday lunch, and make sure we're all on the same page with final tweaks. As you know, our sets are in house and ready"— a couple of people applauded—"and Roz and her crew will be setting them up between scenes so we can all get comfortable with them. Also, use your props. Any questions?"

"Noah?" Susan yelled out.

"Susan?" he replied.

"I got a note telling me to see Monica today about costumes. Is she here?"

Noah looked Roz's way. "Monica will be here at the end of the day," said Roz. "I think around four, four-thirty. A couple of you who still need to see her for fittings besides you, Susan—I think Wayne, Mindy and René. Please see Monica at the end of rehearsal."

"Thank you, Roz," said Noah. "Anything else?"

"Are we going to go over the last scene?" asked Steve. "I know we were waiting for Mindy to get back but I think we still have some things to work out."

"Yes," said Noah. "The last scene of the show is on the top of my list, in fact, that's where we're going to start this morning. I also have an idea for the dream scene that I want to try but we'll get to that either later today or tomorrow. Any other questions, concerns, requests?"

"Any donuts left?" asked John.

"Thank you everyone," said Noah, smiling, "See you on stage in five minutes."

The company worked on the final scene of the show for the entire morning and into early afternoon before Noah called for a break. After lunch, they walked through the dream sequence with the crew moving the sets around but there were some issues getting the suspended *You're A Shmuck, Chuck!* lightbox sign to flash. Noah was not thrilled with the amount of time the crew needed to convert the game show set back into the bedroom. By the time Monica showed up with her duffle bag of size-adjusted wardrobe, everyone was wiped out from the hectic day.

While the actors tried on their outfits for a final fitting in the back room, Noah discussed the crew and lighting issues with Roz and Sue. Roz assured him that the house electrician would be in tomorrow prior to rehearsal to make sure the sign was in good working order and that she would have a talk with the crew about speeding up the set changes.

"I think it was the weather today," she offered as a halfhearted concession.

"Well," suggested Noah, "let's hope the weather is better tomorrow."

On his way out of the Playhouse, Noah was glad to see that the rain had given way to clear skies.

He found Molly lingering outside. "What are you still doing here?" he asked.

"Waiting for Susan and René to finish up with Monica. Thought we'd get some dinner."

"Stay away from the Mexican," he suggested.

Molly pinched his arm. "I love Mexican food." Then, changing subjects, asked: "What are you up to tonight?"

Noah checked the time on his phone. "Not much. I was going to give Jerry a call and see if it was okay to come by. It was a long day. I could really go for a swim."

She smiled at him with a look that was hard to read.

"What?" he asked.

"I don't know."

"What don't you know?"

"Well," she started, "my neighbor told me I could use her pool whenever I want and she and her husband happen to be out of town this week." She let that sink in before continuing. "And, I have to go over there anyway to water her plants and ..." She looked him in the eye. "I could be in the mood for Chinese tonight."

"What about Susan and René?"

"Well, I haven't actually asked them yet to have dinner with me so I really don't know if they're even available."

He sighed, biting his upper lip in the process.

"What do you think?" she asked coyly.

He pondered the invitation. "How do you feel about spare ribs and pork fried rice?"

Noah followed Molly in his car and, when they arrived at her place, she ordered the food from a takeout menu she kept in a desk drawer and asked them to deliver it next door.

"Thirty minutes," she told him. "Something to drink? I've got Chardonnay, beer and TaB."

"TaB?" questioned Noah, a little surprised.

"Roz turned me on to it. It's pretty good actually. Want to try?"

"What kind of beer you got?"

She opened the fridge and began singing the Miller Beer jingle. "I've got Miller and ... I've got Miller. Looks like it's Miller time."

"You know, for a bartender, you don't offer much choice."

She lifted her chin and cocked her head to the side. "Well I'm sorry, Mr. Bass Ale. I'll be sure to stock up the next time I'm *not* expecting you to come by. What's your pleasure, sir?"

"Chardonnay please."

Molly opened her upper cabinet and retrieved two wine glasses. "You're a hard guy to please, you know that?" She pulled the cork out of the opened two-liter bottle with her teeth and poured, then handed a glass to Noah.

"Not really," he told her, raising his glass in front of her. They tapped and drank as they kept their attention focused on one another. At some point she realized the moment seemed awkward and offered him a tour of the house.

"That's where I was going to hang that photo from Newport," she said, pointing to a hallway wall after showing him around. She realized he was still watching her. "But ... then I decided ... you know ...." She looked down, embarrassed by the scrutiny.

"I'm going to get changed," she told him. "Meet you outside?"

Noah went out to his car and grabbed a beach bag with a bathing suit and towel he always kept on hand. He changed in the back seat. Molly joined him a few minutes later, wrapped in a white terrycloth, carrying the open bottle.

He noticed the pretty landscaping in the front of the house. "Nice flowers. Is this your place or are you renting?"

"Thank you," she said. "It's mine after another eighteen years of mortgage payments. Bought it after we were married."

"Didn't know you were married."

"Well, evidently, neither did my husband. Didn't last very long."

"Another woman?"

Molly looked away. "A guy. Would you believe it? My confused, neurotic husband left me for another man. Decided after two years of blissful matrimony that he was bisexual and wanted to give the other side a turn."

Noah grinned painfully to show his support. "That must have been tough."

"I'm pretty tough myself, you know." She swallowed and shook her head. "I got over him."

Noah could tell she was still hurting. "Want to talk about it?"

She looked his way, taking her time. "His name was Cody. Tall, blue eyes, gorgeous. Met him in one of my acting classes. Good actor all right. Fooled the hell of out of me."

He let her have her space.

"Guess it wasn't a total loss. Didn't fight me over his share of the house. Guilt works wonders. Doesn't it?"

"So, I hear."

Molly ended the history session and he followed her next door. She used her spare key and led him through the house to the backyard. Noah, quiet the entire time, decided not to comment further and let the topic drop.

Out back, he admired the glistening blue water once the lights were turned on. "Nice pool," he said. "*And* they've got a hot tub. This is what I'm talking about."

Molly was glad he was pleased.

"And it's so quiet back here," he went on. "And secluded. You're lucky to have neighbors who let you use it when they're not around."

"Kathy and Robert are good friends. They look after me."

He sat at the pool's edge, allowing his feet to dangle in the cool water. "Ah, yes," he cooed. "That feels *so* good." He finished off his wine.

Molly went back inside to turn on the music and, when she returned, was carrying a brown paper bag with handles. "Food's here."

Noah jumped up and joined her at the table, helping to set up the plates and dish out the dinner. On the outdoor speakers, Led Zeppelin's *Good Times Bad Times* played.

"That was delicious," he told her when they were done, "and *my* treat."

"No," said Molly, "you're a guest in *my* house."

"Pardon me, ma'am, but this is *not* your house."

"Doesn't matter," she pointed out, slurring her words.

"Yes, it does," he insisted. "You supplied the wine, I've got the dinner. Do you have a problem with me buying you dinner?"

She studied him for a moment, then relented. "No," she said finally. "No problem. You can buy me dinner if you want. Thank you."

"You're very welcome."

"Now that we've settled that," he said, standing, "how about a swim?" He made his way to the pool's steps and ventured in, stopping on each one so his body could acclimate. Then he plunged in and floated on his back, watching her. "Are you coming in?"

Molly started to clear the table, a bit anxious. "Let me just clean up first."

He watched her pile the plates and gather the silverware. "C'mon, Molly, leave it. I'll help you when we get out."

Molly thought she heard something in his voice. She hesitated then stopped fussing over the table and moved to the top of the steps. She removed her robe, revealing a tiny red bikini and trim body, balanced by symmetrical breasts and narrow hips. Noah's mouth went dry and the burgeoning smile on his face told her he approved.

She swam over to him. He gulped.

"You work out?" he asked, his voice suddenly shaking, his heart quivering.

"You like?" she asked with an expression that could not be misinterpreted for anything other than what it was.

He nodded, realizing he had no control. The few weeks he'd known her, wanted her, had come to this and he realized at that moment that the oversized sweatshirts she wore kept her stunning figure concealed.

She moved in closer and kissed him with ease, winding her arms around him and pressing her lower body against his suddenly snug bathing suit.

"Better than a hot tub," he added, deciding at that moment she could do whatever she wanted to him. He had no power to stop her.

The kissing became more intense as they took turns with the lead. He could taste the duck sauce in her mouth as they playfully dueled with their tongues. She wrapped her legs around his athletic body and pumped herself against him like she was working a machine at the gym. He grabbed her tight petite ass with both hands, squeezing hard enough to etch his fingerprints on her skin, guiding her motions into a collaborative rhythm. From their throats emerged groans, sighs and squeals that were muzzled by their mouth-to-mouth efforts. Noah could hear *When the Levee Breaks* in between muffled shrieks. At some point, their bathing suits sank to the pool's bottom as their movements shifted into higher gear and their grunts became louder.

He entered her without guidance as he stood on the bottom step lifting her with the buoyancy of the water. He wanted her at the shallow end so he could savor her breasts and she accommodated him by pressing them to his face. He licked her flesh and tasted her nipples, and as he did, he felt his penis grow harder as he moved deeper inside her. Noah shifted a step up, her body mostly above the water line, and watched her breasts surge and recoil as their movements accompanied the nearly seven-minute version of *Dazed and Confused,* now throbbing from the speakers.

The thick pine trees and evergreen bushes lining the backyard allowed them to enjoy their lovemaking in private. Eventually, his legs gave out and he sat on the second step and they slowed the pace and went back to what they enjoyed most, soft kisses more with their lips this time.

At some point, he lowered her onto her back on the top step, mounted her like a missionary, and swallowed her breasts one at a time. She grunted louder and lifted her legs thrusting her pelvis forward as the pace of their deep breathing accelerated. They were moaning now—two tenors in a Verdi opera—drowning out whatever Zeppelin song was blaring into the night. He waited as long as he could to ejaculate, hoping she would beat him to the punch, but he was no longer in control. Nature took its course.

After his body stopped quivering and he dismounted, he rolled over on his back, using the cool water as a salve to lower his body temperature. Noah leaned his forehead against her shoulder and spread his arm across her tummy.

He lay there grateful, savoring the warmth of her body, sensing the beat of her heart. Exhausted, they lay motionless—except for a hand that stroked his hair—enjoying a live rendition of *Stairway to Heaven*. He was grinning now, a genuine grin he hoped would never leave.

When the song was over, a surreptitious smile broke out across Molly's face. "I knew you were trouble," she told him, "the moment I saw you at Jerry's place."

He let that linger a moment, gauging his timing. "What are you? A psychic?"

They both broke out in laughter. She first. He bringing up the rear.

"Uncle," she pleaded, wiping away the tears. "Please don't go there. I beg you. That's not fair."

He waited until they were calm again. "You know," he began, lifting his head so he could encounter her reaction and cherish those Siberian Husky blue eyes. "I didn't exactly plan this."

Now it was her turn. "And *why* exactly is that, Mr. Miller? Weren't you attracted to me when we first met?"

He grinned, trying to keep his poker face, then nodded. "I believe you caught me checking you out."

"Oh, yeah. That's right. You liked the way I poured drinks."

He laughed at the memory. He may even have moaned.

"But you didn't come back for another?"

"You were so busy, it was hard to carry on a conversation."

"Poor excuse."

Now he was defensive. "I had just arrived the night before and didn't know anyone except Jerry. Then I started talking to Emma and she seemed to know me. Then Jerry found me on the back deck and wanted to introduce me around and …"

"… Emma?" asked Molly, puzzled. "Emma who?"

Noah tried to recall. "Never got her last name. She's in real estate. Sotheby's, I think. Found the house I'm staying at. Jerry's too. You must have seen me talking to her. Right in front of the bar."

Molly shook her head. "I didn't see you talk to anyone that night, except the crew later. Didn't even see you leave. One minute you were there, then you were gone. And you never came back for another drink." Then she pursed her lips, raised her eyebrows and shook her head again.

By the time they cleaned up, it was after midnight. He walked her back next door and she invited him to stay the night.

He pulled her close to him and they kissed. Long wet ones.

"How are we going to do this?" he asked concerned.

She looked him in the eye. "Is this going to be a problem for you, sir?"

He looked away and sighed. "I hope not, ma'am." She didn't respond. He circled his attention back to her. "I really hope not."

She shook her head. "We don't have to tell anyone, right?"

"Right," he offered, unconvinced.

She broke away from him and turned back. "I know," she said, sounding more hurt than angry. "Why don't we cool it for a while, you know, not see one another until the show gets going? That's only two more weeks."

He placed his hand on her shoulder. "We see each other every day, Molly. Don't you think someone will notice?" He wrapped his arms around her, pressing against her.

"What?" she said, spinning around. "How we look at one another?"

He stepped back. "Yes," he agreed. "That too."

The look on her face told him she noticed his erection. "Oh. Right." She considered their dilemma. "You got to control that thing."

"I'm afraid it has a mind of its own."

"That could be a problem."

Later, in his own bed, it took Noah a couple of hours to fall asleep. Even then, it was a restless night. He had not planned on getting involved with anyone this soon, certainly not one of his actors, and was not sure how to handle it.

He thought about the last time his play was produced in New York City. He was attracted to one of his actors then too but refused to let it go anywhere. He was so in love with his wife and they had this beautiful new baby and there was so much to lose.

But this was different. Jessica was gone and he was still feeling the loss. He had been so isolated from the world and Molly seemed to get him and fill a need. Several needs. And he had to admit that tonight had been fun. More than fun. Incredible. She was an incredible woman and smart and funny and, he realized, not unlike his wife. He enjoyed spending time with her.

But it could all blow up so easily, everything—the play, the relationship, the respect he had worked so hard to earn from the cast, the crew, the people at the Playhouse—if someone found out and questioned his motives or began claiming harassment. It was so easy these days. Sex was always a troublemaker.

No, this had to stop. He had to put a hold on this risky liaison as quickly as possible before it got out of hand.

Then he wondered if it was too late? The look in her face tonight. The feelings. What if he broke it off and she objected? No, not Molly. She wouldn't do that to him. She was too sweet and sympathetic. She understood the situation. A mature adult. She could handle it.

No, he thought, this was not going to end well. This had been a big mistake and it was all his fault. And now, he had no idea how to fix it.

22
Dilemma

The next day, the company proceeded through the remaining scenes in which there were still some issues to be worked out. They followed Noah's suggestions and worked on the final revisions directors often leave for the end to tighten up performances and address obstacles that have been annoying them from early on but have been left unresolved due to more critical concerns. And, as actors have become comfortable with their performance and what to expect from their colleagues in certain scenes, resolving these impediments at this point could lead to further challenges by upsetting the flow of familiarity. But the company came through like the professionals they were and Noah was pleased with the overall progress.

In addition, the *You're A Schmuck, Chuck!* sign flashed on cue—to everyone's relief—and it was evident the crew did a better job moving sets around quicker as Roz timed their progress on her granddad's gold watch.

Noah was business as usual with Molly in front of the cast and crew so as not to give anything away. She followed his lead and did the same and by the time Noah released everyone at the end of the day, the two had not said more than a few words to one another. He called her soon after rehearsal broke to chat and let her know that he was seeing Jerry and Sheila for dinner. He was anxious to discuss Thursday's dry run with

Jerry and what he could expect from the Playhouse brass' upcoming visit to the set. Molly said she understood and left it at that.

Thursday came and Noah still had part of the final scene to run through with the cast. The scene takes place the afternoon following the big dream sequence in the script. Charlie has overslept after a difficult night and missed his Sunday morning softball game. Teammates Billy, Lydia and Stan visit him after the game to find out why he failed to show up. Eventually, the discussion turns to the real problem.

"Where's Stacy?" asks Billy.

"Gone," says Charlie, without a hint of emotion one way or the other. Billy gives Stan a knowing look.

"Can we get you anything, Charlie?" says Lydia.

"No, really, I'm fine," Charlie tells her.

The group gets ready to leave. Charlie, still disturbed by the *You're A Schmuck, Chuck!* dream he had last night, asks them to stay.

Charlie wanders the room, gathering his thoughts.

"When Wendy and I were going out, do you have any idea what was the one thing that scared me the most?"

Billy answers, "Yeah, that she'd find out about you and Stacy."

Stan smacks Billy in the shoulder.

Charlie continues. *"I was afraid of making a commitment. And I can't for the life of me tell you why? That's why I started seeing Stacy."*

"Everyone goes through a relationship in their own way," Stan reasons.

Charlie objects. "But most people overcome their fears. Look where it's gotten me. I lost the one woman I really cared about ... I really loved."

"Let's hold it up there," said Noah, heading onto the set from his downstage seat. "I want you to take your time on that line, Wayne, and get introspective."

"The 'look where it's gotten me' line?" asked Wayne.

"Actually, your response to that line," said Noah. I want the audience to experience your pain. Everyone has been through a breakup before. I want to feel how much it hurts when you say it. So take your time with it, okay?"

"Got it," said Wayne.

Noah nodded. "Okay, let's back it up to Charlie's line—'When Wendy and I were going out …'"

They went through the lines again with the added input until they were back where they had ended.

"I lost the one woman I really cared about … I really loved," admits Charlie, slowing it down the way Noah suggested.

"So you're a schmuck," says Billy. *"What can I say?"*

"You got that right," agrees Charlie.

Stan jumps in. "It's called the game of life, Charlie. Some people play it better than others."

"I'm tired of playing games," admits Charlie.

"Then stop playing," says Lydia.

Charlie gives her a sullen look, then says, "Stan, you dated before you got married. Was it hard giving it up for Cynthia? You know, being single?"

Stan thinks that over. "Not for me. It was something I truly wanted." *He pauses. "But I will tell you where it starts to get hard. It's when things don't work out and you have to reevaluate your life."*

"What are you talking about?" says Charlie.

Stan takes his time here. "What the hell. You'll find out sooner or later. Cynthia had an affair."

"Stanley!" cries Lydia.

"Some guy at work," Stan goes on. *"I suspected it but I didn't have the nerve to confront her. I thought if I put it out of my mind, it would go away. Boy, was I wrong."*

"I'm sorry," Charlie tells him.

"It's okay," says Stan. *"We worked it out. The point is, Charlie, we all have fears we'd rather not face."*

Then Billy decides to confess. "You all know that before I started seeing my little munchkin here, I used to date different girls."

Charlie and Stan give each other a look. It's no news to them.

"Well," continues Billy, *"I never thought I could care about anyone, I mean really care for someone, until I met Lydia."*

"Oh, Billy," says Lydia.

"It was difficult there for a while, let me tell you," he continues. "I kept going from one girl to the next, to the next, to the next ... "

"We get the point," Lydia tells him.

"But I was riding on empty," he admits. "There was never anything in here." He taps his heart. *"You changed all that for me, pumpkin. That's all I got to say."*

Lydia gives him a smile and they kiss.

"That does it," says Charlie. He rises and heads for the phone on the desk.

"What are you going to do, Charlie?" asks Stan.

"Something I should have done weeks ago."

He begins dialing. Suddenly, Wendy is at the front door and enters. "That won't be necessary," she says.

"Great," yells Noah, jumping up again. "Let's hold it there. That was wonderful, everyone. I like where this is going. Just one note. Roz?"

From backstage, Roz stepped out. "Yes?"

"I'd like to get a spotlight on Molly standing in the doorway. Nothing hot but I want the audience to notice her before she says her line."

"Will!" yelled Roz.

Will Hatchwell stepped out on stage from the wings. "Right here."

"Noah wants a spot on Molly in the doorway."

Will ran upstairs to the corner spot and turned it on. "Can we get Molly on her mark?" yelled Will.

Molly took her place.

"Do you want a filter?" asked Will.

"Let me see what you got," said Noah. Will tried the different colored filters and Noah chose amber. "A little wider please," said Noah. "I don't want it too hot. Just enough so she stands out in the doorway."

They rehearsed the sequence several times until Noah was satisfied. When the scene was over, Noah called the cast and crew together on stage. "Good rehearsal, everyone," he said. "We're going to start the run through at 2:30 p.m. and go straight through the entire show. Roz, what time should everyone be back from lunch?"

"Two o'clock," said Roz. "We're going to set up now for the opening so we're ready after lunch."

"Great," said Noah. "Any questions?"

Steve jumped in. "Can we ask for a line if we need it?"

Noah gave Roz a look. She rolled her eyes.

"No more lines, beginning now. You all know the script and what you have to do. Consider this afternoon a live performance. The only thing you won't need are costume changes. Everything else—sets, props, lights, oh yes, and *lines*—is a go. No need to get nervous. The brass knows we still have next week to finish up refining this thing, so just do your best and work the process. If you make a mistake, I promise I won't fire you. Steve, I know you're not going to forget your lines today. No one is. That's an order. But, if by some chance you do, then you need to work it through. You all know how to do that. You've all done it before. Enjoy your lunch."

About 2:20 p.m., five members of the Cape Playhouse staff showed up for the performance and Bobby escorted them to the front row. Noah headed over to say hello and warm them up then found a seat two rows behind. He wanted to be within proximity so they could hear his laughter. That would help cue their own. Being the first official performance of the show in front of an audience—however small—the actors needed to get their timing down and having a responsive audience was a critical step.

Jerry joined Noah in the seat next to him. "Ready for your closeup?" he asked.

"We're about to find out," said Noah.

"How's that money-pit marquee doing that put us over budget? Working today?"

"I don't know," Noah answered. "Keeps blinking on and off. It works, it doesn't work. It works, it doesn't work."

Jerry smirked. "That's an old joke, pal."

"What can I tell you? I'm getting old."

"You can't be getting old," Jerry told him, "because we're the same age. And that would mean *I'm* getting old. And I assure you *I am not.*"

"They say denial is the first sign of old age."

Jerry glanced his way. "Remind me not to work with you again."

Noah took his time. "Memory loss is the second."

The house lights darkened and the curtain for *Committed* rose. Noah listened that the punchlines received the anticipated laughs. The dream scene was nearly flawless and earned applause from the Playhouse execs (with a little help from Jerry and Noah) as the curtain closed. The final scene was a bit unsteady with the changes he had added earlier, but overall the show received a thumbs up from everyone in attendance.

Noah called for a quick meeting after the show. He discussed the notes he had jotted down during the performance and praised everyone on a job well done.

"I'm meeting Jerry in a little while so I'll find out more what our guests thought and will let you know if I hear anything tomorrow. In the meantime, everyone gets time off for good behavior. No rehearsal Saturday morning. I think we're in really good shape and I'm very pleased with your efforts today. Thank you everyone. See you in the morning."

Everyone appeared happy as they congratulated one another and made their way out for the evening. Noah even discerned a sense of relief from Roz.

"Glad that's over with," she told him. "I've been through a hundred of these and I'm telling you these guys have a way of raising your blood pressure. Almost as bad as opening night."

When he turned to get his stuff he nearly bumped into Molly. "Hi there," he said. "Good job today."

"Thanks, Noah. I thought it went well. And congrats to you too."

Standing there, entranced, with his schoolboy-crush look, Noah realized he could be outed and shook it off. "Thank you, Molly. So. Going out to celebrate?"

She studied his face a bit longer than necessary. "A few of us are going back to your favorite restaurant, the Mexican place. Too bad you don't care for it or I'd invite you to join us."

"Thanks, but I'll pass." He started backing up. "Enjoy yourself tonight. And go easy on the sangria."

She didn't bother responding, just watched as he turned and walked away. She was still fixated as René came by to retrieve her.

"Molly? Ready to go?"

She took a breath. "Yep. Who's driving?"

Jerry texted Noah that he was going to be a little late meeting him at The Joint, a quaint local pub he knew of at the east end of Sagamore. Noah took his time getting there, enjoying the winding, coastal route of 6A with its little shops, splendid marsh views, and concealed cranberry bogs. This road was supposed to be driven at a slower pace, as reflected by its thirty-five-miles-per-hour speed limit signs, but drivers often raced it like they were heading for a checkered flag. Even though he was pursued by a number of unwitting motorists on his bumper, Noah pretty much kept to the speed limit. Screw them. Learn to drive. But the roadway was demanding and, by the time he stepped out of his car, he felt like he had just exited a roller coaster ride at Hershey Park.

When he arrived, Noah was led to a table out back under an oversized beige umbrella with *The Joint* logo splashed across it. Jerry had not yet arrived so Noah took the liberty of ordering a couple of Bass Ales. When the waitress delivered the drinks, he asked her to keep an eye out for his friend and show him back to his table.

The evening was warm with a soft breeze in the air. Noah checked out the meager crowd and mostly subdued conversations and enjoyed the recorded James Taylor melodies coming through the outdoor speakers.

After about ten minutes, Jerry made his way to Noah's table. "Is that yours or mine?" he asked, pointing to the pint of beer in front of him.

"I ordered it for you."

"Good," he said. "You read my mind."

He lifted it and tapped Noah's mug. "Thank you. You have no idea how much I need this right now." He downed half the mug.

All of a sudden Noah was worried. "Does this mean our little performance today didn't do as well as we thought?"

Jerry seemed a bit confused, then grinned when he realized the message he was sending. "Huh? No, no, you can relax about that, pal. They thought it was great. A couple of minor things—nothing to worry about—but overall I'd say they liked your play and think you're doing a bang-up job."

Noah relaxed. "Glad to hear it. I feel better now."

"They were giving me a hard time about one thing but I think I calmed their nerves."

"You *think* you calmed their nerves?"

Jerry reconsidered. "Well, when I told them that we didn't have the time to change it and had already blew out our budget, they pretty much relented."

"What? What didn't they like?"

Jerry gulped down the rest of his ale. "Schmuck."

"Schmuck what?"

"They weren't sure about the word 'schmuck.'"

"You're kidding?"

"No, I'm not. They thought it was some kind of Yiddish curse word that might offend people, especially when they saw it drop down from the rafters all lit up."

Noah shook his head. "Amazing. They bring this up now? Didn't anyone read the script?"

"What can I say? There's a big difference between a small word on the written page and the same word flashing across the stage in hot lights. This is the kind of stuff that keeps theater execs up at night."

"So what'd you tell them?"

Jerry raised his hand attempting to get the waitress' attention. "Another beer?"

"I'm still working here," said Noah, pointing.

Jerry motioned for one more. "I told them, first of all, 'schmuck' is not a Rabbinical curse word. I even looked it up on Merriam-Webster on my phone. Found a quote from Paul McCartney using it. That quieted them down. They figured if Paul McCartney used the word then how bad can it be?"

Noah was laughing now. "You see that?" said Noah. "That's why I've always been a Beatles' fan. I knew those guys from Liverpool would save my Jewish ass someday."

The waitress delivered Jerry's ale. "Can I get you boys anything else?" the slender pretty waitress asked. She had dense scruffy eyebrows and spoke with a Texas-cowgirl twang.

"I didn't catch your name?" said Jerry.

"Roxanne," she replied with a slightly bent smile.

"You're a long way from home, Roxanne," Jerry told her. "Where you from?"

She lowered her pad and raised her chin. "Texas. Paris, Texas."

"Oooh la, la," Jerry quipped with a pitiful French accent. "Enchanté."

She apologized. "Eh, I don't speak the language."

"That's okay," said Noah, "neither does my friend."

She giggled along with him.

"Paris, Texas," said Jerry. "Didn't know we had a Paris in Texas. What can you tell me about Paris, Texas?"

"Well," she thought, taking her time. "It's about an hour out of Dallas. And did you know we have our own genuine Eiffel Tower right plumb in the town square?"

"I didn't know that," said Jerry.

"Yes sir," she added. "Eight stories tall! And do you know what's hanging at the very top of it?"

Jerry mulled it over before answering. *The Mona Lisa?*

She laughed. "No. A giant red cowboy hat. You can see it for miles."

"Only in Texas," said Jerry.

Before Roxanne left, Noah ordered a dozen baked clams and another beer. He felt like celebrating.

"You had me going there for a minute," said Noah.

Jerry gave him a look. "What do you mean?"

"Well, when you first sat down, you looked like the Playhouse just went out of business. I thought there was something seriously wrong with the play."

Jerry breathed in through his mouth. "Sorry I frightened you. This deal I've been working on the past two months looks like it's going to cave in. They tell you one thing, then turn around and tell you something else. You can't believe anyone these days. Nothing for you to concern yourself about."

Noah finished off his beer. "Sorry, Jerry. I'm sure something else will come through. It always does."

They sat in silence and enjoyed the music from Crosby, Stills, Nash and Young's *Déja Vu* album until Roxanne was back with their baked clams and Noah's ale.

"I'm ready for another," Jerry told her, holding up his mug. "And do you have mozzarella sticks?"

"We certainly do," she replied. "Best sticks in the state."

Jerry's eyes widened. "Then I'll have to try them."

After she left, Noah admonished his friend. "You know those things will kill you, don't you?"

"It's my dinner," said Jerry. "That's all I'm having tonight. And your clams. That's it. That's all. And maybe some ice cream later."

"That's why you're not losing weight."

"Thanks mom."

"Anytime."

The easy-listening music had a calming effect. Jerry's mozzarella sticks arrived and he offered one to Noah, who turned him down.

"What else did the brass have to say about the show?" Noah prodded.

"Little things, hardly worth mentioning."

"So, you're not going to tell me?"

Jerry gave him a look. "Noah, they're just personal peeves that you don't need to worry about. If I thought you did, I'd tell you. You're the playwright and the director and that's all that needs to be said. Don't let them distract you. What do you care if some little man in a jacket and tie doesn't care for one of the actors?"

"Really? Which one?"

"Why? Are you going to have another audition? This is what I'm talking about. Everyone has an opinion about everything but none of it matters. Only what *you think* matters. Do the play the best you can and let the bodies fall where they may. You're the one the critics are going to castigate if they don't like it and you're the one they're going to congratulate if they do. I don't have to tell you cause you've heard this before. The only one you have to please is Noah Miller."

While Noah finished his coffee, Jerry signaled the waitress for the check. "You ready?" he asked Noah.

"I'm going to hang out a while longer if you don't mind. You okay to drive?"

Jerry smirked. "You see, my friend? There are advantages to carrying around a few extra pounds." He patted his stomach. "I don't need to sit around here and wait for my alcohol level to drop."

"That's clearly an advantage," Noah ribbed him.

"Heard you gave everyone some time off?" added Jerry. "Good way to make friends."

Noah nodded. "They earned it. Besides, we're ahead of schedule."

The waitress brought the check and, after a quick review, Jerry handed her his Amex card. "You know what you need to do to get ready. And, I have to tell you, pal, I'm very impressed with your directing skills."

Noah smirked, pleased. "Me too. I guess those years watching other directors work paid off. I'm sowing my oats."

"Well," Jerry said, more than a bit suggestively, "just be sure to keep the feeding bag where I can see it."

"Speaking of sowing oats," asked Noah, "how's Sheila doing?"

Jerry thought it over. "Better. Thanks."

"Glad to hear it."

"Me too."

Noah leaned in closer with a serious look. "I've been meaning to ask you something."

"What?"

"Do you know someone named Emma?"

"Emma? Emma who?"

Noah started to speak and stumbled. "Your real estate agent."

Jerry made a face. "I don't have a real estate agent."

Noah sat back and stirred his coffee then realized there was nothing left in the cup. Now *he* looked puzzled. "That's funny cause I met her at your house—at your party my first night in town. Attractive woman in her twenties. Looked a little out of place but very confident with herself. Said she works for Sotheby's Realty and was the one that found our houses."

"Seriously," replied Jerry, "I don't know what you're talking about. I got the houses through someone Sheila knows. Guy named Rick. He's the owner. We've used him before. Buys up places on the Cape and rents them out. That's how he pays his bills. Made a killing when the market went south during the recession. Sorry, I don't use an agent. Never have. And I don't know anyone named Emma."

The waitress returned with the bill and, after Jerry signed off on it, he rose to leave. "Maybe I'll see you around this weekend."

"Thanks for dinner."

Noah watched him go then sat there another half-hour to make sure he was okay to drive. Roxanne refilled his coffee cup without asking and shot him a smile. Noah did not even notice. He was too busy weighing the mystery before him. Why would Emma lie to him? And, if she did not work for Sotheby's, how would he find her? Once the reality of the situation set in, Noah realized he had another problem. If Emma was not who she said she was, who was she? And how did she know so much about him?

Noah left a few bucks under his mug and got up to leave. The place had gotten more crowded and louder during the time he was there. Heading inside through the pub, it was Carol King's turn to serenade him. On the way to his car, he was reminded of his first encounter with the now mysterious woman as the wistful lyrics of *You've Got A Friend* followed him out.

23
Erica Naomi Miller

During breaks at Friday's rehearsal, Noah asked Roz and several members of the cast and crew if they knew a young woman named Emma, who attended the party at Jerry's place the first night they all met. No one had any recollection of her. He did some research and found there were four Sotheby's Real Estate Agencies on Cape—in Dennis, Harwich Port, Orleans, and Provincetown—but, after getting in touch with each of their offices, found that none of them employed an agent with her name or description. He was beginning to get concerned.

He devoted most of Saturday visiting the places where he had met her. He grabbed a blanket from his house and spent a good part of the morning at Sandy Neck Beach. No luck. In the afternoon, he explored the Heritage Museums and Gardens, monitoring the visitors he passed along the trails, then waited at the Shawme Pond Overlook for over an hour. Finally, as the day dragged on, he wound up at The Pilot House, where he enjoyed the live music of some local group and a couple of beers out on the back lawn.

But there was no sign of Emma. She had to turn up sooner or later, he figured.

On Sunday, Noah relented and contacted Molly. He needed to get a fresh perspective of the situation and decided Molly was the best person for the job. He could talk to her. Besides, he admitted to himself, he missed spending time with her so he decided to invite her to go on a hike.

Molly picked him up in a vintage Jeep Wrangler, with over two-hundred-thousand miles on its odometer, and they drove out to the Cape Cod National Seashore in Eastham, a natural preserve established by John F. Kennedy, whose family had been vacationing at their Hyannis Port complex for decades. The preserve was part of the Atlantic coastal pine barrens.

When they arrived, they set out along the salt pond on the Nauset Marsh Trail for the more than four-mile round trip to Coast Guard Beach. The morning was just beginning to heat up. Most of the trail had been carved out through thick brush with dense forest coverage. There were few hikers along the way.

"I was a little surprised to hear from you," said Molly, following Noah along the mostly empty trail. "I thought the plan was to play it cool for now?"

Noah was glad she couldn't see his concerned reaction. "It was," he admitted. "But I brought you out here because I wanted your opinion on something." He stopped beside an evergreen, strangled by rampant thorny vines like a calf snared in a barbed-wire fence. He turned to her. "Remember I asked you about a woman, Emma, I met the same night I met you?"

Molly nodded. "The night I was bartending at Jerry's."

He hesitated, piquing her curiosity. "Right. Well, she appears to have vanished. Can't find her anywhere."

"Why do you need to find her?"

He looked away. "I don't know. She knew things about me. Personal things. No one seems to know who she is. You didn't notice her that night. Neither did anyone else. Jerry confirmed that she's not his agent although she said she was. She told me she found our houses. It's all very strange."

Frustrated, Noah continued hiking with Molly in tow. They exited the forest to an open field with a split rail fence overlooking the pond and stopped for a water break.

"You're right," said Noah. "I don't need to find her. I just think it's weird she lied to me. I called the real estate agency where she said she worked—all four offices on Cape—and they told me the same thing. They don't know her. I just don't understand it."

Molly put her water bottle in her backpack. "Maybe you're overreacting. Whatever personal things she knew about you she could have gotten with a little research online, don't you think?"

Noah mulled it over. "I guess."

"And as far as lying to you, well, what's weird about that? People do it all the time."

Noah shook that around in his head. "I get it. But she just didn't seem the type. What did she hope to gain by lying to me?"

"You'll have to ask her that when you find her. Who knows? Some people get off on it."

Noah checked the map on his phone and led them to a secluded spot off the trail behind a wall of bushes. He pulled out a beach towel from his bag and laid it down on a grassy stretch. They sat under the shade of a tree.

"The thing is," said Noah, "I don't know how to find her."

Molly gave him a look. "You seem to want to pretty bad."

Her resentment was hard to miss.

"It's not what you think," he assured her. "I'm old enough to be her father."

Molly moved closer. "Some women are attracted to older men," she said, stroking his cheek.

"Some men are attracted to younger women."

She ran a finger across his mouth. "I could be the jealous type for all you know."

They studied one another before their cheeks swelled, breaking into smiles. Then they kissed and Molly leaned back until her head was on the ground with Noah pressing against her lips the entire way down. They laid there together for some time taking turns rolling on top of one another and giggling.

"I wish we were in your neighbors' pool right now," said Noah.

Molly made a face. "They came back yesterday."

Noah slumped back on his back. "That's too bad."

A while later, he offered her chunks of chilled watermelon, the ideal snack for a summer afternoon. Back on the trail they headed for Coast

Guard Beach, where they stripped down to their bathing suits and jumped into the frigid water, a welcome relief after a sweaty hike. Noah relished the salt water taste. Later, when their suits were about dry, they returned to the trail and made their way back to the Jeep.

It was nearly four o'clock when Molly dropped Noah at his house. While she was hoping their day together would continue into the evening, Noah apologized and told her he had something to do. He would see her tomorrow at the Playhouse. She was a bit taken aback that he would not tell her what it was but she had noticed a change in him as the day wore on. He had become pensive and withdrawn and in a rush to get home. Molly decided to give him his space and not intrude on his privacy.

After she left, Noah changed and got into his car. He drove to Heritage Gardens and made his way back to the Shawme Pond Overlook. He recalled the story Emma had told him about the Mashpee chief and letting his pain out into the pond. Noah had considered doing it that day but decided against it. It was superstitious and he did not believe in that. But today was the one-year anniversary of his daughter's death and he was determined to let go of the pain. It was time. Besides, he decided to put his own spin on the procedure.

He looked out onto the serene water and thought about Erica, that sweet, smart, beautiful child, and how much he missed her. He told her he would always keep her in his heart and was just trying to rid himself of the agony. Then he thought about Jessica and how much he longed for her. He stood quietly there for some time.

He leaned up against the railing remembering them both and the lovely times they shared together. His daughter's last birthday party came to mind as did that idyllic weekend in the Catskill Mountains with the butterfly. But underneath it all, the scarce memories only accentuated how much he missed having his family around. And how lonely he felt each day.

Noah scanned the area and detected no one nearby. He was alone. A cool breeze sifted through the trees causing small ripples on the water. He withdrew his wallet from his back pocket and removed a small ripped piece of paper. He read the Aramaic words—transcribed phonetically into English—deliberately from the folded page almost in a whisper. "Yisgadal, V'yiskadash sh'mei raba ..." It was the *Mourner's Kaddish*, a traditional Jewish prayer for the deceased. When he finished, he lowered his head and said his own silent prayer for the soul of his daughter and pledged to make a charitable donation in her name.

Standing there in the breeze, Noah sensed he was no longer alone.

"Who are you?" he called out, his gaze fixated on the pond before him.

"Erica," came the response from the voice behind him.

Noah turned to find Emma standing there. He did not seem surprised and took several steps towards her. "Erica who?" he questioned, more doubtful than indignant.

She raised her head to meet his gaze and swallowed. "Erica Naomi Miller."

"You're a liar," he roared, more outraged now for her deceit. "You haven't been honest with me from the start."

She took a half step towards him. "You're right. I'm sorry. But I needed to gain your confidence."

He chuckled defiantly. "By *lying* to me?"

She lowered her head, ashamed of her behavior. "I didn't think you were ready."

"Ready for what? What is this about? Tell me who you really are?"

Another step forward. "It's me, daddy. Erica."

"No," he cried, outraged.

She came closer.

He could sense her compromised breath. "Try again."

"I know it's not easy," she told him, "but you have to believe me."

"Why? Why should I believe you? You told me you were from Quincy, had a bloke for a boyfriend and that your parents died in an accident. Everything you've told me is a lie."

"Not everything. Not the part about my parents."

"What do you mean? I'm still here, I didn't die in an accident. Neither did my wife."

He flinched ever so slightly after saying it. She ignored it, not wanting to make him feel any worse.

"I didn't say you died in an accident. I said 'I lost my parents in an accident.' I lost them because ... I died. And the accident was about me."

He pondered her explanation. "Okay, fine, I'll give you that one. But you seem to be forgetting one small problem. My daughter had just turned four when she passed. Sorry, but you don't match the description."

She took her time, peering out at the pond. "I didn't want to come to you as a four-year old. I didn't want you to think of me as a ghost. I wanted to be able to talk to you as an adult so I chose to come to you like this."

"Why? What is this all about?"

She took a breath. "I'm here to help you. I know how much you've been hurting. How much you think about mom and me. How difficult it's been to get over us. Please let me help you."

He laughed. "You're kidding, right?"

She lowered her head, searching for the right words. "I'm not."

"Because it's not funny ..."

"I'm not trying to be funny ..."

"That's a mean thing to do to someone ..."

"I'm not trying to be mean. Please believe me, daddy."

"Stop calling me that! My daughter is dead."

She raised her head towards the heavens then back at him as if she needed the gesture to propel herself forward.

"I know. I died a year ago. Drowned in my friend Monica's pool. Today is the anniversary of my death. My *Yahrzeit*. Isn't that why you came here? To say *Kaddish* for me?"

"What?" Noah took a step back—fear in his eyes—trying to come to terms with her allegation. It didn't make any sense.

"I was with you at the hospital. I could see you and mommy, and Nana and Papa, and Aunt Dee. I could see you all. Please believe me, daddy. It's me."

Noah placed his hands on the fence behind him to steady himself, then stepped further away, plagued by confusion, anger and trepidation.

"How do you know so much about me?" he demanded. "About my daughter?"

She stood there in front of him without responding.

"Who's been giving you information?"

"I'm your daughter. Erica."

"Are you ... with the police?"

"I came back to make a difference ..."

"Follow me here from Long Island?"

"… Answer your questions. Help you move on."

Noah ventured further away. He did not want to hear anymore.

"You're crazy," he said. This time he kept moving.

"You know it's me, daddy," she yelled after him. "You've been wondering why I look so familiar. My hair? My eyes? Why you've had certain feelings?"

"You're nuts, lady," he called in her direction. "My daughter was four years old."

"I'm still four!" she screamed. She was crying now like an obstinate child who did not get her way. Then, under her breath, "I'll always be four."

"Stay away from me," he warned, more to himself. "I don't want your help. I don't need your help."

When he was fifty yards away—at a safe distance—he peeked back. She had not budged. Still standing there crying.

He made his way out of the gardens and drove to the nearest pub, his heart racing, his hand shaking. He needed a drink. Needed several drinks.

24
Fly Like a Butterfly

I was home that day, working on my new play. Jess had taken Erica to her friend Monica's birthday party—a pool party, actually—where they were going to have a clown or a magician or an inflatable bouncy ball pit or all of the above because that is just what kids on Long Island did. Or, rather, their parents did. We were friends with them, lived in the same neighborhood, traveled in similar party circles, saw each other at school events, Trick or Treating, and at other times.

I was grateful to have the day to myself. I hadn't had much time to develop the play, entitled *First Impressions,* so I was relieved when Jessie offered to take Erica for the day and allow me time to work. It was an on-again-off-again thing with me and the play. It was the second one I had written since taking that A.P. job but I was not focused on the last one and Jerry couldn't sell it. So, rather than attempt to rewrite it and try to make it work, I decided to start a new one. But it was taking forever to get it together.

Work was sucking the life out of me. How do these new plays make it on stage? Who is putting their money on the line to back them? They would have better odds with one of those direct mail sweepstakes the postman delivers—or the lottery—both statistically impossible to win. Be that as it may, it was my job to review the shows and I give everyone a fair shot. I mean you never know. But the pressure and stress of my job was getting to me and by the time I got home each night, I had little energy to work on my play. My heart wasn't in it. Just as Jessie had feared.

I got the call sometime after 3 p.m. I remember because I was in the kitchen when it rang, taking my regular writer's block break—a peanut butter and jelly sandwich on a piece of stale egg matzoh. Jessie was on the line and sounded like she was in shock. Had a difficult time making her out but in the end I knew that something had happened to Erica and to get over to Long Island Jewish Hospital. I'm not sure how many red lights and stop signs I plowed through to get to Woodbury without realizing it but got there in one piece without a traffic cop after me.

When I arrived, I found Jess in the emergency room and, when she saw me, she collapsed in my arms sobbing. Without knowing what happened or how serious it was, I began bawling too. A while later, Dee Dee showed up and sat with us in the waiting room. Jessie had called her after calling me. We did not hear anything until one of the doctors came out and told us she had swallowed a lot of water and they did all they could for her. She was on life support now. That was all he would say. It was a waiting game at this point and could go either way. Jessica did not take the news well and Dee and I did all we could to keep her calm and try to get her mind on other things. A little while later, Jessie's parents, Hopi and Melinda, showed up at the hospital and sat with us.

About an hour later, the same doctor we had seen earlier came out and headed toward us. At twenty paces I could see the somber look in his eyes and knew this was not going to turn out well. He told us that Erica's heart gave out and they did all they could to save her. Said he was sorry without looking us in the eye. Asked if we wanted to see the body. He escorted Jessie and me down to the morgue. We all left the hospital together.

Three days later, we buried our precious little girl. Most of her friends showed up at the funeral home for the service so there was quite a turnout. Some did not make it but we figured their parents must have thought they were too young. I noticed that Monica and her family were missing. Heard she was having a rough time accepting what happened, considering it had been *her* party. Not that anyone was blaming anyone. You might think her parents would have at least shown up. Out of respect.

I heard they had a lifeguard at the pool that day, some college kid, but he was probably more interested in keeping an eye on the young mothers and older sisters prancing around. What was he looking at when my daughter needed him to save her life? And where was Jessica at the time? I never bothered asking. I was afraid of the answer.

They found her blowup floaties on the edge of the pool. She had something to prove. Probably figured she was old enough to swim without them.

No one said anything about the drowning all day and everyone was on their best behavior. Several people got up to speak. One person mentioned the tragedy of burying your daughter at such a young age, which I did not appreciate, but what was I going to do? Free speech and all. It was an uncomfortable day and a difficult service and I know everyone was glad when it was over. I know I was.

Later, at Wellwood Cemetery, before we removed her casket from the hearse, I asked that everyone but the pall bearers wait by the grave. Jessica stood beside me. We opened her casket. I wanted to see my sweet little girl's face one last time—the child we had waited so long to bring into this world—before sentencing her to a solitary black hole in the ground. It didn't seem right.

Her life was cut short before she had time to realize her dreams, before she even discovered what those dreams were. She was not going to grow up and become a woman. She was going to be deprived of high school and college and parties and boyfriends and whatever line of work she set her mind to. She was never going to experience the joy of bringing a baby of her own into the world, to become a mother. A grandmother. She was going to miss out on all the highs and lows of life, on everything that makes us human, that connects us to one another and to that beyond our understanding.

Her life was stolen from her. From her friends and relatives. From us. It just didn't seem fair.

I removed the gold butterfly pendant from my pocket, my daughter's birthday present from a couple of weeks ago, and fastened it around her neck. That's where it belonged. With her. Forever. "Now you can fly like a butterfly," I whispered. Then I broke down and Jessie had to help me up.

Perhaps her friend Snort, from that magical summer day, would look after her now and they could play together again and frolic around the lake.

That's how I want to remember her, with a smile in her eyes, laughing.

25
Prediction With Conviction

Noah ambled through the grassy park inspecting the surrounding playground. Children were climbing on monkey bars, skidding down slides, tossing a frisbee, flying a kite. He was barefoot and the cool textured turf helped sooth his tender feet. He must have been wandering for hours.

The park was nestled on the fringe of an island, flanked by a beach and the sea, with nebulous similarities, he thought, to Martha's Vineyard. Mostly children his age were scattered about content on doing whatever amused them on a summer's day. No one was paying attention to him, which made him feel isolated.

Was this a dream?

It was a windy cloudless day. Noah roamed the area searching for a familiar face, someone—anyone—he could ask where he was and what he was doing here. He thought he heard Carol King's *So Far Away* playing somewhere in the distance.

He passed a jubilant young boy, grasping hands with two girls, one on each side. They giggled on their way through the playground. Walking past Noah, the younger of the two smiled at him, filling him with a warm feeling inside. He thought they seemed familiar.

He came upon a maze of picnic tables and discovered Jerry at one, himself no more than ten, devouring a corned beef sandwich, a stack of kosher pickles on his plate. Relieved, Noah approached him but, as he did, overheard Jerry shouting into his phone. Noah decided not to disturb him.

He spotted Molly and Wayne, dressed formally, their table adorned with a tablecloth, candle and a vase of roses. Coming closer, he perceived they were in character as Wendy and Charlie, recognizing their lines from act one, scene three. While Noah stood listening, they began babbling. Towards him. The exchange became heated and he sensed they were berating him and decided to move on.

Wandering around, he bumped into another boy in a Red Sox home jersey who glared at him contemptuously. Noah tried to ease the tension by asking his name.

"Peter," he barked.

"I'm Noah."

"I know who you are," the boy growled, "and I know what you did."

"What did I do?" asked Noah.

Peter began pounding a baseball bat in his hand attempting to intimidate him. Noah scampered away to diffuse the confrontation then turned around to make sure he was not followed. On the back of Peter's uniform he noted the name "Benson."

Discouraged, he headed for the beach. He passed the same boy he saw earlier with the two girls. This time there was only one holding his hand. She wore a blue cap. The pretty girl that had smiled at him was gone. They appeared to be searching for her.

Peering out on the water, he spotted Ed Kaufman's sailboat, buoyed in shallow waters with the moniker "IDEAS" on the transom. Ed and Amy were hosting a luncheon. Noah was about to swim out and join them when he recognized their guest, John Belushi, clad in his Blues Brothers' garb—dark suit, sunglasses, fedora—sipping a mimosa. Nearby, Noah observed a Native American, up to his waist in the water, ignite a raft solemnly with a torch and send it adrift on the outgoing tide. Something on it was shrouded in a colorful-patterned fabric. The native watched as the raft made its way to the portside of Kaufman's boat, igniting the bow in flames. The fire spread and the ship pitched starboard with dense black smoke. While it burned, the native turned and nodded to Noah, appearing satisfied he had achieved his objective: two birds, one stone. Noah recognized his single red feather, scar and long white hair from the graveyard. Horrified, he watched as the cherished sailboat plunged into the nether regions. The last thing he noticed was the moniker now read "IDIOTS."

Now the children in the park were replaced by grownups. He found Billy Corona pushing Lydia Wilkins on the swings at the far end. He drew her back and released her and, when she hit the arc's peak, bolted out into the ocean. Appalled, Billy chased after her.

Noah found Barney Saperstein flipping hamburgers over a smokey grill wearing a Mets cap and chef's apron. He asked him how it was going. "Great," Barney told him. "We don't miss you a bit. Stay out as long as you want." Then Barney began serving burgers to whoever was around but did not offer one to Noah.

At Madam Sweeney's table, a neon sign read *"Psychic Readings— Prediction with Conviction."* Hovering over her crystal ball, fumes began venting out like exhaust from a tailpipe, expanding rapidly, causing the sky to darken. A tempest developed with high winds and rain sweeping across the grounds. Savage waves bombarded the shoreline. Then an angry gust of wind yanked the good Madam, her crystal ball and her neon sign into oblivion. All the while, Noah thought he could hear her laughing.

The chaos did not end there as the storm ravaged everything in its path. People panicked in every direction, slamming into one another as Led Zeppelin was blaring *Trampled Under Foot.* That boy with the two girls was alone now and hysterical. Jerry, Barney and Billy had disappeared. Noah, frantic, could not decide which way to turn.

Then a wondrous event occurred. A sublime butterfly, darting its way without a care through the tempest, touched down on Noah's outstretched hand. Its mellow temperament had a calming effect and Noah's heartbeat fell into a steady beat with the gentle fluttering of its turquoise wings. Noah studied it and was transported into its world of tranquility, no longer concerned about the storm and bedlam around him.

The familiar butterfly appeared to be regarding Noah as well and moved closer. "Prediction with conviction," it said.

Startled by what he thought he heard on top of the fact that it could actually speak, Noah raised an eyebrow. "Did you say something?"

The butterfly stared at Noah's perplexed look then nodded its little head and barked a bit louder, "You heard me."

Then the magnificent insect rose into the air and fluttered away, leaving Noah even more confused.

26
Missed Flight To Saturn

O n Monday, the company was back for their final full week of rehearsals before the following week's tech, dress and opening on Wednesday. Noah mentioned that there were a few scenes that still needed some work but overall was pleased with the progress. At this stage in the production, the one thing he did not want to do was burn out the cast by going over each scene more than necessary.

While on the surface Noah seemed calm and composed, those who knew him a little better noted that he appeared apprehensive. He sensed that Molly was still confused about why he ended their date abruptly the day before and planned on discussing it with her when the rehearsal was over.

Towards the end of Noah's opening remarks, Roz entered the back room and mentioned something to him in a hushed tone. It seemed that John, who played Stan Urlicht, was sick in bed with a fever. Noah announced that Alan White, the understudy, would have to step in until John was back on his feet, which was not expected until at least Wednesday. This was not a good omen and no way to begin the week.

"Better this week than next," said Noah, trying to place a positive spin on it. "Just for the record, no one else has permission to get sick, have a family crisis, or break any bones." Then he added, "are we clear?"

Alan needed to use his script for Stan's part and was rusty with his timing but overall did an adequate job. The cast did their part making him feel welcomed and accepted.

Noah asked Bobby to call Stu Markowitz to sit in the rest of the week as Alan's understudy in case John's health did not improve and Alan had to take over the part for the entire run. He thought it prudent to keep at least one male and one female understudy for the duration of the show just in case.

While people left, Noah went looking for Molly. He found her in the back room having coffee with René and Susan.

"May I talk to you for a minute?" he asked, interrupting their conversation.

Molly appeared reticent, which surprised him. "We're kind of on our way out," she said, holding her ground. René gave Susan a look.

"Right," said Noah, noticing. "But I had a thought about your entrance in the final scene. It'll only take a moment, I promise."

Molly rose from the table. "I'll meet you outside," she told the others and followed Noah to an empty corner.

"You're upset about yesterday, aren't you?" he said.

She tightened her lips and folded her arms.

"I understand," he went on. "I'm sorry I didn't give you an adequate explanation. That wasn't right. Please, let me make it up to you."

Molly appeared uneasy. "Do you really think this is the time and place?"

She was right. This was one of the reasons he was reluctant to get into a relationship with her.

"Can we go somewhere?" he asked.

She lowered her arms in a conciliatory manner. "I told them I'd go out for a drink. How's it going to look?"

Noah took a breath. "Right." He took another one while he devised a plan. "What if I leave and you say you got a call from someone—your sister, let's say—and you're sorry but you'll have to take a raincheck?"

She smirked. "That's a great idea, Noah, except I don't have a sister."

He just kept staring.

"All right," she relented. "I'll think of something. Where should I meet you?"

A half hour later, Molly knocked on Noah's front door. He led her through the house and out to the backyard. The late afternoon sun was still warm and the marsh as static as an unread library book.

"Red or white?" he asked, grabbing two wine bottles, one in each hand.

She checked the labels. "Pinot Grigio."

He poured them each a glass.

She stepped away, gazing out at the high grass and pristine marsh, savoring the view. The sun's reflection was hitting the water at just the right angle, giving it the complexion of a ripe cantaloupe.

"It's so lovely here. That's quite a view."

"You've seen it before. Haven't you?"

"No," she said, her back to him. "This is the first time you've invited me over."

She turned around to catch his reaction. "Well, I … I guess I … *Really? First time?*"

She chuckled letting him off the hook.

"So what was so important you wanted to talk to me about? Problem with my entrance in the last scene?"

He placed his glass on the table and handed her a bright yellow nylon life jacket.

"What's this for?"

He beamed like a novice fisherman showing off his trophy catch. "How do you feel about kayaking?"

"You own a kayak?"

"A two-seater. It's an old one. Found it over there," he said, pointing.

She mulled over his offer. "So, when you say 'old one,' does that mean 'safe without leaks?'"

"I've been out on the water with it several times. Besides, the deepest part of the marsh is only five feet. An old sailor like you knows how to swim, right?"

She tried on the preserver. "I *know* how to swim."

"Good," he replied. "Then let's take her for a spin."

They launched the boat and made their way through the grass and reeds. Noah sat astern navigating. An anxious frog, seeking refuge, moved beyond the boat's wake. A dragonfly buzzed Molly's head. They snaked their way to open waters with a course no wider than six feet until they hit the main canal behind Salt Marsh Road.

Molly had a hard time holding in her enthusiasm. "This is great."

They followed the waterway past Springhill Beach and pulled ashore before they reached Sandwich Harbor. They hoisted the kayak out of the water and laid it on its starboard side.

Molly followed Noah to a cluster of boulders. They sat at the crest facing west enjoying the mellowing sunset. Noah pulled out a couple of tangerines from his backpack and offered her one, which she accepted.

"I'd like to ask you something," began Noah, "but I don't want you to think I'm nuts."

Molly stopped peeling her fruit. "What?"

He took his time.

"Yesterday was the anniversary of my daughter's death."

She shook her head as if she was apologizing. "Noah, I didn't know. I'm so sorry."

"How would you know?"

She didn't answer that.

"When I left you yesterday," he continued, "I told you I needed to do something."

"You don't have to explain. That must have been difficult."

"Please," he urged. "I need to tell you what happened."

She nodded, allowing him to go on.

He stood on the rocks and searched the area taking his time. "I went back to Heritage Park to say a prayer for her." He stopped there for effect. "She was there."

Molly's forehead furrowed. "Who was there?"

Noah gulped. "Remember the woman I asked you about?"

"Emma? The real estate agent. The one you were looking for?"

"Yeah, that one."

"You found her?"

"She was there yesterday."

"Good. That's good. Right?"

Noah peered at her. "Just one problem."

She looked around and Noah realized he was making her uncomfortable.

"What?" she said. "Noah? What is it?"

Taking his time, "She said her name is Erica."

"What?"

"She said she's *my daughter,* Erica."

Molly laughed. *"Right."*

"No. Seriously, she did. She actually believes she's my daughter. She tried convincing me."

Molly looked down as she pondered it. "So that would make *her* nuts. Not *you.*"

Noah walked away and kept going, all the way down to the beach.

When Molly realized he wasn't coming back, she followed. "Didn't you say your daughter was a young girl?"

"She'd just turn four."

"And this woman you met was what? In her twenties? How could she be your daughter?"

"I asked her that."

"And?"

"And she said she didn't want to come to me as a young girl. She wanted to be able to talk to me as an adult."

"You can do that?"

"She thinks so."

Molly strolled along the shore taking her time with Noah in tow. "It doesn't make any sense, Noah. This woman is putting you on."

"That's what I thought. But she knows things about me and my daughter. About the night she died. And nobody has seen or spoken to her except me."

Noah came around so he was facing her now. "You didn't notice her that first night. Neither did anyone else from the company. Jerry doesn't know her. And none of the real estate offices I called claimed to know her. It doesn't add up. She's like … a ghost."

Molly stopped walking. "Don't tell me you believe in ghosts?"

"Well I never considered it. I mean …"

"And *now* you are?"

Noah shrugged and they continued along the coastline.

"There's more," he said.

"More? You mean you think you can top what you just told me?"

Noah made a face. "I had a dream last night. And you were there along with just about everyone else I've met on the Cape. Even Madam Sweeny."

"The Wicked Witch of Newport? Please. I'm still not over that."

"It was some kind of playground near a beach. She was doing her readings with her crystal ball and all of sudden she caused the sky to darken and it started raining and blowing and everyone was running around in a panic. Then the wind swept her and her crystal ball into the sky and she was howling with laughter."

Molly was fascinated. "A happy ending? Good riddance."

"Remember the story she told us about the three kids—the boy and the two girls?"

Molly nodded.

"They were there too. First, the three of them. Then, when I bumped into them later, there were just two. And in the chaos of the storm, it was just the boy alone."

"Just like she told us."

"Right. And in the end, something weird happened."

"Weirder than everything you've told me so far?"

"Yeah. This beautiful turquoise butterfly that I once saw with my daughter landed on my hand and talked to me."

"A talking butterfly? I have to say, you have a vivid imagination. What did it say?"

Noah slowed down for effect. "It said 'Prediction with conviction.'"

Molly scratched her neck. "An educated butterfly. What does it mean?"

"That was Madam Sweeny's tagline in my dream. On her table."

"I like it. Has a nice ring to it."

Noah did not respond.

"So the butterfly was pointing you towards Madam Sweeny ...?"

"I guess."

"... Who told us the story of the three kids?"

Noah nodded.

"Wow. That's a great dream. I don't have dreams like that."

"Molly!"

She laughed. "What? I'm just saying you're a good dreamer. I mean, really, Noah. No wonder you're a playwright. You've got a hell of an imagination."

They made their way back to the kayak while there was still light. As they rowed back, a dazzling palette of colors—amber, pink, violet, and mauve—lit up the sky like a Monet painting.

When they returned to Noah's place they were famished so he ran out to get them a couple of lobster rolls from a local seafood market. He set up a couple of candles on the table and pulled out the opened bottle of wine from the fridge. He got out an old boom box he had found at a flea market and turned to his Classical radio station. They dined outside under the stars.

After they finished eating, Molly prodded further. "So did this Emma … I mean, Erica … whatever her name was … have anything else to say?"

Noah was quiet for a while, unfocused. "She said she was here to help me."

"Help you what?"

He raised his chin, wondering how he was going to break it to her.

"There are some details about my family I haven't shared with you. Yet."

"*Oh?*" she said, surprised.

Noah took his time. He took so much time in fact that Molly figured he had changed his mind.

"My daughter drowned at her friend's pool party. We had waited a long time to have Erica and she was the joy of our lives. When she died, my wife became depressed. A few weeks later, she took her life."

Molly covered her mouth muting a shriek. She was stunned. "Oh my God. Noah. I had no idea." She took his hand in hers. "I'm so sorry. I don't know what to say."

They sat without talking for several minutes while Georg Philipp Telemann's *Viola Concerto in G Major* played.

"This Erica you met said she wanted to help you?" asked Molly. "In what way?"

Noah gave her a blank stare. "I don't know. We didn't get that far. She's under the impression that I'm in great pain. I'm under the impression that she missed her flight back to Saturn."

Molly placed her other hand on Noah's. "Are you? In great pain?"

Noah avoided her eyes. Licked his dry lips.

"It's been difficult. What can I say? I'm managing."

She smiled, filling him with a sense of warmth, a feeling he hadn't felt in some time. "You'll get through this," she told him. "I'll help you."

He appreciated the concern, then poured the rest of the wine with his free hand.

Later, as they laid in bed, Molly could not take her mind off Erica. "She's not a ghost, Noah," Molly surmised. "But she may be your guardian angel."

Noah considered that before saying anything else. "So let me understand this. You question whether or not to believe in ghosts but you *do* believe in angels?"

Molly turned to face him. "No, hear me out. From all the books I've read on the subject, this is what I think. A ghost is a person's soul that hangs onto its life because it's unwilling to move on to the afterlife. For whatever reason. They attach themselves to a particular person or place that's comfortable and familiar. Some might be able to sense their presence but a ghost is in another dimension, on a separate plain, so you can't actually communicate with them. An angel, on the other hand, is a spirit that has already moved on and, through the grace of God, is sent back. The Old and New Testaments are filled with stories of angels that have returned to Earth for one reason or another. And yes, I *do* believe they exist—angels *and* ghosts. I don't think this Erica woman you met is the ghost of your daughter. But she might be your guardian angel."

"Let me guess," he said. "You've read *Dante's Divine Comedy?*"

Molly slapped his shoulder. "I took several classes after college. Fascinating classes. And yes, we did discuss Dante in one of them. All I'm saying is, as incredible as it sounds, I'm open to the possibility. I'm not sure why, mind you, but from what you've told me, it just sounds like she could be ... telling the truth. Think about it. You've been through a terrible time in your life. Maybe she's come back to help you get through it? I mean, you do hear about these things happening now and then. Perhaps that's why you're the only one that's seen her?"

Noah shook his head, unconvinced. "This is crazy. It's insane. I can't believe we've spent the entire night discussing it."

He rolled over on his side, giving her his complete attention. "I appreciate you listening to my tale of woe but I don't believe in ghosts. Or guardian angels. I'm just not wired that way. This is the twenty-first century. I'm not Jimmy Stewart in a scene from *It's A Wonderful Life.* I'm living in the real world, not a paranormal novel."

Molly did not respond right away. Then she got up and got dressed. "You don't have to leave," he told her.

She smiled at him—a fragile smile—like a porcelain plate on the edge of a shelf. "Tomorrow's another work day, chief. I'd better get home."

Noah pulled on his gym shorts and a tee shirt and walked her outside. "I can drive you," he told her. "I'm sorry. I wasn't taking it out on you."

"I'm fine. Thanks." She wrapped her arms around his neck to let him know she was not upset. "You're not alone in this."

Noah sensed she had something more to add and was taking her time.

"I had a brother," she told him. "Gary. My only sibling. He died six years ago."

He delved into her eyes offering compassion.

"When we were growing up, we were close. I looked out for him. My little brother."

Noah recognized her pain as she struggled for the courage to continue. "That must have been tough."

"My girlfriends loved him. We all did. He was so handsome. A Classical musician. Oboe. Auditioned for the Savannah Symphony. Had everything going for him." She stopped there.

"What happened?"

She took her time. "I don't know. Things didn't work out. Some bad breaks. Then he kind of … stopped trying."

She sighed. "I talked to my mother about getting help. Finding someone. We found a therapist. Made an appointment. He said he'd go."

She hesitated, lost within her memory. "One day, he took his boat out. He loved the ocean." She shook her head as if she was watching the end of a movie. "His body washed up three days later."

Noah took her in his arms. They held each other. He kissed her. She took a breath coming back to life then stepped away and opened her car door.

"They called it an accident." She held back a smirk. "But I know better."

Molly got into her Jeep. "I wasn't going to tell you."

"I'm glad you did."

She smiled. Sadly. "Sometimes I get the feeling he's looking out for me."

She turned the ignition and the Wrangler surged to life. "We'll figure this out, Noah. I promise."

He watched her drive off but was not convinced.

Heading back to the house, he noticed the steep-sloped roof above the front door and thought about what Molly had said about her brother. Then he recalled the bumblebee that watched him the day he was late for rehearsal.

While it was after midnight, Noah got out a six-foot ladder he had found on the side of the house and a small tool box and set up in the hallway below where the bumblebee had disappeared through a crack. He used a boxcutter to trace a trapdoor in the ceiling and a hammer claw to extract two oversized nails holding it in place. Somebody not only sealed the attic, Noah thought, but tried to hide it as well. He pushed the painted plywood hatch into the attic and pulled himself up.

Once in, he brushed away the cobwebs and turned on the flashlight on his phone. It was smaller than he anticipated and crowded with stuff—a Victrola phonograph with a large brass horn caught his eye—and there was a pile of clothes in the corner and several cardboard boxes. He used the cutter to slice through the tape of the top box, pulled out an old photograph album and blew off a layer of dust. Then he sat on the planked floor and opened it.

Inside it read: "Mashpee Wampanoag Tribe – People of the First Light" and below it the name "Sagamore," all handwritten with a fountain pen. Noah thought that interesting since his wife's maiden name was Sagamore as was her Great Aunt Cecilia.

He turned the pages of mounted sepia-toned photographs, some dating back to late 19th century. On the last page, he found an oversized faded photo of Native Americans standing around a young girl with one feather in her headdress. He removed the photo from its corners and turned it over. On the back were the words "Cecilia, Sachem Ceremony – 1933." Aunt Cecilia?

Before he could do the math, Noah thought he heard chanting. Tribal chanting. It started as a low hum and grew louder. Noah surmised it was coming from within the walls of the attic, which, to his bewilderment, began to fade away. All at once the photo he had been holding came to life and Noah found himself now sitting within the picture. He was no longer in the attic and had somehow become part of the past. The natives surrounding him were chanting and dancing around them and he watched as one of them painted Cecilia's face. No one appeared to detect him.

After a moment, the scene vanished and Noah found himself back in his attic, his heart thumping. He returned the photo to its place and closed the book. Placing it back in its box, a newspaper clipping dropped out. The date—November 25, 1926—was visible. It was foxing and covered with yellow-glazed tape but still readable, a 250-year retrospective from that date in history about a village attacked by British Colonist with more than 300 natives massacred.

Noah recalled the scene at Abel's Hill Cemetery the day they visited Belushi's grave and wondered if that was what he had seen.

Then he went to bed, taking the clipping with him.

27
The Fallout

J ohn Porter made it back to Thursday's rehearsal after sitting out most of the week with flu-like symptoms. Noah was probably being overprotective with the extra day off but did not want to take any chances that he could spread the virus to someone else with the show's opening only a week away. John did catch parts of Tuesday and Wednesday's rehearsals on Facetime.

At the lunchbreak, Jerry found Noah at a picnic table out back and joined him.

"Hello stranger," said Noah. "How was your trip?"

Jerry and Sheila had been away for almost a week on their annual pilgrimage to Saratoga Springs.

"It was good," Jerry told him. "Good to be away. We won a little at the track, ate well, saw Joshua Bell—the violinist—at the performing arts center and, I don't mind telling you, it didn't hurt my sex life either."

Noah gave him a look.

"Long overdue," added Jerry with a nod.

"No wonder you can't get that silly smirk off your face," said Noah. "Glad to hear things are better."

"Yeah, me too."

While Noah munched on a tuna sandwich, Jerry turned more serious. "How are things here?" he asked.

"All is well. John Porter was out a few days this week with the flu but he's back today. Other than that, it's been quiet."

"Good," said Jerry. "That's good."

Noah could tell something was brewing. "What's up, Jerry? I know that face. Is there a problem?"

Jerry appeared to weigh what he was going to tell him. "Advance ticket sales are in the toilet. The kingpins are having a fit. Doesn't look like we're going to cover our production costs."

Noah sighed. "Well, what a nice way to greet an old friend. Couldn't you break it to me a little softer? Maybe find a way to lead up to it? 'Noah, we haven't sold out the Saturday night performance yet. Or, we're a little behind on anticipated ticket sales. Or, the show is a bomb. We're cancelling the opening. Abandon ship!'"

The two sat there considering the ramifications. "Anything I can do?" asked Noah.

Jerry didn't bother lifting his head. "You wouldn't happen to have 500 or so friends who want to come see your show every night, would you?"

"That bad, huh?"

"Well, the number's closer to 350 if you count season ticket holders."

"See that? Things are looking up already."

"Yeah, easy for you to say."

"Look," said Noah. "You're a producer. I'm sure this isn't the first time you've come up against this. What have you done in the past?"

"Well," said Jerry, "we're running ads everywhere, especially online. And we've invited the press and some of the donors to a cocktail party Wednesday night before the show."

"When were you going to tell me?" Noah inquired.

"I just did."

"Right."

"Serving champagne and hors d'oeuvres—shrimp cocktail, I think— which couldn't hurt. Who doesn't like shrimp cocktail? Hopefully with some good reviews and word of mouth, we'll get through this."

"Sounds like a plan."

"In the meantime," cautioned Jerry, "don't you worry about it. You just do what you can to make it the best show it can be."

Noah listened to his instructions and gave him his sincerest expression. "I'll do everything I can. Promise."

Then Jerry had an idea. "Do me a favor and find out if anyone in your cast is working on anything we could market. You know, is anyone going to be in a movie with a bigtime name? Anyone signed up for a Broadway show? A Netflix original? Anything to use in our ads to attract customers."

"Mindy Russell is doing a movie with Kate Winslet," Noah informed him. "She's got a small part."

"That's right, I forgot," said Jerry. "We had to change the schedule."

"Can you use that?"

"Well," Jerry contemplated, "it's not Ryan Gosling but I'll take it. At this point I'll take whatever I can get."

"Winslet won an Oscar, you know?" Noah reminded him. "*And* she was in *Titanic.*"

"I know," said Jerry. "I said I'll take it. Now if Winslet was in our show, we wouldn't be having this conversation."

Noah watched his friend. "You're worried about this, aren't you?"

For the first time this summer, Jerry appeared lost. "It's my own fault. We should have hired a name. Someone who could fill the house."

"Why didn't we?"

Jerry turned to Noah. "I told you, that was me. I should have made some calls and brought someone in. The budget was so damned tight."

Noah kept his eye on him.

"We couldn't afford a big name," explained Jerry. "But we didn't need a big name. We just needed *a* name. Someone audiences would recognize. Sometimes, that's all it takes to keep a show going."

Jerry shifted on the hardwood bench. "Years ago, Sheila and I saw a play here, I don't recall which, but I do remember it starred Loretta Swit. Remember her from *Mash?* Anyway, the show was a bomb, I mean really bad. People were heading for the exits at intermission. We almost did too. But my point is, the theater remained filled for almost the entire run because it was Loretta Swit. That's all it needed."

Noah let that hang between them. "Why don't you see if Loretta Swit is available?"

Jerry took the bait. "I think she's dead," he said. "If she isn't, she ought to be. Besides, she still owes me for two tickets."

Noah exhaled. "I'll talk to the cast after lunch. See if there's anything else we can use." Then, standing, he leaned in and patted his friend's shoulder. "Don't blame yourself, Jerry. People will come when they hear how good it is. You'll see. That's the other way to fill a house—with a good show. We'll be okay."

Later, when everyone was ready to leave, Noah spoke to his cast. A couple of independent movies were lined up after the summer, some regional work, and someone was waiting for their agent to get back to them on a call back for an off-Broadway show, but there were no big stars or directors associated with any of them.

The following day, Friday, they finished up their regular rehearsal schedule. Noah was pleased. Before leaving for the weekend, he went over the call times for the following week. "Tech rehearsal on Monday will start at 3 p.m. in case the crew needs more time breaking down *Deathtrap* and setting us up. Call time is 2 p.m.

"Tuesday's dress rehearsal and call time are the same as Monday, 2 and 3 p.m." Noah reminded them of the importance of being on time and informed them that everyone, including the crew, could invite up to four guests for Tuesday's dress so there would be an audience. They were also inviting people from a couple of assisted living facilities to help fill the house. He wanted as much of an audience as he could get.

"Wednesday's opening is at 8:00 p.m. The cocktail party is from 6 to 7 p.m. for press interviews for the cast. That'll give you an hour to get ready for the show." He emphasized that Wednesday was extremely important because good reviews would keep the house filled. He advised everyone to get plenty of rest over the weekend.

When the meeting broke, Noah asked Molly if she was free for dinner but she had already made plans to celebrate the end of the schedule with several from the cast and crew. She invited him out to join them.

"Thanks," said Noah, "but I'm going to pass. I'm exhausted. Go, enjoy yourself. Have fun with your schoolmates."

"I feel bad you'll be all alone tonight," she told him. "Please come out with us."

Noah smiled knowing her invitation was sincere. "Thanks, Molly. I'll be fine. Got some leftover Mediterranean in the fridge and a lousy novel I'm dying to finish. I'll be asleep before I get through two pages."

She surveyed the area to make sure no one could overhear. "See you tomorrow?"

"Pick you up at 7:30."

"I'll be ready."

On Saturday morning, Noah was five minutes late arriving at Molly's place. She got into the front passenger seat of his car.

"You broke your own rule," said Molly, the straps of a bathing suit visible under a white cotton top; her hair tied back with a sky blue scrunchie.

"That's the advantage of making a rule," he said. "I can also break it."

He leaned in for a kiss but she impeded his forehead's progress with her hand. "Aren't you forgetting something?"

His eyes darted upwards. "Sorry I'm late?"

"Well, are you?"

"Definitely."

"That's better." Then she cupped her hand beneath his chin and brought her lips to his for a quick peck.

"That's it?" he objected. "That's all I get?"

She nodded. He leaned back and fastened his seat belt. "Well, in that case, I take back my apology."

"Well, then, I take back my kiss."

He started the car. "You can't take back a kiss, silly. You already gave it to me."

She thought that over. "Fine," she told him. "Then I'll just have to withhold the next one as back payment."

He pulled out of her driveway. The two had decided to spend the day in Provincetown and beat the summer traffic with an early departure.

Route 6 East, the Mid-Cape Highway, had little congestion along the way but traffic slowed when they hit the streets off the rotary in Orleans.

"This area is a speed trap, you know," Molly informed him.

"It is?"

"I once got pulled over not far from here for going just two miles an hour over the speed limit."

"Two miles an hour? I've never heard of that. How much was the ticket?"

Molly turned towards her window. "Oh, I didn't get a ticket."

"What do you mean? Why not?"

She chuckled. "The cop was a *guy!*"

"*So?*"

"Well I could give you the song and dance, officer, about how shocked I was to learn I'd been speeding, but you already know what a terrific actress I am. So, suffice it to say that when a woman brandishes her God-given talent, the male species is no match."

She smiled seductively. Noah shook his head. "It's so unfair." Then, "You didn't, you know, do anything inappropriate. Did you?"

Molly made a face. "I don't do anything I don't want to do. Sometimes a little Southern charm is all that's required."

They found parking at an all-day lot and spent the morning hiking up Commercial Street, Provincetown's main thoroughfare. They stopped at a couple of book stores, an art gallery, a huge army-navy surplus shop, where they each bought faux military button-down shirts—his Marines, hers Navy—and a homemade fudge place that offered free samples, walking out with a half-pound of maple walnut.

They spent over an hour at a place called *Shop Therapy*, a throwback to the 1960s, with peace signs, beads, posters, jewelry, smoking accessories, and tie-dyed apparel. For lunch, they ate at The Canteen, with its beachfront patio, and shared a clam chowder and delicious seafood paella. After, they strolled to the west end of town for a peek into the Lands' End Inn vestibule, admiring the antique furniture and spectacular water views, then snapped selfies along the stone jetty at the far end of town. Later, Molly led them to a friend's B&B with a private beach and the two enjoyed the afternoon with quick dips in the glacial sea and napping in the sunshine.

After he awoke, Noah watched Molly sleep. The late afternoon sun warmed his face. Lying next to her, his head resting in his palm, he thought about his wife and wondered if his relationship with Molly was, in some way, inhibiting the mourning process. He had to admit he was having fun. They had a compatible sense of humor. Besides, Molly was beautiful, witty, smart, and interested—nearly everything Jessica was—and spending time with her was certainly taking his mind off his heartache. But was that a good thing? Was it helping him get through his pain or avoid it?

The minutes seeped away without his awareness. When Molly emerged from a deep sleep she found Noah monitoring the incoming tide.

"Been awake long?" she asked, sitting up.

He turned his head and threw her an obligatory smile. "A little while," he said. Then he thought about it. "Actually, I have no idea."

She wrapped her hands around his upper arm and leaned her head against his shoulder. They sat together mesmerized by the passing seagulls, drifting sand, and pummeling waves.

"I think ... Jessie ... thought I ... blamed her ... for Erica's death," Noah confessed, surrendering the words aloud, broken like he was.

Molly's mouth gaped and a sound exited; nothing that anyone listening might describe as incisive.

"And, if she believed that," he went on, his mind at it like a bookkeeper's adding machine at tax season, "it may have been why she became depressed."

Molly still had no discerning response. She peered out on the horizon. In the distance a sailboat tacked through the wind, shrinking in size as it made its run out into the Atlantic.

"She may have become depressed ... because of me."

Neither of them said anything after that until Noah conceded what now became glaringly apparent. "I may have been the reason my wife killed herself."

The first deliberate act Molly made was to release her hands from Noah's arm and squeeze her thighs like a bottle of ketchup as if she was trying to get the blood flowing—against the laws of gravity—towards her brain.

"You're being too hard on yourself, Noah," she told him.

"Please don't tell me that," he said. "If it's true, I'm not being hard enough. I failed her."

"You couldn't possibly know what your wife was thinking."

Noah let that sink in. "You're right," he told her, his voice cracking. "I couldn't have known what she was thinking."

He stood up on the beach peering out on the ocean, combing the throbbing waves.

"I couldn't have known what she was thinking," he repeated, "because we never talked about it."

Then he took a couple of steps toward the water.

"What do you mean you never talked about it?" she asked, coming up beside him.

He turned to face her now, a concession, he realized, he owed his late wife. "I couldn't talk about it. About our daughter. I was too … devastated."

He took a few more steps towards the ocean. She followed him.

"My little baby drowned in a pool full of people. Nobody saw it. Nobody protected her. Nobody saved her. I wasn't there to save her."

"You can't blame yourself for that," she told him. "You weren't there!"

He tried composing his staccato breathing. A losing battle. A lost cause.

"I was supposed to protect her. I'm her father. Isn't that what fathers do?"

He stepped into the murky water. Up to his ankles. The chill shot up his legs like wildfire. She followed him in.

"What happened after that?" she questioned, shuddering from the chilling saltwater. "What happened after your daughter's funeral?"

Noah took his time. "Nothing," he replied, finally, ashamed.

The blood vessels in Noah's face darkened, his complexion more ominous. He looked as though he were about to crumble.

"We never talked about it," he said, his head tottering feebly, his gaze unfocused. "Not a word. I didn't want to hear anything. My daughter was gone. That's all I knew. I didn't want to blame anyone. Not Jessica. She loved Erica. Cherished her. She would have been the only one there looking out for her."

Brooding, he dragged his feet against the current. Needed to keep moving. Needed to escape. "It was an accident. A tragic accident. No one's fault. We accepted what happened and moved on."

Noah stopped moving—he was up to his kneecaps—thinking it through for the first time. "I didn't want to say anything. I was afraid to say anything. Afraid of what might come out." He peered beyond her at the empty horizon. "I was afraid of blaming Jessie ... so I shut her down. Didn't say a word. Wouldn't let her say anything. When she tried, I left the room. Walked out of the house. I couldn't listen to any of it. It was driving me nuts. The pain. Regret. Anger. It was strangling me. Should have been there. Even the look in her eyes. I couldn't. I knew she was hurting. Both of us hurting. I just didn't have the guts to face her."

Then Noah rotated his body to the shore and cringed, turning back to the open sea. From a distance he might have looked like a ballet dancer pirouetting in stages. He whirled again, unable to find asylum.

"She needed to talk. What if she needed me to tell her I didn't blame her? What if she thought ... I did?"

This was the first time he had discussed the fallout of his actions to anyone and the revelation on top of his confession pierced his heart like a silver bullet. He was lost. Too much to bear. And the weight of his anguish rendered him helpless.

Noah Miller sank like he had been taken out by a sniper. He landed on his knees then toppled to his side, his head sinking below the waterline, flooding his throat with a surge of suffocating death not unlike what his daughter must have experienced. Molly bent over and yanked his head out of the water by his collar, precluding his demise. She pounded his back with an open hand, helping him cough it up then waited beside him in the frigid water, his arm strewn over her neck.

"You okay?"

Whether out of shame or remorse or a new wave of guilt, he didn't answer.

It took several minutes before she was able to move him. Molly used every ounce of muscle to support his weight as they made their way back to the deserted beach. He collapsed on the towel and she joined him, an empty look saddled across his face.

Above them, seagulls circled the water hunting for supper. Feeding time. Each took turns skimming the waves and coming up empty. One kamikaze gull, plunging full force—submerging its body into the ocean—soared from the sullied waters with dinner in its beak and flew off to savor its hoard.

The wind blew. The sun slipped. Sand shifted. Remorse lingered.

28
Trons' Eyes

⟨◦❖◦⟩

hree weeks. That's what Barney offered me when Erica died. Three weeks personal paid leave. A week more than usual. A true friend. A good heart. A great boss. Probably would have given me more if he didn't have to answer to anyone.

I mean, how much time does a parent need to overcome a child's death? *A week?* Their only child's death? *A month?* A child we struggled to bring into this world with clinical intervention because we could not do it ourselves? *A year?* A beautiful, sweet four-year old princess who called me daddy? *A lifetime?*

Then again, how long is a lifetime?

So I took him up on it. I had three weeks to take care of matters. Three weeks to bury our child—our only child—mourn her death and resolve whatever challenges we faced moving forward. Seemed like a reasonable amount of time. More than enough. On Monday, I would be going back to my job and my day-to-day existence. But this was Thursday and Jessie and I still had a list of things to finish up.

We drove to the cemetery to pick out an evergreen we wanted planted on her grave and to check out what they were planting on other graves. We didn't need to go there for that—we could have selected one online—but we had made it a point to visit our daughter every day since she died, to let her know we were still thinking of her, still missing her.

I'm not sure if this was a healthy way to mourn our daughter or a compulsive disorder.

After the cemetery, we stopped at Staples to pick up some empty boxes and packing tape. We had decided to give away Erica's stuff to friends who could use it, and whatever was left over—a dresser, some clothes, shoes, birthday gifts, her birthday outfit—we donated to a local thrift shop and a children's charity. Might as well let some other kids benefit from them. We were not going to need them. Then we spent the afternoon cleaning out her room. No use letting it stay that way. That wasn't helping anyone.

We packed it all up and placed the boxes and leftover furniture in the garage. Not that much. The only thing we kept was her plush butterfly, a stuffed bean bag about the size of a paperback novel. We had given it to her on her birthday along with the pendant so she had something to take to bed every night. She refused to go to sleep without Trons. That's what we named it the night of her birthday. Together. It was Snort spelled backwards. She always liked unusual names. Besides, we did not want to confuse it with the actual butterfly we had met that summer day. So the plush was forever known as Trons. But Jessica objected to letting it go. She couldn't. And even though I didn't think it was healthy to keep Trons, it was a small concession I was unwilling to fight her on.

Jessie had been a wreck the past couple of weeks. How could anyone blame her? I knew she was struggling and suggested she talk to someone. She agreed. But that someone turned out to be me and I still wasn't up to the task. I told her that. Told her I couldn't talk about it yet. Was not ready. She said it would help us both if we could. I suggested she see a counselor, a professional. I would even drive her there and pick her up. She said she would consider it at some point. Just not now.

In the back of my mind, I knew she was right. I knew talking about Erica would help her get through it. Me too, probably. But every time I pictured myself sitting down with her, I got this heavy lump in my chest where my heart once resided. And that lump would quickly disperse through my lungs and up my throat and lasso my tongue. Like an octopus inside me spreading its tentacles. Then the tears would start. The entire ordeal smothered me. Whenever I even attempted to talk about it, I would suffocate, like there was no air left in the room, rendering me helpless. It was not just mental impotence. It was physical too. That's how I knew I was not ready to talk yet.

Combing through Erica's things was not easy. It was difficult for me but more for Jess, who appeared to be spiraling into a depressive state. She seemed lost as the days went by, moving further away from me and regressing into herself. She had her good days and her bad. I knew today would be especially hard on her, going through Erica's stuff, but was hoping that as she placed each item in the box, she could look at it and find some comfort. Some relief. A happy memory. A glimmer of positive energy.

Instead it had the opposite effect. While the day wore on, Jessie withdrew into herself as if someone had yanked her plug out of the socket. I knew something had to change. As I watched her wither away, I conceded that avoiding the subject wasn't doing either of us any good and decided that somehow I would find a way to discuss our daughter with her. Tomorrow. I would do it tomorrow. That was all there was to it. I would sit down with my wife and we would talk about Erica. It was the prudent thing to do. A sensible decision. And only fair. I would find a way to discuss Erica with my wife. Tomorrow.

I put Jessica to bed around 10 p.m. By then, she seemed a little more herself, rummaging through some magazines that had piled up on her side of the floor. Dee Dee had stopped by after dinner to spend time with her and I think that had a calming effect. I was grateful to have Dee Dee around so that Jessica had someone else. She was a good friend.

We talked a little about our plans for Friday and I suggested we get out of the house this weekend, maybe to a park or the beach or out east. We could visit a winery. Or Shelter Island. There had been no trips anywhere in a while, since, well, the funeral, and I figured that getting away for the day might be just what we both needed. She said it sounded good but I wondered if she was placating me.

I complimented her ring, anything to help her feel better about herself. She held her hand out examining the sapphire. She had only wanted one ring when we married and preferred this to a wedding band. No argument from me. The ring became the symbol of our struggles. When I proposed, she had promised me she would never remove it, with one condition. I recalled her unlikely stipulation.

After, I went downstairs and brought her some tea, you know, the kind that helps you fall asleep. I put honey in it to sweeten it up. She enjoyed that. Then I went back down to read and checked on her once about an hour later. By then, she had fallen asleep. I removed the journals from the bed and turned the light out.

Sometime after midnight, I turned in. Got undressed in the bathroom, doing all I could not to disturb her. After brushing up, I quietly opened the far window for some fresh air. It was a bit stuffy. Then I climbed into bed and my thoughts turned to Erica and her things we were getting rid of today. They had all been for her. To make her life a little happier, a little easier, a little more comfortable.

I recalled the birthday outfit she wore that day—a puffy mustard yellow blouse and green shorts—and how pretty she looked in it and how she said it made her feel older than she was. It broke my heart that we were giving it away to a thrift shop. No one we offered it to wanted it because they were all at the party and they all remembered her in it.

I laid awake for a while. Too much going on in my mind. The room was quiet. Almost too quiet. I leaned over to make sure the sheet was covering her and that's when I realized she was gone. "Jess?" I said, a little above a whisper. No response. I repeated her name, louder this time. Still nothing.

Then I got out of bed and turned on the lamp and searched the bathroom. The walk-in closet door was ajar, but nothing seemed out of place inside. I called her name again, more desperate this time, as fear began to set in. I flipped on the light switch in the guest bedroom. Still nothing. Only one other place to check.

I opened Erica's door and turned on the overhead light. The room was completely empty except for the beige wall-to-wall carpeting. It was a long, rectangular room with the closet at the far end. Looked bigger without all the furniture. In the corner, one of the sliding closet doors was open. I sensed a peculiar odor in the room.

I headed over to the closet. A little jittery. Wasn't sure what to expect. Then I saw her, naked, hanging from the closet rod, my brown leather belt around her neck. Her knees were buckled, her toes barely touching the floor. Her somber face—her beautiful face—now a pale shade of frightful—a color I'd never seen before and could not begin to describe—

triggered a sense of terror in me. "JESS!" I screamed in full panic mode, loud enough to wake the neighbors. "NO!"

I grabbed her body and lifted, taking the pressure off her windpipe where it was strapped tight. Her head slumped over my left shoulder. She was heavier than I recalled the last time I picked her up—carrying her over the threshold when we bought this house—or perhaps it was my imagination. I struggled to undo the belt with one hand, bumping my head several times on the shelf above.

When I finally got it off, I laid her down on her back on the carpeting. I was in shock and not thinking straight. No time to check for vitals, which would have wasted valuable seconds. I began resuscitating, my hands pumping as instructed in a lifesaving course I had taken at work one afternoon—counting as I pressed down on her chest, one hand over the other—thirty contractions, then two breaths into her mouth. Talking to her the entire time. "Don't die on me, Jess! Don't you do this. Please. Don't do this."

I must have been at it for what seemed like fifteen minutes, screaming hopelessly for help, yelling at her, compressing her chest, unwilling to stop and dial 9-1-1 because I remembered what they told us in class, that if she had any chance of surviving, I had to keep doing what I was doing until I saw some sign of life. Besides, I had left my phone in the kitchen.

When my biceps began to cramp, I abandoned the procedure and placed my ear to her mouth, listening for a breath. I watched her chest for a sign of movement. Then I checked for a pulse on her neck, just below the discolored welt. Nothing. There was nothing. No sign of life. She would not survive this. My wife was dead and there was nothing I could do about it.

I moved away from her and lowered my head, leaning on my elbows to catch my breath, staring at the strands of fiber on the floor, wondering if this was a bad dream, hoping it was really a nightmare. My mind was running amok with endless streams of thoughts but only one I felt compelled to say aloud.

"God damn you!" I bellowed when the shuddering in my body allowed, enraged as if my head was exploding. This was directed at God, not Jessie. Then came the follow-up. "Both?" I protested. "You took them both?" Then the context of that revelation set in, an actuality I had not seen coming. "*Both of them?* FUCK YOU, GOD! How could you do that?"

That was the final question I managed to articulate before rolling over on my back—my heart pounding, my lungs heaving, perspiration dripping on the rug surrounding my head producing a sweaty halo, every muscle in my body depleted of vitality—and losing it. I mean, losing it like no one had ever lost it. No human, alien, animal, bacteria, or protozoa in heaven or in hell or from someone's imagination had *ever* lost it— whisked away at a speed Einstein may or may not have envisioned into the atmosphere, stratosphere, galaxies, or universe, in all the corners of space or God's pockets, or an existence that has yet to be discovered at the end of some goddamn rainbow. I mean, *lost it!*

I don't know how long I remained in that position before returning to full consciousness. At some point I realized I had to call someone. The police. Dee Dee. Jessie's parents. Not sure of the order. Didn't really care.

Struggling to my feet, I noticed something laying on the closet floor and went over to see what it was. It was Trons, the stuffed butterfly Jessie refused to give away. She must have been holding it during the ordeal until her life drained out of her and they were both set free.

I grabbed a robe from behind my door and took the butterfly downstairs with me to find my phone. I sat at the kitchen table to make the calls. Waiting for people to show up, I examined Trons' workmanship. It had pretty colors, similar to Snort, which is probably what attracted me to it. I could see why Erica loved it. I remembered the place where I had picked it up one evening not far from Penn Station. One of those New York City tourist places on Seventh Avenue where they sell everything. They only had one butterfly in stock so I took it home.

Trons had two oversized eyes with full lashes. They reminded me of Jessie's eyes, the look in Jessica's eyes, those disappointed eyes that told me I had failed her. *I had failed her.* No one could see what I saw—the letdown was strictly between us—and the bitterness I sensed cut through me even more than the grief. My own sorrow did not count. She blamed me for Erica's death. I was now sure of it. Somehow it was my fault because I went to work and was not around more; because I was tired that week from doing my job, one she never approved of; because I was busy writing my play. So she took Erica to the pool party instead of me then blamed me for it. And it was all reflected back at me in her eyes. *Trons' eyes.*

Sitting there, I asked myself how was I going to go on without them? I was alone now in the world. No one to grieve with only to grieve for. No Erica around to plan special days for mommy. No Jessica at my side to help me recall pleasant memories of our daughter. My entire family extinguished like a Holocaust victim, who, over time, is callously erased from our mind. Expunged from our soul.

They were both gone. An hour ago I still had Jessica. Now I would have to plan another funeral, choose a coffin, hire the Rabbi, pick out evergreens, visit her grave, say the prayers. Three weeks later. With everyone feeling sorry for me. No, not sorry. They will all be pointing fingers this time, scrutinizing me, comparing me with one of Shakespeare's characters, the sorriest creature in the kingdom.

That is what I was now. That is what it came down to. The sorriest creature in the universe. That poor man. That poor schlub. What a poor shmuck, they will whisper. First his daughter. Now his wife. He'll probably be next. Watch the Steinway fall out of the sky and crush him into the ground. Just leave him there, they will say. At least he can save on the burial fee. But grab his credit card. Need it to pay the Rabbi. Perhaps he'll give me a rate. Three funerals in the same month. You have earned our back-to-the-cemetery special. Call Guinness. See if that's a record.

I opened the cabinet beneath the kitchen sink and searched the butterfly's eyes. Disappointment. That's all I saw. Then I dumped Trons into the pail with the rest of the garbage and slammed the door shut.

29
Quite The Ghost Story

Sunday was mostly quiet. Sheila was busy with her friends that day so Jerry invited Noah over for a swim, a cookout and the Yankees' game, that is, a Red Sox-Yankee game. Noah was still feeling the brunt of his confession to Molly the day before and preferred not to be alone. He arrived at one o'clock and found Jerry out back flipping burgers on the grill and sautéing onions in a small pan.

"Smells good," Noah said, grabbing a beer from the cooler and dunking a couple of chips in the guacamole.

"We aim to please," said Jerry, a chef's toque on his head and a matching white apron with the mantra: *I serve meals three ways: frozen, microwave and takeout!*

"Really?" questioned Noah, "because I'm not reading that on your stomach."

Jerry shrugged, ignoring the comment. "Everything set for the week?"

"All good," replied Noah. He grabbed a few more chips. "What's the story with the media on Wednesday?"

Jerry grinned. "We must have picked a good week to open. Either that or the Playhouse marketing department is better than I thought. Should be a good turnout." He hesitated. "Of course, a good turnout for the Cape means a newspaper blurb, a couple of online blogs, a radio station, and local TV. But I'll take all the free publicity I can get."

"Did Mindy's movie with Kate Winslet buy us anything?"

Jerry lowered the flame and closed the grill hood. "Yes, as a matter of fact. One of the bloggers picked up on it and is featuring Mindy in a story. I believe the angle is 'Local gal heading for Hollywood alongside Oscar winner.' Didn't hurt that she's from Chatham. The Hyannis radio station also requested an interview."

"I know I probably shouldn't ask," offered Noah, "but have ticket sales picked up?"

Jerry stopped what he was doing. "You're right. Don't ask. Need another beer?"

"I better get some food inside me first."

Jerry proceeded into the house and Noah followed.

"It's not all bad news, however," added Jerry. "I called in a couple of favors to see if there were any names vacationing here this week. You'll be happy to know that Luke Wilson and Sandra Bullock have accepted my invitation to the opening."

He placed the ketchup, relish and napkins on the table.

"Anything I can do to help?" asked Noah.

"Sit," Jerry told him.

Noah grabbed a napkin and followed orders. Jerry checked on the burgers. "I've worked with Sandra before and Wilson is always looking for opportunities to appear newsworthy. Keeps his name out there.

"I'm trying to see if I can get Samuel L. Jackson and Meg Ryan, who own houses on Cape, to show up. But they're long shots. Dan Aykroyd's a maybe. He's out on the Vineyard but you never know. I'm glad to say all those names did attract a Boston TV station to cover the opening Wednesday night. So, we're in business."

"Good for you, pal."

"Just doing my job."

Jerry brought two burgers over along with the onions and joined his guest at the table.

"I knew things would look up," said Noah. *"You'll* see. This show will fill the coffers yet."

"I hope so," said Jerry, preparing his burger. "I'm actually starting to feel better about everything."

Noah crinkled his forehead. "Did you forget something?"

"What? What did I forget?"

"Pickles?"

Jerry surveyed the table then rushed inside, returning a moment later with a jar of Whiskey Sour Pickles. "Would I ever serve a meal without a good sour pickle?"

Noah checked the label. "Brooklyn Brine Company?"

"Where else would you find a good kosher pickle?"

After lunch, the two friends made themselves comfortable on the floating lounge chairs with easy access to the cooler and the ballgame turned on. Jerry let his chair float over to Noah's side of the pool. He seemed concerned. "So tell me about you. What's going on? Is it the show?"

Noah was on his second beer. "I'm fine, pal. Thanks for asking."

"I'm not kidding, Noah. A few people have mentioned that you're not yourself lately. Tell me what's going on?"

Noah paddled over to the cooler for another Bass Ale. He needed more alcohol in his blood, even if it was only five percent, to bring Jerry up to speed.

"I'm fine. Really I am. Just have some things on my mind."

Jerry wasn't giving up. "*Uh, oh,* I think I've heard this before. What kind of things?"

Just then, Aaron Judge roped a double into the opposite-field corner and they watched the Yankees' action unfold on screen.

"*Still waiting,*" Jerry said in a sing-song manner.

Noah realized he would have to tell him something. "Remember that woman, Emma, who said she was your real estate agent?"

"Yes, I remember. What about her?"

Noah tried to dislodge some water from his ear. "Well, I found her … at Heritage Park."

"Good. What did she have to say for herself? You did call her on it? About being my agent?"

Noah tilted his head back to let his ear drain and watched the drifting clouds overhead. "I did." He was having trouble deciphering whether the clouds were moving in or out.

"*Noah?*" said Jerry.

Noah gave his friend a long look before opening up. "I told her she lied and asked her to come clean."

Jerry laid there waiting. "Well, did she?"

Noah sipped his beer. "I probably shouldn't discuss this with you."

"What?" Jerry objected. "Why the hell not?"

Noah took a breath. Then he took another, pondering Jerry's reaction.

"Say it, Noah. Just tell me what's going on?"

After a moment, he came out with it. "She said she's my daughter."

Jerry let that settle in. Then he laughed. "You're kidding, right? Toying with me. No, really, tell me what she said."

Noah answered without a hint of emotion. "She said she's my four-year old daughter."

Jerry took a peek at the television to gauge the action giving him time to grasp the concept. "What is she ... insane?"

"That seems to be the general consensus."

"How could any grown woman look you in the eye and tell you she's your four-year old daughter? Your *dead* four-year old daughter?"

Noah didn't care for the remark.

"Sorry," said Jerry. "No offense. I was just ... you know what I mean."

Noah gave him a nod.

"Quite the ghost story. First she lies about who she is, then makes up this ludicrous tale. What's her problem? Trying to convince you that she's ... what? *A ghost?* You kidding me? That's the most ridiculous thing I ever heard."

The two laid there watching the action on the screen.

Then Jerry perked up. "Hey, I just got a fantastic idea."

Noah waited for his friend, still trying to piece together his thoughts. "What?"

"Why don't you invite her to our show?"

Noah did not even bother.

"No, I mean it. She'll be our guest. Our guest ghost. We'll bill her as the ghostwriter. Get it?" Then, raising both hands like a conductor on the downbeat, he announced: 'Let the spirit move you. *Committed*, opening this week at the Playhouse. An ethereal experience.'"

"I don't think she's the type."

"What? It's perfect. This is what we needed. Think of the publicity. It'll be a sellout!"

"She's *not* a ghost. At least I don't think she is. If she's anything, she's an angel."

Jerry appeared cheerful. "Even better! 'It's divine. A godsend. Angels from heaven are fighting to get seats and do they have the right connections. Hurry, get your ticket today before they disappear. Before they've … departed.'"

Noah clapped sarcastically. "A regular P.T. Barnum."

"We'll make her available to the media for interviews. She talks to other people besides you, right? Hopefully, she'll like the show. Well, she's *your* daughter, right? Why wouldn't she like it? I mean, she owes you one, doesn't she? Well, at least that."

"I'm sorry I mentioned it."

Noah knew Jerry was not buying his ghost story but wondered why his friend was not questioning his sanity. He figured he would at least show some concern. He knew Jerry was feeling the pressure. With the show about to open, Noah's job was nearly over and Jerry's reputation was on the line. He must have assumed it was Noah who was teasing him.

"What?" said Jerry. "You don't like it?"

Noah continued staring at him.

"Okay," conceded Jerry, "we won't use her. But I think we're missing out on a fabulous opportunity."

Noah opened the cooler for another beer.

"Don't I have a say in this?" came a familiar voice behind him.

Noah turned to find Emma sitting on the edge of the pool.

"Shit," he screamed, startled—and kicked his feet to get away as if he had spotted a Hammerhead Shark—splashing Jerry in the process.

"What are you getting all worked up about?" yelled Jerry, wiping his face and reaching for a towel. "I was just giving you a hard time. Serves you right after that meshuggener story."

Noah's heart was pounding. He looked at Emma then at Jerry, his mouth ajar.

"What's gotten into you?" asked Jerry. "You look like you've seen a ghost."

Noah pointed at their guest. "Or an angel."

Jerry turned in the direction he was pointing. "What? What are you pointing at?"

"Her."

"Her, who?"

Noah gave him his *you have got to be kidding me* face. "Our ghostwriter."

"You mean she's here?" asked Jerry. "Now *you're* putting *me* on, right?"

"He can't see me," she explained.

"He can't?" questioned Noah.

"He can't *what?*" asked Jerry. I certainly *can.* Are you talking to her?"

"She says you can't see her," Noah told him.

"Well why the hell not?"

Noah gave Emma a look.

"This is between you and me," she explained.

"So only *I* can see you?" he asked.

Emma nodded.

"What are we living in a feudal society?" asked Jerry. "You better than me or something?"

Noah ignored him. "What about that guy in the park? The one who waved at you?"

Emma laughed. "He wasn't waving at *me.* "

"What guy in the park?" asked Jerry.

"And the waitress ... at the restaurant?"

Emma shook her head.

"What waitress?" asked Jerry. "Do I know her?"

"Sorry," said Noah. "I'm not buying it."

"Do I have to prove it to you?" she questioned.

"Buying what?" asked Jerry. "Is she trying to sell you something?"

"Try if you want but it's not going to do any good."

Emma thought a moment.

"I'm not playing this game anymore," said Jerry. "No more questions from me."

"Ask your friend," she said taking her time, "about the affair he had with mom."

"What?" said Noah, startled. *"What affair? What are you talking about?"*

"Affair?" said Jerry. "Someone had an affair?"

"Go on," Emma urged. "It happened before you were married. See what his reaction is."

Noah looked over at Jerry.

"What?" asked Jerry.

Noah bit his top lip trying to keep from saying it. "Did you have an affair … with Jessie?"

"What?" said Jerry, flabbergasted. "What are you talking about?"

"Before we were married?"

"Why would you ask me that?"

"Did you or didn't you?"

"Where's this coming from?" he said. "Did Casper put you up to this?"

Noah continued his fixed gaze. "Just answer the question, Jerry."

"No. I refuse. Can't believe you'd ask me that. I thought we were friends."

"So did I."

Neither one said a word for the next minute.

"Seems to me," said Noah, "you would have denied it by now."

Jerry lowered his head and took a deep breath, then finished what was left of his beer. "It happened once a long time ago after you two split up." He took his time, searching for the words. "She called me."

Noah felt that lump growing, this time in his throat.

"I didn't plan it," Jerry went on. "She was feeling down and I went over as a friend to talk. That was all, I swear."

He leaned his head back on the inflated pillow, staring up at the clouds, then puckered his lips like he was going to whistle and exhaled.

"It was just after you two had discussed marriage and you wouldn't give her an answer and she broke it off."

Noah massaged his temple and still had nothing to add.

"She was vulnerable, I know, and I'm sorry Noah. It just happened. We were sitting there and she was crying and I wiped the tears and held her and I was just trying to comfort her as a friend. I swear to God. I never meant for it to go any further than that."

Noah glanced Emma's way but she was gone. He paddled to the shorter end of the pool and got out, picked up his towel and dried off. Then he got dressed.

He started to head inside then turned back. "Thank you for telling me." He took a step towards the house and stopped. "You know," he added, his voice cracking, "she used you ... to get back at me."

Noah stood there a moment to gather his strength. Then he went home.

30
The Fourth Wall

On Monday morning, Noah took a ride up to Plymouth. He had gotten in touch with Jessica's Great Aunt Cecilia's caregiver, Silver Fox, on the reservation where they lived. He had saved the phone number from when he and Jess were contacting family and friends for Erica's funeral. Her aunt could not make it to that one, but did show up to Jessie's a few weeks later.

On the passenger seat lay the photo album Noah had found in the attic. He wanted to know if it was really Aunt Cecilia in the picture, and, if so, what she could tell him about the ceremony, and what Jessie might have known. He was also curious how it may have affected his wife and daughter. He had questions about the documents he had found in the boxes—land deeds, tribal citizenship papers, plaintiff's motions and court opinions over the course of more than 200 years—an entire history of the Wampanoag Nation and Mashpee Tribe, all packed up in the back of his car.

Aunt Cecilia was pleased to see him and the family album. She confirmed that it was her in the photo the day she was designated sachem or chief of the Algonquian people and Wampanoag Tribe, shortly after her father's passing. She also explained that the documents he found in the attic belonged to the "Keeper of Records," who lived in the old house Noah was renting, a century ago. The records had been thought lost and her people would be grateful they had been recovered.

She explained that her ancestors were the ones who greeted the Pilgrims at Plymouth Rock. She recounted the story of Metacom, chief of the Cape Cod tribe, who wore one feather in his headband—the feather of the magical Thunderbird—a bird so powerful, according to legend, it could scoop a white whale out of Nantucket Bay and carry it off in its talons. Noah recalled the bird from his dream.

His wife's aunt informed him how the Colonists stole wood and provisions from her people and encroached on their land, making it difficult to hunt and fish. When the settlers implicated three Wampanoag warriors for a murder they did not commit, Metacom had seen enough. He plotted with the Algonquin and Narragansett tribes and together tore out on a rampage of revenge in late 1675, decimating settlements from Massachusetts to Maine.

Upon Metacom's return, the surviving Plymouth Colonists pleaded for a peace. They invited him and his bravest warriors to a three-day gathering for a reconciliation alliance. But it was a diversion. When Metacom returned home to Mount Hope, Rhode Island, he found his entire village bludgeoned to death along with his wife and only son. Noah recalled the massacred women and children he had seen that day at Abel's Hill Cemetery and the Native American hovering over two bodies. He handed Cecilia the newspaper clipping he had found.

She told him that since she never married or had children, Jessie, as next of kin, would have inherited the honored designation of sachem that would have passed down to Erica. She added, "It's a shame the bloodline ends with me."

Noah could see she regretted the admission and changed the subject. Then he mentioned what happened in the attic. "While I was studying your photograph, I heard chanting. Then the walls of the attic disappeared and I found myself ... *in* the photograph. I mean I was there with you and your tribe. And that's not the first time something like that happened."

"You have been chosen, Noah."

"Chosen for what? By whom?"

"There are many names. The Great Spirit and God of Light are two by which we refer to our Creator. You may know him as God."

Noah appeared a bit dumbfounded but did not take her seriously.

"As for why you were chosen," she continued, "I have not been consulted so I couldn't say. But my guess is that you have become part of our story. Perhaps it has to do with my great niece."

Before leaving, he asked her what became of Metacom.

"Two tribes, the Mohawks and Mohegans, joined the Englishmen and together overcame the Wampanoags. Many of my people surrendered and were sold into slavery. When Metacom died, his rebellion died with him." She stopped for a moment, gathering her emotions. "He was hung, beheaded, drawn, and quartered, and his head was displayed on a spike at Plymouth Colony—as a trophy—for many years."

On his way back, Noah considered what Aunt Cecilia told him about the challenges her tribe has faced over the centuries with recovering land the federal, state and local governments illegally absconded. He was moved by the story of the Wampanoag people.

Back at the Playhouse, the tech rehearsal went off without any major headaches. Whatever hitches did arise as far as lighting and music cues and any other tech issues were resolved so that the crew was in complete sync with the director's wishes and the cast knew what to expect. If the particular cue didn't work as planned, they tried it again until they got it right.

Noah wanted the lights brought up a little slower in the restaurant scene and gave explicit instructions to the lighting tech when to turn on the flashing *You're A Schmuck, Chuck!* sign towards the end of the show. When it was over, he asked Roz to please remind her crew to be on top of set changes during the game show scene so the actors would not have to wait. Other than that, everyone seemed pleased with the progress and the company appeared ready for the dress rehearsal the next day.

The theater was about a quarter filled for the dress rehearsal on Tuesday afternoon. Most of the audience were acquaintances of the cast, crew, and theater staff. A friendly crowd. The Playhouse also engaged two buses to deliver residents from assisted living and rehab centers in the area, those who had no way to get to the theater on their own. It was good public relations and another means of promoting a positive word of mouth to friends and relatives. It also gave the actors a sounding board before the paying customers showed up.

The show proceeded well with just a couple of minor concerns, par for the dress and welcomed since a flawless rehearsal before opening night was historically bad luck. Steve missed a line in the first scene but Susan discreetly covered for him. Wayne had the wrong costume change late in the second act, but neither miscue was discernible to the audience. One of the set changes also took longer than it should have but Noah saw Roz jotting a note to herself and knew she was on top of it.

When the curtain was lowered, everyone seemed pleased with the overall performance and the audience—those that were able—gave the actors a standing ovation. The cast took their bows in the order that Noah had arranged and breathed a sigh of relief they had made it to this point. They were all excited and looking forward to opening night.

Noah gave them time to socialize with their friends and family that showed up and let the cast know there would be a final meeting in the back room in half an hour.

Jerry stopped by to congratulate Noah and inform him that the brass was impressed with the job he did and encouraged by the publicity the show was receiving. Left unsaid, but on everyone's mind, was that tomorrow was the key to determine whether the show survived. Noah chose not to say anything more about their difficult conversation that weekend.

Once the theater was cleared, Noah met everyone in the backroom. He was not pleased with Steve for missing a line or the way he handled it but at this point in the schedule knew he needed to be tactful. He brought up the two slipups and, while he did not name Wayne or Steve in his remarks—he had no intention of embarrassing them in front of their colleagues—he wanted to make sure that everyone was clear on what happened and prepared to rectify any future issues should they occur.

To emphasize his point, Noah raised a topic that most of the actors probably had not thought about since their high school theater days. If ever.

"Before I let you go, I have a question. Feel free to shout out your answer."

Intrigued, everyone gave Noah their full attention.

"What's behind the fourth wall?" he asked them.

The actors turned to one another with curious blank stares.

"Dead bodies," yelled Steve. Everyone in the room laughed.

Noah allowed them their moment. "No. Seriously. Who can tell me what's behind the fourth wall?"

After some hesitation, Mindy asserted: "*We* are."

"That's correct. Thank you, Mindy. *You* are behind that wall. The little story we've created; Charlie and Wendy and Billy and Lydia. All of you. The fourth wall separates you from your audience. It's invisible, but that doesn't mean it's *not* real. I believe that invisible curtain is as genuine, as tangible, as anything on stage. It keeps you within the reality you've established. It can be your best friend if you let it. But, if you forsake it, it comes crashing down, and your private universe disappears. The fantasy we've created vanishes."

Noah nodded giving himself time to formulate an example. "Picture yourselves in a movie theater—in a dark room—your attention focused on the big screen. You're all caught up in the action, completely engaged in the movie. And then the projector breaks down and the lights go on shattering the moment. That's what happens if you breach the fourth wall."

He took a sip of his tepid coffee giving everyone a chance to absorb the concept.

"I'm sure you're wondering why I'm bringing this up now. It's to emphasize the need to stay on *your* side of the wall. In *your* reality. Especially if you flub a line or miss a cue. Don't lose it. Don't hesitate. Keep the action moving in context. Look to your fellow actors to help you get back on track. You're all in this together. Whatever you do, don't surrender to it because the moment you cross that line, knock down that wall, you lose them—the lights go on—and that fourth wall can no longer protect you. And then all you have is a bunch of dead bodies buried behind a wall. Right, Steve?"

The reference broke the tension and everyone breathed in the jovial air, laughing it off.

Noah stopped there fearing he might say too much. He asked if anyone had anything to add. No one took him up on it.

"You've all done a hell of a job the last few weeks," he asserted, "and I appreciate your hard work and for bearing with me. I'm proud of you guys." He underscored that point with a smile, gazing at each of his assembled cast members.

"Thank you one and all." Then he added, "Have a great evening. We'll see you tomorrow at six sharp for the opening."

Everyone appeared touched by his last words, no one more than Molly, who had a gleam in her eye. But Noah had noticed a bewildered expression from her moments before and wondered what she was really thinking.

31
Déjà Vu

Later, after most of the company had left, Molly and Noah had dinner at Scargo Café, a colonial-style tavern and one of Molly's favorite restaurants, directly across 6A from the theater. They had planned to walk there but changed their minds at the last minute. While the front lot was completely full and they had to park his car in the reserved lot, they were escorted to a table as soon as they arrived.

"I've never had to wait for a table here," said Molly. "They're one of the few establishments that honor your reservation to the minute. That's one of the things I like best about them, besides their delicious specials. Wait until you taste the food."

The restaurant seemed busy to Noah for a Tuesday night. Molly explained that the place was always crowded. She was glad they were sitting in one of the back rooms where they could carry on a conversation. The tavern area was bustling and loud. Noah wondered how people hooked up these days when you couldn't hear what the person in front of you was saying.

They ordered drinks and picked out their entrées—Noah the swordfish, Molly the roast duck—and, after their drinks were served, the waitress brought over hot rolls and a bowl of seafood chowder, which they shared.

"How you feeling about everything?" asked Molly. Then, before he had a chance to answer, "I thought the rehearsal went well."

But Noah seemed preoccupied.

"Noah?"

He focused on her. "Huh? Sorry."

"You okay?"

He ripped a piece of his roll and dunked it in the chowder.

"I'm fine. Just a few things running through my head."

"Anything I can do to help?"

He gazed at her adoringly. "You're doing it, Molly. Believe me. I don't know how I could have gotten through all this without you."

She tried suppressing a smile and failed.

But while he tried to convince her—and himself—that all was well, he knew better. He was still nervous about the show and what he was going to do with himself once they closed. And then of course there was Molly. And Emma.

"Everything's delicious," he told her. "You were right about this place."

She beamed. "I thought you might like it."

"I do."

"Then tonight's dinner is on me," she insisted.

"Thanks, Molly, but you don't have to do that."

"But I want to. You've been paying for everything since we've started dating."

"That's because I make more money than you do."

She donned her serious face. "Let me do this. Please."

Their eyes rendezvoused and Noah's concerns for the moment subsided.

"Thank you."

"You're very welcome."

Later, as they were finishing dinner, Noah glanced around the room then looked at her. "I was thinking that we could go back to your place after dinner because I'd like to show you just how much I appreciate everything you've done."

Molly beamed. "Well, I certainly like the sound of that."

"So, no objections?"

She pushed out her lower lip and rocked her head side to side. "None that I can think of."

"Good. Why don't we get the check and dessert will be on me?"

"I think you'd make an excellent dessert," she told him.

Molly searched the restaurant. Her hand shot up to catch the waitress' attention when she spotted her.

Waiting for their waitress to return with the bill, Molly took a more serious tone. "I know you've had a lot on your mind lately so I didn't bother mentioning this to you before."

Noah gave her his full attention.

"Remember that story about the three kids in the park we heard from the Newport Madam?"

He nodded.

"Then they showed up in your dream."

"What about them?"

"I think I know who they represent."

Noah straightened up with some tension, anxious for her to continue.

"I think the two girls represent your wife and your daughter."

Noah's head turned awry as he considered that, before shifting back in place.

"And the boy?" he inquired, having already surmised the answer.

Molly looked straight at him and gave him what he wanted. "The boy is you, Noah."

He stared at her for a while as her theory took shape.

Molly continued. "That's why she asked us if the story had meaning. She didn't even bother with my tea leaves. She was talking about you."

Noah was still busy processing it. "And what about the third girl in the story?"

Molly began to smile gauging his mindset. "The third girl in your dream is … me."

He watched her for a moment. *"You?"* he asked.

She raised her brows and nodded.

"What makes you think it's you?"

She looked away, formulating her answer, then said matter-of-factly, "What makes you think it's not?"

"Noah?" said Dee Dee Donaldson, standing beside their table. "Is that you?"

Startled, he jumped to his feet.

"Dee Dee, how are you?" He kissed her cheek and they hugged. "What are you doing here?"

Before responding, she gave Molly half a nod and a forced smile.

"I'm sorry," he apologized. "Let me introduce you two. Molly Talbert, one of the actresses in our show, this is Donna Donaldson, a dear friend of my wife's."

"Dee Dee," she corrected him as the ladies shook hands in a cordial manner.

"Nice to meet you, Dee Dee," said Molly, who remained sitting.

"I would hope I'm a dear friend of *yours* as well," said Dee Dee, watching him.

"Of course you are," he replied, a bit embarrassed. "How long you in town?"

"Well, we've got tickets to the opening tomorrow tonight. We came by earlier to pick them up and read the reviews about this place and decided to hang out and try it. Jimmy and I are renting a house in Truro for the week."

"*Jimmy?*" asked Noah.

"My new boyfriend," she explained. "Well ... acquaintance. Actually, I don't know what you call it these days. We've only been dating a couple of months. I told you I'd be back for your show."

"You *did.* And I'm so glad you brought Jimmy with you. I look forward to meeting him."

Dee Dee gave Molly a glimpse that Noah caught. "Me too," she replied, almost slyly. "Sorry I interrupted your dinner, Molly, but when I stepped out of the ladies' room I saw Noah and had to say hello."

"Of course," said Molly. "You didn't interrupt us. We were just getting ready to leave ourselves."

Almost on cue, the waitress placed the bill and credit card beside Molly's plate. Dee Dee smiled. "I see."

Noah took a half step away from the table. "So we'll see you tomorrow night?"

Dee Dee's gaze was a little too long. "Until tomorrow then," she said, giving them each a look. "Break a leg."

While making her way to the door, the eyes of all the men in the room—and a couple of the women—followed her out.

Neither of them said anything at first. Molly added a tip to the bill, signed her name, and put her card away. "You want to get out of here?"

Noah appeared distracted, back in that lost world she had found him in when they first sat down. Again, she called his name to get his attention, and again he had a similar reply. "Huh?"

"Noah, are you ready to go?"

He raised his head to meet her eyes but his focus appeared blurred. Without knowing, he placed his hand on his stomach. "You know, Molly, I was thinking ..."

Before he could finish the sentence, she appeared disturbed. "What's gotten into you?"

Noah looked at her blankly. He was really torn and at a loss how to proceed.

Molly tried to smile but her sincerity did not shine through. "I thought we agreed to take this back to my place? You wanted to show me something? Remember?"

Noah knew he was on shaky ground. "I did. I'm sorry. I do. Believe me."

"So what's the problem?"

"Nothing. No problem. It's just that I've got a lot on my mind and could use a good night's sleep."

"I could help you with that," she said, her eyes making promises she planned to keep.

Noah dropped his head. "I'm sure you can. But listen, tomorrow's a big day and I've been thinking ..."

Molly's temperament began to erode. "Does this have anything to do with your friend, Dee Dee?"

This time he had no answer, clever or otherwise.

"What is it, Noah? Something you want to tell me?"

He had never seen this side of her and wondered from where this apparent jealously emerged. A cheating boyfriend? An unfaithful lover? Her duplicitous husband? He decided to take the high ground. It was sincere and, he figured, the only thoroughfare to an amicable solution.

"Don't you think we'd both be better off with a full night's rest? I mean, if I come over, let's face it, neither one of us is going to get much sleep. And we should be at our best tomorrow. So why don't we put this on hold and save it for tomorrow night?"

His answer did not appease.

"I noticed the way she looked at you."

"What? What are you talking about?"

And then she just came out with it. "Did you and Dee Dee have an affair?"

The expression on her face would have shattered the marrow of a lesser man.

"What? *No!* Of course not!"

She reloaded. "Let me rephrase so we're absolutely clear."

He had just enough time to inhale half a breath, his only armor to withstand the blow.

"Are you having an affair with her?"

Noah could not believe what he was hearing. *"No,"* he told her emphatically. "We are *not* having an affair. We have *never* had an affair. And I'm not planning to have an affair with Dee Dee Donaldson. Is that clear enough for you?"

She crossed her arms indignantly. This time she did not hold back. *"Absolutely."*

Noah knew he was going to lose this battle although he wasn't quite sure why.

"Maybe I was wrong about the third girl," she said as she rose to her feet.

"Huh?"

"Thanks for joining me for dinner." With that, she threw her napkin on the table and barged out.

"Molly!"

Noah realized at that moment just how much he had laid on her plate—his wife and daughter's deaths, the psychic reading, his follow-up dream, Erica's haunting presence, the show's opening, their relationship, and now Dee Dee's conjecture about the two of them—and it was more than she could handle. What was he thinking?

He deliberated how he was going to resolve this but there was something else. Something nagging at him. Something familiar about this moment. Something she had said. Then he recalled Madam Sweeney's claim. Or was it a prophesy? A warning, she had told them. The third girl moved quickly and went ahead of him. Noah regarded the doorway where Molly had exited then jumped to his feet and dashed out.

When he got outside, he glanced towards the back lot but she wasn't there. He chose not to call out her name because he wasn't sure if Dee Dee was still in proximity and did not want to cause a scene.

He spotted Molly plodding towards Route 6A at a determined pace. It had started to rain. Panicked and shaken, he ran towards her. Then Noah watched in stunned silence as an SUV came racing around the curve. He screamed her name. Molly hesitated and turned in time to witness the car screech to a stop, slamming into her.

"MOLLY!"

The driver, seeing Noah rushing towards him, took off. Noah pulled his phone from his pocket and snapped a picture of the car speeding away. Even though he was in shock, he had the presence of mind to note it was a light-colored vehicle but that was all. He did not catch the license plate.

Then he dialed 9-1-1.

Molly was lying on her stomach on the dirt road on the far side of 6A. She had been propelled at least twenty feet from where the car had struck her. She was unconscious and he could detect no sign of life but was afraid to turn her over and possibly inflict further damage.

He squatted beside her and lowered his head. "Molly?" he whispered, alarmed. "Can you hear me?" No reaction. "Molly, it's Noah. Say something … please talk to me."

He felt the pulse on her neck. It was low but still beating. She was alive. Barely. He noticed scrapes on her face where she'd hit the ground and blood. Parts of her clothing were torn.

Customers from the restaurant, who had heard the crash and his scream, emerged to see what happened.

He could not help but feel déjà vu. A woman, lying on the ground, checking the pulse of her throat, dialing emergency services. Oh, God. It was all coming back to haunt him.

Noah got to his feet and wandered to the double yellow lines on the road. What had he done? He had told her they would celebrate, then reneged. He would put it off another day. That's what set her off.

Then he yelled "HELP ME! GODDAMN IT! SOMEBODY PLEASE HELP ME!"

Overcome with a new wave of guilt, Noah Miller collapsed to the ground.

32
History Repeated

Noah turned on his hazard lights and followed the ambulance to Cape Cod Hospital in Hyannis. He had told the police he would meet them at the hospital and finish the report there. Inside he was reeling but was able to hold it together for appearance sake and convince the two officers to let him go ahead. They agreed and hung around to question other witnesses.

Driving there, the gravity of the situation pulled Noah out of his stupor. No time for criticism or blame. Some hard decisions needed to be made.

First and foremost was Molly's health and Noah was determined to discuss that with the doctors when he arrived. Next was tomorrow night's opening and the fact that they were now minus their lead actress. Noah realized he needed to call Jerry right away.

He voice-dialed Jerry's cell phone. He did not want to mention any names, afraid that his friend would freak out, only that there had been an accident. He told him to meet him at the hospital.

But Jerry was insistent. "Who went to the hospital?" he demanded. Noah knew what this would do to him and needed time to figure it out but was too upset right now to worry about that. He also knew that key decisions would have to be made and that Jerry would probably be the one making them.

"Molly," conceded Noah.

"What happened? Is she okay?"

Noah told him he didn't know her condition and tried to diffuse Jerry's fears as best he could. "She was in a car accident. She was barely conscious when they put her in the ambulance. I'm on my way now. See you there."

Jerry rattled off three more questions without waiting for answers. Noah felt no remorse when he cut off the call.

On the way, Noah followed the ambulance through several red lights gunning its alarm as it crossed. Approaching the hospital, the guilt began to seep in. It was all his fault. He had made the suggestion to go over to her place after dinner, felt guilty when Dee Dee showed up, retracted the offer upsetting her, then hesitated, waiting too long to follow her out the door. This was entirely on him. And because of that, Molly was fighting for her life.

But there was something else—another matter that was now plaguing him—a more shameful one. He had not only discovered his role and responsibility in *this* tragedy but in his wife's death as well. He had realized it as soon as he told Molly that he wanted to put their celebration off until "tomorrow."

He remembered thinking similarly when he decided he would discuss Erica's death with Jessica "tomorrow." He owed her that. But he never expressed it in words and tomorrow never came. His reluctance cost his wife her life. Now this. It was another failed lesson and squandered repeat of history.

At the hospital, they rushed her into a surgical unit. It was nearly ten o'clock. They had to phone the surgeon on call, whom, Noah was told, lived less than ten minutes away. They needed that time anyway for triage, x-rays and to control the bleeding.

Noah had no idea what her blood type was or what medications, if any, she was taking, and was barely helpful with personal history. The nurse pointed him to the waiting room where he was asked to fill out the admittance and insurance forms. All he could offer was her name, address and phone number. He was not aware of any health insurance or whether or not she carried a card. He never noticed a wallet. At the restaurant, he thought he saw her pull her Visa from her back pocket. He could not believe that after spending so much time with her the past month, he hardly knew anything about her.

He thought about calling Pete Benson and Roz Harris, both of whom had worked with her before to see if they knew anything or even whom to contact as far as Molly's family was concerned. In desperation, he called Mindy Russell, who said she would make some calls and meet him there as soon as she could. Noah asked her to be discreet.

While he waited for Jerry and Mindy, the two police officers on the scene found Noah in the waiting room holding a cup of black coffee. He was just staring into it. It was going to be a long night. Noah answered their questions as best he could and texted one of them the picture he had taken of the car.

"Had to be going sixty," said Noah. "Maybe seventy."

"We'll have a better idea of his speed from the skid marks," said the tall one with a slight lisp.

"Can you read the plates from the picture?" asked Noah.

"We'll look at it at the station. We have software we use to clean it up. It's a good lead." They thanked him for his help and told him they would be in touch.

Fifteen minutes later, Jerry showed up carrying Molly's file with whatever personal, medical and insurance information she had given him. After Jerry gave the hospital what they needed, he marched Noah to a corner of the waiting room. It was pretty empty, a slow night. Not slow enough as far as Noah was concerned.

He gave Jerry a rundown of the past hour and admitted it was all his fault.

"Sounds like the driver of that car is the culprit," said Jerry. "I hope they catch the bastard."

Noah sat there staring at the floor. "It all happened so quickly. I still can't believe it."

Jerry put a hand on his shoulder. "Stop kicking yourself. I'm sure they have good doctors here and Molly's going to get the best possible care. She'll pull through this."

Noah sat up, swallowed, and nodded in agreement.

"We need to make decisions, pal," Jerry told him, "and I need your help. Have you had any time to think about how we're going to fix this?"

Just then, Noah spotted Mindy coming towards them. The two men rose. She walked up to Noah and gave him a long, heartfelt hug. "Oh my God," said Mindy, shaken. "Any news?"

"She's still in surgery. I think it's going to be a while."

She gave Jerry a hug. "I can't believe she was hit by a car on the night before we open. This is a disaster."

Noah wasn't interested in prophecies. "What did you find out?" he asked.

Mindy caught her breath. "Molly's mother lives in Georgia. Her dad passed away a few years ago. I was told there's a brother but couldn't get anything on him. I wasn't able to reach her mom but left a message."

Jerry stepped in. "Thank you, Mindy. Would you please give the hospital whatever contact numbers you have and please text them to me. Then I'd like you to go home."

"What?"

"I need you to get your rest tonight. Sorry. Tomorrow's going to be a long day."

Mindy looked to Noah for help.

"He's right," Noah told her. "You need to get your rest. Nothing more you can do here. We're just going to be sitting around, waiting. I promise I'll call you if anything changes. Please. Go home. And thanks for your help."

Mindy nodded without another word.

After she left, they took their seats. "I'm sorry I've got to be the bad guy here, Noah, but I need you to concentrate." Noah knew they were compelled to make some hard decisions about the show. "Assuming Molly won't be able to make the opening tomorrow," said Jerry, "we'll need a Plan B. Who's the best person to fill her spot?"

Noah took a deep breath and considered his options. René Powell, who played Charlie's girlfriend, Stacy, was Molly's number one understudy and the best choice for taking over the role. She had been there from the beginning and had played Wendy's character several times during breaks and once when Noah wanted to get a different read on a scene. Noah was not positive but thought she knew the lines. Most of them anyway. That would leave Linda Hart, the extra, to take over René's role as Stacy.

"We're going to need several walkthrough rehearsals tomorrow," said Jerry. "We'll only work on Wendy and Stacy's scenes. No costumes. We'll have René bring her own outfits. We'll start at ten and finish no later than two. That will give everyone a few hours to relax before the open. I'll call Roz and get the ball rolling. She'll get the word out. Would you call René and Linda and give them the news? I think it should come from you."

Noah's head was spinning but he did what he was told. He was relieved that Jerry was at the helm making decisions because he was in no condition. Ostensibly, Noah was still in control but inside he was completely flustered—like a surging tsunami against a pile of sandbags—and there was little holding him together.

He called René and explained what happened. She was heartbroken to hear about Molly but assured Noah she would do her best to know her lines. Then he called Linda. After that, he dialed Bobby to inform him of the situation. He would need to be on script tomorrow backstage to feed René lines if she needed them during the rehearsals and the show. Too much at stake now. It was critical that the opening go well to bring in the audience. The timing could not have been worse.

Around midnight, Dr. Stuart Millenberg came by to update them on Molly's condition. Said there were several broken bones in her left leg, three cracked ribs, and some internal bleeding, which was under control, but no major organ damage. She was going to be in the hospital for at least two weeks, maybe longer, and then another four to six months in physical therapy. When it was over, she may have a small limp but he thought she was going to pull through okay. Noah asked if he could see her but the doctor said she would be asleep for several hours. Best to come back in the morning.

Jerry and Noah stood as still as two marble statues in the Borghese Gallery following the doctor's departure down the hallway.

Jerry took a breath coming to life. "Guess we'll be going with Plan B, huh?" He turned to Noah. "You okay?"

Noah stood there transfixed. "Could have been worse. Right?"

"Absolutely. Sounds like she's going to be fine."

Noah dropped his head. Jerry placed his arms around him and patted him on his back. "She's going to be okay, Noah. You'll see."

"It's all my fault."

Jerry grabbed Noah's upper arms and held him at a distance. "That's enough of that, pal. It was an accident that you didn't cause. Really, Noah. You can save what you have to say for Molly but right now I need you to get a hold of yourself. We have a big day tomorrow and you need to be on top of your game if we're going to get through this in one piece. *Please.*"

Noah looked him in the eye. "You're right. I need to focus. I got it."

Jerry watched him. "Why don't you follow me home and we'll get some rest? We're both going to need it. You want to stay at my place tonight?"

"Thanks, no. I'll be all right."

He shook his head in no certain direction and walked away. "I'll meet you outside," he called back. "Just want to find out about visiting hours."

Jerry waited by the front door so they could walk out together.

At ten after one in the morning, Noah flopped into bed after a quick shower. He let out a big yawn. Tomorrow was going to be the longest day of the year. Maybe of his life.

He was asleep in less than five minutes.

33
Cosmic Coincidence

⌘

There was no note. No answers. No explanation. No clues. My wife never told me why she took her life three weeks after our daughter drowned.

I didn't think that was right. I mean, if you are going to kill yourself, the least you could do is leave a note behind for your husband to help him through the ordeal. I guess there was no sentimental obligation, no "early withdrawal" language, no mandatory small print in the marriage certificate that compelled you to explain why you were checking out prematurely.

Unless, of course, your intention was to drive him insane.

After Jessie's funeral, I decided to go back to work. I needed to get into a routine and sitting home alone staring at nostalgic family photos on the walls was not my idea of a healthy lifestyle. Overnight, our house had been transformed into a prison cell and living there was beginning to feel like some kind of solitary confinement.

I wanted to stay busy, proactive, do something that felt normal again. But Barney would not have it. He and Dee Dee and a couple of other friends sat me down and made it clear that I needed to talk to someone, get my feelings out and resolve the guilt. And the pain. And the anger and grief, and any other hazardous emotions that might be lying dormant, waiting to rise up and revolt like a French Revolutionary mob on Bastille Day.

They suggested I go to the place. That's how I referred to it: "the place." It was upstate somewhere—I never bothered to know any more than that—and everyone who was anyone in my life agreed that it was best for me. I was in no condition to debate and, frankly, would have taken an elevator down to the depths of hell if that was the only option out of my house. Not ready to accept that I was now utterly alone in the world. So I packed a bag and went.

I was told I could stay as long as I wanted, similar to the old Catskill Mountains hotels—Grossingers, Kutshers, The Concord—an all-inclusive resort where you paid by the week, thanks to my decent health insurance. There was no time limit or locked doors, at least not for me because I was voluntary. I could come and go as I please unless they thought I presented a danger to myself or to someone else.

In the end I decided I had to survive this for no other reason than to keep Jessica's and Erica's memories alive and to try and make sense of what happened. Otherwise, with all three of us gone, it would have been one of those pathetic tragedies that nobody ever wanted to talk about, only write about in a bestselling novel that somehow winds up in the psychological thriller genre section. I could not have that. I loved them too much to give up on them, to have us remembered in that way.

The property was in the middle of nowhere. Nothing for miles. I'm not even sure it was part of any town. The gated estate was exquisitely landscaped like a grand villa in Tuscany with cypress trees, flowering bushes and fountains. Classical sculptures and teak benches stood beside the pathway leading to the private garden so you could sit, meditate, and take it all in.

Some affluent family, trying to make a name for themselves, had left all their money to a trust fund and persuaded their wealthy acquaintances to donate as well. A bronze plaque at the entrance to the main building told their story and the benches were all inscribed with supporters' names.

The place was surrounded by a forest with a hiking path that included streams and ponds for fishing if you bothered to bring your rod. Morning aerobic and tai chi classes were available on the grounds outside, ongoing volleyball and basketball games throughout the day, and plenty of other things to keep you busy. The place really was comfortable.

We were free to spend the day as we pleased with only one stipulation—a one-hour counseling session each day—either one-on-one or in a group setting. I wasn't ready to discuss anything with anyone, certainly not in front of a group, so I opted for a private therapist session at four in the afternoon.

My doctor's name was Gideon and I would have to say we hit it off pretty well. He wasn't pushy like some shrinks who try to force you to see things their way, or disengaging like others who refuse to say a word and expect you to figure it all out yourself. Gideon was somewhere in-between. He had been apprised of my situation and, for the first couple of weeks at least, was consoling and supportive. We stayed away from discussing my feelings, just sort of skimmed the surface so that he could get to know me better with background and details of my life.

By the third week, Gideon was urging me to open up and talk more about my relationship with my wife and daughter. That is when it got tough. And even though I was aware of how important it was to discuss them, I still wasn't up to the task. The trauma of losing my daughter, then my wife checking out without any explanation, had left me empty inside. No, not empty exactly. More hard rock, a cement block, like one of those statues outside. That was closer to how I was feeling at the time and it would have taken some sort of cathartic sledgehammer to break through.

That is where Gideon came in. Instead of describing the cause and effect of what I was feeling or formulating a complete breakdown of the emotional and psychological correlations involved, he instead offered a more simplistic approach. He asked me merely to discuss what was on my mind. What was I thinking? That is all he expected of me. He anticipated that eventually my mind would make the connection and we'd be able to delve deeper into the heart of the matter. But the pain and anger that ravaged me at the time and left me feeling abandoned was too much to bear. Or talk about.

Over the six-and-a-half-weeks I was a resident, there was no psychological progress in any of my personality traits or disorders that would have left Sigmund Freud smirking on the sidelines; no pages to bookmark in his textbook to delineate the distinctions between my conscious and unconscious minds. Gideon did not fix me or give me a better understanding of myself and how to move forward or even sideways to circumvent what now felt like a meaningless existence. I did not leave feeling more confident that there was any kind of behavioral breakthrough or that I was now more prepared to step out and face the world again.

But something did happen that gave me some peace of mind and a little hope. It occurred my last night there. I had gone out for a walk after dinner. It was still light when I left and I stayed on the path so I could find my way back. I had a lot on my mind as I strolled the countryside and failed to pay attention to the direction I was heading. I guess you could say I was lost. Rather than continue, I stopped in an open field with a full view of the evening sky and laid down on the grass. The colors at dusk were magnificent and, for the moment, I was content.

I thought about Jessica and Erica and wondered where they were. Was there an afterlife? Were they together? I asked God to give me some sort of a sign that they were all right. That's all I wanted—to know that my wife and daughter were in a good place—that they were safe and looking out for one another. That's all I needed. That's all it would take to make it a little easier to go on without them.

I did not expect an answer but asked anyway for the hell of it. I had never asked Him for anything before and figured maybe He, too, was taking a walk in His garden at that moment and happened to notice me. And if He did, perhaps He would have pity for a guy whose life had been turned upside down and inside out and was struggling to make sense of it.

Then I saw it—well, I saw something—just above the horizon, a tiny light moving from twilight to darkness. I blinked to make sure there was nothing in my eye. I was not even convinced I'd seen anything. Then it happened again. It shot across the sky like the Starship Enterprise at warp speed and then it was gone; a pinpoint of light racing across the universe. Fast. I must have watched it ten times before it dawned on me—a meteor shower—with one blaze of light after another shooting through the cold dark universe billions of miles away.

Was it possible? Was that it? My sign from the Big Guy?

Incredible as it seemed, I figured this had to be the answer to my prayers. I mean, it was a cosmic event timed perfectly, like I had dialed God's private number and He actually picked up and talked to me. Not like I was sitting around for years or months or even hours waiting for something to happen. It was asked and answered without delay. One sign requested, one sign delivered in real time. *When does that ever happen?*

I did not even mind if it was the night of the Perseid or Orionid Meteor Showers. It could have just been a cosmic coincidence for all I cared.

I laid there watching until there was no more movement. The heavenly window had apparently closed and the sky turned black, the light turned off. I closed my eyes and thanked Him, my gratitude overwhelming. It was like being handed a lottery ticket on your birthday and you wind up having the winning numbers.

So many emotions were running through me I did not know if I was laughing, crying or dreaming. I had just had a one-on-one conversation with God. *The* God. *The one-and-only God.* With that incredible display, He not only answered my questions about Jessie and Erica, but also let me know that He was looking out for us. All of us. And it was okay to go on, that life had meaning, and there was a reason to look forward to tomorrow.

What an amazing feeling overcame me at that moment—bundled with warmth, love and hope—like nothing I had ever felt before or would ever feel again. But it was all right because at least I got to touch it. Once.

You can't buy that in your neighborhood bodega.

When I looked again, I found myself staring at a breathtaking sight. Stars were everywhere—more than I ever imagined—just me and a billion stellar points of light. I could even make out some of the constellations. Eventually, I was able to pull myself away and follow the North Star, which helped lead me back to "the place."

I sensed that the realization of what had just occurred had helped me somehow, like it had struck a nerve, perhaps started a crack in that cement block inside me.

I decided then that I was ready to go home, that this one event—this one magical moment—was more than I expected to find here and more than enough to give me hope for what lay ahead. The fear had drained out of me.

Jessica and Erica were safe. God was looking after them. And me, as well. And while my heart was still shattered because I missed them so much, I decided that somehow I had found the courage to live with that.

34
Bells, Beeps And Buzzers

Noah woke early on Wednesday after a rough night. He kept waking, rising, reliving the accident, and falling back onto his pillow, missing out on some much needed REM sleep. He knew he was going to be busy all day and wanted to see Molly before the day got away from him.

He grabbed a strawberry Pop Tart and hurried out to his car. He had just over an hour-and-a-half to drive to the hospital, see Molly and get to the theater. On his way, he called Roz to make sure everyone had been notified about the emergency rehearsal and asked how they had handled the news. She assured him that the team was behind him and up for the challenge, and of course were upset to hear about Molly.

He asked her what she thought about René taking over Wendy's role.

"She's a good actress," said Roz tactfully. "She'll be fine. The only question is: can she learn all her lines in a day?"

Noah mentioned that Bobby would be backstage feeding her lines if she needed them.

"Do you think he's the best choice?" she questioned.

"I think so," said Noah. "He's been doing it up 'til now. I don't see why we'd change it."

"I know," she said. "But it's a timing issue. He'll have to be on top of every line and feed it to her so it appears natural."

Noah evaluated her concern. "Do you think there's someone better qualified to handle it?"

"I do," she told him, stopping there.

Noah waited. "Well, don't keep me in suspense. Who do you have in mind?"

"You."

"Me? Why me?"

She chuckled at his surprise. "Noah, you wrote the damn script. You know the timing of each scene. If you're asking my opinion, I think you're the best person for the job."

Noah pulled into the hospital parking lot. "I'm at the hospital."

"Tell Molly we all send our love."

"I will. And Roz …"

"Yeah?"

"I'll consider your suggestion."

"See you later."

He stopped at the ground-floor gift shop and bought a pretty summer bouquet with a miniature teddy bear hanging from the vase. While he waited for his credit card to go through, he signed the card "Love, Noah." Then, aware that others would see it, he ripped it up and grabbed another card. "We're all pulling for you. Feel better, Noah." He made his way to the main desk to find out her room number and took the staircase up to the second floor.

Molly was in a bed by a window in the Intensive Care Unit. She appeared to be asleep. A nurse, who looked as though she might still be attending high school, had just finished checking her IV as he walked in. He counted five beds in the room with only three occupied.

"How's Molly? Molly Talbert?" asked Noah, as he approached her.

The RN turned but did not respond until she had given him the once over. "Stable," she said in a curt almost dismissive manner. "Blood pressure, heart rate, breathing, all normal."

"Is she asleep?"

"On and off since I've been on duty."

"Is the doctor available?"

Noah had apparently reached his limit. She whisked past him. "We're changing shifts."

"Thank you," he said as she exited the room.

Noah placed the vase on the windowsill and slid a chair closer to her bed. He peeked out of the window beyond the shade but all he could see was a parking lot and a drab overcast day. He noticed a disinfectant odor in the air though it was not as pronounced as other hospitals he had visited. The room was quiet and, at that time, there were no other family members there.

He sat down next to her and noticed her hand. An IV was plugged into the back of her right hand with a finger monitor keeping track of her heart rate or temperature or whatever it was designed to keep track of. A blood pressure monitor was wrapped around her upper left arm that continued to inflate every few minutes, sending new numbers to the tote board above her head. An ensemble of dissonant sounds—bells, beeps and buzzers—played throughout the room as if the band conductor had just given up and left the stage.

Noah checked his phone. He had about twenty minutes before he had to leave. He leaned in close, looking past the scrapes and bruises. She was so beautiful. "Molly?" he murmured in a tender voice lacking the courage to wake her. Nothing. "Molly, can you hear me? It's Noah."

He saw her face begin to twitch and fidget. Once more he repeated her name. Her eyes opened and he watched as they came into focus. She moaned softly when she saw him though he wasn't sure if it was from pain or she was just glad to see him.

Her tenuous smile was enough. He took her idle hand in his and clasped his other one over it. "That's okay," he said. "I'll do the talking for both of us." He told her that everyone was concerned about her and sent their love. "I'm sure you'll be seeing them in the next few days." He mentioned that Mindy and Jerry had been to the hospital last night.

Then Noah turned serious and delved deeper. He swallowed and considered his words. "I am so sorry about last night," he said, his voice cracking. "For upsetting you like that. I had no right to take you for granted and treat you the way I did. It was all my fault."

His voice was soft and tender. While he spoke his eyes welled up.

"I was feeling guilty when I saw Dee. It was childish of me, I know, and it shouldn't have affected our plans. But I let it. And I am so sorry I overreacted and upset you."

She managed to raise her hand, touching his lips, and shake her head sluggishly. He smiled at her gently and kissed her hand, his eyes never veering from hers.

They sat that way until a male nurse interrupted them, explaining that the doctor had ordered an MRI. He told Noah she would be back in about twenty-five minutes. Noah stood and moved away from the bed, staying within her field of view.

"I have to go anyway," he told them. "But I'll check in on you later." He waited while the nurse unplugged Molly from her monitors and rolled her bed out of the room.

Before opening the door of his Rogue for what he knew was going to be a difficult day, Noah raised his head towards the sky. "Thank you," he said. Then he added a silent prayer before getting in and driving off.

35
Showtime
〜◦◦〜

When Noah arrived at the theater, everyone was already there, anxious to hear about Molly. He assured them that she was resting comfortably and was going to be okay and that she probably would not be back in time before the show closed so this was the lineup they were going with. He thanked everyone for their understanding and asked them to please stay focused on what they had to do today.

He told them they were going to run through all of Wendy's scenes without costume changes and Stacy's two scenes until everyone was comfortable. He assured René that Bobby was on book and would feed her lines if she needed them.

"We've come a long way together the last few weeks," said Noah. "I'm sure we all feel thrown by Molly's accident but this is live theater and these are the cards we've been dealt. We can fold our hand and give up, or do our best and make it work. If we all put our minds to it, I'm confident it's all going to work out in the end. But it starts with today. Today is the most important day of the entire run and will determine the next few weeks what with our opening tonight and the media on its way."

He looked around the room taking his time. "Don't do it for me. But if you need extra motivation think about how far you've come as a professional actor and how sometimes in life we're thrown curves and have to deal with them, have to rise to the occasion. Don't do it for me, or even for yourself. How about we make a pledge that we're doing this for Molly. Let's do it for her and make her proud. She probably feels like she's let us down by not being here today. I would rather she not feel responsible for something that was out of her control. Do you agree? Let's not let Molly down."

He hesitated there, a bit emotional. "I promise that ten, twenty years from now when you look back on this day, you'll know that you didn't allow adversity to get the best of you. You can look yourself in the mirror and say 'we did our best that day as an ensemble and made it work.'"

Noah still had more to say but hesitated, and before he said another word, someone started to applaud. Then another followed suit and before long everyone was up on their feet giving themselves a standing ovation. There were tears too. Then the hugging began—everyone either needed one or the moment just seemed to lend itself to it—and Noah was encouraged he had gotten through to them.

"Let's go to work," he announced to the room and everyone headed for the stage with a new confidence.

Following the group out the door, he saw Jerry, who had been standing in the back of the room. Jerry just smiled and nodded his head and Noah realized his friend was as touched as everyone else. Then Jerry gave Noah a big bear hug he was not expecting. "Go get 'em," he whispered.

On his way to the stage, Roz stepped in line with him.

"I want Bobby to handle the lines," he decided. "I talked to him about timing and I'm confident he'll be fine. Besides, I need to be out front to watch the action."

Roz nodded accepting his decision. "That was a good speech," she told him. "Just what we needed." He thanked her for the kind words.

They spent the next four hours going over each scene Wendy's character appeared in. René had learned her lines well and only needed help a couple of times that morning. She told Noah that she and Bobby would spend the rest of the afternoon running lines until she had it down cold.

When they were done, they rehearsed the two scenes with Stacy's character and Linda, too, did a more than adequate job. Noah reminded her that Bobby would be in the wings with the script during the show if she wanted help and Linda assured him that would not be necessary.

True professionals. He had picked them well. Noah was relieved he had insisted on having two extra actors at every rehearsal. He recalled that when Peter was running the show, paying a couple of extra actors to sit around all day in the early stages was not a priority for him and Noah wondered where they would be today if the situation had not changed.

Mindy, Wayne, Susan, and Will mentioned they were going to visit Molly after the rehearsal so Noah decided he would return to the hospital after the performance that night, hopefully with good news that would set her mind at ease. When he got to his car, he noticed that the cloudy sky he'd observed from Molly's hospital window that morning had dissipated and left a beautiful August afternoon in its place. Before heading back to relax for a couple of hours, he stopped at Sandy Neck Beach. He was in the mood for a swim even though the water was still too cold for his taste. He jumped in anyway and it invigorated him. Then he went home for a shower and a quick nap.

He returned to the theater at 5:45 p.m. Before the house opened to the press, Noah checked in with Bobby, Roz and the tech and stage crew, then chatted with the actors backstage. Everyone appeared focused and ready for the opening. He made it a point to talk to René to see how she was doing and was gratified to find she was as confident as ever.

Mindy mentioned that Molly was feeling better and was pleased they had stopped by. When they left her room, Molly told them to "break a leg," then changed her mind saying she had already taken care of it. Noah was glad to hear she had not lost her sense of humor.

Jerry, Noah, the cast, and a couple of the celebrities Jerry had invited were available to greet the media for interviews. The turnout was encouraging. Noah understood how crucial a positive review was for the health of a production. A show lived or died by it. He knew this because he did it for a living and it did not matter if it was New York and the Associated Press or Massachusetts and the *Cape Cod Times.*

They discussed how they were going to handle the news of Molly's accident. This was not the kind of publicity they were after and they feared the media could use it as an alibi to disparage the production. Jerry had had the theater send out a press release that morning acknowledging the cast changes to help mitigate the likely stunned reactions.

They also were aware how important it was to stay upbeat for their interviews. "We were all deeply shocked by Molly Talbert's unfortunate accident last night," explained Jerry to a *Times'* reporter, "but her doctors have assured us that she's going to come through this okay."

Noah, too, made sure he remained optimistic. "We have an incredibly talented cast who have worked extremely hard and pulled together under very difficult circumstances," he told one of the local radio stations. "In this business, as you know, the bottom line is 'the show must go on,' and there was never a doubt with this group. We believe the audience is in for a treat."

While there was nothing Jerry could do about the printed theater programs being distributed, he did have the staff insert a page acknowledging the revised cast. He also had the billing changed on the marquee to reflect the modifications. The last thing he wanted was for it to appear as if René and Linda were stand-in replacements for this performance only.

Later, after the party broke up and the house had opened, Noah made his way to the back of the theater and bumped into Peter Benson.

"Miller," said Peter.

"Benson," he reciprocated.

"Sorry to hear about Molly."

Noah suppressed a response, staring at him coldly.

Then Peter smirked. "Bet you wish I was still running things, huh?"

All he was missing was a baseball bat, thought Noah. He considered taking the high road. Brushing past him, Noah smiled. "Fuck you, Peter." That felt so much better.

Opening night. This was it, everything Noah had worked towards since taking a leave from his job, moving up to the Cape, usurping the director post, and getting the show ready for the stage. Showtime. He found an empty spot behind the center orchestra seats, his preferred place to view the action. He leaned against the padded back wall, a prime vantage point to gauge the audience's response.

With all the excitement of the past twenty-four hours, Noah surprised himself with his mood and mindset. He was not nervous. Too much had happened in the past six weeks—in the past twelve months—to rile him now. He was proud of his own composure, mostly because, at that moment, he was thinking about Molly. Her recovery was more important than the show and he could hardly wait for this to be over so he could go see her.

Jerry came out on stage—it was a full house after all—to thank everyone for coming. He had done it a thousand times. "One final note before we begin," he said, his voice wavering just enough for Noah to pick up on it. Then he went off script. "Some of you may be aware that last night, Molly Talbert, who was supposed to play the female lead in our show, was in a car accident." A startled wave circulated through the crowd. Noah's heart missed a beat. "She's going to be okay but, unfortunately, will not be able to resume her role." Visibly shaken, Jerry took his time. "The cast, crew and everyone here at the Cape Playhouse would like to dedicate tonight's performance to Molly. We wish her a speedy recovery and look forward to seeing her again back on our stage. Thank you."

The spotlight remained on center stage after Jerry's exit. Noah suspected this was done deliberately to allow the audience to give Molly a tempered ovation—they did—but more to give the company time to compose itself.

After a moment, the spotlight slowly faded out. Then, James Taylor's *Fire and Rain* began playing throughout the darkened theater. The curtain was pulled and scene one began.

36
Facing The Enemy

T he next day, Noah stopped off at Jerry's house before heading to the hospital. He wanted to thank him for his opening remarks. He did not get a chance to talk to him or anyone because he had rushed out to see Molly after the show; just after Wayne and Mindy escorted René downstage for an exclusive curtain call in which she received a standing ovation. The entire company joined the audience, moved by the remarkable effort she had made on their behalf. It was a touching moment that affected everyone who attended and a perfect ending to an emotional evening.

"You inspired me," said Jerry, sitting in a bathrobe by the pool with his morning coffee, a satisfied look on his face. "Believe me, I only thought of it after your little talk at yesterday's rehearsal. Before that I had no plans to say a word about it."

"It was very sweet," Noah told him.

"Well, take some of the credit," Jerry insisted, pouring him a mug of French Roast coffee with a hint of hazelnut. "What can I say? We make a good team."

Noah mixed in a little sugar and stirred. "I think you put the audience in just the right mood."

Jerry passed him the milk. "I did more than that, my friend. The reviews are in. Care to hear them?"

"Not particularly."

Jerry opened the Apple MacBook next to him. "Like hell you don't." Then he gave him a rundown of several of the better critiques. "And here's the one from the *Times:*"

> *There was not a dry eye in the house, partly because of the emotional strings that were played but mainly because of the hilarious lines and predicament presented in Noah Miller's romantic comedy,* Committed, *which opened last night at The Cape Playhouse. This is a show that must be seen by anyone who has ever been in a relationship. Even if you have never been, you should still go simply for its clever dialogue and heartwarming message...*

"We're a hit," boasted Jerry. "Tickets started selling at the bell this morning and haven't let up yet. This is good. This is *very* good."

Noah appeared unimpressed. "Glad to hear it."

Jerry was elated. "I've got three interviews lined up for us today plus the NBC affiliate station. They want us both down there at 5 p.m. in time for the evening news."

"I don't think so," said Noah.

Jerry did not say a word, just looked at him with an expression you might find on a first-time crook who had been nabbed by waiting cops.

"Sorry, pal," Noah added.

"What do you mean 'sorry pal?' This is the payoff. What we live for. What we hope for. The Baked Alaska!"

"Huh?" replied Noah, confused.

"The icing on the cake. It's called success. It could put your writing career back on the map."

Noah waited for a break in the discourse. "Would you mind handling the interviews for me?" He finished off his coffee and stood up. "And I've never heard anyone use 'Baked Alaska' that way."

"*What?!* What did you say?!"

Noah stepped away from the table. "I'm sorry to do this to you, Jer, but I'm pulling rank. As my manager, I need you to handle this. Believe me, in my current state of mind, you're the best man for the job. I mean that sincerely. I've got nothing left."

Jerry stepped towards him. "Look, I understand how you feel but, as your friend and manager, I'm telling you, don't do this. Don't walk out on success. You never know when it'll come knocking again."

Noah smiled. "Thanks for understanding, pal."

Jerry refused to leave it there. "I think you're making a big mistake."

Noah headed into the house. "See you around."

"Wait a second," Jerry called after him. "You didn't eat anything. I've got lox and bagels. Who walks out on lox and bagels? You want to walk out on success? Fine! But no one walks out on my lox and bagels!"

Noah spent most of the day in the hospital with Molly. She was sitting up when Noah arrived to an inviting smile he had not seen in a couple of days and was encouraged by her appearance and attitude. The color in her face was almost back to normal. He was curious to know how she slept and whether she had been informed of any updates on her condition.

But all Molly wanted to talk about was the show. Noah had already mentioned Jerry's tribute to her, René's performance and the overall audience reaction when he saw her last night. She had been relieved to hear that René came through and the show went off well. Now she wanted a rundown of the reviews. Noah gave her what she wanted and also mentioned the added interest for additional interviews.

"Maybe Jerry's right," she said. "I mean, it'll certainly give you more exposure and you never know who might be listening. I think you should reconsider."

"I'm tired," he told her. "Physically and emotionally drained. I don't think I could even fake a good interview today."

"Oh, I don't know" she told him, her eyes lighting up. "I think there's an actor in there somewhere."

Noah just grimaced and shook his head.

"Seriously, Noah, this is your moment. Don't throw it away."

He looked up at the dotted ceiling panels and sighed. "I'll think about it."

They spent the day working on a crossword from a book Mindy had brought, and after, he read to her from a bestselling thriller he found on her nightstand. With more persistence from Molly, he agreed to meet

Jerry at the studio later. Before leaving, he asked if there was anything she needed.

"Just you," she told him, her eyes twinkling.

He sat on her bed and kissed her gently.

"Are you going back to the theater tonight?" she asked.

"I'll stop by for the first act, at least. I know Jerry plans to be there later."

"I hope *I* get to see it before it closes."

"Me too." He considered that. "Of course, tickets *are* selling fast. Do you know anyone with connections?"

She laughed at that and kissed him again until they were interrupted by her dinner.

"Mmmm," said Noah, uncovering the platter. "Looks delish."

"Would you like to help me eat it?"

"Love to. But I've got an interview, remember?"

"Then scoot. You don't want to be late."

Later, after leaving the television studio with Jerry, Noah was in his backyard having a quick bite before getting ready for the theater. The interview had gone well and he was glad he had relented. It could only help sell more tickets and, who knows, maybe help him with his career.

Noah heard someone at the door and ran inside to open it. "Dee Dee, what a pleasant surprise. How are you?"

They exchanged hugs and she followed him out to the backyard.

"I didn't get a chance to tell you how much we enjoyed your play. Must have missed you after the show."

"Sorry," said Noah. "I ran out of there pretty fast to get back to the hospital."

"I'm so sorry to hear about Molly. How's she doing?"

"Much better, thank you. I spent the day with her. Pretty banged up but the doctors feel she's going to come out of this all right. A *full* recovery."

"I can't imagine what you've been through," she went on, "and how you found another actor on such short notice. She was amazing. The entire cast was amazing. And the show was wonderful, even better than the first time. Congratulations!"

"Thanks. I appreciate that. It was touch and go there for awhile but everyone came through."

She asked him if she could stay a few minutes and they sat at the table. He offered her a glass of red wine from the other night.

"Definitely. I never turn down a glass of wine."

She was quiet after that and Noah noticed an odd look about her. "Something on your mind, Dee?"

She gulped down her drink in a hurry. "I have something for you."

Dee Dee opened a dark purse on her lap, removed a small beige envelope and handed it to him. This time she met his gaze. "It's from Jessica."

He took his time examining it. "I don't understand. Why you giving this to me now?"

She breathed in deeply before replying. "Those were her wishes."

He shook his head, not fully comprehending. *"What?"*

She touched his hand to give them both strength. "The night she … died, I was at your house."

Noah affirmed the memory with a nod.

"She called and asked me to come over. She was pretty distraught when I got there but we talked for awhile and she seemed a little better by the time I left." She stopped there momentarily, taking a superfluous sip from her empty glass. "Before I left, she handed me that envelope and told me that if anything happened to her, I should give it to you on the one-year anniversary of her death."

Noah jumped to his feet, livid. "You waited an entire year to give me this?"

He waited for her reaction.

"Noah, please. I'm sorry."

Then his anger surged like a breached dam. "Do you have any idea what I've been through?"

He moved about the room. "I was lost. No answers. No reasons. My sanity in question. *Are you kidding me?*"

She was prepared for his resentment. "I understand. Noah, please, I'm sorry. I don't blame you for being angry. Really. I'm truly sorry. But these were Jessie's wishes. I was only doing what she asked of me."

He sat down, deflated. The tension in the room was suffocating. He tried to control his emotions. "You knew she was going to kill herself and didn't say a word to anyone?"

"I didn't know anything, I swear. I asked her if that was her intention and she promised me it wasn't."

"And you believed her?"

She poured what was left from the bottle. "I didn't know what to believe. She said she was feeling better, more like herself, and I believed that because that's what I wanted to believe."

Noah peeked at the envelope and back at Dee. "So why the note? And why did she ask you to wait?"

She was beginning to whimper now, flustered. The emotional confrontation had unsettled her. "She didn't tell me anything else. Just asked me to give it to you. It's a few days early, I know, but we're leaving tomorrow and I wanted to make sure you got it. I swear Noah, I didn't know what it was. I thought it might be a password or an account number she wanted you to have. For all I know, that's all it is."

Noah shook his head. "So why wait a year to deliver it?"

Dee Dee did not respond.

After she finished her wine, she tried one last time to convince him. "She asked me not to read it. That was the hard part. I picked it up a thousand times, but in the end I respected her wishes. Because ... I had given my word."

Noah assessed his wife's closest friend trying to unravel the truth. She was the last person Jessie had opened up to before ....

He watched her. She was clearly upset.

When nothing more was said, she stood and headed for the door. He followed listlessly. She gave him a sympathetic hug and kiss on the cheek but he was too rattled to reciprocate. "I'm so sorry, Noah."

They stood in the doorway, peering at one another until the quiet was disturbed. "Why a year?" he said, still shaking his head.

"Perhaps," she told him, as tactfully as a surgeon delivering bad news, "the answer is in your hand."

He forced a smile out of courtesy. Then she left.

He went back into the house and found his seat in the parlor. He turned on the lamp beside the leather chair and held the envelope up, dreading what was inside. An explanation? An accusation? A confession? His stomach began to grind and he noticed his hand was shaking.

Sitting there wondering what was inside—and what prompted her to wait an entire year to have it delivered—he could feel his heart bumping up against the wall of his chest. He felt warm and started to sweat. For a moment he thought he might pass out. He looked at the envelope in his hand. All these thoughts and memories ran through his head but there was no one there to answer his questions. He was desperate to know what was inside but alarmed as well, almost too terrified to find out. Right now he was surviving without any insight of why she did what she did. But that was about to change and he would have to live with that knowledge forever. Surrendering to fate, he decided to open it and face the enemy he feared most.

He used a pocket knife to slit open the top and carefully extracted the textured rice paper. He removed several pages, detecting the scent of her favorite perfume. *J'Adore.* She was setting him up. Seducing him. Pure Jessie. He unfolded them, immediately recognizing her handwriting, then leaned back in his chair and brought his leg across his knee. He inhaled the aroma to calm his nerves and sense her presence beside him.

Noah never made it to the theater that night.

37
Dagger Of Blame

Darling Noah,

As I sit here writing this, my hand trembles and my heart has been ripped to shreds and I am grieving not only for our beloved daughter but for you, my love, as well.

Please know that I do not wish to leave you. I love you with all my heart and am hoping by the time you get through this you will better understand why I am compelled to carry out this most egregious and unforgiveable act.

Please pardon my delay in getting this to you. Knowing you as I do, I thought it would be wiser to wait. I'm not certain that you would fully comprehend my reasons if you had received this note together with the news of my death.

I want you to be in a better place and hope now that you've had some time and distance from what must have been the most distressing and painful period of your life, I pray that you are of a more sound mind to hear what I have to say.

For as long as I can remember, it has always been my dream to have a child of my own. I knew early on that no matter who I wound up with, that would always be my number one priority. It wasn't an easy journey for us but we persevered and found a way to make it happen and I am so grateful it was with you.

The happiest day of my life was the day our Erica was born. She was the most beautiful baby I'd ever seen and to know she came from you and me made it all the more special. I cherished our four incredible years together. Every milestone. Every memory. Every treasured moment.

She was a precious little girl in so many ways and I loved everything about her. I loved her laugh and her mind and the way she'd look at you when she didn't understand something and the wonder in her eyes when it began to make sense.

It made me alive inside to be with her and there was nothing I wanted more than to spend the rest of my life knowing you were both with me.

When our darling Erica passed away a few weeks ago, something inside me died with her. I've been trying to rid myself of my demons but can't seem to overcome the depression that has ravaged me. And I'm not sure I ever will.

No matter what help I receive, the fact remains that our little Erica is gone forever and I will never be able to look at her and tell her how much I love her ever again.

I know that you've been suffering with the trauma of our loss and it's been a most challenging time for you as well. I had hoped that we would find strength in each other to get through this but I know now that even if we were able to overcome our struggle and move on, it would still be without Erica.

And I can't live with that.

The most difficult part of all of this is trusting in a God who could take our innocent baby away after all we've been through. It's indefensible. There's nothing to justify it. If the God of Light truly exists then I detest him for depriving us of our time together. He is not the compassionate one I imagined and I no longer believe in him and his benevolence. If there is no God, then it's all random chaos. There's no plan. No hope. No heaven.

Either way, our little girl is out in the universe by herself. What is to become of her? Our dear, sweet child has no one to hold her hand, no one to guide her, no one to help her find her way. She is wandering through a precarious eternity alone. And I can't bear that.

That's why I must go to her.

I was responsible for giving her life and I take responsibility in her death. Whether or not you choose to incriminate me for this horrible tragedy, I want you to know that it doesn't matter. I condemn myself. I know you too well to know that you would never accuse me to my face;

perhaps in your heart but never in words. You are too sweet, Noah, to assail me with the dagger of blame.

But the fact that you haven't been able to confront our daughter's death speaks volumes. I can feel your disappointment in me and sense your bitterness. While I can't blame you for your reticence, I only hope you can find it in your heart to forgive me.

Please don't be angry, my love. I do not want to abandon you but I'm looking out for Erica in the only way I know how and hoping, dear Noah, that someday you come to accept my reasons for doing so.

I pray with everything that is precious to me that you find someone special to spend the rest of your life with, live a happy life, and fulfill the dreams in your heart.

Farewell my sweet darling. I entrust our memories and souls to your custody and encourage you to find the strength to go on.

For we shall endure through you.

My eternal love,

Jessica

38
'Til Death Do You Part

T he vibration of the phone in his pocket aroused Noah from a bottomless sleep. He did not answer it. He did not respond to any of his calls that Friday.

He had no idea what time he fell asleep but knew it must have been late. He remembered dozing off and waking several times with the indulgence of a good night's rest just out of reach, rendering him as unwelcome as an uninvited guest.

That morning, he found himself on the heavy leather chair in the parlor, where he had sobbed, grieved and mourned again before the relief of slumber reprieved him from his torment.

He noticed the letter—the incriminating testimony implicating him in the case—staring at him as if a prosecutor had just waved it before a jury. He considered burning it, disposing of the evidence of his culpability, but decided instead to bury it in an abandoned book he had rescued from a dresser drawer—*The Grapes of Wrath*—perfect, lying on the coffee table.

While he now understood the motivation behind his wife's suicide, the insight only caused him more agony and he was left with the revelation that his own fears and cowardly neglect had conspired in her demise. Noah was devastated.

There was nothing he could do. The deadline for a solution had passed. No do overs. His window of opportunity expired. Jessie was gone, *again*, and Noah had to live with himself and the understanding that he might have been able to stop her if he had just found the courage to address the torment for their innocent little girl. But he had lingered too long. He had ignored the problem and a possible remedy, and the evidence was now glaring at him.

He leaned forward in the chair and lowered his head, placing his elbows on his knees. He lifted his hands to his face and tried grinding the sorrow out then paused when he realized what he was trying to do was mitigate the shame. But that could not be extracted. Noah sobbed once more with spasms of resentment and betrayal. The lump in his chest had returned along with his remorse.

Had Jessica been right? Was God not the just and forgiving Almighty Being Noah believed tended the universe? Did God exist at all? Whom had he been praying to all this time? Who was up there minding the store? And what about that meteor shower Noah had witnessed? Was that a coincidence? A diversion? A red herring? Had God become a free agent, moving on to greener pastures in a bigger universe with a better offer? Who was his agent?

Noah decided not to visit Molly that day. Regrettably. He turned his phone off and resolved not to speak to anyone. He was too ashamed. His wife's unheralded sermon had been delivered with the answers he'd been seeking but not expecting, pointing a condemnable finger at the true culprit. *Be careful what you wish for.* Now he had to live in this new world with the truth of what really happened, wishing he had been left in the dark.

This disturbing development opened a wound he had spent the entire past year trying to close. He was out of options. No one to appeal to for absolution; nowhere to turn for redemption. No recourse at all in sight. The game was over and the players had all showered and gone home. The jury had determined their verdict and been discharged. The judge had pronounced sentence.

And now he learns that God, too, had left the building and there was no one left in the office to petition for clemency? Where was justice? Where was closure? Where was the gravedigger to point out the spot where his heart was buried?

Noah felt like his entire existence had come to a dead stop and this new universe made absolutely no sense. It was all coming apart as if he was out on an open field and it started to rain bricks. And the bricks were getting larger. And there were no trees around to hide under. And whoever heard of raining bricks?

Noah was reeling, coping to hang onto his own personal attributes that had plummeted him to the bottom of the food chain. He had been a loving husband and father, a motivated artist and critic, an empathetic friend and neighbor. Who was he now? Where did this rank him on the index of indifference? On the Richter Scale of irresponsibility? Which circle of hell had he landed in?

He made a mental note to fast that day as a gesture of repentance. Not to score points—was there anyone still up there keeping score?—but as a first installment of reparations. He needed to escape this surreal prison cell he had locked himself inside. Noah pulled out of the driveway as if he was late to his best friend's wedding and was holding the rings. He headed east on Route 6A with no destination in mind, just wanted to distance himself—quickly—as far as he could away from ... *that* letter.

The sky had darkened that morning to a somber grey, reflecting his torment. He followed the winding road mindlessly through Barnstable, past Brewster, towards Orleans and Eastham, until he tired of driving and made his way to the Great Island Trail, a hiking path along Wellfleet Harbor that juts south into Cape Cod Bay. The last time he was here Noah recalled finding remnants of Pilgrim and Native American graves on the trail. Perhaps the ghosts of Cape Cod's past would ease him from his misery.

He headed out onto the sandy road of the seven-mile course, hiking his way through indigenous shrubs and evergreens that led him past massive dunes and reputedly buried pirate ships. This was old Cape Cod during its heyday—the Silicon Valley of the Seventeenth Century—when whaling and exploration and merchant trade were the industries of the day. After nearly an hour of walking, he found himself on an abandoned beach. No sign of life anywhere. Even the sea fowls snubbed this place.

Noah tried not to think about Jessie's letter and his complicity in the events leading up to her death. But that was impossible. His world had been shattered and he had no idea how to return home to a normal life.

Where was home? What was normal? He felt like he had to keep moving—a felon on the run—no longer knowing whom to trust.

This was Noah's new reality, retribution for his tactless and misguided attitude when his wife was at the end of her life and needed him most. Who but his own conscience was stalking him now?

How could he have been so insensitive as to think that ignoring his daughter's death would make it go away? Why had he been so dismissive when all Jessica wanted was to talk to him about her pain?

And yet, even in distress with her grief, she was still able to offer words of encouragement, hoping to inspire him to make the most of his life. But how could she expect him to find happiness after this? Make the most of what life? He had reached the ocean floor and his oxygen was running out. This was hopelessness. This was helplessness. This was Noah Miller at the crossroads of despair. He never felt smaller than he did just then.

The wind had picked up since he arrived, assaulting him like an angry Medieval mob on his way to the chopping block. That is where he felt it had come to, on the way to his final solution. Noah collapsed on the empty beach watching the storming tide close in. The menacing waves seemed to be growing louder as they broke and rain pellets began to descend (or were they bricks?), striking their intended target.

He was delirious with remorse and dismay. Possibly delusional. Noah watched a giant octopus—or was it a squid?—rise from the sea. It seemed to stretch the entire coast before him, ascending higher and higher until its bald head brushed up against the clouds. He sensed it was laughing at him, amused by his quandary, pointing tentacles his way, harassing him with accusations and innuendo. Noah's heart pounded furiously.

"The truth can be a bitter pill to swallow, don't you think?"

Somehow finding that woman—Emma or Erica—beside him at that moment did not surprise him. He was bereft, too heartbroken to speak and nodded sheepishly. He glanced back at the water. The tide was still furious but the fallacious invertebrate he had imagined had disappeared.

Just then, the wind delivered a feather that brushed up against his leg. He reached for it before it could blow away.

"You read mom's letter?"

Her voice was tinged with empathy. This time he did not have the nerve to nod. The tears welled up behind his grimace.

Noah sat there, admiring the vividly colored feather. It appeared ancient, as if it had navigated its way through time.

He shrugged, resignedly, with soggy eyes. "I know who you are."

She turned her head his way, curious.

"You're a figment of my imagination," he told her. "That's how you know so much about me."

He twirled the feather between his fingers, guessing at its age.

"That's why no one else can see you. You're haunting me, aren't you? I've created you from my own remorse ... for my wife's death."

Emma took her time, waiting for the right moment as if to swat a fly. "Do you remember what you said to me at the gravesite?" she asked.

Noah did not bother answering, raising a wall of resentment.

"You whispered something ..."

He tried ignoring her, scrutinizing the blood-red plume. He had never seen one that color.

"... In my ear."

Whatever it was, he did not want to hear it. But that didn't stop her. "'Now you can fly like a butterfly.'"

He bit his lip as he digested the memory then swallowed finding his courage.

"Of course you know what I said to my daughter. You're inside my head. Right there when I thought of it."

"You gave me something, too," she reminded him, tears sliding down her cheek.

"No," he begged, almost inaudible, willing her not to, positive he didn't want this to go any further.

She raised her chin and reached beneath her cotton shirt. He could hardly bear it yet could not look away.

"No," he pleaded again, this time his voice trembled and the tears came. "Please ... no."

She lifted the testament concealed below her neckline and displayed it against her blouse.

"My God!"

Just then, a lightning bolt blazed across the sky, unleashing a pummeling downpour. Noah covered his mouth with his hand, releasing the feather. He reached, hesitantly, for the evidence—the gold pendant spelling the name "Snort."

The blood vessels in his eyes reddened, similar to the hue of the departed feather. He peered at her incredulously, seeing her for the first time, noticing her hair and those pale green eyes. Noah threw his head back and ran his hands through his scalp. Then it all came gushing out and he buried his shame once again as thunder reverberated across the heavens.

The Great Thunderbird's venerable feather tumbled along the beach returning, in all likelihood, to its provenance.

When the sobbing had settled, Noah lifted his head. His eyes glistened. Beside him sat his four-year old daughter.

"Is it really you?" he asked, hoping she was not about to disappear like the octopus.

She nodded.

"Erica?"

They embraced and he held her, no longer any doubt in his mind. They both cried—consoling tears—shivering in one another's arms, neither in a hurry to let go. The deluge had eased leaving a soothing, steady drizzle.

"I love you, daddy," she told him.

"I love you too, baby. I've missed you so much."

They sat like this for some time. When they were able to pull themselves apart, Erica could not take her eyes from his. "You must have some questions."

It was difficult to approach the subject considering his ordeal last night but somehow Noah found the willpower. The questions had not changed. The questioner had. "What are you doing here?"

Erica took a deep breath, her expression sobering. "I can't imagine what you must have been through, daddy. First me. Then mommy. No answers. No warning. Everything taken away. Alone. It wasn't fair. None of it."

Her tone did not sound like that of a little girl but more like the mature young lady he had met. "I came back to help you understand what happened so you can try to get past it. I don't want to see you lose hope."

That cut him. He looked away, avoiding her gaze.

"I don't deserve your help. I screwed up. I don't deserve anyone's help."

Erica nudged his chin with her fingers, forcing him to look at her. "You didn't do anything wrong. You were both going through an impossible time. You were mourning me the only way you knew how. What mom did, she did for me. Like she said in her letter. She didn't want me to be alone. You couldn't have done anything different to stop her."

That didn't seem to help. Noah was still feeling the effects of his new awareness. "Why didn't mommy come?"

Her warm smile faded quickly. "It's complicated. I don't know. Something to do with the way she died. I'm sorry. Not really sure."

"But ...." Noah started then stopped. He considered his words carefully. "But, she sacrificed her ..." And could not finish the thought. "Shouldn't that count for something?"

Erica was heartbroken. "It does, daddy. What she did was selfless. True love. *It counts. Believe me, it counts.*"

Noah was still unconvinced. Erica placed her hand on his shoulder. "She doesn't blame you for what happened. She knows you weren't ready."

He sat there biting his lip unable to come to terms with her claim. She had hoped her words would absolve him from his self-inflicted torment but realized it was going to be harder than she thought. Undaunted, she held out her fist, palm up, a curious expression on her face.

"What's that?" he asked.

There was a gleam in her eye as if she was presenting him a gift. "'Til death do you part."

She took her time, lowering her fingers collectively. And waited.

Noah stared at Jessie's ring—the crystal blue sapphire ring. His heart chilled, his gaze fuzzy and unfocused. He took the ring from her hand and examined it. "She promised she'd never take it off."

Erica's voice cracked. "And in this family ... we keep our promises."

They smiled painfully at one another through misty eyes.

"She said you'd understand."

Noah recalled his wife's bizarre condition the day he proposed. "She'd only take it off ..." Then he whispered to himself ... "'to save me.'"

He let that sink in. How did she know?

He peered into the crystal blue stone once again, into the bottomless prism that always reminded him of Jessie's eyes. He no longer detected disappointment. At that, he sensed the heavy anchor around his heart—that had been dragging him down for over a year—release and float away.

Erica perceived she'd broken through his wall of resentment. She rose to her feet. Noah joined her and took her hand. They ambled along the shore in silence.

"Is God real? Is he looking out for us? And what about heaven?"

She considered the questions thoughtfully. "I can answer that but it's different for everyone. It sort of depends on what you believe. I think you're supposed to figure that out for yourself."

They spent the afternoon strolling the beach. Erica answered his questions as best she could. The rain had stopped at some point though the clouds and breeze lingered.

"Will I see you again?" he asked.

She nodded affectionally.

Then he took her in his arms one last time and embraced her, holding her for several minutes. He never wanted to let go. "Thank you for coming back, sweetheart."

She squeezed him lovingly. "I'm glad I was able to help. I know mom will be too."

She took a step back. It was time. Noah noted the hope in her eyes and could feel it in his heart, which, he realized, had started beating again. They shared a final smile before she moved on.

"Erica," he called.

She turned giving him her full attention.

"Tell your mother ..." He swallowed hard. "... I'll do my best."

While he watched his daughter, the Native American with coconut white hair Noah had seen that day at the cemetery (and again in his dream), came up beside her. The ancient warrior squatted down and picked up the drifting feather. *His sacred feather.* He fitted it into his empty headdress. Then Metacom turned to Noah, raised his hand—a sign of thanksgiving—and nodded. Noah reciprocated, gratefully.

He watched them make their way down the crescent coast until they vanished into the summer afternoon.

Noah took a deep breath filling his lungs with briny air. He felt rejuvenated—better than he had in over a year—restored like a newly painted room. He searched the area around him, a little surprised he was alone.

The tide spilled onto the beach in a dragging motion. He stood there awhile as the sun peeked out from the clouds and, sometime later, he watched as it disappeared into the Atlantic. A swarm of seagulls, flying in formation, passed overhead. A warm breeze caressed his face. He removed his sandals and stepped into the ocean. The tepid water was welcoming. About time, he thought.

Then he began jogging along the shoreline. He was hungry and decided to pick up some Chinese food on the way back.

He thought Molly might enjoy some too.

39
Not Part of The Equation

Noah had gotten the call that morning. Molly was being released from the hospital that afternoon. She had come a long way in the past few weeks and the doctors were pleased with her progress. He promised he would be there to take her home.

There was no need to hang around the Cape past the weekend. *Committed* would be closing after Sunday's performance and Noah still had not made up his mind what would come next. The success of his show had opened some doors as Jerry predicted—a screenplay option, another play, an adjunct professor position at a community college, teaching a writing course—but that meant making decisions about his job at A.P., his house in Northport, his life in New York.

The summer was winding down and several of the cast would be off to other productions they had signed up for by the following week. Others would be returning to their part-time jobs or seeking temporary work until the next audition came along. A cast and crew party was scheduled on the calendar for Sunday evening and Noah was hoping that if Molly was up for it he would take her to the closing show and surprise everyone at the farewell celebration.

He drove over to Jerry's place to say his goodbyes. Sheila had returned to the city a couple of days earlier and Jerry was heading off to L.A. that evening for a quick junket before joining her.

"I've been meaning to tell you," said Jerry, out on his deck at the table munching on a day-old sesame bagel. "You look great."

Noah eyed his pal suspiciously. "What do you want, Jer?" he asked, reaching for the slab of Philadelphia Lite cream cheese and the small butter knife posing as a paperweight on one of Jerry's work folders. Noah retrieved the knife and replaced it with a fork.

Jerry laughed complacently and raised his right hand. "Nothing, Sherlock. I swear. Everything's a conspiracy with you. I just wanted you to know that, lately, you've been looking good. You seem like your old self again. That's all. Can't a friend say something nice anymore without a hidden agenda?"

Jerry held out for as long as he could. "By the way, I'm having lunch with a producer friend of mine tomorrow," he added.

"Here it comes," Noah conceded.

Jerry ignored him. "They're looking for a writer for a new production. Some kind of sitcom-slash-reality-slash-variety show. I don't even think they know what it is yet. I'll find out more tomorrow. Anyway, I sent him your script along with the reviews and there may be some interest."

"Where?" asked Noah, convinced he already knew the answer.

Jerry took a sip of his coffee. "Where do you think?"

Noah bit into his bagel. "I'm not relocating, Jerry. Not to L.A. anyway."

"Well I don't think they'll be shipping their sound stages to the east coast for *your* sake. If you get it, you'll have to move to Hollywood."

That appeared to end the conversation and for the next twenty-three seconds the two enjoyed their bagels, lox, cream cheese, and capers in silence.

"It wouldn't have to be for the entire year, you know," Jerry mumbled. "Just a couple of months."

Noah glanced at his friend. "How *many* months?"

Jerry poured himself more coffee without looking up. "I don't know ... six, eight, maybe nine. It's not the entire year."

"Not interested," Noah told him.

"I'm just saying, you may want to keep your options open."

Jerry finished what was left of his bagel. "And I wasn't kidding before. You do look better."

"You said I looked *great.*"

"You do, Noah. Really. You look great. Relaxed. Better than I've seen you in some time." Jerry scratched his neck although it didn't itch. "And I'm still pitching you to my friend despite your objections. Wait to see if they make you an offer, okay? *Then* you can turn them down."

After breakfast, Noah joined his friend in the pool.

"So, let's say you don't move to L.A. for this gig," said Jerry. "Any idea what you're going to do with yourself?"

With effort, Noah pulled himself up onto a floating raft. "Haven't made up my mind yet. I need a few more days."

Jerry removed his sunglasses. "You're not thinking about settling here? Permanently? I mean … are you?"

Noah didn't answer right away. "I'm still considering my options."

"Be serious, Noah. You know we love the Cape too but … live here? *Year round?* What would you do with yourself?"

Noah paddled away. "I'm not sure. I might take that teaching job at the college."

"What teaching job? What college?"

"Didn't I mention it?"

"Not to me."

"Well, remember that interview we did for NBC?"

"Of course I remember it. I insisted you go."

"Well, someone at Cape Cod Community College saw it and called me. Asked me if I'd be interested teaching a playwriting class."

Jerry was shaking his head. "I'm not going to say I told you so."

"Thank you."

"You're welcome."

"No, I mean thank you for not saying it."

"You really are hopeless."

Noah flashed him a smile. He loved giving his friend a hard time.

"So? Are you going to take it?"

"I don't know. Could be fun, you know, imparting my wisdom on the next generation." Noah hesitated there. "*And* … I started working on a new play."

"*Ah hah,*" cried Jerry, gratified. "Now *that's* the kind of news I enjoy hearing. What's it about?"

Noah splashed his face and ran his hands through his hair. "It's about ... twenty pages. But don't worry, I plan to make it a little longer."

"You're hopeless."

Noah gave him his Cheshire cat pose. *"Oh,* you mean what's the play *about?"*

Jerry shook his head, unamused. "I hope it's not a comedy."

Noah smirked. "Let's see. It's about this down-and-out off-Broadway producer who gets indicted for hiding cameras in his actors' dressing rooms."

"I have a good mind to call my lawyer."

Now Noah was laughing. "Actually, it's about the Native Americans on Cape Cod."

"What?"

"Yeah, I'm researching the plight of the indigenous people who've had their land stolen by the government. The play will help publicize their struggle. If I decide to stay here, I'm thinking of getting involved with the Wampanoag Tribe."

"Wow. Who'd have guessed?"

"Jessie's family belonged to that tribe. I'd be doing it for her."

"I don't know what to say. They're in the news lately. Timing could be good. Send it to me when you're done and I'll see what I can do."

It was a seamless late-summer day, ideal for relaxing at the pool. September was just a week off. The two friends spread themselves out on comfortable lounge chairs, content with cold beers and low-sodium veggie chips. Jerry had decided to finally do something about his health. Noah read a book he brought along and Jerry took a snooze.

"Do you need a lift to the airport?" Noah asked Jerry sometime later.

"Thanks pal, but I wouldn't ask you to drive me to Logan. I've got someone picking me up."

Noah turned a page. "Well, don't say I didn't offer."

"I thought you had plans tonight?"

Noah grinned. He was so looking forward to spending time with Molly outside the hospital, where she had been confined for nearly a month. He was going to cook lobsters at her place and had ordered an ice cream cake.

"I do," Noah told him, checking the time. "That reminds me … I've got some things to take care of. I should be going." He sat up and put on his sandals.

"I thought we were hanging out?" Jerry said.

"We were. And now I'm leaving. Sorry, but I've got to get home and shower, change, and get everything ready for later."

Jerry accompanied him to his car.

"Sorry you're going to miss the cast party," said Noah. "I'll be sure to send you the bill."

"Thanks buddy. Have a good time for me. Tonight too. Send Molly my love."

"Will do."

They stood there smiling at one another until the smiles evolved into laughter. Then they embraced.

"Thank you," Noah said sincerely. "I'm glad you talked me into coming up here. It was just what I needed."

Jerry pulled back to make his point and watch Noah's reaction. "You see? You should listen to me more. I'm smarter than you are."

Noah laughed it off, looking away. "Well, I don't know if I'd go *that* far."

Jerry placed a hand on his friend's shoulder. "It was a good show, Noah. And you did a hell of a job stepping up and keeping it together. You earned your director's stripes."

"Thanks," said Noah. "We picked a hell of a good cast."

Jerry used his pedantic teacher voice. "It's okay to take some of the credit."

Noah nodded as he got into his car, started it, and lowered the window. "Good luck in L.A. Let me know how it goes."

"Will do."

"And, when you get a chance, Jer, send me the number of your shrink." Jerry appeared surprised. "Hey, you never know," added Noah.

Jerry waved to his friend as he pulled away, gratified that Noah was over the worst and poised to move on with his life, whatever that was.

Noah stopped to pick up the food and decorations before heading to Molly's house. She had given him her key when he mentioned he wanted to get the place ready for her. He threw out a bunch of stuff from the fridge and freezer to make room for the pair of three-pound lobsters, the magnum of wine and the cake. Then he set the table with candlesticks and attached the mylar balloons to her chair. He put up some festive decorations around the room, unrolled the "Welcome Home" banner and hung it where she would see it when she entered. He wanted this night to be special. Before leaving, he gave the apartment the once over with a dust rag, vacuumed the floor, and opened a window.

When he arrived at the hospital, a bon voyage reception had commenced in Molly's room. She had made a few friends during her stay. Hanging out were two doctors, four nurses, a resident, a technician, a physical therapist, and a few others from the clerical and maintenance staff. Noah noticed a couple of open bottles of nonalcoholic champagne on the overbed table and what was left of a chocolate layer cake.

Molly was on crutches when Noah entered the room. She introduced him around. Several had seen his play and were pleased to make his acquaintance.

About ten minutes later the party broke up—they were, after all, on the clock—and, once they went over the discharging procedures, Noah escorted her downstairs in a wheel chair.

"Feels like I'm busting out of prison," she said, looking up at the building behind her. "Can't believe I've been holed up here over three weeks."

"Be nice to be back in your bed," offered Noah.

"*I know,*" she agreed.

"I was talking about me."

Molly smiled. "We'll see about that."

After the drive back, Molly was glad to be home and genuinely touched by Noah's thoughtfulness. She loved the sign he hung in the living room, relished the fabulous lobster dinner, and laughed when she read the inscription on the ice cream cake: "Molly, 'Break A Leg' is just an expression!"

After dinner, she made herself comfortable on the living room couch with a light blanket and pillow. The bottle of Chardonnay came with her. Carly Simon was singing *You Belong To Me* from Bluetooth speakers. Noah was exploring the titles of books on the built-ins.

"Did I mention I spoke to Barney, my boss, yesterday?"

"No," she replied. "I don't believe you did."

He sat down in the matching pinstriped loveseat adjacent to the couch. Molly leaned on her elbow so she was facing him. "Yeah," continued Noah, "I'd been meaning to call him the last few days to catch up. He wants to know what my plans are."

Molly breathed in her wine and sipped it slowly. "So, *what are* your plans?"

Noah refilled his empty glass. "I told him if I was coming back it probably wouldn't be until the Tuesday after Labor Day."

"*If* you were coming back?"

"Right. *If* I was coming back."

"What did he say?"

"Sounded a little confused."

Molly gazed at him pointedly. *"Him or you?"*

Noah did not bother responding.

"So was that it?" she followed up.

"Not entirely. No."

She raised an inquisitive eyebrow without bothering to elaborate.

"Said he wanted me back in the office as soon as possible and that I could continue writing my theater column or we could discuss other writing assignments. Or, if I wanted, I could edit. Said he was open to whatever I was interested in doing."

"Wow. That's great, Noah. Guess he wants you back pretty bad."

A lull in the room ensued. Molly finished off what was left in her glass, giving him time to assess his next move. "So, what are you going to do?"

Noah got up, returning to the spot of books where he had left off, evading the question as long as he could. Carly was crooning *Haven't Got Time for the Pain* off her *Greatest Hits* album.

"*Noah?*"

He turned so he could see her. "I don't know, Molly. I really don't. There's a lot to consider..." He sat next to her. He was jumpy. "...The house, my friends, an income ..."

She stared him down with her poker face. He leaned in closer, detecting the hope in her eyes. "... *You.*"

She peered at him dumbfounded, her expression vulnerable and helpless. "*Me?*"

Her reaction was so innocent, he was sure that if he didn't take her in his arms at that precise moment she was going to lose it.

"*Yeah, you!* What do you think? You're *not* part of the equation?"

Then they embraced eagerly as they considered what their lives would be like moving forward. Together.

They made their way into the bedroom soon after with Noah sweeping her off her feet like a willing new bride. He told her he was okay just holding her all night but Molly was not content with that. She wanted him inside her. Noah didn't argue. They made love. Mindfully. Passionately. Cautiously. He was so worried about hurting her that he felt compelled asking her permission before touching her. She found that incredibly sweet. When they were finished they laid in bed, physically drained but still awake.

"What ever happened to that woman?" asked Molly.

He didn't answer right away. "*What woman?*"

"You know, the one you were looking for? That real estate agent? Did you ever find her?"

He moved his head from side to side. "*What are you talking about?*"

He seemed genuinely confused so she rephrased. "The one who said she knew things about you? Said she was ... your daughter?"

Noah turned in her direction. *"My daughter?"* He chuckled, a bit flustered. "Seriously, I have no idea what you're talking about."

Molly left it there. She dropped the subject. Forever.

There was no more conversation after that. She took Noah's arm and leaned her head against his shoulder. Moonlight spilled into the room between the flowery curtains, closing out the world beyond. He was grateful. Carly serenaded them with *Well That's The Way I Always Heard It Should Be.* Molly fell asleep first, quietly, peacefully, and Noah soon after.

On the tree outside her bedroom window, a single leaf was snatched from its branch by a surging gust. It soared into the night before gravity seized it, forcing it to flutter back to earth, where it was raked up by the gardener that Tuesday morning and bagged along with the mowed grass, weeds and pruned shrubs. It eventually found its way to a compost pile that was delivered to an organic farm where, a year later, a grassy landscape began to rise.

The following July, an exotic turquoise butterfly darted its way through the area and descended onto one of its blades of grass.

About the Author

Originally from Coney Island, Brooklyn, Michael Solomowitz has cherished his roller-coaster ride as a professional writer. He began writing scripts for Manhattan Cable-TV and worked for Warner Brothers in Hollywood. As a freelance sports journalist, he has published dozens of articles in national and trade publications and contributed to two non-fiction sports books. As a playwright and director, his plays have appeared on stages from California to Long Island. He resides on Cape Cod with his lovely wife Katharine. *Behind the Fourth Wall* is his debut novel. Please contact him at: michaelsolomowitz.com.

Note from the Author

Word-of-mouth is crucial for any author to succeed. If you enjoyed *Behind the Fourth Wall*, please leave a review online—anywhere you are able. Even if it's just a sentence or two. It would make all the difference and would be very much appreciated.

Thanks!
Michael Solomowitz

We hope you enjoyed reading this title from:

BLACK ROSE
writing™

www.blackrosewriting.com

Subscribe to our mailing list – *The Rosevine* – and receive **FREE** books, daily deals, and stay current with news about upcoming releases and our hottest authors.
Scan the QR code below to sign up.

Already a subscriber? Please accept a sincere thank you for being a fan of Black Rose Writing authors.

View other Black Rose Writing titles at www.blackrosewriting.com/books and use promo code **PRINT** to receive a **20% discount** when purchasing.

CPSIA information can be obtained
at www.ICGtesting.com
Printed in the USA
LVHW032233080122
707889LV00007B/321

9 781684 338603